Also by Julian Lees

The Bone Ritual

The Burnings

Julian Lees

Constable • London

CONSTABLE

First published in Great Britain in 2017 by Constable

This paperback edition published in 2018 by Constable

1 3 5 7 9 10 8 6 4 2

Copyright © Julian Lees, 2017

The moral right of the author has been asserted.

A CIP catalogue record for this book
is available from the British Library.

ISBN: 978-1-47212-313-8

Typeset in Bembo by Photoprint, Torquay
Printed and bound in Great Britain by
Clays Ltd, St Ives plc

Papers used by Constable are from well-managed forests and other
responsible sources.

Constable
An imprint of
Little, Brown Book Group
Carmelite House
50 Victoria Embankment
London EC4Y 0DZ

An Hachette UK Company
www.hachette.co.uk

www.littlebrown.co.uk

The Burnings

Prologue

It's three in the morning and there's blood everywhere.

Behind the 100-watt bulb shining into the back of Ruud's eyes, searing his retinas, stands a man.

A dimly outlined figure.

Hovering like a giant predatory bird.

He calls himself The Physician.

A smile reveals cramped white teeth, pink gums.

'Let us get down to business.' The teeth glisten. 'Are you ready to answer my questions?'

Ruud barely hears what's being said. His focus lies elsewhere, on the thing protruding from his flesh.

There's a twenty-centimetre finger ring retractor stuck in his shoulder. It is made of stainless steel with a cam ratchet lock that draws back the tissue and exposes the surgical site. The curved metal arms twitch to the beat of his heart.

Ruud eyeballs it. Half-terrified, half-fascinated.

His circumflex humeral artery's been punctured and the pain is almost unendurable.

The man, backlit, gives the instrument a little nudge and Ruud hears himself roil and blow.

The wound is deep. Mariana Trench deep. Each time his heart contracts the Weitlaner retractor shivers and a spurt of blood sprays up. It splatters his face and chest, douses the barber's chair, spills down his bare shanks onto his ankles and feet. Untended, the blood gluts the spaces between his toes, pooling on the footrest. It's as though someone clever has done a magic trick and concealed a water pistol inside the top of his collarbone. *Stffff-stffff. Stfff-stfff.* Squeeze the plastic trigger, cowboy! Quick Draw. *Stffff-stffff.*

Ruud wrestles against the wrist and neck straps and tries to move his head.

But the buckles hold. His legs are secured too.

Haemorraging. The blood spatters.

So much red. Suffocating, fungal-metallic red. It reminds Ruud of when he and Arjen tricked their mum by slathering their faces with ketchup and super-gluing rubber scabbards to their ears. Arjen clattered into the kitchen screaming blue murder. Mum, who had her head in the fridge, sorting stray Brussels sprouts from the back of the veg compartment, almost fainted. Arjen laughed so hard he choked on some spittle and had to lie down after. Ruud lifted his eyes to the ceiling – God, they should have spent more time together.

Only natural to reminisce, only normal to assess things and have regrets.

Now that I'm dying.

If only the cuntish tosser with the knife would shut the fuck up.

But he likes to talk to Ruud as he goes about his cutting and paring.

Sixty-seven types, he says.

The Physician raises a scalpel, held softly between the thumb and forefinger of his left hand. Silver in the spotlights.

He tells Ruud there are sixty-seven types of scalpel blades.

Blade No. 12, for example, has a sharp crescent-shaped tip – he shows Ruud – and is used to disarticulate small joints during digit amputation or for cleft palate procedures. He picks up another. While No. 15 here has a small curved tip used to make short precise incisions – good for excising skin lesions or opening coronary arteries.

The Weitlaner retractor shivers.

A slow hissing sound of pain escapes Ruud's mouth.

The Physician attempts a few practice stabs with his wrist. He is starting to enjoy himself. Then, pumping the foot pedal of the barber's chair, chatting about this and that, he slices Ruud open.

Chapter One

FSSST.

A hot electrical charge. It popped behind her eyes, a sharp explosion of static in her skull.

She stirred.

A fuzzy cognizance, followed by a voice in her head.

Her own voice.

Urging her to wake up.

FSSSSSSSST.

Gasping, swallowing blood, tasting copper, her eyelids snapped open and she made out a curved black panel mere centimetres from her face. Dazed, she blinked once, twice and quickly lost focus.

FSSSSSSSST.

Her chest jolted with a startled heave.

Awake now.

She heard an engine. Discerned movement, sensed wheels bumping beneath her.

The boot of the car stank of old carpet. The inside temperature, unbearable at the best of times, must have been nudging 50° Celsius with the motor running. There was no air. No ventilation. Nothing but stale breath and fumes from the exhaust pipe.

4

Everything appeared unnaturally dark. But gradually the darkness began to shimmer. There were thin chinks along the weather strips of the boot door and through them she saw the city rush by, streaming past in a kind of molten slow motion. The colours from streetlights played out across her forehead. A flicker show of sharp reds and yellows.

She was not sure how long she'd been out. Perhaps a couple of hours.

What she recalled was leaving work, walking through her building's underground car park, hearing the squeal of balding tyres in the distance and then . . . choking, flailing. The hand over her mouth had smelled of rotting mango. Struggling, she'd raked his shin with her heel, but he soon had her by the hair, snapping her head back and toppling her to the ground.

Had he struck her? He must have done because her face felt sore. All bashed up. She couldn't see out of her left eye. Her nose was so smashed in that when she inhaled through it she made a wet *klik-klik* rattle deep in her nostrils. And whenever the wheels hit a bump it was like a nail gun to the temple.

Instinctively, she went to touch her face. One wrist pulled on the other, causing both hands to move in unison, the left hand mimicking the right. A momentary confusion. She realized she lay curled in a foetal position, head bowed, back curved, with her limbs fastened in front of her – lower arms secured to ankles with thick cord. Bound like a trussed fowl.

She tugged wildly at the rope, jerking her knees right up to her chest. Elbows knocking against ribs, she brought her fingers to the underside of her chin. Straining on the cords, she probed with her fingertips, finding congealed blood and a band of plastic, which was smooth beneath her touch. A strip of duct tape ran the length of her mouth. A little higher, the pulpy flesh around her left cheekbone was sticky like a popped peach.

A car horn blasted. A motorbike roared by.

One thing was unmistakable: the streets had darkened. Night was falling fast.

The car stopped.

An aluminium shutter clattered down over a door and windows. The small shops were closing; people were making for home following the end of evening prayers.

Bucking, she heaved and yanked and tugged at her bonds. She dug her nails into her cheek, into the corner of the tape at the edge of her mouth, snatched at it. After several attempts, the adhesive came away.

She screamed. The blood from her nose slipped down her throat, turning her cries into a gurgle. She butted the boot door, hesitated, and then did it again. She battered it until her crown bled, desperate to be heard. She buffeted, bumped and slammed herself against the catch. Nothing she did sprung the lock.

The car moved off once more.

Shivering, the trapezius muscles along her spine juddering, she begged for her mother.

She groped the floor. Her bag and purse were gone. Her phone had been taken too.

She shifted her weight, knocking her pelvic bone against steel, twisting to get onto her front. The carpet was loose here. With the ends of her fingers she wrenched at the interior lining, first peeling the black polyester away from the false bottom and then the flexible rubber material to expose the metal underneath. Even in the darkness she could tell the spare wheel, the plastic trim and the spare wheel tools had been removed. But she was not interested in them. It was something else she was after.

She ripped away the final bit of rubber and there it was: the tiny hole. Only just big enough to shove her thumb through.

It was only a small rupture in the floorpan.

Regardless, it gave her hope.

She tried to force the casing open, thrusting the pads of her thumbs into the hole, prizing, wresting. But to no avail. The opening refused to get any larger.

Through a blur of tears she stared at the small gap. At the blacktop whipping by.

Once more, she tried to wrestle with the breach but it wouldn't budge.

A sickening sense of free-fall took hold.

The night grew darker as the sedan made its way out of the city. The sky became a bruised shade of purple.

By the time she noticed the motorway lighting columns flash by, she had thought up a plan.

Using her mouth she freed a silver ring from her finger and spat it through the hole. It disappeared, vanishing from sight as it ricocheted off the asphalt and bounced away. There was another silver ring, a midi ring, that sat below the first knuckle on her right forefinger, but it was stuck tight and she couldn't remove it, so she opted for the next best thing. She tore off her earrings and fed them into the opening, followed by her narrow wristwatch, which she jammed through the cavity.

A spasm of doubt shot through her.

The midi ring. She had to get them to see the midi ring.

Again, she tried desperately to pull it free. But to no avail. Ever since she'd damaged the top joint of that particular finger playing softball she hadn't been able to loosen the ring, and it still refused to budge.

And then she made up her mind to do the unthinkable. She had to leave a piece of herself behind. It was the only way to be sure.

The woman scraped the flesh of her right forefinger along the sharpest edges of her canines, crammed the finger hinge between her teeth and bit down hard. The pain tore her apart, shooting though her like an electric current.

Grimacing, she inspected the digit. She had barely made a dent.

She bit. Even harder. Splitting the epidermis. Drawing blood.

Her head swam. Tears and snot soaked her face. She was close to passing out.

She positioned it between her teeth, exactly where the ligaments met below the middle phalanx. She took a deep breath, held it and chin-butted the floor.

It did not crunch like a raw carrot. The cartilage did not crack like a chicken-wing joint. Nevertheless, when she drew apart her jaws, she had gone through.

Although not completely.

Bits of dermis and muscle remained attached. She had to work on the fat and connective tissue like a dog worked on a bone.

Until the knuckle came away.

A broken country byway. Tall yellowing grasses brushed the sides of the car. The woman heard the grinding sound of small stones being flattened as the wheels slowed. Every jolt-ing bump in the road drove the breath out of her in ragged pants. When the car came to a stop she strained her ears, terrified what she might hear. But all she could make out was the insect hum of the hills.

She remained stock-still, like a child in a secret place play-ing Christmas hide-and-seek. Senses on heightened alert, listening for footsteps, voices.

Several minutes elapsed. Her chest was trembling. Everything around her spun. Her wounds were making her woozy.

Hearing nothing, she silently prayed to God and Jesus and her recently departed grandmother.

She waited, inhaling slow, shallow gulps. Her chest rising and falling.

The dormant car ticked as the engine cooled.

Her face ached from crying.

A minute passed. And then another.

Her hand pounded with each beat of her heart. Even in the dark she saw that blood was smeared everywhere. It was pooled around her, congealing, sticking to her clothes and hair. Very quietly she bandaged her pulped finger with the end of her sleeve. Bloated and raw, it twitched un-controllably, making her wince. The throbbing – she clenched her jaw to numb the pain – was driving her out of her mind. But she refused to black out.

Several more minutes went by.

She knew she mustn't give up hope.

The sun would be up soon.

She began screaming for help again.

She screamed and screamed and screamed.

To the point that her throat gave out and only a flaccid

croak escaped her. She was aware of the heat, aware of the dark, but after a while, all she could think of were her parents. Memories flashed through her head. She wondered if she would ever see them again.

The insect hum of the hills grew louder.

And louder still.

Crickets and katydids and other night-singing bugs chirped and whirred. The noise was amplified a hundredfold in the dark.

They chirped and whirred and fizzed.

But.

Then.

Suddenly.

As though a needle had lifted off a record.

It all went quiet.

A jungle hush blanketed the car. It was the sort of hush that only occurred when a predator approached.

She held her breath.

In the new silence, her skin quivered.

She waited.

And she heard it. The crunch of feet on gritty earth.

She twisted her body into a half-kneel and peered through a chink in the boot door.

The moonlight reflected off his shoulders. Drawing him in full silhouette. He was clad in black PVC. The outfit was tight and tear-resistant, like a gimp's bondage suit, and on his head he wore a hideous rubber pig's mask.

He was standing there. Staring right back at her. About ten short steps away.

The car keys jingled in his hand.

He whispered three muffled words: 'Oink! Oink! Oink!'

And advanced towards her.

10

Chapter Two

It was a steamy Javanese morning; the sun in the sky was over the tree line, already the colour of a dark orange egg yolk. Ruud Pujasumarta parked his blue Toyota Yaris by the police sawhorse and approached on foot. The first *inspektur* was perspiring profusely. The sweat dribbled down his back and into his cotton underpants. He ran a palm across the nape of his neck; it came away glistening. His shirt stuck to him like a second skin.

Along the road he passed a boy clutching a live rooster and tugging a goat by a rope halter. '*Selamat Pagi!*' cried the boy.

Ruud wished him a good morning.

Up ahead, he heard the sound of idle chatter. A pair of Sabhara street cops stood in the shadow of a thorny acacia smoking Djarum Blacks and siphoning cold coffee from plastic bags. They acknowledged him by tapping their berets.

Ruud did not stop to debrief them. He kept on walking towards the ladder trucks.

At the bend in the broken road he spotted his colleague waiting for him by the edge of the slope. Leaning against a fire engine, Detective Aiboy Ali rested the back of his head in a casual manner on the first 'K' of the gold-leaf decal – DINAS KEBAKARAN FIRE RESCUE. When he saw

Ruud he banged on the fleet markings and stepped into the sunshine. His gait was stiff.

He raised a black leather biker cuff. 'Hey, *Gajah*.'

Ruud nodded, noticed the new Megadeth T-shirt – Killing Road 2016 – and prayed he wouldn't have to listen to the horrendous clatter on Aiboy's car stereo later on. 'What have we got?'

Aiboy Ali used both hands to pull his long hair from his eyes. 'Burned-out car. Must have skidded off the road. Went over the cliff, smashed into a coconut tree and *whoomp*! We think it's a Japanese sedan, but it's pretty difficult to tell. The registration number's fried. Whoever was inside got flame-roasted too.'

Ruud gazed at the view overlooking the Puncak valley, at the tea plantations and the higgledy-piggledy houses squashed up against the hillside. 'How many people in the vehicle?'

'One adult.'

'Male or female.'

'Can't tell.'

Ruud saw a second ladder truck positioned by the cliff verge. He looked up. Nearly six metres from the ground a fireman perched on his truck's tower ladder drawing on a *kretek*.

Ruud neared the escarpment, cocked an eyebrow. 'Long way to fall.'

'A good fifteen-metre drop. *Pemadan kebakaran* had to use foam to douse the flames. It spread to the vegetation beyond. Took them about an hour to get the fire under control.'

'Where's the body?'

'They pulled it up in a body bag. Solossa was here with

the forensic team. The coroner's van took it away fifteen minutes ago.'

'Does Solossa suspect foul play?'

Aiboy Ali made a low guttural sound. 'Why do you think we were called? Something tells me this is going to get complicated ugly.'

'Let's not start jumping to conclusions quite yet.' Ruud studied his friend's face and saw something he didn't recognize. 'What's the matter?'

'What do you mean?'

'You good?'

'Why?'

'You seem, I don't know, as if you're not yourself.'

'Leg hurts.'

Ruud nodded but knew that wasn't it; Aiboy had been acting out of sorts and troubled for months now. He hadn't been the same since the shooting – more withdrawn and a great deal quieter.

Ruud crossed his arms and stared at the ground, the sticky heat on his back. 'You should talk to someone about it.'

'What's there to talk about?'

Ruud noticed his colleague's fingernails were bitten to the quick. He made light of the fact and tossed it to the back of his mind. Taking a tentative step closer to the precipice, he bent at the waist, peeked over the edge and quickly took a pace back.

'You know you are going to have to go down there, don't you?' said Aiboy.

The thought startled Ruud. He had no appetite for heights.

A scorched stench of rubber coiled atop the wreckage. When the wind soughed through the trees, flecks of torched plastic and chargrilled crumbs of upholstery fell like snowflakes on their skin. The smoke permeated everything, leaving an acrid taste at the backs of their throats.

The lead firefighter strode across, removed his cream helmet to reveal a hairline damp with sweat. He touched hands with Ruud. He had a clammy handshake. 'Salam, *Inspektur Polisi Satu*. A nasty business for sure. We belong to the Creator and to Him shall we return.' His voice resonated like a Surabayan fishmonger's. 'My name is Sidiq. I tell you how it happen. The car came round the corner and through the bend and drop, hitting the big coconut below like an accordion.' He pressed his fists together. 'The collision with the tree ruptured the fuel tank and . . .' He folded his fingers and thumbs together and then sprang them apart.

'*Babang*,' said Ruud.

'That's what most people will think. But you know, vehicles they do not blow up the way they do in the movies. No massive bim-bam-bam.'

'No?'

'No. Sure-sure, when you have a collision hot slivers of metal get shoved into the gas tank, fuel lines get cut. On occasion a spark will fly, setting off the fuel leak, but no huge bang. What you will get is a fireball. Though very rarely will it spread throughout the car if gravity is involved, *sih*?'

'You think an accelerant was used?'

Sidiq inclined his chin. 'The car crashed, came to rest at such an acute angle.' He tilted his elbow to 45 degrees. 'Gravity would pull the blazing petrol downward. Yet in this case the vehicle was fully engulfed. Carpets, seat foam, seat plastic, all alight! Even the tyres erupted from the heat, and the airbag melted down to white liquid, just like palm syrup, you know? After that the shock absorber struts exploded.'

'Sounds like one helluva mess.'

'Also the windows were open. If windows were closed the interior fire would burn itself out from no oxygen. But I ask you, *meh*, who drives a nice car with their windows open in this country?'

'Was the body found on the driver's side?' asked Ruud.

'Yes.'

'Which direction was the car travelling when it left the road?'

'East. Heading downhill. And you know what's missing? Brake marks on the road.'

'The rain may have washed them away. If it rained.' Ruud raised a finger. 'Bear with me a second, will you?' He called Werry Hartono. 'Werry, it's me. Do me a favour and check with the Meteorological Agency if it rained in Puncak last night. Yes, *Badan Meteorologi*. Thanks. Call me back.' Ruud returned his attention to the firefighter. 'So you suspect someone doused the cabin with lighter fluid, tossed in a lit cigarette then pushed the car over the cliff?'

'Either that or suicide. Throw petrol over yourself and strike a match as you roll down the cliff.'

'Sounds unlikely.'

'It is possible, *sih*?'

'Someone wanted this to appear like an accident.'

'Well, our job here is done. Lucky for us the wind direction was in our favour, otherwise we'd have struggled to control the blaze.' The fireman glanced at the sky and made a face. 'Looks like the clouds are rolling in. Listen to me, if you are going to examine the crash sight wait another hour or so. There are gasses and toxic chemicals such as hydrogen cyanide and hydrofluoric acid about from the cooked plastic. Better not tamper with anything for a while. And if you do go down, leave your mobile phones with us. Fuel vapours and wireless devices do not mix.'

The murder of crows took flight from a hollow tree trunk, soaring on an updraught. Quick darts of black against the sky. They reached a current of warm air and then glided. Ruud counted six of them way up above, drifting on thermals, wings extended, circling like buzzards.

Aiboy Ali was the first to abseil down. Then it was Ruud's turn. He wore a handkerchief across his nose and mouth to prevent inhaling hazardous fumes. Even so, the smell of burning was pervasive.

'Right,' he said, 'let's smash this.' Gripping the rope for dear life, peering over his shoulder, eyes bulging from their sockets, Ruud rappelled the ridge, negotiating a metre at a time. Anchored to the fire engine twelve metres overhead, he hopped and crabbed his way lower, more than a little scared even though the line was paid out in a controlled fashion and he had a climbing harness secured to his waist. The static rope bit into his palms. Singed leaves swished up to meet him. The fire crew assured him it was safe. All the same, he wondered aloud whether he should have worn protective headgear and kneepads.

He felt watched, scrutinized. Ever since he'd become a minor celebrity by solving the Mah-Jong Master killings, Sabhara cops and traffic patrolmen ogled him with unnatural interest. Ruud didn't like the attention but he didn't let it bother him. Even now, as he scrabbled along a bank of tall yellowing grass, he caught them staring from above, eye-balling him like birds of prey.

His vision grew milky at the edges.

To make matters worse, Ruud became conscious of his breakfast of *roti bakar* with cheese threatening to repeat itself. Don't you bloody chunder, Pujasumarta, don't you bloody dare!

As he descended, the vegetation, once riotous and dense, became brittle and bare.

When he reached Aiboy Ali, Ruud planted his feet on the tiny ledge and prodded the earth with his shoe. A twig snapped in two. He let out a long breath and his head swam a little.

'You okay, *Gajah*?'

Ruud spoke in a faint tremor. 'I'm good.'

Although logic and common sense urged him to take a moment to regain his composure, what Ruud did was spin around and take a bold stagger-step stride towards the blackened car. His foot slipped, his legs cycled in thin air and he almost toppled onto the blistered roof of the sedan.

Fortunately, he remained attached to the rope and received a faceful of toasted elephant grass instead. The dry plants crackled under his clumsy grasp and he heard laughter from high up.

Ruud stumbled about a bit. 'Legs have gone all wobbly. Got disco knees.' He found himself talking at the top of his lungs.

The stench of charred rubber was overpowering, even through the handkerchief. He had bits of ash sticking to him, gritting his tongue. The ambient heat pierced Ruud's shirt and trousers, through his clothing to his skin. It was as if the air itself was roasting.

'Is it safe to poke about?' Ruud asked.

'They've secured the frame and wedged chocks under what's left of the wheels, so I hope so.'

Both men leaned at an angle of approximately 45°, touching shoulders. Neither looked left towards the bamboo grove by the rock pool nor right towards the low houses clustered in the distance. For a long while they stared at the empty incinerated shell in sullen silence. Everything was crumpled and deformed. Where the tyres had once been, only steel belts remained. In the back, the rear drive axle, the body side moulding and platform frame appeared wilted, and the back glass had melted. While in front, the bonnet had curled up, peeled away like a sardine tin.

'Jesus,' hissed Ruud as he batted away a beetle. 'Check out the windscreen.' The windshield was so twisted and bubbled, globules the size of onion bulbs burgeoned from the laminate.

'You going in for a closer look-see?'

The harness chewed into Ruud's waist. 'On second thoughts, we should leave this for the pathologist and the forensic boys,' he said. 'When they haul the car upwards, make certain the recovery team protects the integrity of the vehicle and whatever evidence is left. Let's get ourselves back on solid ground.'

Ruud made a circular, swooping gesture with his arm, as though lassoing a horse, and prepared to be winched skyward. The static rope tautened, and seconds afterwards he was lifted off his feet. He'd ascended about halfway when he heard his name called.

'*Inspektur Polisi Satu* Pujasumarta!' Ruud looked up. One of the Sabhara street cops was waving a phone in the air. 'Telephone call for you! It's Police Commissioner Witarsa! He says we have a *saksi*, a witness. Someone has contacted *Polisi Lalu Lintas*.

'Who?'

'A blind woman! You have to return to Central HQ on Jalan Kramat Raya straight away!'

'What?'

'A blind old lady who lives nearby. Says she heard a woman screaming. Says she knows what happened!'

Ruud's stomach convulsed. A blind witness – this could only happen to him!

Fuck, thought Ruud, his heels dangling. Things just got complicated ugly.

Chapter Three

Ruud waited with the other detectives in the Incident Room for Police Commissioner Joyo T. Witarsa to make his entrance. On the bulletin board someone had put up red and gold Imlek decorations to commemorate Chinese New Year.

Methodically, Ruud arranged the plastic chairs in a circle, before taking the seat closest to the door. He took a moment to appraise his teammates.

In stockinged feet was Werry Hartono, perched in the chair opposite, applying boot polish to his leather shoes with a stiff brush. The young second lieutenant wore a blue Prince of Wales check shirt, immaculately pressed and starched, together with a black knitted wool tie. Quite sensibly, he had a dishcloth draped across his knees to protect his knife-edge trousers from stains. To his right sat Aiboy Ali, a bagelen bread roll held to his lips. Beside him, Officer Hamka Hamzah, looking scruffy in his brown police uniform, picked his teeth with a matchstick.

'Must you do that in public?' admonished Ruud.

'Do what?' Hamzah slid the matchstick into his tunic pocket with his cigarettes. There was a curry stain on his shirt cuff.

'Excavate.'

Hamzah glowered, coughed a bronchial cough and then belched loudly. 'Sorry, *neh*, this morning's *bubur ayam*, a little too much peppercorns. They get stuck in my molars.' He made a sucking noise and ran three fingers through his centre parting. 'You acting tired, like only have five-watt left,' the little man exclaimed. 'Tired and grouchy. What, not getting enough sleep? Twenty-four-seven servicing your *bule* girlfriend, *nih*? She keeping you up late? How is she? You two still living water-buffalo style?'

'We're not engaged yet, if that's what you mean,' said Ruud.

'*Wai-yoo-yoo*, she is a fine woman. Good ankles and calf muscles. So many women have legs like rhinos nowadays. Not her. You *elok bertunangan*. Ask her father's permission, get a *mahr* agreed upon. Better sooner than later. What do you think, Hartono?'

'What do I think? I think the world has gone crazy!' He wobbled his roly-poly cheeks. 'Benedict Cumberbatch in nineteenth-century London, *ya ampun!*'

'What you talking, *meh*?'

'*Sherlock*. Last year's Christmas Special. I just watched the YouTube trailers. How can the story take place suddenly in Victorian times? Seasons One, Two and Three are in modern-day Britain and then the bloody writers do something so *bodoh* and set the story in the past.'

Hamzah gave his colleagues a sideways glance and did a circling motion with his index finger at the side of his head.

'They even have Martin Freeman wearing a ridiculous moustache! *Bodoh*, I tell you. *Bodoh*.' He kissed his pinky ring, the one embossed with the logo of the Indonesian National Police.

'You know what he is talking about, boss?'

'Of course he doesn't,' said Aiboy Ali, chewing his bread roll and swallowing noisily. 'You think he has the opportunity to watch TV?'

'I never understand those foreign shows. I can't read the subtitles fast enough. My wife likes to watch *Preman Pensiun,*' continued Hamzah. 'You seen it, boss?'

Ruud ignored the question. He never watched the local soap operas. Instead, he swept a hand over his mouth, clamped shut his eyes and allowed his mind to wander.

Hamzah's comment about women's ankles got him thinking about Imke. She did have good legs, he was right. Whenever she stood on tiptoes in the kitchen, reaching up to grab the cast-iron pots on the top shelf, her calf muscles flexed, looking as if they wanted to break free. It always lit a little fire in his chest.

That very morning Ruud and Imke had had sex from five thirty until daybreak.

He was reliving the memory when all of a sudden a scowl of displeasure etched itself on Ruud's face.

Three times during their lovemaking, Kiki's face appeared over the edge of the mattress, once with one of his socks in her mouth.

'I think she thinks you're giving me a very vigorous tummy rub,' said Imke, giggling. 'Probably wants one herself too.'

Ruud smiled and resumed his position.

And that was when Kiki began licking his feet.

Ruud had to laugh.

This wasn't the first occasion it had happened either. Once she even jumped on the bed and tried to join in.

'She just wants some attention,' Imke had said.

Ruud couldn't perform after that. Not with a pair of

spaniel eyes watching him. It was like a gush of iced water had spilled on his lap.

In the eighteen months they'd been together, they'd tried shutting Kiki out of the bedroom, but Kiki had been Imke's roommate since she was a puppy, and she hated being barred from sleeping beside her mummy. If they lured Kiki into the bathroom and closed the door, she would start whining. And five minutes later she'd be howling like a nomadic wolf. So loud the street cats would join in, setting off a cacophony of bellowing, screeching and caterwauling so spirited you'd think they might raise the dead.

It was, if nothing else, a mood killer.

Ultimately, for that reason, they allowed Kiki back into the bedroom. It was either that or shagging with bits of cork stuffed in their ears. There was no way they could endure another second of incessant mournful baying.

Consequently, Ruud was eternally clenching his buttocks tight in fear of a cold canine nose poking between his toes.

He hadn't mentioned anything to Imke yet, to spare her feelings, but he might have to soon.

Really, the situation was unmanageable. Quite absurd. Thinking about it made him laugh softly. He couldn't help himself.

'Boss?'

Yes, he was overreacting. Of course he was. It wasn't Imke's fault. It wasn't entirely the dog's fault either. In spite of that, it wasn't something he could gloss over. How could he continue making love to Imke with the dog's beady orbs on him, black gums glistening, sizing him up as if he were a juicy pork chop? Wasn't this kind of thing borderline depravity? Ughh! It gave him the shivers. He read in a report once that bestiality was legal in Japan and in Finland. Japan and Finland – two of the most socially advanced countries in the world – what the hell was wrong with these people? And why weren't the animal rights activists in Tokyo and Helsinki doing anything about it? Probably because they were constantly blotto, getting hammered on sake and Finlandia vodka, swinging and swaying in their saunas.

'Boss?'

There was this Kiwi bloke last year that was caught doing things with a Collie. He got three years. The guy must've been a right sicko.

'Boss!'

Ruud's eyes sprang open.

He was back in the Incident Room.

Before Hamzah could press him any further, Police Commissioner Witarsa blundered in, grumbling and grousing like the baseball coach in *The Bad News Bears*.

Hartono stepped into his lace-ups and leapt to attention. '*Komisaris Polisi!*' he cried in greeting.

The senior officer waved him down. 'AT EASE, at ease,' he said, shambling past the circle of chairs to the whiteboard, his tall frame bent forward as though battling a stiff wind.

Ruud studied his chief's hangdog face. He looked shapeless and jowly, almost half-asleep. Walter Matthau on Quaaludes.

A young woman in a brown police tunic and black skirt appeared at his shoulder. She also sported a beige hijab, worn high like a badge of defiance.

'FIRST THINGS first,' Witarsa announced. His voice dwindled downward, almost to a whisper. 'I'd like to introduce the new member of our unit.'

The woman took one pace forward, chin raised. Her expression was focused on the far wall.

'This is *Ajun Inspektur Polisi Dua* Alya Entitisari.' Witarsa offered her a modest bow. 'Alya joins us from Commercial Crimes Division, Section Eleven. It appears she found insurance fraud too boring. So be nice.'

Murmurs from the assembled. The men exchanged the remotest of frowns. So this was to be Vidi's replacement, a year and a half following his death. Corrupt, distrustful, troubled Vidi, who'd stolen to pay for his stricken wife's cancer treatment, who'd had his throat cut from ear to ear. The appointment, owing to departmental budget cuts, was a good twelve months overdue.

Ruud, surreptitiously, gave Alya the once-over. She was slight and trim – medium height with caramel-coloured unblemished skin. She had arched brows, long lashes and full, meticulously outlined lips. Ruud thought she was very pretty. What's more, she looked familiar. And was that a scent of freesias in the air?

'Thank you, *tuan*.' She glanced at Ruud and smiled, very sure of herself. '*Apa kabar?* How are you?'

Ruud replied in the affirmative and all of a sudden he remembered her. They'd met several times at the police shooting range at Cijantung. She usually occupied Firing Lane 5 whilst he favoured Firing Lane 6. If memory served him she consistently hit the lower left torso on the human silhouette target, which was a symptom of jerking the trigger.

He hadn't recognized her without her safety goggles.

'Nice to see you again, Alya,' he said.

'And you.' And then, with a studied awareness, she addressed his teammates as a group. 'Hello everyone.'

'Hello.' They replied in unison.

Confident, not showing any of the usual skittishness associated with young female officers, Alya Entitisari pulled up a plastic chair and sat down next to Werry Hartono, who straightened his tie.

'Right, listen up.' The commissioner clapped his hands. 'Earlier today a body was pulled from a burned-out car in the hills of Puncak. The preliminary findings from the fire investigators indicate foul play. Solossa and his team are working on the assumption that our victim was alive before the car hit the tree and went up in flames.'

'Man or woman, boss?' asked Hamzah.

'Initial signs point to the *korban* being a woman.'

'Do we know her name?'

'Identifying the corpse is proving tricky as fingerprints are not a viable option. Forensics have fragments of dental evidence so we will pursue that line of enquiry by checking with hospital records to try and match dental X-rays.'

'What about the car?'

'There's not much left of it. We're attempting to identify the make and model by the car's overall design and engine shape. We're also looking at the exhaust system and the wheel rims. Preliminary evidence suggests it may be a Mazda.'

Witarsa handed out several colour photographs of the ruined vehicle and the surrounding area. Everyone gawked at the images.

'A few hours ago', he continued, 'we received a call from an old lady who lives in the area. Her name is Gita Lindo. She is in her seventies and she is blind.'

Hamzah groaned.

'Yes, she's blind. However, she claims to have heard something. We will send a car to collect her tomorrow. Ruud, I'd like you to speak with Mrs Lindo when she comes in.'

'Why tomorrow, sir?' Hartono queried. 'Shouldn't we question her this evening?'

'This evening I am attending a police fundraiser with First *Inspektur* Pujasumarta. I'm confident Mrs Lindo can hold on until then. Furthermore, you'll all be pleased to learn that due to recent developments the Code of Ethics seminar scheduled for tomorrow will be postponed till next month.'

Alya flicked nonexistent dust from her long skirt, which she tugged down, making a rustling sound. From where Ruud sat, none of her little movements escaped him. She kept catching Ruud's eye and smiling. Smiling from under her lashes and biting her bottom lip.

Ruud distracted himself by studying Officer Hamzah's centre parting, admiring the shiny black hair that was as glossy as damp varnish.

Alya raised an arm to ask Witarsa a question, shifting forward in her seat, sending wafts of freesia-scented air Ruud's way. Ruud tried not to look at her as she spoke, yet, like a finger that cannot help but worry an angry pimple, he found his gaze returning time and again to her face. Alya. Alya Entitisari. He rolled her name silently off his tongue.

Chapter Four

The fundraiser was held in the Hotel Kempinski's oval-shaped Bali Room. Over 700 people had gathered to toast the development of a new mosque complex on Jalan Rawasari Barat.

The General Authority of Islamic Affairs and Endowments had agreed to sponsor the construction project but they had come up short and needed to raise another RP 10 billion to complete the dome and south wing.

A tiny nervous tic made Commissioner Joyo T. Witarsa's eyelid hop. He surveyed the sea of grey suits. The place was swarming with fawning officials and grizzled bureaucrats.

'Fucking politicians,' he grumbled under his breath.

The very sight of them and their flummery made him blanche.

Ruud often wondered why his chief operated in a near perpetual state of disgruntlement. Well, here lay the answer.

He mistrusted them, scorned them, abhorred their grip-and-grin toadying. If he could he'd gladly feed their carcasses to the Komodo dragons at Ragunan Zoo. Every year during the departmental budget proposals, Witarsa had to battle these men. They hid behind the police generals, pulling the strings, trying to get some of his people sacked by reducing the number of officers per department. Every year he'd had to fight them tooth and nail. This year alone, investment in technology and communications systems had been slashed, while training opportunities for rookies had been axed. There were even neighbourhoods in Northern Jakarta, like Koja and Cilincing, where the police had stopped responding to vehicle thefts and burglar alarms.

Witarsa shambled up to the bar, then returned, splay-footed, to stand by Ruud's side. He clutched a glass of mung bean juice and was decked out in *teluk beskap*, the Javanese jacket and sarong worn on special occasions.

'I hate these things,' muttered the police commissioner.

'Well, I think you look exceedingly smart. Your mum would be very proud.'

'Look at them all. Every sycophant, bootlicker and yes-man in Jakarta is here. I tell you, Pujasumarta, it's enough to make your head spin.'

'You didn't have to come.'

'I was told I had to. Compulsory. Orders from the very top.'

'Brown-noser.'

'Piss off.'

Ruud contemplated the sweep of people. There were cabinet ministers, civil servants, industrialists, doctors, imams and mullahs all crammed into every square metre of the venue.

Many of them, however, were bunched around a raised lectern where the Minister for Religious Affairs was about to speak.

Attention focused on the man, and there was a scattering of applause as he began. 'Ladies and gentlemen, *bipak-bipak dan ibu-ibu*, honoured guests, thank you for your attendance

29

this evening. Eighteen months ago we embarked on a project to build a fine new *masjid*, a house for the pleasure of the Creator, a structure to accommodate the community's growing needs. A landmark building with modern facilities . . .'

Ruud grew restless. These gatherings bored the crap out of him. He and Witarsa took a couple of turns around the room.

'. . . together with an updated interior comprising energy-efficient cooling systems,' continued the minister, 'and a state-of-the-art women's prayer hall.'

A sprinkling of cheering and clapping.

Ruud was gagging for a beer.

He stopped a waitress doing her rounds with a tray of soft drinks. 'Excuse me' – he eyed the metal name plate pinned to her uniform – 'Yuliana. Do you have any cold Bintangs or Ankers stashed away at the back?'

'Sorry, sir,' said Yuliana in a quavering voice. 'We are not permitted to serve alcohol at this function.' Her words quivered as though a feather fluttered in her chest.

'Inshallah,' the minister at the podium proclaimed, 'the building will become a focal point for the district's brotherhood and sisterhood. So hear my appeal! We need your help, your continued generous support and *dua*.'

Cue massive applause.

Witarsa helped himself to another glass of mung bean juice. A minute later, his cheeks turned cauliflower-white.

'Oh, no,' hissed Witarsa.

'What?'

'Pariah dogs. One o'clock.'

Ruud saw three men approaching; two fifty-year-olds accompanied by a younger man in full ceremonial naval dress. The commissioner drained his glass and prayed for a shepherd's crook to extend from offstage and yank him away.

The three men extended their hands to Joyo T. Witarsa. He pressed each palm deferentially and said, 'May peace be upon you,' before introducing the first man to Ruud. 'Lieutenant General Fauzi, Director for International Cooperation, Ministry of Defence. Allow me to acquaint you with First *Inspektur* Ruud Pujasumarta.'

Ruud dipped his chin and touched his chest with his right palm.

'A pleasure,' said the lieutenant general, a solidly built man with peppercorn-grey hair and lugubrious lips. '*Senang bertemu anda.*' He cocked his head at the navy man. 'My son. Captain Noah Fauzi of the Second Marine Cavalry Regiment.'

The captain frowned at Ruud as if he were a fly in a glass of water.

'And this is H. W. Rusmin, director of KPK,' continued Witarsa, 'the Corruption Eradication Commission.'

'They call us the "law mafia",' chimed the KPK official in a high-pitched voice. His smile revealed small, even teeth. Ruud didn't like the look of his fat, greasy face. He had a large bulbous nose and wide-set features. It was, thought Ruud, like peering through the peephole of a hotel bedroom and seeing Mr Blobby through the fisheye lens. 'Your reputation precedes you, First *Inspektur*. I was greatly impressed with your handling of the Mah-Jong Master investigation.'

'I'm flattered.'

'I'm sure my friends at the Ministry of Tourism cannot thank you enough. Cases like that can be very damaging to the tourist industry and to Indonesia's reputation abroad. And right now, in light of last month's grisly ISIL attacks, we need all the help we can get.'

'Detachment Eighty-eight will sort out ISIL, don't you worry,' said Fauzi junior.

'Quite right,' agreed Fauzi senior.

'If only the First *Inspektur* could do the same with the bloody *shabu* pandemic,' said Rusmin. He reached out and touched Ruud's sleeve. 'You know what, we should stick Pujasumarta in front of the *shabu* dealers. Scare the hell out of the buggers. Catching serial killers and hired guns is all well and good, but what we really need now is a drug tsar, a strongman at the helm.'

Witarsa groaned into his empty glass.

'The country is crying out for it. Witarsa, give your man Pujasumarta here a promotion and get him to clean things up. This *shabu* is destroying us.'

'With all due respect, director,' said Ruud. 'I'm a homicide detective.'

'What, a doctor can't pull a tooth? A plumber can't change a light bulb? Don't give me that nonsense. Witarsa, have a word with General Haiti. If Pujasumarta here is the best we have then utilize him. Utilize him!'

'Rusmin has a point,' said Lieutenant General Fauzi. 'I'm told there is more methamphetamine produced in Southeast Asia now than in any other region in the world.'

'The BNN can't cope,' argued Rusmin.

'In which case organizations related to narcotics control should step up their game,' said Fauzi. 'The coastguard, the airports security service, the Kalimantan border constabulary, the customs department.'

'Your reasoning is flawed,' trilled the KPK man. 'Who gives a damn about the coastguard and border control? Much of the narcotics hitting the city streets is produced in Indonesia. We have to stop domestic production before tackling frontier issues.' He grabbed Ruud's arm. 'Listen to me, Pujasumarta, pack in homicide and transfer to narcotics. You could go far. Very far.'

Ruud turned to Witarsa for help, but the police commissioner looked as though he'd swallowed a worm. Something in Ruud's pocket trembled. He thanked the heavens. 'Gentlemen, if you will excuse me, I must take this call.'

Ruud stepped out of the Bali Room and into the relative calm of the hotel foyer. 'Pujasumarta here.'

'*Tuan* Ruud?' A female voice. 'It's Alya. Can we meet for a coffee?'

He was surprised to hear from her. He glanced behind him to see if Witarsa had followed. There was no sign of the commissioner.

'What's the matter?'

'I need someone to talk to. First-day nerves. It's been a tough initiation and I think I may have made a mistake transferring from Commercial Crimes.'

'It's late.'

'I know. I wouldn't have called if I didn't have to.'

Ruud closed his eyes. What was he getting himself into here? His heart pounded. He remembered that smile, the meticulously outlined lips, the jiggling calf. His mouth went dry. The phone felt hot against his ear. 'You know Kopi Tuku across from Toodz House? I'll meet you there in half an hour.'

The finger couldn't help but worry the pimple.

Yuliana put down her metal serving tray for the final time. It had just gone eleven at night and the air conditioning in

33

the staff changing rooms was already shut off. The room was very warm and the lamp dangling from the ceiling made the heat in the basement worse.

Dripping with perspiration, Yuliana yanked off her uniform and slid into her civvies. It was now 11.07. If she hurried she'd make the 11.15 bus and be home before midnight. But first she had to run the gauntlet of Perdana and his female assistant. Mr Perdana was the hotel's safety and security manager and right now he stood up against the rear wall checking every employee as they left, searching their bags and pockets for hotel cutlery and kitchen provisions.

It irked her, this mistrust. True, she was only part-time staff – brought in at short notice on the minimum wage – but she'd never stolen anything in her life, and at the age of twenty-three she wasn't intending to start. Honesty was something she instilled in the children. Better to share than to take, better to give than to appropriate. Suddenly, images of the boys and girls in her kindergarten class filled her head and she smiled. Her role as classroom assistant at ACG School in Ragunan was one of life's delights. Not having kids herself made the experience all the more special. Soon, she hoped, she'd be promoted to KG 2 Teacher, which meant entry into the faculty common room and a 10 per cent discount in the canteen.

When she reached the rear exit Perdana gave her handbag a cursory glance and waved her through without the usual pat down. Everybody seemed eager to get home tonight.

Yuliana nodded her thanks, shoved against the steel door and escaped into the hotel's dark side street, where the night was heavy with vent smoke and carried the greasy smells of the Kempinski's kitchens.

The moment the steel door clanged shut behind her and she stepped outside, she felt a chill despite the warm air.

Winged bugs bumped against a caged filament lamp secured to the wall. But their frantic swishing wings weren't the only sounds she heard.

To her immediate left she perceived movement. Something dark and indistinguishable disturbed the shadows. She caught herself with a jolt and stopped in her tracks. She waited.

A pair of glistening black eyes watched her.

She steadied herself and groaned with disgust. '*Enyahlah!*' she yelled, clapping her hands. A glass bottle tipped over and something bristly and rough scuttled across her path. A long thin tail slinked into a hole in the wall.

Yuliana's smile turned into a grimace. She hated rats. They repulsed her; the mere sight of one made her skin crawl. The trick is to stamp your feet, she said to herself. Scare the damn thing off. She took several forceful steps and grimaced once more. Her feet and ankles ached from all the walking she'd done. The fundraiser was scheduled to last from 7 to 10.30 p.m. She hadn't eaten or sat down for the entire stretch and she must have circumnavigated the Bali Room a hundred times. When she reached home the first thing she'd do was soak her toes in a bucket of warm salty water.

The thought of a soothing footbath made her forget about the rat.

Up ahead, she heard the dull sound of traffic. A group of people mingled under the shelter. Most likely, the bus would be standing room only.

Just as she began to trot toward the bus stop a car horn bleated behind her. At first she was concerned she was in its way, but then she noticed the headlights weren't on and the car was stationary.

She stopped and turned to look at the car. It was parked beside a tall metal rubbish bin. The car made the low growl of a predatory animal.

Yuliana stiffened.

Growing up in Jakarta had taught her never to let her guard down. She gripped her handbag tightly to her side, ready to employ it as a shield or wield it like a weapon.

There was minimal street lighting, but she could make out a man at the wheel. A sinister-looking figure.

'What do you want?' she snapped. The feather in her chest fluttered forcefully. Her first impulse was to run. She was about to leg it to the bus shelter when the man's face and deep-set eyes became visible in the open window. 'Hello,' he beamed, wiggling his fingers at her. 'I almost nodded off. Good thing I spotted you.'

Her breath caught in her throat. 'Bayu!' A smile like sudden sunshine. 'What are you doing here?'

'The hotel was on the way home. You mentioned you'd be finished before midnight so I thought I'd come pick you up.' Bayu's voice was subdued, as though fearful that speaking in the dark might wake somebody, but his tone was warm. It lifted her heart.

He squeezed her to him as she climbed into the passenger seat of his Perodua Kenari. Once thin, she'd become joyfully tubby since marriage, much to her husband's delight. True, parts of her wobbled now when she ran and a few of her tops were tighter than before, but she didn't consider herself fat. Shapely, curvy even, but not fat.

'You should have gone back first. I was happy to take the

bus,' she said with mock disapproval. She touched her husband's arm.

'No problem! *Tidak apa-apa!*'

'You are too good to me, my handsome husband.' She laughed with a side-to-side waggle of her lips.

'*Hnnn* . . . such sweet compliments, pouring like syrup from the mangosteen tree. Keep them coming.'

'Now your head is getting inflated.'

Bayu manoeuvred the car into the main road. 'I called your mother to say I'd collect you,' he said. 'She cooked *soto* in case you were hungry.'

Yuliana and Bayu shared a small but clean apartment with her parents. The couple wished they could have a place to themselves but couldn't yet afford a one-bedroom walk-up, so they had to put up with the sagging mattress and creaking armchairs for now.

'I'm not hungry, but I'll eat a little to make her feel good.'

'She also mentioned one of the budgies died.'

'Which one?'

'The smaller of the two, Kacang. Your mother has wrapped it in newspaper.'

Yuliana gazed at Bayu. His receding black hair was lank and his eyelids were swollen from overwork. The erratic shift arrangements and frequent hours on call seemed to be exhausting him. Like the good wife she was she asked about his day. 'How was it today?' She gave him a gentle tug. 'Sunny side up or scrambled?'

He chuckled. There was a Japanese restaurant in Kota Kasablanka that went by that name. Yuliana passed it every morning on her way to Ragunan. 'My day was sunny side up. A quiet stretch. No broken legs or gunshot wounds to report tonight.'

Bayu worked four evenings a week at the military hospital on Jalan Abdul Rahman Saleh, treating servicemen for a range of ailments from fevers to ingrown toenails to fractured limbs. He was one of ten general medical officers at Gatot Soebroto Army Hospital training to be flight surgeons. The pay was rubbish, the benefits worse, but Bayu had wangled an angle. And it was starting to pay off.

Yuliana eyed her husband, studied his features. When the words rose to her lips she said, 'You seem energized tonight.'

'Can't a man be energized when he sees his wife?'

From the day they met he'd had a savage intensity about him, a fire burning in his eyes, bright as coals. He told her repeatedly how he wanted to achieve success, make a name for himself, and that he wanted to do it quick. Quick, quick, quick, he'd say, snapping his fingers.

He was prepared to do anything to get ahead. If it meant stealing vials of fentanyl to sell on the streets or peddling bottles of Versed to rich junkies, then so be it. And so long as his superiors were kept in the dark, so long as Yuliana didn't know, all would be well.

'I know you're not hungry but I bought this for you,' he said, handing his wife a bag of tamarind candy.

'You have blood on your sleeve, Bayu.' She held his arm up to the tip of her nose.

'Hmm? Oh, that must belong to the *kopral* who stepped on a nail. He checked in at nine o'clock. Nice young man from Malang. Eleven stitches and a tetanus shot.'

'You told me everything was quiet tonight.'

He said nothing.

'I'll soak it in cold water for you. You wouldn't like it to stain.'

Expressionless. 'I would hate that.'

The car turned into a well-lit street. The backwash from the streetlights illuminated his knees and feet. It was only then that he noticed the blood on his shoes.

He'd have to dispose of the shirt, as well as his trousers and shoes, and use oxygen bleach to remove any blood evidence in the car.

Now, more than any other time, he needed to be sly with the truth.

Chapter Five

The following day Ruud climbed out of bed before dawn and was out of the house by seven.

He hadn't got home until well after midnight, creaking in at around 1 a.m., which hadn't gone unnoticed. 'Why so late, *hè*?' Imke had asked, propped up among the bedroom pillows. 'I waited up, spent the evening folding laundry and eating Frosties straight from the packet.'

'Work.'

'I thought you were heading back straight after the police fundraiser.'

'Something came up.'

'Do you want to talk about it?'

'No, not really. Listen, I was looking in the mirror just now. Do you think my forehead's got bigger?'

'If you mean are you losing your hair, then no, you're not losing your hair.'

'Good.'

He was asleep within a minute; he hadn't even bothered to kiss her goodnight.

His odd manner naturally meant that Imke tossed about for ages, unable to sleep.

Worse was to come when Kiki suffered a sneezing fit at 4 a.m., waking the entire household.

And then came the sound of Ruud's 6 a.m. alarm call.

He crawled into the shower, muttering that he felt like a zombie.

She stayed in bed and catnapped.

Which meant that when Djoko, the head of the K9 special unit, rang at seven telling her she had fifty-five minutes to meet the police chopper at the Military Provost helipad at Menteng, Ruud had already left.

Tossing back the covers, she scrambled out of her pyjamas. No time for breakfast. No time to feed Kiki. Just enough time to pee, clean her teeth and drive like the clappers via Jalan Pemuda to avoid the rush-hour traffic.

All in all it had been a topsy-turvy morning for Imke Sneijder.

She looked at her watch. It was 10.50 a.m.

Earlier, the police helicopter had deposited them in the nearby, long-disused playing field, landing on a patch of scrub. The pilot told them he'd be back in ninety minutes. As it took off, the chopper whipped the dirt off the deck in concentric circles, the air pressure from the rotor blades flattening Imke's hair against her pate. She huddled in a crouch with her arm wrapped around Kiki protectively.

Imke watched the Airbus H135 take off and rise high in the sky. And the higher it went, the angrier she got. She couldn't believe Ruud hadn't left her a note. No note, no card, not even a text, and when she checked her phone there were no missed calls. Nothing.

When he'd left, all he'd given her was a careless peck on the forehead as she lolled between the sheets, half-asleep, one eye open to the world, her hair looking like a scraggy rooster. No minute of snuggle time, no pat on the bottom, not even a hug. One little smooch and a hasty sayonara before the front door swung shut.

Surely he wouldn't have forgotten. She'd only mentioned on – when was it, Thursday? – that she didn't want a cake. Was he that forgetful?

Pushing those thoughts aside, Imke concentrated on the here and now. She peered down the dark tunnel.

From the very start, everything about the search had felt peculiar, off-kilter. The abandoned lead smelter on the eastern outskirts of Greater Jakarta was a pretty spooky place to explore at the best of times, consequently having to reconnoitre two kms of unlit basement passageways alone, armed with nothing but a flashlight, really gave her the creeps.

Ducking low as she entered the mouth of the duct, she let out a stream of expletives.

Lifeless moths lay scattered at her feet, their brittle wings shedding scales like dead poppies dropping pollen. There were spiders, too; spiders, caterpillars, rats, monitor lizards and possibly even snakes.

It didn't take long for her eyes to adjust to the gloom. The underground passage was cramped and fusty and smelled of decay. Water leaked into the shaft and the ceiling was too low for upright movement. Parts of it were wider than it was high. Advancing in a half-crouch, she shuffled along for about a hundred metres. Having to stoop like a hunchbacked hockey player for such a long period made Imke's lower spine stiffen up. Soon her entire backbone started to ache.

Outside the wind blew and gusted, the air fresh; below ground it was dead. Ventilation was poor. With every step, the air grew worse and breathing became a struggle. No breeze. No draught, just a suffocating Javanese heat.

She cursed Djoko, the unit head, for giving her this assignment. Since taking up her position with Kepolisian Indonesia K9, she and Kiki had met with unparalleled success. Between them, they'd earned two certificates of merit and one unit citation. However, success brought its own added pressures. BNN – the National Anti-Narcotics Agency – utilized them whenever they could, as did Homicide and Detachment 88 anti-terrorism, which meant the job became more demanding, with increased hours, fewer days off and higher expectations.

What she craved was a hiatus, some downtime, a pampering weekend at a spa in Ubud. Not 7 a.m. calls from Djoko telling her to hotfoot her arse down to the helipad at Polda Metro Jaya. Did he have any idea how many pairs of shoes she was wearing out? Her beloved Bally flats were testament to that. She'd worn a hole in the left heel, which was costing RP 50,000 to get mended. That was why she now donned an old set of all-terrain Reeboks.

And why did she have to do this on her own? Why did the three National Anti-Narcotics Agency officers stay above ground, smoking and chatting, while she recoiled each time her torch illuminated a monstrously hairy eight-legged *laba-laba*? The answer, like so much in Indonesia, remained a mystery. Conceivably, BNN were planning to inspect the plant building, examine the idle blast furnace or the lead sintering machine for clues, although she doubted it very much.

Kiki, nevertheless, was having a ball. The dog led Imke through the tunnel, darting left and right, tail wagging, nose to the ground, twisting and turning.

Several sections of the tunnel walls were crisscrossed with cobwebs. And was that mushroom growth on the floor?

Imke shuddered at the thought. She decided she wouldn't be eating mushrooms on toast for some time. The further she proceeded, the more closed-in she felt. It was dark down below. So dark it was almost palpable.

It was in this tunnel that a police informant – a man codenamed SquarePants – insisted a Maluku smuggling ring had stashed 15 kgs of crystal methamphetamine.

The demand for crystal meth, or *shabu*, was soaring in Southeast Asia. Its production was relatively simple and did not require any elaborate equipment. Much of it was produced in home-made laboratories. In 2015, Indonesians consumed an estimated 16.2 metric tons of the massively addictive narcotic. According to one UN report, crystal meth seizures rose 82 per cent the same year.

Fifteen kgs of crystal meth had a street value of US$1.2m.

Imke checked her phone one more time. She had the faintest of signals. The artificial light shone on her face. Two voicemails: one from her father, Thys, calling from Amsterdam, the other from Stop'N'Go shoe repairs informing her that her Bally flats had been reheeled and were ready for collection.

She could hardly contain her disappointment. At least her mother had rung earlier. She could always rely on Mama to call first thing – be it on Christmas Day, New Year's or her birthday.

A split second later Kiki's tail went rigid. The spaniel came to an abrupt stop and sat down, her torso elongated. 'What have you got there, Kiki? Is it the drugs?'

She saw a mound of newsprint. Imke stooped lower and nudged the object with the toe of her shoe.

But she didn't find any *shabu*.

When she peeled away the layer of damp newspaper she found a head.

A head encased in clingfilm.

Imke's hand jogged the bundle and a roach scurried into the shadows. She grimaced before leaning in for a closer look. The clingfilm distorted the face, crushing the pair of blue saucer-shaped eyes, mashing the two buckteeth and stretching the mouth into a rictus grin. Alarmed, Imke directed the torch beam down the tunnel shaft, sweeping the ray to and fro like the swift gliding of a snake. She searched the blackness, beyond the range of the flashlight, staring into darkness.

No sounds. No movement.

Satisfied there was nobody else there, she aimed the light once more at the head. She examined it intently with troubled fascination. It was rectangular shaped, canary yellow in colour and resembled a kitchen sponge. When Imke prodded the bundle with her shoe, the soft load tipped onto its side. That was when she saw a second face, then a third, one behind the other, all of them identically wrapped in clear plastic.

There must have been a dozen pair of eyes staring back at her.

Something burned in the hollow of her stomach. Whoever had done this had a very peculiar brand of humour.

'Made in damn China! Mother of bitches!' spat the senior BNN officer. He ran his pocketknife along the back of the stuffed toy, pulling out white fistfuls of synthetic stuffing. He'd craniotomized seven SpongeBob dolls already. This was the eighth.

'Any sign of the *shabu*?' Imke asked in her semi-proficient Bahasa. Having dusted herself off, she bent forward slowly then leaned backwards, stretching the soft tissues along her spine and releasing the tension from her lower back muscles.

The officer's lips formed a *moue* of disapproval. He was ankle-deep in a sea of artificial wool. 'What does it look like?'

'It looks like your informant's had his cover blown, *hè*?'

'That fucking SquarePants. If the Maluku boys don't kill him then I sure as hell will.' He tore the shades from his face. 'I'll wring his *goblok* neck if I ever get my hands on him.'

Imke shrugged and lifted her chin to the midday breeze. She and the three BNN agents stood in the shadow of the sentry box, under the cover of its corrugated-iron roof. Having escaped the confines of the tunnel, the gentle wind was like a blessing.

'Something tells me you're too late. The Maluku *preman* sent you a message with these dolls. Odds-on he's already fish food.'

One of the agents barked instructions into his mobile.

The senior officer sucked his teeth. 'What is it?'

His colleague got off the phone. 'She's right, our canary is dead. He was found at home with three bullets in his chest. Someone sold him out.'

Imke decided to remove herself from the conversation. This was BNN business, not K9 Animal Police's.

She checked her own mobile – still no text or voicemail from Ruud.

She felt desolate.

They'd been living together for a year and a half. He'd said he was ready. She believed him, believed they shared something special; she still did. But lately he'd become increasingly aloof, less bouncy on his toes. Quitting those awful HeadStart energy pills hadn't helped. Without them he grew cranky and lifeless. She wondered whether he was suffering from withdrawal symptoms, but he blamed the job, claimed it was sucking him dry.

Being on call 24/7 exhausted him. Most homicides in Jakarta occurred between 11 p.m. and 4 a.m., which meant he rarely got a decent night's sleep. The mandatory overtime shifts were wearing him down, too. What he needed, he said, was a tummy-full of her delicious chicken casserole and several days' hibernation.

It dawned on Imke that she was pretty exhausted as well. There was no point finding fault with Ruud. Because of the Nakula case the couple had come under public scrutiny.

Nakula.

She was reminded of the terrible ordeal once again. Her crazed half-brother had drugged her, tied her up. Naked and spread-eagled. With a ball-gag jammed into her mouth. She was sure he was going to kill her.

Sometimes she could still taste the rubber on her tongue. If it weren't for Ruud she would probably be dead.

But it was Nakula who'd died.

After that, there had been police debriefings and hours and hours of cross-examination by PROPAM, the internal affairs division.

Then came the newspaper and TV interviews, the endless telephone calls from foreign journalists. But that was, thankfully, all behind them now. These days it was the demands of their respective jobs that consumed them. They hadn't had a holiday in months – Indonesia being a Muslim country meant that both she and Ruud only enjoyed a single day off at Christmas. In addition, because the homicide squad was short-staffed, Ruud did not fly to Melbourne this year to see his brother Arjen and his parents; not spending the Yuletide week with them – a family tradition – had made him even more cranky.

He was knackered and she was knackered. Both of them were bone-tired. Clearly, she had her own dreads and desires, her own crazy demands, but right now she had to be strong. She knew full well that being a cop's girlfriend was not for the frail. There was no room for the self-absorbed, the needy and the insecure. Being a cop's girlfriend often meant eating alone, sleeping alone and watching TV alone, but most of all it meant learning to live with the bigger picture. She'd read online that a policeman's spouse developed an unusual resilience to loneliness.

Bluebottles rested on Imke's bare arms. Cicadas shrilled deafeningly in the trees. She kicked a loose pebble with her instep; clenched and unclenched her fist.

So why was she feeling this way? She never felt dependent on Ruud. Of all the women she knew, she was by far the least clingy.

Sure, she missed having his shoulder to lean on or his ear to bend. But she understood what she was getting into from the start.

He had a tough job. An ugly job. Every day he met with emotional pain, fear and stress. Sometimes he had to just bottle things up.

Yet she had to wonder if things were changing between them.

She thought about this for several minutes and then smiled. No, nothing had changed between them. He still made her laugh and wanted to make her laugh. He still called her *Putri Salju* – his little Snow White. They continued to tease one another, feed each other bits from their plates, read aloud extracts from magazines. And she was certain he really, really loved her. She could see that in the way he looked into her eyes.

But that didn't mean she didn't want to wring his neck sometimes. You'd think the bloody bugger would've remembered to buy her a card at the very least.

Perhaps she should speak to Hartono and find out whether Ruud had turned up at Central or if he was out in the field. Was he on a stakeout, at a murder scene, in a firefight? The last thought chilled her. What if . . . ? No. Imke shook the thought away. She didn't want to dwell on the dangers of his profession or overthink things. But she couldn't help herself. Police casualties were on the rise. Gangs were getting increasingly violent. He'd promised to wear a ballistic vest – one that was stab- and bulletproof – and he'd assured her that if things got too hot to handle, they'd call in BRIMOB, the special response unit.

Imke kicked another pebble, booting the fears and forebodings from her mind.

Instead, she filled her head with spurious theories.

Theory A: he'd fallen down a well. Verdict: unlikely. This only happened in *Lassie*. When said dog ran to the local farmer for help to save a boy named Timmy.

Theory B: in aid of medical research, and because he yearned for a nice long sleep, he agreed to be cryogenically frozen for a year. Verdict: possible, but horrifying. What if the freezing chamber malfunctions and he wakes in fifty years' time having not aged, looking young and healthy, only to find she'd become a dry old crone. See *Forever Young* starring Mel Gibson.

Theory C: he'd self-combusted.

She paused, remembering something she'd learned ages ago at school. The last semester of VWO, preparatory school education, *Cultuur en Maatschappij*, English literature class, taught by Mr Van den Droog. They'd spent six months reading and discussing Dickens. Van den Droog spoke about a character spontaneously combusting in one of the books. Some fellow who'd had so much booze in his gut he lit up like a flare. *Bleak House*, wasn't it? Yes, she nodded, yes, Mr Krook, the alcoholic landlord. *Bleak House*. How apt.

Imke groaned.

Kiki, sensitive to Imke's moods, sat on Imke's feet reassuringly and gazed skyward.

Twin turboshaft engines shook the air, followed by the *wop-wop* sound of spinning blades. Imke looked up. The drug enforcement agents did the same.

Floating through sunshine, the Airbus H135 hovered above them for some seconds before coming alongside some twenty metres away. The chopper landed on its skids, the downwash from the main rotors sending dust flying into their eyes.

Turning away from the chopper, Imke punched Ruud's number into her mobile. After six rings it went to voicemail.

She muttered an expletive, grabbed Kiki and stormed towards the aircraft, ducking her head as she mounted the step and climbed into the cabin.

Chapter Six

Imke stepped out of the Airbus H135 and found herself back on the tarmac of the Military Provost helipad at Menteng, just south of Merdeka Square in downtown Jakarta. She walked across the apron, over the pavement markings, and ducked behind a rusting Enstrom F-280FX parked on the hardstand.

A man in a blue jumpsuit was waiting. They exchanged smiles and Imke handed Kiki over to the K9 official, who led the dog towards an idling van.

Imke waved farewell to Kiki then checked her phone.

Ruud still wasn't responding to her calls. Was there a reason he'd turned his mobile off? She couldn't understand it. And because there was no way she was leaving another voicemail (she'd left four by now) she decided to call Hartono.

'Second Lieutenant Werry Hartono speaking,' he announced in English, deliberately enunciating each syllable.

Imke climbed into her car, which was parked in the forecourt. 'Werry, it's Imke. Where's Ruud? Christ, it's hot in here. Hold on while I get the aircon working, *hè*?'

She fumbled with the climate control panel.

'Sorry about that. I was asking about Ruud?'

51

'First *Inspektur* Pujasumarta is currently not at his station.'

'Can you tell me where he is?'

'No.'

'No you can't or no you won't?'

'I do not understand the question.'

'Is he at a crime scene? Nothing's happened to him, has it?'

'He seemed in good health this morning.'

'Do you know where he is?'

'He took an early lunch at his desk but has been gone now since about noon. He comes and goes like the wet-season rains.'

'I'm trying to find him, Werry. It's important.'

'He may be job-juggling.'

'What does that mean?'

'Miss Imke, sometimes police detectives have to follow multiple leads.'

'When is he due back?'

'He is interviewing a witness, Mrs Gita Lindo, at 6 p.m. today, so I expect him back at Central before then. She is blind, you know.'

'Are you near his desk?'

'A blind witness, who would have thought? There was an episode of *Sherlock* called "The Blind Banker", but I doubt there is any similarity with this case.'

'His desk. Are you near it?'

'I can see it.'

'Please go over and open his logbook to today's date.'

'Miss Imke, this I cannot do. He is my commanding officer. It is against—'

'Just do it!' She steadied herself. She could almost see

Hartono anxiously stroking his puppy-fat gills. 'Please, Werry. I'll explain later.'

'First *Inspectur* Pujasumarta will have my head if he finds out,' he bleated.

'I will take full responsibility.'

'That is what you say now but when he—'

'Werry!'

'OK, OK.'

Imke heard Hartono's footsteps clomp through the office, a door swishing open, a door slamming shut and a desk drawer sliding free. A bit of paper rustling followed.

'His logbook says, "Meeting AE at Suparna Hotel."' He pronounced the word 'hottle'.

'The Suparna?'

'"Room six-oh-five. Four forty-five p.m."'

'*Who's* AE?'

'Miss Imke, I am sorry I am not meant to say.'

'Who is AE?'

'She is . . .'

'She?'

'You are not meant to know about her.'

'AE is a she! And I'm not meant to know about her!'

'I am sorry, but I cannot be of any more assistance. I have already crossed the line.'

And with that, he hung up.

Two minutes later Imke called back Werry Hartono.

'Me again.'

'I cannot be of any more assistance,' reiterated Hartono.

'I'm not calling about Ruud, I'm calling about you.'

'Me? What about me?'

'It concerns your promotion.'

Her response seemed to confuse the young detective. 'Promotion, what promotion? I'm not due for assessment for another six months. I'm still studying for my *Inspektur Dua Polisi* evaluation.'

'Ruud told me to tell you it's been brought forward. There are a few things the top brass feel you need to work on, but I can help you. Meet me at the Suparna Hotel at five p.m. sharp.'

Chapter Seven

Ruud parked his blue Toyota Yaris at the Masjid Al I'tisam. The moment he got out of the car his shades fogged up. He slapped a KNRI entry permit on the windscreen before pausing to admire the white stone dome and fifteen-metre minaret. It was a quiet period, between prayer times, and only a handful of people dotted the courtyard. The last time he'd stood in the grounds of the mosque was to commemorate the previous year's Eid al-Adha, a festival honouring Ibrahim's willingness to sacrifice his son, Ismail, as an act of obedience to God. Along with his fellow officers, he'd watched the chief of police offer a cow to the imam. The cow was one of several chosen for *qurban*, the sacrificing of an animal, the police would donate to the surrounding community. It was all over the local press.

His phone vibrated in his pocket. Ruud sniffed when he saw the caller ID.

He couldn't trust himself to pick up. He'd have to lie and he wasn't good at lying to Imke. There was no way he could tell her who he was about to spend the next hour with.

He quickened his pace. The hotel was up ahead.

He crumpled the page he'd torn from his notepad and tossed it down an open drain. 'The Suparna. Room 605.' He looked at his watch; it was after five; he'd kept her waiting twenty minutes. He repeated the room number in his head several times to commit it to memory.

The Suparna was an elegant and tranquil hotel; a haven of unhurried calm in the bustle of the city. Two red marble sculptures of Garuda crouched at the entrance, legs cocked, arms drawn back against the wings. Their reproachful eyes bore into Ruud.

Placing his phone and Heckler & Koch 9 mm in the tray provided, he stepped through the metal detector and flashed his warrant card at the security personnel.

He scoured the main lobby, scanning left and right for anyone he knew. He observed two newspaper-reading tourists, a pair of Jakarta socialites on their way to Tamarind Seed, a flunky in a white uniform attending to some orchids, a little boy in shorts staring at the decorative water feature, a fat man picking his nose. The coast was clear. Moving nonchalantly, doing his best to avoid being recognized, he strode past the hotel boutique and the coffee shop that smelled of fresh lilies and took the mirrored lift to the sixth floor. Before stepping out of the lift, he checked his hair in the reflection.

He was both excited and nervous. He'd never done anything like this before. The yellow light pinged. The lift door opened.

Spring-heeled, he strode forward.

The hallway stretched out ahead.

Chapter Eight

Meanwhile, in Ruud's absence, the forensic pathologist arranged to meet Aiboy Ali in the bowels of the Persahabatan General Hospital. It usually smelled of powdered bleach down here, and it was always freezing. But Aiboy had come prepared, fortified in a leather biker vest to ward off the 4 °C chill.

The moment the detective entered the autopsy room he was greeted by a blast of cold air and the swinging blues-based vibrato of a jazz saxophone.

'This way, please,' said the diener, a young man named Hussein.

'You still working here, Hussein?' said Aiboy.

'Believe me, nobody is more bewildered about this fact than I,' Hussein replied. 'Come, the boss is expecting you.'

Solossa, short, stocky and forever cheerful despite his profession, was hunched over a body. He wore green scrubs with his trousers crammed into half-length wellies. There was also a 3B pencil tucked behind his left ear.

On seeing him, the medical examiner set aside his skull chisel and extracted a comb from his scrub suit pocket. He ran the comb through his scalp, before sidling up to Aiboy Ali. 'Welcome to the meat locker! You'll forgive me if I don't shake hands. I just completed scoring the skullcap of a blunt impact victim. Messy business.' His gloves were plastered with blood, as were certain portions of his comb-over.

'You wanted to see me?'

The music blared. The hard bop jazz seemed far too cool for someone like Solossa. As if reading his thoughts, the *dokter forensik* smiled. 'Hank Mobley. *Soul Station*. Released in 1960 by Blue Note Records.'

'Sounds wild.'

'It's an important album for me. When I first heard this I was completing my second year at University of Indonesia. People assume I'm just a mouldy old fig. You should come and hear me play. A few of us get together once a month and perform at the Red White Lounge.'

Aiboy Ali didn't want to say that his musical tastes were a little darker, although he might be persuaded to listen to groove metal from time to time.

The forensic pathologist yanked off his sullied gloves, tossed them in a bin, and directed the detective across the tiles to a slanted stainless-steel operating table. He pushed aside a set of weighing scales hanging from the ceiling. Aiboy Ali winced when he saw the blackened figure lying on the slab. It was scorched beyond recognition. All skin and hair was burned clean off, the flesh melted and the eyes poached down to the lacrimal bone, dried up, shrivelled into their sockets.

'Is this the stiff from the car fire?' He tried not to look at the cadaver. Its insides resembled a split dead tree trunk – a dark gurgled mess of charred snag covered in black fairy inkcaps.

'Yes.'

'It's like her body's been cooked and turned on a huge

spit. Why', Aiboy asked, swallowing, 'are the hands twisted like that?'

'We call that the pugilistic attitude. In extreme heat the muscle proteins coagulate, contracting the muscle fibres, causing the arms to flex at the elbows and wrists. The same thing happens to the hips and knees.'

'Do you have anything solid to give me?'

'Solid, eh? Well, we have established our little friend here as female,' remarked Solossa. 'Notice the larger sub-pubic angle of the pelvis. Larger than a man's. Moreover, take a look at the skull; the chin is pointy and the forehead quite rounded. Usually, this indicates a woman's skull. The male chin tends to be squarer and the forehead slants back ever so slightly.'

'Well, that's a start,' Aiboy managed. 'Anything else?'

'Lean in, can you smell that?'

'I'd rather not.'

'There's a very faint residue of kerosene on her, embedded in her bones.'

'Which confirms an accelerant was used.'

'We will have to apply several chromatography tests on the skeleton to be sure.'

'But it's likely.'

'Yes.'

'Any clues to her identity?'

'Naturally, because of the fire, we found no KTP card or any form of ID on her, no driver's licence, no credit cards.'

'Jewellery?'

'None.'

'That's strange. Mobile phone?'

The older man shook his head.

'What about the remains of a handbag? House keys?

There must have been keys. Even in an extreme fire keys don't just melt. What are they made of?'

'Brass with nickel plating.'

'What temperature does brass melt?'

The diener, Hussein, who also acted as Solossa's assistant, looked up the figure on his screen. 'Brass liquefies at nine hundred and twenty-seven degrees Celsius. You want to know about jewellery melting? Nine hundred and sixty-one degrees for silver, one thousand and sixty-four degrees for gold.'

'A burning car can reach peak temperatures of nine hundred degrees. Rarely higher,' stated Solossa, 'at least not for a sustainable period.'

'So we should have found a set of house keys and jewellery.'

The diener adjusted the body block under the corpse's back so that the breastbone jutted forward while the rigid arms and head fell away marginally.

When Hussein completed his task, he bowed low with his right hand touching his brow. 'May the Almighty dwell her in *Jannatul Firdaus*, in the most beautiful of paradises.'

'Thank you, Hussein,' said Solossa. 'You may leave us now.'

Solossa and Aiboy Ali watched the man depart through the metal door and pull it shut behind him.

'Hussein likes to eavesdrop on my conversations,' said Solossa. 'I wouldn't be surprised if he's got his ear pressed to the door.'

With a pair of hardware store pruning shears, Solossa cut through the ribs, snapping them one by one, and lifted off the chest plate until the ruined heart and lungs were exposed.

'Was she dead before the fire?' asked the detective.

'Hard to say. Carbon monoxide levels in the blood would tell me that. Or soot in the lungs. But given the state she's in I'd be pushed to get anything concrete.'

'How are we going to identify her?'

Solossa tapped the cadaver's mouth with his pencil, tapping as though it were a percussion instrument.

'Teeth,' said Aiboy Ali, answering his own question.

'Yes, through her teeth. Teeth can sustain very high temperatures, but heat contractions have locked the jaw rigid so Hussein here will have to excise the lower mandible.'

'*Sangat bagus*, but to identify her we will need her—'

'Dental records. Either that or a sample of her DNA.'

'How are we going to get her dental records if we don't know who she is?'

'You're the detective.'

'And hasn't all her DNA been cooked?'

'A fire rarely destroys a body completely. True, the dermis and hypodermis layers are gone and her organs are fried, but don't despair. I'll go deep to see if any tissues are intact. As you can plainly see, there's not much left of the heart, lungs and liver.

'I suspect I'll have to get the trusty electric saw out and see if I can collect a sample of her DNA profile from her bone marrow.' Solossa stepped to the far side of the table. 'One thing I did find peculiar was this.' He drew Aiboy's attention to the right hand. 'See anything strange?'

Aiboy Ali stole a glance at the charcoaled digits, which were hooked like claws.

'The top half of one finger is missing.'

'Correct. *Digitus primus*. The top and middle sections of the right index finger have been removed.'

'A trophy?'

'Possibly.' Solossa leaned in, hovering over the cadaver's midsection. 'But you know what?'

'What?'

'That's not all that's gone. Ordinarily, I might find some parts of her uterus intact. The uterus has a thick musculature and is well protected by the pelvis in these situations, but I can't in this case.'

'Why not?'

'The colon's been cut through. Most of her lower abdomen is missing. Whoever did this took out her womb.'

Chapter Nine

Imke was drawn to the hotel. If her natural curiosity hadn't already kick-started her overactive imagination before, it sure as hell was set on overdrive now. Curiosity had her by the throat.

Ruud's aloofness, for one, should have tipped her off, but it was Hartono's words that calcified her suspicions.

She wrote Ruud a text:

Is something going on I shld know about?

But she deleted it at the last moment.

What was it, a sixth sense? A premonition? A funny feeling?

It was hard to rationalize, but Imke felt it in her bones. She was sure Ruud was seeing someone else.

She couldn't do this over the phone. She had to confront him face to face.

The traffic driving over did not help alleviate her stress. Stuck behind a POS INDONESIA delivery van for half an hour at the Jalan Veteran junction, she'd grown more and more agitated by the minute. She'd considered picking up a pair of car jockeys on the side of the road in order to use the three-in-one carpool lane, but decided against it. There was something distinctly odd about paying complete strangers to act as passengers-for-hire.

Her mood lightened, however, when she saw an *ojek* pass with the motorcycle passenger balancing a queen-size mattress on his head. She pulled up to take a snap of them. So much for health and safety. Only in Jakarta.

She spent another ten minutes negotiating the bottleneck at Juanda, where a hawker thrust a clutch of pens against her window, until finally, at 5.10 p.m., she reached the Suparna Hotel.

She rode the speed bumps and parked at the hotel entrance, right in front of the Garuda sculptures. As soon as she tossed her keys to the hotel doorman, he whistled for a parking attendant and led her to the security post. Imke threw off her shoulder satchel and placed it in the tray provided. Seconds later she walked through the body-scanner machine.

The lavish lobby of the Suparna was all marble columns and curved wood panels. The scent of fresh lilies sugared the air.

Imke circled the decorative water feature a couple of times, then marched beyond the reception desk and the glass ornaments, before coming to a stop by the overpriced coffee shop to check her reflection in a mirror. God Almighty! She blanched. Look at the state of you! Worzel bloody Gummidge! The helicopter had done a right number on her hair. She fumbled a hand through her locks, patting and pulling bits into place. She hadn't thought to carry a brush.

'Sorry I am late, Miss Imke.'

It was Werry Hartono.

'You're not late, Werry, you're bang on time.'

'It is thirteen minutes past the hour. Where do you wish to discuss the prospects of my promotion?'

'Upstairs.'

'Upstairs?'

'With Ruud. Upstairs.'

'This isn't about my promotion, is it?'

'No, Werry, sorry. I misled you.'

'Is it about Aiboy Ali?'

'Why should it be about Aiboy Ali?'

'I am worried for him.' It was the kind of worry Watson experienced in episode three of series two after Moriarty had humiliated Sherlock, but Hartono refrained from saying this. Instead he said, 'He's been acting strange. I am worried for him because he is my friend and a very good colleague.'

'What do you mean by strange?'

'As if he has been pushed off-balance. He is keeping things to himself. Bad things. Usually, he talks and jokes all day, but no longer. He frets a lot more, and talks about football and music a lot less. I think it is because of Farah.'

'The girlfriend.'

'Yes.'

'How miserable is he?'

'What do you mean?'

'Is he hide-away-in-a-dark-corner miserable or hang-yourself-from-a-light-fitting miserable?'

'I don't know.'

A gamelan quintet played in the foyer cloister, performing a *balungan*, a skeleton melody. Two ladies armed with tiny mallets knelt on a rug playing a bronze metallophone and a *gambang kayu*, a girl plucked a *siter*, another drummed a *kendhang*, while a little old lady at the back struck a series of gong chimes. The hauntingly beautiful music with its textural melodies mesmerized Imke.

Hartono adjusted his tie. 'So you're telling me this isn't about Aiboy?'

'No, Werry, it's not about Farah and it's not about Aiboy Ali. You're here because of First *Inspektur* Pujasumarta.'

His eyes widened. 'Is he in some kind of danger?'

'If Pujasumarta is doing what I think he's doing then, yes, he's in a helluva lot of danger.' Thoughts of strangulation entered Imke's head.

She stopped, gathered herself. 'Right, are we ready?'

'For what?' said Hartono, plainly confused.

'We're heading up to room six oh five.'

She gave a little nod of decision and blew out her cheeks, knowing the next hour could determine the rest of her life.

Cracks appeared at the corners of her mouth. Her thoughts were running out of control. She shook off a terrible image of packing a suitcase, tossing her toiletries into a pillowcase and moving to budget lodgings on Jalan Cikini Raya.

Imke squeezed her eyes shut, listened to the tempo of the *kendhang*, the woody ringing of the *gambang kayu* and its echoing, onomatopoeic rhythms. The music in the background fell into a pattern, growing stronger and louder, soaking her up.

Before she knew it, she was lost in the moment, lost in the resonating chimes of the *gambang* keys and the rounder thuds of the gong.

The marble floor lapped at her feet. Imke experienced a tingling in her hands and a collapsing sensation, as if she were sinking through the floor. It came upon her in a rush, as if she were on some spiralling marijuana trip.

'But I did not bring my firearm,' said Hartono, breaking the spell.

'What?'

'If the first *inspektur* is in danger, won't I need my firearm?'

'Just stay by my side, Werry.' She grabbed his arm and pulled him towards the lifts. 'Come on, follow me.'

At the lift lobby, a set of shiny panels slid open and Imke and Werry stepped into the mirrored interior. They took the elevator to the sixth floor. The music of the gamelan piped through the speakers. Imke watched the numbers change colour, turning from grey to orange. The bell pinged on six, made a *bing-bong* noise, and they stepped out of the elevator and onto the hall carpet.

The shiny panels slid shut behind them. The sounds of the gamelan receded.

Imke took several deep breaths.

She wanted to be sick. Rather than head straight to room 605, she roamed the corridor, fretting, geeing herself up. She must have paced about for ten minutes.

Werry, meantime, checked his phone for messages.

She fidgeted, swallowed, swallowed again, fanned her cheeks. Biting her lip, she realized she'd been holding her breath. She ran her hands through her hair. God, her palms were clammy. And then she found herself in front of the door, transfixed.

You'll go mad, she told herself, you'll go mad if you don't knock on that door.

A physical ache settled in her stomach. She had to be brave.

She leaned forward to rap on the door, hesitated, pressed her ear against the mullion, took a step back, leaned forward again.

Her knuckles struck three times.

Tap. Tap. Tap.

Unbreathing.

Her mouth set hard, a thin line, as thin as a hairpin, sealed against the hurt she knew was coming.

She heard voices. Conversation. Laughter. Someone padding behind the entrance. And then the door to room 605 opened with a swish.

Ruud gaped at her; his face a picture of bewilderment, alarm and awkward resignation.

'Imke,' he said quietly. 'What are you doing here?'

She puffed her chest up. 'What am I doing here? I'm here to see you.' Her tone was firm. She kept her anger at bay. 'And to see who you're with.'

'I don't know what you're talking about.' The colour drained from his cheeks.

'Hi boss!' shouted Werry from the hallway.

'Oh, you're here too, Hartono. What a strange day this is turning out to be.'

'Yes,' said Imke, 'isn't it?'

They stood facing one another. He didn't move from the doorway. She didn't move from the threshold.

'May I come in?'

Ruud stayed quiet. Instead of speaking he glanced over his shoulder.

'Are you going to let me pass?' Imke continued, her voice vibrating. She glared at him and couldn't help notice the strange glimmer in his eyes. What was it? Discomfort? Embarrassment? Amusement?

'Look, I can explain.'

She bulldozed past him, jostling him to one side, passing

the bathroom on the left, the mini fridge to the right and through to the bedroom.

What she saw on the bed made her stiffen and stop dead in her tracks.

Her jaw fell open.

'Oh God!' she squealed, gawking at the unthinkable. 'What the hell? I don't bloody believe this!'

'Oh God!'

A woman in her fifties, dressed as a man, bounced up and down on the bed. Hopping like a bunny, doing cheerleading arm rotations, she performed a low touchdown, followed by a high touchdown. 'Give us an H, give us an A, give us a P P Y,' yelled the besuited woman.

An explosion of joy. 'Aunty Ecks!'

Erica Sneijder leapt off the mattress and into Imke's arms. 'Ta-daah!'

'I can't believe it!' cried Imke. 'This can't be real. I thought you were attending an art conference in Utrecht.'

'What, and miss congratulating my niece on her thirtieth birthday? *Niet in een miljoen jaar.*'

They stood and embraced for a long while, saying very little.

It was Imke who broke the silence. 'This is crazy. Oh, Aunty Ecks, I'm so . . .' She was lost for words. 'I can't believe . . . what are you doing here . . . I thought Ruud was . . . Ruud had . . . he was with . . . and then you . . . I thought, oh I don't know what I thought.' She was prattling, talking at a rate of knots, but she couldn't stop, didn't want to. She jumped for joy.

'Can I go now, boss?' came a voice from the hallway.

Ruud replied with a laugh, 'Yes, Werry, go. And thank you.'

The two women embraced again. Imke felt her aunt's

narrow shoulder blades through her jacket, twin little formations under the cotton material. They stood and stared at one another, joggled each other by the arms.

'How? I mean, how did all this happen?' said Imke, giddy, her fingers trembling at her mouth.

Aunt Erica jutted her chin towards the mini fridge.

Imke spun on her heels to find Ruud grinning hugely, retrieving a bottle of Prosecco and laughing at the expression on her face. Without her seeing, he'd slipped on a conical party hat. 'Surprise!' He blew on a foil blowout, which made a tooting noise before recoiling back into position. 'Happy Birthday, *Putri Salju*.' He smiled from ear to ear.

'You planned all this?'

'Mmm-hmm.' He twirled an imaginary moustache. 'But of course.'

The room was lined with crêpe-paper streamers and balloons. A banner ran the length of the window and there was enough bunting for a Jubilee fête. The only thing missing was a sparkler.

Imke, with a hand on her forehead, said, 'Sorry, I'm struggling to take this in.' She wiped away a tear. 'Look at me, I'm leaking.'

Ruud slipped a *Birthday Queen* paper crown on Imke's head. Immediately, her muscles loosened and relaxed. 'But how did you know I'd turn up here?'

'It was a long shot. I guessed you'd try to track me down. Hartono told me you called him. The silly fool almost gave it away.'

'Was he in an awful panic?'

'Like a submarine taking on water. He said he may have unintentionally misled you to think I was shacked up here with some young floozy.'

'Rather than an old floozy,' quipped Aunt Erica.

'He said you sounded pretty peeved,' added Ruud.

'Not surprising. And after the way you've ignored me the last few days.'

'What, you mean I haven't been my usual bright-eyed and bushy-tailed self?'

'No, you bloody well haven't!'

'Sorry about that. I didn't mean to ignore you. There's a shitload happening at work, as you know. I got all your texts and voice messages, by the way. I didn't reply because my battery kept dying on me.'

'But I still can't figure out how you knew I'd take the bait?'

'What, that you'd come here? We didn't. But Erica was sure you'd turn up when Hartono let the cat out of the bag about the hotel. You're like a sniffer dog. There's no hiding anything from you.'

'I call it a healthy curiosity,' said Erica.

'I'm sure she checks my phone records when I'm sleeping, Erica, and goes through my wallet, my papers, my trouser pockets . . .'

'Rubbish!' Imke guffawed, pinching his chest.

Ruud beat a retreat, taking three steps back and rubbing the flesh near his right nipple. 'Anyway, if you didn't come here, I'd planned to surprise you at the restaurant tonight.' He pulled her in for a kiss.

'Which restaurant?'

'One Thousand Flavours. It's booked for eight thirty p.m.'

'Seribu Rasa,' Imke declared. 'My favourite!'

Seribu Rasa, an old establishment serving excellent local food, was situated in Menteng, Ruud told Erica.

Imke's face glowed with delight. 'You're a bloody arsehole, Ruud Pujasumarta.' She slapped his arm and kissed him back.

Erica chortled. 'Look at you both. And to think that only minutes ago she was glaring at you like Clint Eastwood at a gunslingers' duel. You've been in a strop all day, I'll bet.'

'Let's just say I was planning on murdering a homicide detective.'

Ruud clasped his throat theatrically.

Imke turned and gave her aunt another hug, wriggling delightedly in her arms. 'When did you arrive?'

'This morning on Garuda Air. I landed at Soekarno–Hatta a little before noon.'

'How was the flight?'

'Monstrous! I sat next to a hideous bore from Hoorn who wouldn't stop talking. He even tried to engage me as I slept. It was like listening to Latin Mass whilst strapped to a dentist's chair. But the stewardesses were marvellous. They did their best to keep me in chocolate for fourteen hours. Fourteen hours with the human talking clock in my ear! Can you imagine? But I'm here now, none the worse for wear and in the full flower of health.' She plucked a wrapper from her breast pocket. 'Fancy a Rolo?'

Imke declined. She had so many questions to ask.

'How long are you staying?'

'A fortnight.'

'All this way to see me.'

'Well, there's this art festival in Bali I've been invited to speak at. But I can't possibly go without you.'

'I don't think I can take any leave.'

'No.'

'Or can I?'

Both Imke and Erica laughed.

Soon, Erica was explaining to Imke how Ruud had been plotting the surprise for ages. 'He paid for my flight, I'll have

72

you know, and even tried to persuade your father to join. But Mathias didn't feel ready to return to Jakarta just yet. And your mother ... well, that Nakula thing shook her badly. Ardy suffered one hell of a shock seeing you tied up on the bed like that. She thought she was going to lose you. She refuses to have anything to do with Indonesia now, especially following the terrorist attacks last month. Awful what these IS people are doing.'

Imke let the words hang in the air.

'I didn't think you'd ever come back,' said Imke, 'given what happened before.'

'And miss the prospect of another adventure? Never in a million years!'

Erica rattled on about how she'd dined out on the Nakula story for weeks and weeks.

Imke listened, smiling. In truth, she was thankful her father had stayed home. The two of them had gone some way to mend fences, but the foundations of their relationship remained wobbly.

'*Nu dan*, before I forget.' Erica gave Imke a small parcel wrapped in shiny orange paper.

'For me?' Imke weighed the present in her palms as if it were a bag of coffee from Albert Cuyp Market.

Once, when she was very young, Aunty Ecks had given her a stuffed animal for Christmas. 'Is it Humpty Dumpy?' Imke had asked, not recognizing the animal.

'It's an octopus.'

'What's an octopus?'

'A cat with eight legs.'

Imke, sitting on the floor by the Christmas tree, threw her legs in the air with glee. At the time it was the best joke she'd ever heard. These days, at birthdays and other celebrations, they'd restage the whole thing to one another's delight, even though nobody else got the joke.

Imke tore off the wrapping. 'What have we here then, *hè*? A round of Gouda.' She placed the cheese on the table. 'Some *rookworst*, yummy, and, what's this? Dogbreath dental treats.'

'Those are for Kiki.'

Imke gave her aunt's hand a squeeze. 'Yes, I gathered that.'

Ruud uncorked the bottle of chilled Prosecco and handed each woman a champagne flute.

'*Proost!*' sang Imke.

'And let's not forget . . .' From under a cloth, Ruud flourished a dish stacked high with frosted doughnuts, with a single candle at the crest.

'Oh goody!' cried Erica, licking her lips and poised on her tiptoes. She nabbed the top doughnut, coated in icing sugar and sprinkles. 'This one is dusted with *hagelslag*, my favourite.'

All three tucked in.

For a little while the only noise was the sound of Imke making *mmm-hmmm* moans as she chewed.

Then, bang on cue, Ruud's phone buzzed. He took the call then rang off thirty seconds later.

'That was Witarsa. I've got to go. The Australian Embassy has lodged a missing person's report. A woman called Jillian Parker hasn't been seen for two days. She's the First Secretary's cousin. Witarsa thinks the dead body we found in the burned-out car is the same woman. We may have ourselves a diplomatic incident.'

Chapter Ten

With his bad leg hooked over the arm of an office chair, reading the badminton pages of the *Jawa Pos*, Aiboy Ali was getting in a few precious minutes of much-needed downtime. He'd been on the go since breakfast, and until now his lunch had sat on his desk, uneaten and cold. He bought his lunch most days from the same three-wheeled cart that parked at the corner of Kramat Raya and Kramat Sentiong. Today it was *tahu telor* on the menu – deep-fried bean curd coated in egg and served with spicy onion gravy.

His fingers knotted.

His mind strayed.

For a few wonderful weeks last summer, his girlfriend prepared his food for him. Mondays and Wednesdays she cooked fried duck with sweet chilli paste (*bebek goring*); Tuesdays and Thursdays it was *gado-gado* and prawn crackers; on Fridays she made him *mie celor* – a noodle and egg dish seasoned with pepper and salted fish. She would prepare these meals for him in her mother's kitchen and deliver them on her way to work.

But then, suddenly and unexpectedly, she grew ill. They'd been away together to the coast – a long weekend away – and soon after returning things went downhill. She started off with a rash, and after that came muscle pain and severe headaches. She was admitted to hospital, where the doctors treated her with electrolyte therapy and gave her a blood transfusion, but on day three she went into shock.

She died of dengue hemorrhagic fever.

He couldn't help her.

He couldn't save her.

They'd only been dating for six months. Her name was Farah. She was a nurse at Persahabatan General. They'd met in the infirmary canteen during his rehabilitation.

Three times a week he'd gone for therapy on his injured leg. He did everything from heel slides to knee extensions, wall squats to hamstring curls. After which he would wait by the nurses' station for her shift to end, then drive her home in his car.

Housing rents were too high for Farah to have a place of her own, so she lived with her parents and two sisters in a modest apartment in Tanah Abang.

Once in a while, to Aiboy's delight, she'd stay over at his, telling her parents she was on night duty. She kept a pair of pale blue canvas shoes at Aiboy's place, together with a toothbrush and a little pile of underclothes.

He still had her shoes in a cupboard.

In his head he could see her wearing them.

The memory scraped away at him.

She was twenty-six.

He'd never told her that he loved her.

And now she was nothing more than gravedust.

As always, a hot blast of panic shot through him when he thought of Farah. A reflex. He saw her hospital bed, the cardiac rhythm machine jumping and then flatlining across the monitor. Two-tone alarms going off. The nurse hitting the red button. The stampede of activity.

'Fuck it!'

He tossed the *Jawa Pos* into the bin and got to his feet.

He hated it, this feeling. Of being sad. It breathed down the back of his neck.

He clamped his gaze on the wall clock.

The time was 6 p.m. and Mrs Lindo, the blind old biddy from Puncak, was in the conference room waiting to be interviewed. Dressed in maroon pyjamas, she was thin and wiry and wore large Ray Charles shades that covered half her face. She also had a spinal curvature, which made her sit awkwardly, left elbow partially raised as if braced for a blow.

'Good evening,' said Aiboy.

'Hello there.' She rested her white cane across her lap. 'I have never once been in a police station before,' she wheezed. 'This is hugely exciting for me.'

'How nice for you,' said Aiboy.

'I can tell by your accent that you are from Madura. My grandmother came from there.'

Hartono made her a cup of *bandrek*, prepared from a ready-made packet with just the right amount of coconut sugar and ginger, and told her First *Inspektur* Pujasumarta was on his way and would not be long.

'I'm in no hurry,' she said.

Hartono gave a little *harrumph*. He wanted the interview concluded quickly. Earlier he'd received an online tip that the bison skull 'as seen on Sherlock' was about to be sold on eBay. Perhaps he could place a low bid. But what if there was a reserve price? And did eBay even ship to Indonesia? He wanted desperately to return to his desk and find out.

The old lady sipped the hot sweet beverage.

Hartono studied his watch.

Impatient, unable to sit still, Aiboy Ali went to the office pantry and heated up his lunch in the microwave. The tea lady, Mrs Hapsari, plucked a spoon from the draining board and tucked it into his hip pocket. A few minutes later he entered the conference room with his rectangular ceramic pan of savoury bean curd in hand.

He took a seat across from Mrs Lindo and dipped the spoon into his food. The sauce turned the cutlery the colour of saffron.

Mrs Lindo sniffed the air. 'Are we in the police canteen?'

Aiboy Ali wiped his oily fingers on a paper napkin.

Moments later, Ruud barged in, flustered and full of apologies.

Everyone gathered around Mrs Lindo as Ruud introduced himself and settled into a chair. 'So, Mrs Lindo, tell us what you saw.'

'I did not *see* anything.'

'Right, of course not. Please tell us what you heard.'

'I live with my sister. My eldest daughter visits me from Cengkareng twice a week. She reads to me.'

'The night in question, Mrs Lindo, what can you tell us?'

'Yes, yes, I am getting to that.'

'Please do.'

'Our house is at the bend in the road, just past the Mang Ade coffee shack. I was feeling restless. I think perhaps I ate too vigorously the durian my daughter prepared. At any rate I fancied a walk.'

'Time?'

'I left the house around four in the morning.'

'So early?' remarked Aiboy Ali. 'Why go for a walk in the middle of the night?'

'It is always the middle of the night for me, young man. And I prefer the air between four and six. Fresher, less city fumes.'

'How did you know it was four a.m.?' Ruud challenged.

'I consulted my timepiece.' She smiled a thin smile. 'Ahh, I think I know what you are asking Mr First *Inspektur*.' She waggled her wrist. 'I wear a tactile watch. It contains a magnet that moves two ball bearings around the watch face. The fatter ball shows the hour, the smaller one the minutes. It is very expensive, I can tell you. My son bought it for me. He is a success and works for an American petroleum company.'

'What time is it now?'

'You want to test me, is it?' She dragged a finger across the dial. 'Six twenty-two.'

'How do you know if it's morning or evening?'

'For such things, I rely on the radio news and the heat of the sun on my face. Now, if you can refrain from asking any more *kampung* idiot questions, I would like to tell you what I know.'

'Of course. Please go ahead, Mrs Lindo.'

'As I say, I went for a walk. Seven hundred and thirty steps from my front door, on a gentle descent. There are potholes on the road so I have to take care. I was sitting on the bench the kind people from the village put near the bus stop. Simply taking in the sounds of the insects – crickets and night-chirpers make wonderful music – when a car's engine rumbled and came to a halt some fifty or sixty paces away.'

'Did the car pass you?'

'No. It was coming up the hill and stopped before it reached me.'

'So the driver of the car did not see you.'

'I presume not.'

'Please carry on.'

'By now the Fajr had commenced. From the mosque across the valley I could hear the sound of the muezzin's call to prayer.'

'So we are talking about a quarter to five in the morning?'

'Yes. As I say, the car came to a halt. At first I thought little of it, but then I heard muffled yells coming from somewhere. It was like listening to a voice coming from behind a locked closet. Then all of a sudden someone was walking about and the car's trunk opened, then I heard a woman screaming. No muffling on this occasion. It was a full-throated scream.'

'Was it a cry for help?' Aiboy queried.

'And did she call out in Bahasa or in English?' Ruud added.

'It was a short, loud *arghhhh*. No words. A shriek of terror like a beaten dog. It lasted for no more than two or three seconds before it was deadened by a hand.'

'You made this out distinctly, audibly?'

'The one true God may have taken my sight, but in His infinite wisdom He has blessed me with very good ears to compensate.'

'Carry on, please.'

'Well, I kept statue-still, I can tell you. What could I do? A blind old lady. I was terrified.' Her hands went instinctively to her mouth. 'Terrified he might spot me. But of course, thinking back, I should have yelled out something.'

'He didn't see you, you're sure.'

'If he had I wouldn't be sitting here today. I'd be dead. Chopped up with bits of me hidden in a woven basket. I imagine I must have been sitting in complete darkness because he just carried on doing what he was doing.'

'It's possible,' said Ruud to Aiboy. 'There aren't any street-lights along that stretch. What happened next?'

'There was a struggle, a lot of thrashing about. He struck the woman a number of times, smack, smack, until she was silent. After that there was a kind of cloth tearing, which went on for a bit. Then I heard something being dragged, her body I suppose, followed by the sound of liquid pouring from a metal can. It is a distinctive noise. A kind of tinny *glug-glug* sound.'

She broke off, deep in thought.

'Could you smell it, Mrs Lindo? Was it kerosene?'

'Fire. I could smell fire. And burning flesh. I lived near Tomohon as a child. They used to cook dogs on open fires. I know the smell. It was very frightening, I can assure you.'

'So he poured something on this woman and set her alight.'

'But before that,' she inclined her head, 'the attacker grunted.' The Ray Charles shades slipped a fraction down her nose. 'It was a grunting, a snorting. An *oink, oink, oink*. Like the sound of the *babi*.'

'A pig?' Ruud turned to Hartono and Aiboy Ali. 'Why a pig?'

'Because the pig is *haram*,' replied Mrs Lindo. 'The dead meat and blood, the flesh of swine is an abomination before The Prophet. This poor woman must have been an apostate, *fasik*, a committer of great sins.'

'He imitated a pig?'

'Yes.'

'And that is all he said?'

'That is all he said.'

'Then what?'

'A crash. One of your officers explained the car rolled down a cliff, which is what I must have heard. A great toppling-over crash.'

'And then you returned to your house?'

'No, I waited. I waited to make sure this accoster, or whatever he was, had gone first. I held on until I heard his footsteps make their way down the road.'

'So he left on foot, down the hill?'

'Yes.'

'Did any cars pass while you sat there?'

'No. It is quiet on that road until the bus comes for the school children.'

'He went down the hill and you went in the opposite direction, up the hill.'

'Yes. Oh, but I forgot to mention something. When he was leaving I heard his pocket telephone ring in the distance.'

'Did you hear his voice?'

'No, but the telephone ring was a distinctive tune. My daughter's pocket telephone trills out duck quacks when somebody calls her. This man's phone was quite different.'

'What was the sound?'

'It was the music from a television cartoon they used to show a long while ago. It went a bit like this.' Her dry old voice clattered out a few bars: '*Dee-dum-dum-deebee-deebee-dum-dum, deebee-dum, toot-toot.*'

'Sounds a bit like "Popeye the Sailor Man",' said Aiboy.

'Yes, that's it,' cried Mrs Lindo with glee, clapping her hands. 'The spinach man. My children would go round to the neighbour's house to watch it.'

'So tell me,' said Ruud. 'What time did you get home?'

'Exactly quarter past six. I immediately called my daughter to tell her what had happened.'

There was the clang and clatter of an upturned tray from the hallway. Witarsa thundered into the conference room

82

with the violence of a honey badger fleeing a hornets' nest. '*Sialan!* Hot, hot!' he yelled.

Aiboy Ali threw him a box of Kleenex.

Jiggling and joggling, Witarsa furiously mopped scorching tea from his shirtfront. 'PLEASE look where you are going, Mrs Hapsari!'

'Me? You are the one with the clumsy slap-slap walk,' came a voice from the corridor.

Witarsa tossed a wad of sodden tissues into the waste bin and shook off his dead-eyed exhaustion. 'Gentlemen, we have a new development. I need to see all of you now! My office!'

Mrs Lindo lurched upright from her seat, cane at the ready. 'Is the building on fire?'

'No, there's nothing to be alarmed about,' said Ruud.

'My goodness, well that is a relief. One can never be too careful with these tall structures. The man who just entered, shouting and stumbling like he has both feet in the same boot,' croaked the crooked little lady. 'The commissioner, I imagine?'

'Yes,' replied Witarsa, composing himself and patting Mrs Lindo's limp hand gently. 'Begging your pardon, I apologize for my outburst. A thousand thanks for your assistance today. I am in no doubt that everything you shared is of vital importance. I will have someone escort you home.'

'What, already time to go home? Oh, what a shame. *Inspëktur Polisi Satu* Pujasumarta, are you still here?'

'Yes, Mrs Lindo.'

'Will you promise to tell the commissioner how the man made a pig-snorting noise?'

'I promise.'

'And the thing about the spinach? You'll tell him about the spinach, too?'

Ruud was at the door, offering Witarsa another tissue for his tea-spotted trousers. 'I will Mrs Lindo, I will.'

Witarsa paced splay-footed around his desk. 'RIGHT!' he boomed, plucking at his damp shirtfront. 'Can we start?'

The detectives crammed into his office; it was standing room only.

'This is what we have so far. Six hours ago the Australian Department of Foreign Affairs alerted Paspampres of a lost adult female. This could be a coincidence,' his words faded out, 'but as we have little else to go on, we are making preliminary inquiries.'

'Do you think there's a link between the two events?' asked Alya.

'Too early to say.'

'Who is she, sir?' Hartono enquired.

'Her name is Jillian Parker,' apprised the police commissioner, holding up a colour photograph of a woman with short pale-brown hair. 'Australian citizen. Born in Sydney. Aged thirty-five. Divorced, no children. Lived in Jakarta for seven years. Started working for Fitness Extreme Gym in 2009 before branching out on her own. She rented retail space on the second floor of Grand Atlas Towers. Eleven employees. Owned a strata title condominium on Jual Sewa and leased a weekend house in Puncak. Drove a green Mazda six two six LX. The duty sergeant is circulating these details to police stations in the Greater Jakarta area.'

Hamka Hamzah sparked a match and sucked a *kretek* to life.

'You say she left Fitness Extreme to branch out on her own. What line of business?' queried Aiboy Ali, squatting like a weightlifter, his iPad balanced on his right knee.

Witarsa referred to his notes. 'She became a Pilates and yoga instructor. According to her bank records she was doing very well.'

Werry Hartono raised his hand eagerly, like a defender appealing for offside. 'Any recent large withdrawals or deposits, sir?'

'Nothing out of the ordinary.'

'When was she last seen, sir?'

'At five p.m. on the night of Monday, February fifteenth, when she left her studio. She was reported missing at eleven p.m.'

'What? And the Australian Embassy got in touch so fast?' said Alya Entitisari. 'The process normally takes five, six days.'

'She was expected for dinner as a guest of the Ambassador. Ms Parker, you see, is the cousin of the First Secretary. When she did not show, they called her mobile, but no one picked up. Yesterday they phoned her friends, her colleagues, her clients and her family back in Sydney, after that they contacted the hospitals. When they drew a blank they called the police first thing this morning. The Ambassador is very concerned, he spoke to General Badrodin Haiti himself.'

'Do you think she's our corpse?' said Aiboy Ali.

The commissioner's desk phone bleeped. 'WHO KNOWS? It's possible.' He ignored the ringing and the flashing red light. 'But the chances are she picked up a man at a hotel bar and will turn up all apologetic and embarrassed later today. So for now,' he cleared his throat. 'For now it is to be our initial line of inquiry, so get busy, people. I have the Ministry of Home Affairs breathing down my neck. They want answers.'

Ruud butted in. 'May I have your permission to speak with the Australian ambassador?'

Witarsa shrugged.

Ruud checked the time. He had twenty minutes to get to Seribu Rasa by eight thirty. Imke and Erica were already on their way to the restaurant.

The desk phone bleeped. Alya Entitisari suggested someone grab it.

Witarsa mumbled something under his breath, snatched the receiver and pressed it to his ear. 'Police Commissioner Joyo T. Witarsa.' A dark cumulous cloud broke across his face. 'Yes. So? What do they want? Who? No. You serious? On the where? No!' He replaced the handset.

The nervous Herbert Lom twitch, the tic that made his left eyelid jump, reappeared, doing overtime.

'Trouble?' asked Ruud.

The commissioner looked shell-shocked. 'That was the duty sergeant,' he said, jowls wobbling like turkey wattles. 'There is a class of high-school students from SMA Negeri 8 waiting at the front desk. They say they found a human finger on the road near the entrance to their school. They say it could be the work of ISIS and fear for their own safety and are threatening to inform the press.'

'So? Let GEGANA handle it. What's this got to do with our investigation?' asked Ruud.

'There's a silver ring attached to the finger. On the shank there's an engraving that reads, "To J.P. Love M&D". I think it's Jillian Parker's finger.'

86

Chapter Eleven

Ruud arrived at Jalan H.R. Rasuna Said on foot. The Australian Embassy was a stubby cream structure shielded from the road by a six-metre wall and a string of mango trees. Having identified himself to the diplomatic police in the stationary red Ford, he scooted around the bollards and found himself at the guard post.

The entire homicide unit was working flat out: Hartono was interrogating Jillian Parker's office and studio staff; Aiboy Ali was searching her condominium on Jual Sewa; Alya Entitisari was trawling through email and phone records, and Hamzah was at her weekend house in the Puncak hills, going door to door, asking people if they'd seen anyone acting suspiciously on the night of 15 February or the morning of the 16th.

Ruud checked his phone. No leads as yet, but he had received a sweet message from Imke, thanking him for dinner the night before.

> food at seribu rasa so yummy
> I gt my sambal hit
> thks for surprise and g8 time

my cheeks r sore frm laughing
luv U xxx

He was pleased the evening had gone well, but a lot had happened since then and he needed to keep his mind on the job.

Earlier, he'd experienced a ticking off from Witarsa. 'A human finger outside a school! A *finger*? This sort of thing makes headlines, Pujasumarta, *memek busuk* headlines. The papers will have a bloody field day with this. I've already got the top brass leaning on me. If we don't do this properly heads will roll, do you hear me Pujasumarta? Heads will roll.'

A face appeared behind the security grille. Ruud unclipped the handcuff pouch and his Heckler & Koch 9 mm from his waist and slid them through a tray slot to one of the guards. Next, he registered his name, rank, purpose of visit, and ticked the box beside the name of the diplomat he wished to see. He scanned the consular list. 'Is Ambassador Beale in?'

No response.

'I have an appointment with the First Secretary,' he added, speaking into the glass partition. 'I'd like to see the ambassador, too, if possible.'

'You wear this,' came the reply. 'Wait here.'

Ruud looped the visitor lanyard over his head.

While he waited, his phone rang. It was Solossa. 'The finger definitely belongs to Jillian Parker. We compared it to her KTP card biodata.'

'I'm a little bit lost here. How on earth did her finger get from the car to the school?'

'Maybe it was a bungled kidnapping.'

'It doesn't make any sense.'

'We also managed to get hold of her dental records.'

'I'm listening.'

'It's her all right.'

'OK.'

'There's more. Bite-mark analysis on the finger matches teeth belonging to the victim.'

'What, you mean she bit her own finger off?'

'Yes.'

'Christ.' Ruud tried to picture the scenario in his head. 'So what do we do next?'

'I'm running some tests on her bone marrow.'

'Why?'

'I'll explain later.'

'Right you are. Listen, I have to go. I'm being shepherded through security.'

Ruud chucked his phone through the tray slot and pushed against the heavy metal turnstile. He raised his arms above his head. One guard ran a hand-held detector up and across his body while another patted him down. Once through the checkpoint, a female member of staff welcomed him to the complex and led him through the outdoor areas, and into the building proper.

'You are here to see Mr Waters?'

'I am,' he confirmed.

'My name is Diedre. I'm the First Secretary's PA.'

She ushered him into a square whitewashed space, roughly the size of two badminton courts. 'The embassy is very busy at the moment with official receptions, exhibitions and trade displays. We're also in the process of relocating to our new complex in Patra Kuningan about a kilometre away. It opens next month.'

In the middle of the white room was a massive solid

teak table. A stainless-steel bust of Barry Humphries sat at its centre.

'Usually, we use this part of the embassy to host business missions,' she said, 'but we're presenting an exhibition of contemporary Australian artists next week. I love it in here. Every piece tells such a brilliant story.'

The walls were lined with vibrant canvases and Aboriginal tribal sculptures. 'May I fetch you a tea, detective? A coffee?'

'Coffee would be nice, thanks. Black, no sugar.'

'Mr Waters will be with you shortly.'

Ruud listened to her heels clip-clop out of earshot.

He approached a large oil depiction of Hobart's night-scape. Two youths in hoodies were grappling with an elderly man. It appeared as if a carjacking was taking place. The subject matter bristled with noirish undertones. He found it unsettling.

'That's a Stewart Macfarlane,' a gruff voice resonated from the doorway. Ruud saw a heavyset man with thick dark hair. 'And that one to your right is a Marie Hagerty. We have thirty-seven pieces on display all over the complex.'

'It's quite a collection.'

The man lumbered towards Ruud, arm outstretched. 'Shane Waters.'

'Ruud Pujasumarta.' They shook hands. Ruud immediately noticed a recent scratch mark running along the man's right wrist.

'Yes, we're very lucky. We don't own the pictures, of course. Artbank leases them to us. It's a government support programme that acquires the works and rents them out to public- and private-sector clients.'

'Gives the artists a wider audience, I expect.'

'Precisely.'

'I know someone who'd really appreciate a viewing.'

'Then we'll have to have you back some time.'

Shane Waters was a big bloke. Stocky and barrel-chested, he had a neck most prop forwards would be proud of. 'Thank you for coming, First *Inspektur*.'

'I'm sorry about the circumstances.'

'Can you confirm it's definitely her?'

'Yes.' He refrained from going into detail about the finger.

After a respectful silence the Australian said, 'Where did you find her?'

'Out of town. In a car in Puncak.'

'Puncak?'

'Is that significant?'

'Jillian owned a weekend house in the Puncak hills. She went every other Friday to escape from the city.'

'How many people knew she had a place there?'

'Not many. She did most of her entertaining in Jakarta. She used the weekend pad in the hills as a place to relax and unwind.'

'Have you been there?'

'No.' Waters sighed. 'She kept it very private, a kind of sanctuary.' He shook his head. 'A tragedy. And what a grisly way to go. I can't believe it's happened.'

'She was your cousin, is that correct?'

'A distant one, but yes.'

'And you were friends?'

'Yes.' Ruud noted how quietly Waters suddenly talked. 'It's going to be tough on the family. We've arranged for her parents to fly to Jakarta tomorrow. And the DFAT will inform Jillian's ex-husband in due course.'

Ruud didn't waste any time. He began by quizzing the First Secretary about the night Jillian Parker disappeared.

'The Trade Council hosted a dinner, thirty, thirty-five people. When she didn't appear I knew something was amiss. She wasn't a no-show type of person. Not if she could help it. I called her but she didn't pick up.'

Diedre returned with a pot of black coffee and a pair of mugs.

As soon as she'd finished pouring the coffee, Ruud asked a host of questions about Jillian Parker's character, and quickly established that she enjoyed a good night out. 'We met up about once a fortnight,' said Waters. 'She was a lot of fun. Ambitious. Driven. Perhaps a little too driven sometimes, but a lot of fun and not at all self-conscious. The sort of person who would order bean soup at a cocktail bar because she felt like it.'

'She didn't care what people thought of her.'

'Precisely.'

'Did she have a boyfriend, a lover?'

'Ever since her divorce she'd denied having a new man in her life.'

'Do you believe her?'

'She was very aloof about her love life, but I thought she was seeing someone.'

'Any idea who?'

Waters indicated a no.

'And did she dress provocatively? I ask because often in Muslim countries people can take offence.'

'She liked showing off her legs on occasion.'

'Did she have any enemies? Someone who might have held a grudge?'

'Who, Jillian? Course not.'

'Did she gamble? Owe people money?'

'No to all the above.'

'What about stalkers? Did she ever feel like she was being followed?'

Shane Waters shook his head.

'Was she on any medication? Was she into drugs? Recreational use?'

The First Secretary crossed his arms. 'I can't really say.'

'Why the hesitation?'

'Aw look, you know what people can be like. She might have had the odd choof from time to time. She was very fit. She looked after herself. Liked to play softball with the other expats; hardly drank, but some of these yoga holistic types like a bit of grass from time to time.'

'So she had her secrets.'

'Everyone keeps secrets, First *Inspektur*.'

'Anything about Jillian I should know? Did she have any odd habits?'

'No odd habits, but she didn't like elevators much.'

Ruud tilted his head, not comprehending.

'Confined spaces. She didn't like being in small, dark rooms.'

'Tell me about yourself, Mr Waters. How long have you been in Indonesia?'

'A year and a bit.'

'Married?'

'No, not any more.'

They were interrupted by a knock on the doorjamb. Ruud saw a limp silhouette at the threshold.

A man in a beige suit ambled into the room.

In contrast to Shane Waters, the Ambassador was sinewy and lanky, like a long-legged wading bird. He stood nearly two metres tall, with thinning blond hair and the red and blotched nose of a habitual boozer.

A much shorter man with a ruddy-black crew cut and sallow skin accompanied him.

'Ah, you're both here,' said Waters. 'Allow me to present Detective Pujasumarta.'

'Your Excellency,' said Ruud.

'Glenn Beale. Call me Glenn. I've just spoken with General Badrodin Haiti. He's told me the latest.'

'We are doing all we can to find Jillian's killer.'

'Your efforts are greatly appreciated.'

'And this,' continued Waters in a raspy voice, 'is Murray Pocock, our press relations officer.'

They exchanged handshakes. Ruud noticed the mono-grammed *MP* shirt cuff. 'Thanks for meeting me,' said Ruud. 'I'd like to start with a few questions.'

'Fire away.'

'Do either of you have any inkling why anyone would want Jillian Parker killed?'

Beale made a face. 'None at all.'

'Was Jillian Parker outspoken on social media? Did she have any radical views? Any anti-Islamic leanings?'

'That's a strange thing to ask,' asserted Beale.

'Her death might be politically motivated or an act of religious extremism. I'm trying to look at this from every angle.'

Beale, half a head taller than Ruud, narrowed his eyes. 'Are you implying Jillian's death could be the work of pro ISIL forces or Jemaah Islamiyah, detective?'

'Perhaps.'

'We're talking abduction here, detective, abduction and murder. It doesn't fit the pattern of recent IS aggression. Last month's bombings and gunfire shook Jakarta. Five men, all heavily armed with grenades and handguns, rocked the capital. They targeted Starbucks, a police traffic post and the financial district. Then you have Paris, Copenhagen and Istanbul – all mass shootings or suicide bombings aimed to inflict widespread slaughter. Don't get me wrong; we're on high alert here. We've advised our citizens travelling to the region to exercise a high degree of caution. Rumours persist that terror cells in Sulawesi and Java remain active, so further violence is a real possibility. ISIL have made that perfectly clear. And we take the suspicious death of any Australian national very, very seriously. However, we'd be foolhardy to classify Jillian's murder as an act of terror before being certain of the facts.

'We know there are about five hundred Indonesian Jihadists fighting in Syria at the moment. And we're very aware of the threats this sort of extremism poses. The hotel bombings in 2009, the Bali nightclub bombings in 2002 and the attack on this very embassy in 2004 are testaments to that, but abducting and murdering foreign non-combatants here in Jakarta? Our intelligence doesn't point to anything of the sort.'

'I still think it's something I should explore.'

'You're half Australian, isn't that so, First *Inspektur*?'

'That's correct, Mr Ambassador.'

'So, you'll understand where I'm coming from.'

'I understand I have a job to do.'

'Look, for years Indonesia's toiled to discard its image as a centre of Islamist terrorists. Last month was a ghastly wake-up call to the country. A game-changer. Their intelligence people fucked up. BIN, the state intelligence agency, didn't do its job. Despite the limited casualties, the Joko administration lost a hell of a lot of face. The last thing they want is to have one of its neighbours accuse them of incompetence. I have to make sure we don't rub their noses in it.'

'Rub their noses in what?'

'The new government's got a chip on its shoulder, detective. They can't stand being belittled. Australian–Indonesian ties are at a particularly rocky juncture. We're miles apart when it comes to climate change, refugees, agricultural trade, drug smuggling and loads more. So for me to propose that Jillian Parker died at the hands of ISIL and their people knew absolutely nothing about it? Well, that makes them look stupid, and they hate being made to look stupid. President Jokowi's administration would put us in the diplomatic doghouse, so to speak.'

'The Indonesian hierarchy is fickle and hypersensitive,' said Pocock, running a hand over his crew cut.

'Be that as it may,' Ruud contended, 'let's concentrate on finding Jillian's killer first and your diplomatic concerns second.'

'We must mind our step and tread lightly,' warned the press relations officer.

'Too right,' said Beale. 'We had one ambassador recalled in Twenty Fifteen following the Bali Nine executions. We certainly don't want another.'

'I see.' Ruud turned to Waters. 'Well, we mustn't rock the boat, must we?' The sarcasm crinkled his eyes and nose.

'I'm a diplomat from the old school, First *Inspektur*,' Beale said, his hard mouth stretching the third vowel – *Inspect-euur*. 'I don't upset the apple cart. I leave that to the politicians.'

The mention of school made Ruud think of the students from SMA Negeri 8 who'd found Jillian's discarded finger on their doorstep. 'First Secretary Waters, did Jillian have any dealings with schoolchildren in Jakarta?'

'Schoolchildren?' The First Secretary gave a series of long blinks and gazed at the ceiling to think. As he lifted his chin, Ruud spotted another scratch line running down his throat.

'No, I don't think so. Not that I'm aware of.'

'And Your Excellency, sorry, Glenn, how would you describe Jillian?'

'She was a good woman. Kind. Thoughtful. Even-tempered. Not given to drama. Popular with her peers.'

'Gentlemen, you have been very helpful. Thank you for your time.'

'Not at all.'

'I'll ask Diedre to see you out,' said Shane Waters.

Ruud exchanged handshakes once more and left his coffee untouched.

As soon as he retrieved his possessions and walked out of the complex, Ruud called Aiboy Ali. 'It's me.'

'Yes, *Gajah*.'

'Shane Waters. The Australian First Secretary. Get me all you can on him: rumours, gossip, allegations.'

'But he's a diplomat.'

'I know, so watch yourself.'

'What's happened?'

'I've just spoken to him and there's something not right. He's hiding something. I can see it in his eyes. He's not telling me the whole story.'

'What do you think he's hiding?'

'I can't tell for sure. He was either keeping something back because the ambassador was in the room or he's lying about his relationship with Jillian Parker.'

'What do you want me to do?'

'Do you have a problem putting a tracker on him?'

'Not one bit.'

'OK, but we keep this to ourselves. If this gets out Witarsa will have our balls for breakfast.'

Chapter Twelve

'A herbal medicine kiosk?'

'She says it will ease your jetlag.'

'Ease me into a body bag more like.'

The Dutch women stood at the corner of Jalan Bukit Duri Tanjakan and Gg Langgar in South Jakarta's Tebet district. It was early in the afternoon. Both smelled of coconut sunblock and wore wide-brimmed sun hats pulled down over their ears.

Aunt Erica ran a battery-operated hand fan over her hair. 'Anyway, I think it's frightfully odd that you're on such good terms with Ruud's mother-in-law.'

'*Ex* mother-in-law.' Imke, who had Kiki on a lead, bent down to tickle the dog's tummy. 'She's very kind to me. Every Sunday she brings breakfast, brandishing a stainless-steel tiffin carrier full of *nasi goreng* and sunny-side up eggs, except she calls them cow's-eye eggs. She seems to have an uncontrollable urge to feed me.'

'Mrs Panggabean sounds quite intriguing, I'll give her that.'

'She's intriguing all right,' said Imke.

A *bajaj* trundled to a stop by the *Toko Beras* rice store. The driver hissed to get their attention. 'Psst! Psst! Where you go?'

'No, thank you. We have a car.'

'Maybe tomorrow.'

'Yes, maybe tomorrow.'

The sun beat down. Erica took refuge in the shade of a tree. The pavement around her was ruptured where the roots pushed through. 'I feel like one of Dalí's melting clocks.'

'It's not that hot.'

'That's what Joan of Arc said when they tied her to the stake.'

Kiki's tail started thrashing.

'Oh, there she is.' Imke waved.

'Yoo-hoo!' yelled Mrs Panggabean, waving back from across the road. She threw out a laugh. 'Look-see, I am here!' She'd grown rounder and fuller over the last six months, and the extra padding strained the seams of her dark mauve *kebaya*.

'*Goede God* above! It's an Asian Ma Larkin,' said Erica with a broad grin.

Smiling, cheeks like plums, Mrs Panggabean marched over and immediately embraced Imke and Erica. The bosomly matron's smile was so joyous it crinkled up her eyes.

'*Halo, apa kabar?* It is so nice to meet you, Nyonya Aunty Erica,' she said with almost irrepressible joy. 'I have heard so much about you and I admire very much your portrait of President Susilo Bambang Yudhoyono. It was featured in many magazines.'

'Thank you, my dear. I have heard great things about you too. How you care for my niece and feed her wonderful food.'

'Your niece is like a daughter to me. Actually, she is nicer than my real daughter. My daughter always complaining with a sharp tongue, like knife cutting my morning newspaper.'

'Imke says you cook the best eggs,' said Erica.

'She has a good appetite.'

'Speaking of appetite,' interrupted Imke. 'You are looking happy and prosperous, *hè*?'

Mrs Panggabean tossed her head back and chortled. '*Eeyee*, I think you are teasing me, *nuh*? I need to lose weight. Look at me.' She pressed bits of her Tiger Balm–aromaed chest. 'I'm bulging all over, as if I've been stuffed with papayas.'

'Better than looking like a raggedy old scarecrow like me,' said Erica.

The women chuckled.

'Enough chitty-chat!' exclaimed Mrs Panggabean, dragging Imke by the elbow. 'OK, we go!'

Two hundred metres away, down a tiny alley, they found a young woman in a conical straw hat pushing a bicycle cart.

'This area is mainly Ahmadiyah neighbourhood. They are a Muslim minority and get badly treated in Indonesia. As the country becomes more hardline, these people suffer more and more from religious intolerance. I like to support them as much as I can.'

'I thought Jokowi appointed ministers who were progressive and open-minded?' said Imke.

'All talk, no action. The truth is things are becoming worse. The local authority and Satpol PP shut down their mosques. They have nowhere to pray now,' Mrs Panggabean said. 'Not only happening in Jakarta, same thing in Papua and in Madura Island, and Christian churches being attacked in Sleman too.' She touched the young woman's forearm. 'This is my *jamu* lady. Her name is Yayuk.'

Yayuk greeted them and rummaged through her bundle of goods. The front basket of her bicycle was stuffed with cinnamon sticks, turmeric powder and tamarind roots. The rear basket held an assortment of rhizomes, leaves, tubers and tree bark, while the rattan saddlebags rung with the sound of Johnnie Walker bottles knocking together each time the wheels juddered.

Imke peaked at the bottles, which were filled with multi-coloured concoctions.

'*Jamu* dates back long, long time,' said Mrs Panggabean. 'Conceivably even to the time of the Buddhist temples of Borobudur.'

Kiki lay on the ground by the cart with her paws in the air.

'Yes, we have the malls and the shiny Starbucks shops and good doctors with modern medicine. But people here cannot do without *jamu*.'

'What goes in it?' blustered Erica.

'Family secrets.'

'That fills me with confidence.'

'Imke tells me you cannot sleep well because of jetlag.'

'A minor issue, really. I don't think we need to trouble the good woman.'

Ruud's ex-mother-in-law held up a quieting hand and turned to speak with Yayuk.

'What did you say to her?' said Erica.

The *jamu* lady popped the cork on a bottle of black syrup, then rattled out a string of information, which Mrs Panggabean translated. 'Galangal for seasickness and vocal cords. Good if you are a singer on a cruise liner. This one, turmeric for snoring and body odours. This, lemongrass for alertness. Over here, tamarind for constipation, and ginger for detoxing body.'

'They all look like sweepings from a carpenter's floor.'

'She has one that aids breast milk production.'

'No, thank you.'

Yayuk pointed with her thumb at a cloudy liquid.

'This one to lose weight and look sexy.'

Then she jiggled a packet of green powder. 'This with egg yolk is the one for you to try.'

Yayuk ground some tree bark in a mortar and pestle, then poured the granules into a cup. She threw in the raw egg and the green powder and stirred it with a spoon.

She handed Erica the cup.

Erica took it with a scowl. Her face puckered. '*Ophhh*, I'm sure if I gulp down a melatonin pill tonight I'll be fine. Honestly, after one of those it will be milk rusks and beddy byes for me.'

'Drink.'

Imke placed a hand over her mouth to hide her amusement.

'May I have a dash of sugar in it?'

'Must never be sweet.'

'Blasphemous!'

'No more delay,' urged Mrs Panggabean. She mimicked drinking with an exuberant slurp.

Aunt Erica's body drooped. She hunched over the cup and glared at the swampy liquid as if it were a demon.

Imke began to chortle. She tried to quell it but the giggling welled up in her throat. Erica shook her head as her scowl turned into a smile. 'Can I pinch my nose as I swallow?'

'Drink!' ordered Mrs Panggabean.

Tears of laughter ran down Imke's cheeks.

'I don't know what you find so funny,' said Erica, laughing

herself. 'Have you smelled this? Actually smelled it? It's like poking your nose into a mildewy potting shed.'

She swallowed the mixture in two gulps.

'Tasty?' asked Mrs Panggabean, nodding.

'Lucrezia Borgia!' Erica heaved, scrambling in her pocket for a Rolo chaser. 'And you wonder why these people are persecuted?'

By now all four women had dissolved into laughter.

'Tonight you will sleep soundly,' determined Mrs Panggabean, passing Yayuk a blue banknote.

Erica ran a Kleenex across her lips.

Nearby, a stall selling fried jackfruit fired up its grill. The aroma of charcoal smarted in Imke's nostrils.

'Anyone hungry? Let's have snack,' suggested Mrs Panggabean.

'Can't we sit somewhere', Erica requested, wiping her brow, 'that has air conditioning?'

'What? You are hot?'

'Oh, heavens, I am simply wilting. Perhaps you can re-suscitate me in a refrigerator.'

Mrs Panggabean plonked Imke's aunt down on a plastic stool. 'Please unlace shoes and take off socks.'

'You expect me to walk about like a barefoot Kalahari tribesman. What is this, torture Erica Sneijder Day?' She cast Imke a pleading look. 'What are you going to ask me to do, run over hot coals?'

Mrs Panggabean relieved Erica of her brogues and socks.

'I keep telling her,' confided Imke, 'to wear flip-flops in this climate, but she refuses.'

'Appearances, my dear.'

'Toes in the air,' said Mrs Panggabean, withdrawing a tin of Tiger Balm from her bag. 'I try not to tickle.' She slathered

Erica's feet with ointment. 'Now, put socks back on. This way your feet will feel icy cool even on such a hot day. You see? No more wilting.'

Erica lifted one of her feet for inspection. 'It's all tingly and mentholated. Smells like Fizz Wiz popping candy' – she sniffed – 'mixed with a Polo mint.'

'All this talk-talk about sweets and candy making me hungry.' Mrs Panggabean wiped her hands with a Wet Ones. 'OK, *boleh*, as clean as a whistler. Now we go eat!'

Chapter Thirteen

The setting sun dipped below the city skyline, bathing the clinker-brick building a darker shade of red.

Twilit, in silent misery, Aiboy Ali waited in his vehicle watching the shadows lengthen. His car was parked next to a crumbling concrete wall. He had been waiting there for quite some time, but he was patient. Patience was something he'd been blessed with. He rubbed his arms and elbows.

The time was 6.56 p.m. The giant outdoor speakers of the Masjid Istiqlal crackled with static as the muezzin began summoning the faithful to their knees. The crier recited the *adhan*, but the permanent background sound of traffic dulled the call for *Isha* prayers.

As the sun sank, the evening clouds bled out like a butchered goat.

Dusk gathered quickly. The night birds were out in numbers. For a few seconds Aiboy Ali watched the trilling swiftlets barrel roll and spin while crows gathered on the telephone lines.

An hour crawled by. Followed by another.

A small red ant scurried across the dashboard.

He used his thumbnail to trap the ant and snap its body in two.

The car interior smelled of salty sweat. He had been on duty for fifteen hours straight and he was desperate for a shower, aching for a few hours' sleep.

Aiboy Ali looked over his shoulder. Still no sign of the black saloon with the diplomatic corps licence plates.

The dashboard clock clicked to 9 p.m.

When he finally spotted the Mercedes park up ahead he smiled to himself. The driver climbed out and disappeared into a coffee house.

Aiboy Ali sat tight for another two minutes and then got out of his car. As soon as he opened the vehicle door the heat and humidity engulfed him, fogging up his shades. Languidly, he strolled along the street. Unnoticed.

With a clandestine casualness, the policeman buried his hands in the pockets of his cargo pants to conceal his leather gloves. Because of the heat and closeness, no one wore gloves in Indonesia apart from garbage collectors and jockeys.

When he reached the black Mercedes he bent down low and knelt, dropping one shoulder to lean his weight on one arm. He craned his neck sideways. The road surface was smudged with oil. A torn plastic bag cavorted in the breeze.

Effortlessly he attached the rectangular box to the underside of the Mercedes. He felt the magnetic pull and let go. The high-strength magnets held firm.

Rising to his feet, he slapped the dirt off his trousers, pulled the hair from his shades and looked up. The coffee shop was quiet. Nobody had seen him.

Several minibuses and *mikrolet* cabs rushed past, their amber headlights glowing pale in the Jakarta haze.

The coffee-shop door swung open.

He tensed.

No, all was well.

106

Two men, neither of them Western, materialized from within.

He made a mental note of the two men as they exited the coffee shop: one headed down the street away from him, the other man lit a cigarette and fiddled with his hair.

Aiboy Ali lowered his head and walked back towards the crumbling concrete wall.

As soon as he returned to his car he opened the boot and tore off his gloves, tossing them inside.

Slamming the boot door shut, he fished out his phone and pressed a button. Seconds later, a detailed city map appeared on the phone display. He adjusted the zoom-in feature and a red dot blinked to indicate the vehicle ahead.

The tracker was working fine. Shane Waters was in play.

Chapter Fourteen

Dinner was over and the washing-up done.

Slices of watermelon glistened in a bowl, untouched.

The television was on in the corner of the room.

Yuliana's mother fanned herself with her hand. 'Is the air conditioner not working, Papa?'

Papa, a nervous little man who often detached himself from company to read his horror novels, blew out his cheeks.

'Working but not cold. Man coming tomorrow to fix it,' explained Yuliana, putting away the dishes. 'Said it would cost quite a bit to replace the expansion valve.'

'No, no, no,' groaned Yuliana's father, rolling his tongue around his mouth. 'More expense, Shinta.'

Shinta, their neighbour from downstairs, had joined them for a late supper. She was a widow with a mouth full of questions. Lounging in her sarong, she said, 'I try not to use aircon during the day. Standing fan is just as effective.'

'Don't worry, Bayu will pay for it, won't you Bayu,' said Yuliana. 'I didn't marry a doctor for nothing.' The lines along Bayu's jaw hardened a fraction.

'The neighbour patted him on the shoulder. 'Tell me, ah, are you still working at the military hospital?'

'Yes, of course I am. Why do you ask such a thing?'

'My cousin's son, Neri, was admitted yesterday morning with stomach pain. Turns out he had a gastric bug. Anyway, my cousin's son asked after you and you know what they said? They said you left; said you no longer held a position there.'

Bayu went pale. 'Who said that?'

'The woman at reception desk.'

Yuliana laughed, her lips waggling from side to side. 'That woman, the skinny one with the bunched-up hair, is it? Oh, she is always teasing people.'

'Well, that's what she said,' insisted Shinta. 'Why would she do that?'

A quickening in Bayu's gut. A hot stab of scalding panic that beat its wings and surged from his groin to his navel and up to his throat. 'Please, Shinta,' he said, striving to keep the anxiety at bay. 'I'll ask you not to spread ridiculous rumours about things you don't know.'

'Neri thought it was true.'

'I will deal with it.'

'But he—'

'I said I will deal with it.'

Yuliana's eyes met his. There was not a hint of suspicion in her gaze. Her thoughts were on the following day's classroom activity – making patriotic pinwheels out of pins, straws and bits of coloured paper.

Bayu fiddled with his lank black hair and turned his attention to the television.

'Husband, are you coming with us on Sunday to visit Aunty Puri in Depok? We're taking the early train.'

Bayu folded his arms. He pretended not to hear, so Yuliana

repeated the question. Bayu made an impatient grunt and glanced at his phone.

The news started on SCTV. The lead story was all about the government drawing up tougher anti-terrorism laws in Indonesia.

Bayu's mobile made a *ting* noise. He pressed the navigation key and scrolled to his inbox.

The incoming text read:

meet me outside

His heart leapt. He stared at the phone.

now

Head fizzed and his deep-set eyes grew liquid. Instinctively, Bayu covered the phone with his hand.

He got to his feet and walked to the front door. He did not grab his car keys or his umbrella.

'Where are you going?' asked Yuliana.

He slipped on his shoes. 'Work.' He released the locks and the deadbolt.

'At eleven at night?'

'No problem! *Tidak apa-apa!*'

He shut the door quietly as he left.

Chapter Fifteen

Thursday morning and Ruud's MP3 was blasting 'Get Up Offa That Thing' at full volume. He was alone in the apartment. Imke was having breakfast with her Aunt Erica at the Suparna coffee shop, which meant he could crank up the tunes and temporarily lose himself in the music. He'd spent the night mulling over Jillian Parker's murder; he badly needed some chill time.

He climbed out of the shower and ran a towel over his body. Steam escaped through a gap in the tiny window. Through it he heard the tooting of a bus, the incessant sounds of traffic.

The water dripped off him as he performed a dozen thigh lunges followed by a dozen push-ups. After this he did some stretching exercises, reaching up high to extend his arms, bending down low to touch his toes.

Ruud bobbed his head as James Brown sang. Before he knew it the detective was boogying, doing the Mashed Potato, sliding his feet across the tiled floor with snaky in-and-out moves, rolling his hips this way and that.

The trumpet and saxophones kicked in.

Naked, with only the bath towel draped across a shoulder, Ruud jerked his head back and forth like a chicken.

He span and whirled. Clapped his hands. Threw his elbows in the air.

Getting down. Grooving. He shuffled and swivelled with all his weight on one foot, gyrating to the drum and bass, to the funky beat.

Performing to his imaginary audience, he mouthed the lyrics, grunted and screamed. And then, just like Soul Brother Number 1, he fell to his knees.

He was about to jump into 'Sex Machine' when the landline rang.

Instinctively he reached for his mobile and realized the battery was dead again.

He scurried into the bedroom and picked up the receiver. It was Witarsa. 'Your mobile isn't working!'

'Sorry,' he panted.

'We have a bad situation here. There's been another murder. Same as before, all smoke and ash.'

'Where are you?'

'JAKK. We've had to close it down.'

Jakarta Kota Station was the city's largest rail station, operating several of the intercity lines running across Java. It was also the busiest terminal in the country as far as passenger usage was concerned, providing half the commuter rail service for the Jakarta metropolitan area.

'It's the middle of rush hour,' said Ruud.

'*Sialan!* Tell me about it.'

Ruud's hair was still damp when he reached the crime scene.

And he wasn't surprised to find the old colonial building's façade teeming with *bajaj* three-wheelers, *mikrolet* cabs and *ojek* taxis.

When he got inside, he was met by a tidal flow of humanity. Five of the twelve tracks had reopened, but the backlog of disgruntled commuters was overwhelming. They jammed the six platforms and caused gridlock in the main hall, choking the stairways, blocking the exits, spilling out onto Jalan Lada and the adjoining streets.

Ruud had to thrust his forearms into people's backs and throats to get through. Here and there a channel of undulating bodies moved, surging sporadically like an intermittent stream. Some rolled away just as others rolled in.

A terse announcement on the station Tannoy urged the crowd to make way for emergency services. The words reverberated around the hall, bouncing off the barrel vault roof. Ruud held aloft his KNRI police badge and shouted for those up ahead to make way. The throng shifted a fraction. Ruud shoved some more but he was wary of causing a crush.

Then from somewhere behind him a police motorcycle blared its siren. The public address system repeated the earlier announcement and there followed a brief swaying as the herd shifted. Seconds later, the horde split in two and parted down the middle. Ruud took his chance and sprinted across the concourse to Platform 2.

Aiboy Ali was waiting for him, squinting and pointing to the huge station clock.

'My phone died on me.'

'I guessed as much. The forensic team arrived half an hour ago. We have the crime scene secured.'

'Well?' demanded Ruud. 'Tell me what's happening.'

'There's a body on the tracks.'

They walked to the far end of Platform 2, through the hot metal stink of idling engines, and climbed down onto the track's ballast shoulder. Their shoes crunched against tiny stones.

'The station was closed for servicing,' said Aiboy, 'between midnight and four a.m.'

'What time was the body discovered?'

'The four a.m. from Bogor arrived at five thirty on Platform six, as scheduled. No problem. The first commuter train to leave was the five forty Red Line from Platform two. As he pulled out, the driver saw something on the tracks and sounded the alarm.'

Ruud stumbled on the narrow-gauged track.

'It's easier to walk on the sleepers,' said Aiboy Ali.

The morning sun hit Ruud full in the face. He took in the grey towers and the elevated highway to the south, and the low bank of earth to the west. There was nothing to stop people from walking across the tracks. This wasn't North Melbourne or Amsterdam Centraal or London Waterloo. Public safety was not a high priority in Indonesia. Only a few kilometres from here, in the shanty towns, families lived five metres from the rail lines, bathing their children in buckets, foraging for food and collecting garbage.

The gravel bit into the soles of Ruud's feet. 'How far?'

A conductor's whistle shrilled the air.

'Not far. Look.' Aiboy levelled his gaze at the silhouette sixty metres ahead. Ruud saw Officer Hamka Hamzah standing over what looked like three camel humps of grey concrete, waving his arms, shooing the crows away.

A locomotive horn hooted. A puff of dirty diesel smoke drifted by.

Ruud covered his mouth and coughed.

In the near distance, Ruud heard the wheeze, squeal and slam of cogs, of brakes, of slamming carriage doors.

'Are we safe here? We're not going to get run over, are we?'

'We're fine, *Gajah*. Sabhara has cordoned off the area. Tracks three and four are closed until further notice.'

The pair straddled the yellow *garis polisi* barrier tape.

Aiboy called out and several people appeared from a white tent erected on the track side by technicians. They included the police pathologist, Solossa, Commissioner Joyo T. Witarsa and Alya Entitisari.

Solossa raised an arm in welcome. '*Selamat Pagi* to you, First *Inspektur* Pujasumarta.' The pathologist wore a pair of yellow goggles and held a UV flashlight in his hand. Ruud recognized the 380–385 nm flashlight; it was used to detect accelerants such as petrol, diesel and kerosene.

Ruud went straight up to his chief. 'Same guy?'

'He's struck again,' said Witarsa, looking miserable. 'It's bad, very bad.' His expression resembled a trampled towpath. 'The victim's name is Anita Dalloway. She's British. We think the perp parked beyond the earthen bank and carried the body down.' Ruud looked towards the bank and saw a line of press photographers held back by Sabhara cops. 'We're checking for tyre markings and shoe prints. There's no CCTV beyond the main station and no traffic cameras in the vicinity.'

Another whistle shrieked behind Ruud.

A train from Platform 5 moved off. First-class compartments in the front. Female-only coaches at the back. It was the delayed 07.20 Red Line to Depok and Bogor. The gut-rumbling sound of its engine shivered the ground. Ruud watched the 07.20 commuter pass the south junction signal box with about a hundred pairs of eyes staring his way. Passengers, young and old, had their faces pressed against the train windows, gawking, hoping to catch a glimpse of the action.

Witarsa paced along the ballast, too wired to keep still. He was muttering to himself, trying to regain his self-control.

Ruud had never seen him like this before. 'Are you all right?' he asked.

'Where's Hartono?' barked the commissioner, his eyes wild.

'With the IT boys,' said Aiboy Ali. 'He's going through the station's security tapes.'

'Anything so far?'

'No,' Aiboy admitted, 'but he only started on the tapes half an hour ago.'

Ruud felt a hand on his hipbone. It was Solossa. He still wore the yellow goggles over his eyes. 'I want to show you something.'

'What?'

The pathologist removed the goggles and extricated a comb from his breast pocket. He ran its teeth across his scalp.

'Come,' urged Solossa. 'Take a look at the *korban*.'

'Is it the same MO as before?'

'Yes and no,' reflected the pathologist, pulling on a pair of latex gloves.

'How do you mean?'

'See for yourself.'

The stench of the burned corpse hung heavy in the air. Ruud shoved a handkerchief to his mouth and nose.

The figure, or what remained of it, sat cross-legged with arms folded across the lap. Most of the skull and torso was scorched a hellish colour, burned so black it looked wet and shiny, but there were areas near the forearm joints and knees where patches of rust poked through, reddening the over-hanging bits of skin.

Ruud couldn't help thinking he'd seen this image before. It reminded him of the Buddhist monks who voluntarily set themselves alight in Tibet. It was a horrible sight. But what was most worrying to Ruud was the banner that lay, unfurled, by the corpse's feet.

Next to a bright-yellow Versa-Cone, Ruud saw a dark-blue tarp, about sixty by ninety cms, with white Islamic writing scribbled across it.

'Can you read Arabic script?' asked Ruud.

Solossa said he couldn't. 'But one of my men took a photo and downloaded a translation app on his phone. See this here? That's a verse number.'

'It's the *Quran.*'

The older man referred to his notebook and read aloud, '"Indeed, those who disbelieve in our teachings, we will burn them with fire. Every time their skins are roasted through we will replace them with other skins, so they may taste the punishment once more. For God is majestic and all-wise."' He stopped and looked hard at Ruud. 'Surah An-Nisa. Verse four: fifty-six.'

Ruud sank to his haunches. Right beside the unfurled banner was Anita Dalloway's undamaged passport, the royal coat of arms with the gold lion and unicorn glinting in the sunlight. It had been placed there deliberately.

'Oh shit.'

'Oh shit, is right. He's targeting Christians.'

Chapter Sixteen

'Are you certain nobody found anything like it at the Jillian Parker crime scene?' Ruud shouted into his phone. It was a weak signal and he could barely hear Hartono's response. 'Not even a scrap of paper or a message scratched into the earth?' Indiscernible squawking. 'I see. OK. Thanks.'

He hung up and turned to gaze at Imke, who was driving, her eyes fixed on the road. She drove with her hands low and only her forefingers on the steering wheel. They were on their way to the Puncak hills with Ruud in the passenger seat and Kiki sprawled out in the rear chewing one of her squeaky toys.

'Look at her back there.' Imke grinned. 'Stretching out like she's in First Class.'

'Thanks for coming with me.'

She swerved to avoid a pothole. 'I was going to have a late lunch with Karen at Bakmi Aheng, the noodle place on Petak Sembilan.' Karen was a new friend who worked as a guest relations officer at the Mandarin Oriental Hotel. 'But one of the front-desk staff called in sick, so she has to cover for him. We postponed lunch to next week.'

'I could do with a fresh pair of eyes.'

Imke smiled. She knew the real reason she'd been asked

to come – Ruud needed Kiki to work her magic. Perhaps what forensics and Sabhara had missed, Kiki might find. 'I hope Djoko doesn't mind me kidnapping you.'

'It's good to get out of the city.' She glanced across at him. 'So tell me, what's this all about.'

Ruud filled her in, telling her the finer details of the two homicides.

'But when you searched the hills you found nothing.'

'Not a thing. A dingo's breakfast. That's why I want yours and Kiki's help, to re-examine the site and expand the search parameter. Why would the perp lay out a strip of canvas with words from the *Quran* for Anita Dalloway, but leave nothing when he killed Jillian Parker? It doesn't make sense.'

'It does sound odd, I must admit.'

He looked at the rear-view mirror to ensure they weren't being followed. 'I can't work out why the pattern doesn't match. It doesn't fit.'

'Perhaps Anita Dalloway's murder was more personal.'

They came to a bend in the broken road and Imke slowed. She parked by the ridge, opposite the bus stop where Mrs Lindo had sat on the morning of 16 February. The road had been cut into the hillside, with a picturesque valley below and trees and scrub bushes on both sides.

Ruud carried a thermos in his hand. He walked up to the cliff verge and sat on his haunches, looking down the slope. He took his time, taking it all in, getting a feel for the place again. The burned-out car was gone, winched up and hauled off to the scrap merchants, but the scarred imprint remained. The long rectangle of disfigured earth was dry, parched and blackened.

Imke shielded her eyes from the sun, admiring the view of the tea plantations across the valley. 'Nice to see a bit of lush greenery for a change,' she said, Kiki at her heels. 'So this is where it happened, *hè*? It's quite a drop. You'd think they would have erected a fence or some bollards.'

'That's the Ministry of Public Works for you.'

Ruud drew a slow breath and searched the tops of the branches. Over to his left, a bruised papaya fell to the ground with a thump – a squirrel had taken a chunk out of it. Ruud considered pinching a fat yellow one for his breakfast the following day.

He unscrewed the thermos cap with a soft popping sound and tipped hot Earl Grey out of the vacuum flask into a melamine cup.

'Tea, vicar?'

Imke declined with a smile.

He took a cautious sip, careful not to scald the roof of his mouth.

The tea calmed him, made him think more clearly.

Growing impatient, Imke said, 'Can we see if Kiki can find anything?'

'Be my guest.'

'OK, let's start.' Imke patted the side of her leg to get the dog's attention. 'Who's a good girl? Yes, Kiki.' Imke gave her a treat and unclipped the lead.

Ruud passed Imke the plastic bag containing an article of clothing, an old T-shirt taken from Jillian Parker's apartment. 'Strictly speaking, Kiki's a cadaver dog. She can pick up the smell of a dead body with no trouble whatsoever – through concrete, under water, buried fifteen metres underground – you name it, and she can do it. She's not so good as a scent-discriminating dog, however, which is picking up the scent of a particular person. But I'm sure she won't let us down. As long as there's even a hint of sebum or blood, she'll find it.'

Kiki buried her nose in the T-shirt then looked up, her attention focused on Imke's words and hands. Imke clicked her fingers and signalled. 'Find, Kiki, find!'

The spaniel sprang away, twisting and turning. A few seconds later Kiki came to a stop by a ribbon of well-trodden grass. She plopped her bottom down and stared hard at the ground.

'Good girl! She's picked up the minute trails of skin cells. Good girl, Kiki.' Imke gave the dog another treat. 'My guess is Jillian was placed here at some stage. You said her insides were removed. It's not inconceivable that she was still breathing when he transported her, but then he pulled her from the car and killed her, right here, on this little patch of sod. Even if the perp covered the space with plastic, some of the skin rafts and blood molecules would have gone windborne. Some might have spilled. Tiny traces would have collected along this part of the ground.'

Ruud got down low and sniffed the grass. 'Very slight smell of kerosene.'

'What do you think?'

'I think he abducted Jillian from her office car park and drove her to this spot. He took Jillian from the car alive. Mrs Lindo, our witness, said she heard the victim scream, so Jillian was certainly alive when the Mazda drove up. I think our perp then beat her unconscious and dragged her out. He then laid out some plastic, placed her on it and cut her open. There's no sign of blood so he must have used waterproof plastic. Then he poured kerosene over her and carried her back to the car, placing her in the driver's seat.'

'Sounds about right, *hè*? After which he released the handbrake, lit her up and rolled her over the cliff.'

'He probably used Builder's Roll. Unravelled several metres of it from here to the car, but because she was soaked in both blood and kerosene some of it dripped off her skin and splashed onto the grass, leaving a residue.'

'You know what, you should be a detective,' said Imke. 'You have a talent for this sort of thing.'

'That's what my mother keeps telling me.'

'Okey-dokey, let's see if Kiki can come up with anything else.' Imke slapped her thigh. Immediately, Kiki's body elongated, her tail grew stiff and she was off again, nose to the ground. She trotted a kilometre or so up the road, poked her head into some bushes, made a beeline for an iron-wood sapling, gave it a sniff, dismissed it, did an about-face, and scuttled towards the cliff edge. After another two minutes of heading this way and that, Kiki doubled back and came to a halt at Imke's feet. 'Good girl,' exclaimed Imke, ruffling the dog's ear. 'She's telling us, this is the only spot where Jillian Parker left a trace.

Ruud nibbled his thumbnail, deep in thought.

'Do you have a plan?'

His eyes focused on the thicket. 'The tarp has got to be in those trees somewhere.'

'Why are you so convinced he left a message?' said Imke.

'I just am. I'm going down the hill to check it out again.'

'You can't do it without a harness and rope. It's way too steep.'

'Not if I take it from there.' He indicated a spot with his hand about a hundred metres away. 'The angle's not so sheer. I'll climb down where those rocks are and make my way across.'

Imke didn't look convinced. 'Are you sure about this?'

He didn't reply. On impulse, he jogged over to the slanting rock scarp and slithered over the lip, sliding down on his bum, taking it a few centimetres at a time.

'Are there snakes out here?'

'Cobras, banded kraits, pit vipers, the lot. If I'm not back for supper, call for backup!' he yelled, before disappearing completely behind a sea of hip-high crowngrass.

For several minutes Imke searched the clumps of green for movement. The vegetation was so thick and tall it was hard to see anything through the canopy. She made out some nesting birds, a jangle of jade. Little else.

A light breeze combed the treetops, cooling the perspiration on her skin.

The sun shone in her eyes, distorting shapes, making it difficult to see.

Then she saw the top of his head appear and she sighed with relief. Moving through dapples of sunlight and leaf shadow, he was making slow progress. She could hear him cursing. 'Bloody thorns!' he yelled.

'Try to avoid the prickles and the skin-blistering weeds!' she shouted.

'Now you tell me!'

'And you know what they say about poison ivy. Leaves of three, let it be.'

For a while all she could see was the top of his head bobbing about. At regular intervals he turned his eyes up to look at her, offering a little wave of assurance. Even from up here she could see the sweat pouring off him, soaking his shirt. The tall scrub enclosed him. She suspected he couldn't see more than three or four paces ahead. He struggled through a screen of flame trees and copper pods, tripping over saplings, circumnavigating a high palisade of lofty bamboo. Until, finally, he broke through into the open and was standing directly below her, about fifteen metres down, in the rectangle of charred earth.

Ruud went down on his haunches once more. The nearby soil was grainy, pitted with the marks of heavy raindrops. 'Must have rained here this morning,' he said.

Insects buzzed about.

'Did you bring any mozzie spray? I'm being eaten alive here.'

'See anything?' Imke asked.

'Nope, just an ocean of jungle vines. Wait a minute.' He climbed onto a low-hanging neem branch. 'If the canvas went down with the car it couldn't have been blown off course very far.'

'Do you think it could have been incinerated in the fire?'

'Forensics performed a full chemical analysis test. They went through the vehicle with a fine toothcomb, and they didn't find any traces of woven polyethylene.'

Ruud looked around once more. He peered up at the sky. Clots of dark clouds charcoaled the horizon. 'Gonna rain soon.'

'It's not here, is it?'

'No.'

'What now?'

'Now I have to make my way back, which should be fun. I'll retrace my steps. Meet me over by the rocks, will you?'

Twenty minutes later he was scrambling up the cliff wall. 'Let me help you,' offered Imke, kneeling, reaching over the verge. 'Take my hand and hurry up, you're making me feel dizzy.'

'Thanks, *Putri Salju*.'

She hauled him over the top and hugged him close, wrapping her arms around his back. He smelled of wet earth mingled with Imperial Leather. For a while he sat on the ground panting, dusting himself off and picking thorns and grass seeds from his shirt. He shook his sleeve, jettisoning a few more prickles.

His trousers were torn at the thigh and his elbows were bruised. Imke kissed him on the ear to make up for the scraped elbows. 'Edmund Hillary eat your heart out,' he grunted. 'Remind me to pack a ladder next time.' He ran a hand through his damp hair, which now stood to attention in crests.

Imke fished her phone from her pocket and held it at arm's length in front of her. She had her back to the valley and was aiming the zoom at Ruud.

'What do you think you're doing?' he protested.

'Taking a picture of you.'

'Why?'

'I like the bedraggled, unkempt, dragged-along-the-jungle-floor look.'

'Get off!' he laughed.

'Oh, come on, I have to have a record of this. Ha ha ha! The state of your hair!' She stopped short and focused on a point in the distance. 'Oh God!'

'What now?'

'You're not going to believe this.'

'What?'

'Behind you.'

Ruud wheeled round to see what she was looking at. 'What?'

'Up there. I see it.'

The first *inspektur* stared at the trees that grew on the upper slopes of the hillside. At first he saw little but dense foliage, tangles of creepers and climbers, fir spinnies, underbrush, the sweep of an Indian cork tree. 'I don't see anything.'

'There.' She pointed.

His shoulders stiffened. He tried again, scanning the branches and boughs, concentrating, sifting through the shadowy shades of green and brown, and then he saw it. Thirty metres above the road. A canvas tarp slung between two limbs. Sagging. Looking as sad as a deflated weather balloon. Almost folded in two. White Islamic writing on a dark blue background.

'What the hell is it doing up there?'

'You were all so busy looking down the hill the other day, you must have forgotten to look up.'

'That can't be.'

'Well, it is. Plain as day.'

Grabbing Imke by the waist, he kissed her on the lips. 'You bloody beauty!'

As he dashed off to retrieve the tarpaulin, he was forced to scrabble through even heavier clumps of foliage, a tussock of spiky grass and knots of weed, causing his trousers to tear further. He raised an arm to shield his face from the sharp, scraping branches.

'Shit!' he cried. The ground was marshy here, slick and slimy, blanketed by a light drift of damp leaves. Mud coated his feet up to the ankle bone. Ruud fought his way through some rushes, slipped on moss and had to crawl over a fallen pine, but eventually he got there. A mosquito landed on his sweaty neck. 'You're not going to believe this!' he shouted to Imke who waited by the road.

Jillian Parker's KITAP permanent-stay permit card was

nailed to the base of the tree. The blue card was waiting for him; it was like being awarded a prize for coming first in a treasure hunt.

'Need any help?' yelled Imke, hands on hips, her voice croaky.

'No, I'll manage.' A bug flew into his ear. He swiped it away and gazed skywards. The tarpaulin was hooked round a crooked tree limb; it was sodden and speckled with bird shit.

Only when he'd got it down, using his pocketknife to cut through the rope, did he start to question himself and his team. How had they not seen it before? How could they have missed something this size? And then a thought struck him: what if it wasn't here the other day? Suppose he had come back. Suppose the perpetrator had come back.

Chapter Seventeen

Back at Central HQ on Jalan Kramat Raya later that night, the Incident Room was buzzing.

Twenty-six men and women — a mixture of Sabhara cops, warrant officers, homicide detectives, CID, Serious Crimes and Detachment 88 agents — converged around the whiteboard.

They all looked at Ruud as he entered.

Wordlessly, he stuck half a dozen crime-scene photographs to the adjoining corkboard, before focusing on the white-board itself. Then, with a sharp glare, he dug his fingers into a box of coloured pens and used a red marker to write Jillian Parker's name, address, approximate time of death as well as the identity of the first responder. He did the same for the second victim. After this he put up an elongated map of West Java and drew a long red line connecting Puncak to downtown Jakarta.

Turning to the gathering, he said, 'For those of you who don't know me, I'm *Inspektur Polisi Satu* Ruud Pujasumarta.' Half of the faces were unfamiliar to him. 'I'll be SIO in the inquiry for the Jillian Parker and Anita Dalloway murders. Jillian Parker, Australian, aged thirty-five. Anita Dalloway, English, aged twenty-three.'

'Where is Commissioner Witarsa?' demanded one of the warrant officers.

'He's meeting with Police General Haiti and the Minister of Home Affairs. OK, any more interruptions? No? Good.' It was time to seize everyone's attention. 'Death by burning.' He jabbed his finger at the photos on the corkboard with an air of determination. 'A punishment historically meted out for acts of treason, heresy and witchcraft. These women were burned alive. Roasted until their blood and marrow bubbled, until the dermal layers of their skin exploded and their brains boiled in their skulls.'

He regarded the sea of faces and knew he had control of the room.

'Ninety kilometres, ladies and gentlemen. That's the distance between our two homicides. Jillian Parker was discovered in Puncak. Anita Dalloway in Jakarta Kota. Killed three days apart.' He pointed to the photograph of the tarp with white Islamic writing scribbled across it. 'And he's left us calling cards. The messages were handwritten using ordinary house paint. We've sent them for ink analysis.'

The red marker was still in his left hand. He tossed it on the table. 'How are these women connected? Did they know one another? Why did the killer choose them? That's what we have to find out.'

'Are we seeking one individual or several?' asked Tjo from Serious Crimes.

'Too soon to say, but experience tells me this is the work of one person,' said Ruud. 'However, we cannot confirm if these are the acts of a serial offender, a jealous lover, a pyromaniac sadist, a misogynistic madman or a terrorist, nor whether they're racially motivated, sexually motivated or propelled by religion.'

He inclined his head. 'But initial evidence suggests it is a hate crime based on the victims' faith. In his eyes these women are an affront to God, and he is punishing them for their transgressions, using fire to cleanse them of their sins.'

'Punishing them for being Christian,' reflected the warrant officer. 'So he's a misogynist pyromaniac Muslim who hates Christ worshippers?'

'Yes. Hence we've upped the police presence in all major tourist spots and hotels, and increased patrols near churches.'

Werry Hartono had a question. 'Apart from the lengths of canvas with the Quranic writing, is there anything else to go on?'

Everyone eyed Ruud keenly.

'We are following the usual protocol, calling for witnesses, looking into the victims' finances and medical data. We're also speaking to their relatives, associates and work colleagues, past and present boyfriends, the places they travelled. You know the form.'

'I'm told the perp took their mobile phones. If he still has the devices, can't we locate him using GPS?' asked the Serious Crimes man.

'We believe the phones have been destroyed,' said Ruud. 'They've been smashed up or tossed into a river, which means, of course, that we can't retrieve any of the texts. If we could recover the victims' last text conversations we might have a better understanding of who they were going to meet and where.'

'Maybe he just removed the SIM cards.'

'If he'd removed the SIM cards, we'd still be able to track the phones. Every phone has an integrated group of identifiers that allow it to be detected via Stingray devices or IMSI catchers.' Ruud paused. 'Any other questions regarding the mobile phones?'

He took a sip of water from a plastic bottle and looked about for a familiar mop of hair. 'Aiboy, what did you find at Jillian Parker's flat?'

'Apart from a very hungry cat, an overflowing laundry basket and some seriously dehydrated pot plants, not much.' Aiboy Ali passed around several black-and-white enlargements of the apartment interior. Ruud regarded the images; the first enlargement showed Jillian's home office; he saw karma stones, crystal wands, books on feng shui, a brass Buddha on a green velvet cloth; nothing appeared out of the ordinary. 'No indication of a forced break-in. Everything looks the way she might have left it,' said Aiboy. 'Full of spiritual-healing crap. No sign of her phone or laptop, though. And she had a pretty sad collection of CDs – no punk or metal whatsoever.'

'So the place appeared undisturbed?'

'Yes. However, a few objects seemed out of place, as though someone had rummaged about and put things back again carefully, but not carefully enough.'

'Explain.'

'Some of the books on the bookshelf were upside down and I found dust marks where heavy furniture had been moved.'

'You think someone forced their way in looking for something?'

'It's possible.'

'OK, let's leave this for now. Remind me who's checking Anita Dalloway's place?'

'We are, sir,' one of the Sabhara cops replied. 'She took a room in a hostel round the corner from Jalan Jaksa. She was travelling with two other backpackers. They claim she went missing two days ago, never turned up for late-night drinks. We're still going through her things.'

'Take your time. Be thorough. Yesterday, the Minister of Home Affairs informed the British Ambassador of her death and the UK Foreign & Commonwealth Office was quick to offer assistance. We've already received Miss Dalloway's old dental records and matched them to the body.' Ruud paused again, reining in his thoughts. He didn't want to rush the words. 'Furthermore, as in the case of Jillian Parker, we're taking the view that Anita Dalloway was alive when set alight, or at least still breathing.'

'What are you basing this on?' asked the warrant officer.

Solossa, the *dokter forensic*, answered: 'Time of death in these situations is notoriously hard to determine because post-mortem hypostasis, rigor mortis and body temperature cannot be appraised. But we found smoke in her lungs. She had a CO-Hb level of seventy per cent, indicating she was alive when the fire started and was able to breathe in the fumes.'

'Is the way she's positioned on the ground, with arms and legs folded, relevant?' asked the Sabhara cop.

'Too early to say.'

'What about forensic evidence?'

Solossa again. 'After hours of fruitless searching I'm afraid we have nothing. *Kosong.* No tyre markings and no shoe impressions at either site. The fire destroyed all hair and fibre evidence, so we've drawn a blank with that too. As for the canvases, the passport and KITAP card – they were all wiped clean of body fluids and fingerprints. The words on the canvases were handwritten with ordinary house paint, so nothing to go on there. We found several hundred discarded cigarette butts within a hundred-metre radius of the second victim, but the chances any belong to our man are slim to nil.'

Ruud spoke over him. 'We have little on the witness front too. Officers went house-to-house, knocked on over a hundred doors. Nobody saw anything. The train station was closed between midnight and four a.m. He made his move between those times, so he has a working knowledge of train times. He also knew there was no CCTV coverage beyond the train platforms and no traffic cameras in the area. Everything points to a man who is cautious and selective in his movements. The bloke's smart, he knows about police procedure, knows how to clean up after himself. He's a risk-taker, but not a rash risk-taker. His MO is quite simple. He incapacitates his victims and then burns them. Obliterating all evidence.'

'Yet, we have one major oddity,' said Solossa. 'Both victims had their insides removed.'

'You mean they were mutilated?' said Babar from Serious Crimes, his throat sounding dry and parched.

'I mean their lower abdomens were cut out. He removed their reproductive organs.'

'Like Jack the Ripper.'

'Yes, Babar,' said Solossa. 'I suppose you could say that.'

'And you're suggesting they were both still alive when he set them alight, even after being mutilated?'

'Yes, it would appear so. Which indicates the perp must have cut open Jillian Parker and Anita Dalloway only moments before setting them on fire.'

'Are we to assume he hates women?'

'Possibly.'

'If they weren't burned to death, do you think the women would have bled to death?'

'Most probably.'

Babar exchanged glances with his colleagues. 'Anything else you want to tell me?'

'Yes,' said Ruud. 'We think our man was wearing a pig mask.'

'A *what*?' blurted a CID officer in the corner, laughing.

'We have a witness who claims she heard the perp making oinking noises. So logic dictates he might have been in a costume of sorts.'

'You mean like Porky Pig! A fire-worshipping Muslim dressed as Porky Pig. How *bodoh* can you get. Who is this *saksi*?'

Ruud smiled. 'It's merely a theory.'

'Any other lines of inquiry?'

Ruud thought about Shane Waters and the curious scratch marks on his wrist and throat. 'Not at the moment.'

'Sir?' Werry again, sounding dead serious. 'How do we proceed?'

'I've spoken with the top brass and our instructions are to tread carefully. We will release information that two women have been killed in separate incidences, but as far as details go we're to keep it vague. For the moment it's imperative everything is kept tight and in-house. The last thing we want is a media circus, so there's to be no talking to the press. No talking to colleagues outside of this room. No sharing of information with anyone. Is that clear? Just for the next few days until D88 can explain whether this is or isn't a terrorist act. Understood?'

There came a murmur of assent.

'If they confirm this is a terrorist crime, we'll hand over

to Special Branch and D88 as instructed by BRIMOB POLRI. But until then we are to treat this as a category B investigation, using normal police resourcing avenues.'

Ruud turned to the two strapping Detachment 88 agents. 'I know it's early days, but what can you tell me?'

'Next to nothing,' the taller of the pair said. 'Often we'll get wind of an imminent attack – not the precise where-abouts, nor the date – but Intelligence will be aware of an impending threat. Not this time.'

'Has there been any chatter about this?'

'Not a thing,' said one.

'Quiet as a mouse,' said the other counter-terrorism specialist. 'Metadata has drawn a blank. No electronic chitchat whatsoever. Whoever's responsible isn't talking or boasting about it.'

'Strange, don't you think?' said Ruud.

'Very strange. Usually, if it were, say, Jemaah Islamiyah, they'd be cock-a-hoop about this. We've heard nothing, for example, from Santoso or his rebels in Sulawesi. My feeling is it's the work of a single individual – not a member of IS or JI, but someone acting alone.'

'Very well, let's move on,' urged Ruud. 'As I said, we have to be discreet. For now, treat this as if it were your common curry-sauce variety homicide.'

'Where do we start, boss?' asked Hamzah.

'We start with you, Hamzah. I want you to talk to the imams, the ulema scholars, sit them down, be forceful if you must, ask them if there have been any extreme people mak-ing themselves heard. Go to every district, from Cakung to Tebet. Don't tell them why you're asking, but get me some answers. Can you do that?'

'Yes, boss.'

'Good. Alya, where's Alya?' She raised a hand. 'I want you to work with CID and get me a list of those underground blogs that publish all that anti-Western sentiment crap, you know the ones – *Antikristus* and *Asing Pulang* and . . . what's that other one?'

'*Aturan Islam.*'

'Get me their IP addresses. I want to know everything about these people. I want to know who they chat to, who they write for, who funds them, together with a list of all registered followers and subscribers.

'Aiboy, can you check with the radio stations, especially the late-night call-ins, for any nut-job callers. See if they've had anyone ring in who might fit the profile. The producers usually keep the phone details of anyone who's been particularly weird or abusive.'

'Sure, *Gajah.*'

'And contact the Ulema Council, the Muslim clerical body. The MUI regularly conduct religious appraisals on the clergy. Find out who they've censured in the last year for militant preaching. I want the names of anyone even remotely extremist.

'Listen up, everyone. Whoever did this has experience. Whoever did this has killed before and has a background in killing. Whatever the motive might be, he knows how to extinguish life. What he did yesterday took guts. Setting fire to someone in full view of people takes balls. He's done this twice now, and more than likely he's going to do it again.'

Ruud gazed at everyone, allowed them time to take it all in. Then he raised his eyebrows and lightened his tone. 'I have distributed individual task notes to each of you with specific duties. Please speak with the office manager regarding overtime, cancelled rest days and travel costs. Soentoro will act as OM.' Soentoro waved his arm to identify himself. 'Is that clear? Good. If you have any follow-up questions, come see me afterwards. Well, that's me done for now.' A tired grimace cracked across his face. 'Right then. It's been a long day and it's going to be a long night and tomorrow's going to be another long day. So, who's hungry?'

The entire room seemed to respond in unison.

Earlier on, his ex-mother-in-law had brought in several boxes of gooey *dodol*, the sweet, toffee-like treat made from palm sugar, coconut milk, screwpine leaves and glutinous rice flour.

'If you all head into my office you'll find Mrs Panggabean and Mrs Hapsari waiting with some treats and tidbits to keep you going. We'll regroup tomorrow for a briefing at fifteen hundred hours.'

Chapter Eighteen

Eight a.m.

Anita Dalloway's hostel, The Paradies, behind Jalan Jaksa, was far more upscale than Ruud had expected. There was a coffee nook, a bar, a snooker room, a book exchange and even a roof-top garden. The first and second floors housed six-bed dorms, the third-floor rooms were six- and eight-bed dorms, whereas the entire fourth-floor space was reserved for the budget-conscious, with two dormitories each containing sixteen double bunk beds.

'I always thought these places were dark and dingy and full of druggies,' hissed Aiboy Ali under his breath. There was no one else in the small bright lobby but he couldn't help whispering.

'They still are,' said Ruud. 'The druggies just have more money these days.'

Aiboy flicked through a brochure he'd picked up at the front desk.

'What are you doing?'

'Checking the nightly rates. If it's cheaper than where I'm renting, I'm moving in.'

'Who runs it?'

'German fellow. Gerhard Vosseler. Married a local.'

Ruud went behind the desk, across flooring corked with sugar palm bark, and approached the door bearing a brass sign saying 'STAFF ONLY'. He rapped three times.

A man with curly grey-blond hair appeared. 'Gentlemen! How are you this sunny Friday morning! I am Gerhard, the proprietor.' He was dressed casually in baggy shorts, polo shirt and sandals.

Ruud showed him his warrant card. 'You got our call?'

'*Ja.*' His smile was welcoming but his eyes suggested he wanted them gone. 'The room where Miss Dalloway stayed has not been touched. The police came yesterday and went through everything.'

'I'm sorry to inconvenience you again. We're from the homicide unit.'

'For me it is not a problem.'

'We'd like to take a look around for ourselves.'

'*Natürlich.*'

They took the stairs.

'How many guests are currently in residence?'

'Thirty-three. Well, thirty-two now because of the, erm . . .'

'And my men from yesterday retained all of their passports, is that correct?'

'*Ja, ja.* Some of them were hoping to travel elsewhere later on, but I think everyone is in too much shock to complain.'

'No reason to complain,' reflected Aiboy, still thumbing through the brochure. 'You run a very clean, cheery establishment. Very upmarket for a hostel.'

'The Paradies is not your common backpacker sanctuary. There are many of – how does my wife say – *losmen*, low-cost inns, nearby, but we steer away from that model. For sure, we are a little more expensive, but we give you the all-round product. We encourage everyone to socialize and make party. That is our situation here. This is not simply a place to sleep. It is a place to cherish.'

'Nice sales pitch,' said Ruud. 'Married long, Herr Vosseler?'

'Since six years.'

They stopped at the second floor.

Gerhard Vosseler smiled, drawing his lips back to reveal the gum lines. 'Please, along this corridor until the end.' He showed them to the entrance of Anita Dalloway's six-bed dormitory, which was fortified with yellow *garis polisi* barrier tape.

Ruud straddled the tape and stepped into the room. He flipped the light switch. Above his head a fluorescent tube blinked on. He saw no locks on the door, so anyone could come and go at will. There were three bunk beds, each with a three-step wooden ladder leaning against the top mattress. Folded blankets and towels rested atop the sheets, and a mirror hung on the wall between. Everything looked neat and tidy. Ruud stood in the centre of the windowless space. 'Where are all her possessions? Her clothes? Her personal items?'

'Bagged and itemized,' said Aiboy Ali. 'They're running tests back at the lab.'

'Who was sharing this room with her?'

'Her travel companions,' said Vosseler. He stood at the threshold, watchful. 'At this moment they are in the room opposite. Until now they have not left the hostel.'

'I want to speak to them.'

'Of course,' replied the German.

Jade Watson and Timothy Greenleaf were playing cards in

the adjacent dorm, sitting on the floor, barefoot, listening to music. They did not rise when the policemen entered.

Ruud introduced himself and asked them what game they were playing.

'Gin rummy,' said Jade, her tone flat.

'Who's winning?'

'We're not really keeping score.'

'Mind if I sit with you?'

Timothy lifted his chin, then let it drop. 'If you like.'

Ruud tugged off his shoes and left them in the corridor with Vosseler. He bent at the knees and sat cross-legged next to Jade. He guessed she was about the same age as Anita Dalloway, around twenty-three. Timothy could have been a bit older but it was hard to tell. They both looked tired and wan, the man especially. His eyes seemed to have receded into their sockets.

'I have a couple of questions,' said Ruud.

'One of your men went through everything with us yesterday,' insisted Timothy. 'He seemed extremely interested in the fact that Jade's last name is Watson and asked her several times if she'd been to Baker Street in London.'

'That's Second Lieutenant Hartono. His line of questioning can be a bit odd sometimes.'

'You're telling me.'

'I'm sorry about your friend,' said Ruud.

'Why would' – Jade emitted a hitching cry – 'anybody want to hurt her?'

Tears welled in her eyes. She lowered her head and strands of brown hair fell over her face. The playing cards dropped into her lap.

Timothy reached across and touched her forearm.

The air conditioner rattled.

'Were you her boyfriend?' Ruud asked Timothy.

'No,' said Tim. 'Anita's boyfriend's in London. His name's Ben. Ben's studying to be a chartered accountant in London. That's why he's not here.'

Jade Watson wiped her face with the back of her hand and said, 'It's Tim and I that are, you know, like, a couple. We met Anita at uni.'

'Can you tell me when you last saw Anita?' said Ruud.

'Wednesday night.' It was Timothy who replied. 'Five, maybe six in the evening. It was still light.'

'What were you and Jade doing at the time?'

'Hanging around. We'd finished our showers, grabbed a bite to eat and were waiting to go out.'

'Anita was meant to join you?'

'She wanted to do some shopping at the night market so she went for a walk.' Jade blew her nose into a tissue. 'We arranged to meet later on at ten for drinks.'

'Do you know what she took with her? Phone, purse?'

'She had her belt pouch round her waist,' said Jade. 'Passport, cash, all that shit. She carried it with her everywhere, even to the bogs.'

'Do you remember what she was wearing?'

'Shorts and T-shirt,' said Jade.

'A purple T-shirt,' added Timothy.

'And she wore that tartan Alice band, didn't she, Tim?'

Ruud nodded. 'Why didn't you call the police when she didn't show at ten o'clock?'

'Because', bawled Jade, 'we thought she might've met someone and gone to his room.' She grabbed the pillow from her bunk and buried her face in it.

Ruud thought about this for a while. He let the silence stretch out.

'Was there someone here she fancied? Another traveller maybe?'

They shrugged.

'But you obviously tried to call her?'

'We rang her mobile but she didn't answer. Jade texted her, too.'

'Sometimes', said Jade, 'she liked to read in the coffee nook downstairs, but she always had her phone with her.'

'What time did you become worried?' asked Ruud.

'Eleven o'clock. I said to Tim that we should go look for her.'

'Did you?'

'Yes. We went to the bars close by.'

Jade exhaled noisily. 'The other policemen asked us these exact questions yesterday. Why do we have to go through this all over again?'

Ruud ran a hand along the nape of his neck. 'Jillian Parker. Does that name mean anything to you?'

'No. Should it?'

'What about Grand Atlas Towers. It's an office building on Jalan Rambutan. Was Anita anywhere near there last Sunday evening? Did she witness anything unusual?'

'No. We were here for Sunday dinner. We ate in. Stir-fried noodles, wasn't it, Tim? Anita cooked.'

'Yes, noodles,' he said flatly.

The police detective scratched his chin. 'The night Anita disappeared, Wednesday, did she say what she was going to buy? Where she was going?'

The pair looked at each other. A message passed between them. 'No,' said Jade a little too loudly.

Ruud stared into her eyes, stared right through her as if he could read her thoughts. 'There's more to this, isn't there?'

'What d'you mean?'

Ruud felt a peculiar anger take hold. He didn't know the first thing about Jade Watson, but he knew she was lying. Over the years he'd acquired a talent, an almost animal instinct, for sorting the liars from the truth-tellers, the charlatans from the straight-talkers. And if Jade Watson wasn't bullshitting then she was definitely holding something back. 'Listen.' His tone left no room for debate. 'I know this is a difficult time for you, but I don't have the patience to tiptoe around. Anita was brutally murdered, burned alive.' The image of the woman's scorched skull and ruined torso remained seared on his eyelids. 'The killer's still out there roaming the streets. It's crucial you tell me everything.'

'We have told you everything,' said Timothy, but his eyes suggested otherwise.

'How long have you been in Jakarta?'

'A week. We're meant to be in Lombok on Monday, but we don't know what to do now. I spoke to my parents. They want me to fly home.'

'But we can't,' cried Jade, squinting back tears. She balled her hair in her fists. 'Because you have our bloody passports. I hate this place. I want to leave. I want to see my family.'

Ruud talked over her. 'Did Anita often head out by herself? Did she go out alone the previous nights?'

They both said they weren't sure.

'And you expect me to believe you don't know what she went out to get? She didn't go on a random walk, did she?'

Timothy blenched and seemed to wince.

Out in the corridor Ruud heard Aiboy Ali interrogating one of the cleaning staff.

Ruud's mind circled a number of likely scenarios and he played them out in his head. 'Do either of you smoke?'

'No.'

Ruud spied a packet of Marlboro Lights by the bed, nestled under a magazine.

One of Timothy's fingers twitched and he made a throaty sound.

Ruud reached over and placed his hand over the cigarettes. 'Are these Anita's?'

'Yes.'

The detective opened the packet and found some loose rolling papers among the cigarettes. 'Did she smoke marijuana, too?'

No reply.

'I asked you a question.'

'We don't want to get into any trouble,' said Jade, regaining her composure.

'This is a murder inquiry. I couldn't give a toss whether you all shared a joint or two. My job is to find Anita Dalloway's killer. So tell me,' his tone hardened. 'What is it she went out to buy?'

A few moments later Ruud got his answer.

Chapter Nineteen

As soon as they left the hostel the two detectives stopped to buy coconuts from a makeshift stall fashioned from bamboo poles and sheets of tin.

Ruud and Aiboy Ali stood in the shade of a canopy bleached white by the sun, under the sagging cords of telephone cable overhead.

The vendor balanced a coconut in his left hand and, using a machete, hacked through the top of the husk with his right. He dug a small groove, tore off a strip of fibre and plugged the hole with a paper straw.

Aiboy took a sip and smacked his lips. 'Hits the spot.'

Ruud fanned the neck of his shirt. He fished into his pocket for a HeadStart energy tablet and then remembered he'd given them up. 'Fuck!'

'What?'

'Nothing.' He massaged the bridge of his nose. 'Well, I think it's pretty evident Anita wasn't carried off from The Paradies,' he reflected. 'There's not much to indicate the hostel was the scene of the crime. I think it's as Jade Watson said. She went out to buy some dope, somewhere close by, and never came back.'

'Do you believe she just wandered out on a whim?'

'No, I'm guessing she had a contact, or knew where to find it. Someone in the hostel would have told her, perhaps one of the staff or another backpacker.'

'Who works this area?'

'Hmmm.'

'Problem?'

'No, give me a second and I'll find out.'

Aiboy Ali made a call. The men kept walking, passing shops and convenience stores, doing a tour of the neighbourhood. The sound of Indonesian pop music spilled from open doorways. An old lady swept her steps with a besom.

The hot February sun was high in the sky. Ruud hurried along, fighting the urge to shrink back from the heat and find shelter in an air-conditioned shopping mall.

Aiboy spoke into his phone and was told to call a different number. He stood beneath the red neon of a money exchanger. Within a minute he had a name.

'They call him Suparman. He's a deadbeat, a small-time dealer. Speaks OK English, a scrap of German and Italian. Most of the young travellers who pass through Jalan Jaksa buy their shit from him.'

Ruud and Aiboy Ali walked along the street, sucking coconut water through straws. It was another stifling day. The sun beat down, wobbling the air.

Motorcycles and *bajaj* buzzed past, burping smoke.

'So let's say she came out to buy a few grams of weed from Suparman. Let's say she did the business but then got snatched on the way back to her room.'

'If you were going to abduct her where would you do it?'

'Somewhere dark, somewhere quiet, where I could drive my car.'

They passed the homestays, the 24-hour boarding houses,

a tiny eatery with red stools called the Wateg Wisma Delima, a laundromat, a *soto ayam* hawker selling spicy chicken soup, and reached the corner of Gg. 8. At the mouth of the alley they took a left after the Circle K convenience store, coconut water sloshing, and strolled all the way down the crooked lane, where Bagus Auto Mechanics and Motosikil Repair spilled out onto the pavement.

Here Ruud, Aiboy and other pedestrians scooted around the stacked tyres and hopped over misplaced wrenches. The lane was also a gathering place for children. A group of youngsters in colourful clothes kicked a shuttlecock about and played a finger game called Elephant, Man, Ant.

'Not much down here, *Gajah*. Let's head back.'

'Not yet,' said Ruud.

They turned right and right again into one of the many skinny alleyways, wandered another fifty paces along the tapering road and stopped where the pavement ended. Ruud pointed at the construction site, which had once housed the JK Café. 'Somewhere dark and quiet like that, you mean?'

'Yes, I suppose so.'

Ruud shielded his eyes from the sun and took in the scene. He made out a low wire fence that had fallen into disrepair. It surrounded a detached one-storey shoplot, which had seen better days. The outer walls of the building were moss-smeared and crawling with ivy. There were holes for windows. A rusting portable cement mixer lay stranded on its side in the forecourt. A little further on they found a yellow hard hat with the name Stabilitas Contractors printed on the side.

'Looks abandoned.'

'Happens all too often these days, *Gajah*. They start a project, then run out of money midway through.'

Half a minute later the two policemen were checking out the property. They walked past the portable cement mixer. The metal clanged as Aiboy gave the towing tongue a kick. Ruud bent low and snapped off a handful of dry grass. He fixed his gaze on the hollow windows and rubbed the stubble on his chin. Both men scowled into the sunshine.

They resumed their search and inspected the rear of the building. There was a small section that was hidden from the road and it was here that something caught their attention. The tall weeds were partially flattened; some of the stalks were bent double. Ruud reached down and touched the soil. There was a remote impression on the ground. 'Looks like something heavy lay across here.'

'A body?'

'Maybe.'

Ruud moved forward. His eyes scoured the wild grass. Seconds later he stopped abruptly. 'Well, well, well, look what the tooth fairy left us.' He unrolled an evidence bag from his pocket and scooped up a plaid-patterned, horseshoe-shaped object.

'Anita Dalloway's Alice band.'

'I think we hit the jackpot, Aiboy my friend.'

'Here, let me take it.'

The moment the words left Aiboy Ali's mouth they heard a clattering sound from inside the building.

'What was that?' Ruud said, looking at Aiboy, who suddenly appeared disconcertingly pale.

Ruud unclipped the Heckler & Koch 9 mm from his belt and released the safety. Forefinger to his lips, he took two steps forward, then made a crouch gesture with his hand.

Aiboy Ali clasped his Glock 17 and cocked his head.

Wordlessly, they scampered round to the front of the building, keeping tight to the wall.

Tense, Ruud edged toward the main entrance and, stooping, placed his fingers against the door. With his free hand, he gave it a push, but it didn't budge. The first *inspektur* leaned forward and turned the knob. With a nudge, he opened the door wide with his heel. It made a creaking sound.

Keeping low, both hands gripping the Heckler, he burst in, pointing the firearm wherever he looked. '*Polis!*' he bellowed into the darkness.

Aiboy scurried ahead, zigzagging left and right, eyes bulging. 'Front hall clear!'

Another clanging sound. A clash-clatter of metal. Like somebody shaking a cutlery drawer then hurling it against a wall.

Ruud raised his left hand, indicating a room to the left, and spread his fingers wide. Aiboy seemed to hesitate then sprang forward, charging; kicking down a door with such force the hinges gave way.

The door crashed to the floor.

'Shit!' cried Aiboy.

'What is it?'

'A bloody cat!'

A brown tomcat had made a home in two discarded cooking pots.

'False alarm?' shouted Ruud.

'Yes, all good,' came the reply. 'False alarm.'

A minute later, having searched every room and cubbyhole, they holstered their weapons.

There was a mouldy smell to the place, of lichen and

mildew. Plants grew out of the electric sockets. Graffiti tagged the brickwork. Bird shit ran down the walls.

The front room was dark and grey with dust. Aiboy ran his palm along a partition. 'Lights don't work.'

'What do you expect?' Ruud shot him a glance and cut across the puddles of rainwater that pooled on the concrete. 'Pretty creepy spot. If you were a woman would you come here alone at night to buy a bag of weed?'

'You'd have to be either very stupid or very brave.'

Ruud directed a penlight into the nooks and crannies. 'Call for forensic support and get them to tear the place apart. I want it turned inside out.'

'Will do, *Gajah*,' Aiboy Ali whispered. He went quiet. He leaned against the doorjamb to maintain his balance and placed his hands on his knees.

Ruud looked at his colleague. Aiboy was completely out of breath. He was deathly pale and his lips shook.

'You OK?'

Aiboy nodded. 'Need some fresh air. Feeling a little dizzy.'

'Deep breaths, mate, deep breaths.'

'Like I've been turned upside down.' He gave an embarrassed smile. 'A monkey hanging from a tree by its feet.'

Ruud rubbed his back.

'I keep thinking I'll get over it.' He threw his head to the side, tossing the hair from his eyes. 'But whenever I do a house search or chase someone down a dark alley, I see it.'

'See what?' said Ruud.

'The muzzle flash.'

Ruud placed his hand on his friend's shoulder and gave it a firm squeeze.

Aiboy flinched. The gunshot wound that had ripped open his leg still tormented him. He remembered removing his police ID card from his drill pants pocket and holding it up. Seeing the man, backlit against a window at the far end of the long corridor. He was carrying plastic grocery bags in each hand, about twenty metres away. The man stopped and did nothing, just stared back. Then he grabbed at his waistband.

Even now, over a year on, Aiboy couldn't work out how it had happened so quickly. Once again, for the hundredth time, the thousandth time, he heard the discharge, the three thunderclaps that split and warped the air. Two of the bullets took bites out of the doorframe by his ear, showering him with splinters. The third . . .

It was like being spun upside down. He felt his right knee kick sideways from under him. Heard Ruud firing in response, his ears ringing, the spent shells spilling onto the floor. He saw his thigh burst apart with a red hole punched through the cotton and a lump of flesh hanging out the back. Then Ruud moving fast, removing his belt and tying it above the entry wound and shouting to 'Keep pressure on it!' He swore he could actually feel the blood warming his fingers.

Aiboy stared at his hands now, at the tattoos in the webbing of his fingers. Slowly, he turned them over. But of course, the blood was gone.

Ruud cricked his neck left and right. He had recommended trauma counselling following Aiboy's hospitalization, but Witarsa said they didn't have the budget for it. In reality, the Indonesian National Police remained unsophisticated and outdated when it came to helping troubled officers. The notion of providing police psychologists, clinical services and peer support groups for traumatized cops was nothing more than a pipe dream.

Aiboy Ali blew out his cheeks. 'It sneaks up on me sometimes, more often than I want it to.' He pretended to laugh,
his tone void of joy. 'Aiboy Ali, the hard man, the one people
call an XTC heavy, suffers from panic attacks. Who would
have thought?'

'You received a serious gunshot wound.'

'Yeah, missed the artery by a whisker, lucky to be alive,
blah-blah-blah. It's been well over a year now, *Gajah*, why
the fuck am I still acting like a pussy?'

'It takes time.'

'I'm not cracking up or anything.'

'I never said you were.'

'It just creeps up on me.'

'And then there's Farah.'

'Farah dying has nothing to do with this.'

'I'm just saying . . . you've had a lot happen to you. Up
until then you were the most level-headed person I'd
ever met.'

'Yeah, *Gajah*, up until then.'

'You've had to cope with a lot of shit.'

'And I'm doing that. I'm coping.'

'When did you last draw your weapon?'

'*Gajah*, I'm fine.' But it was a lie. He was far from being
fine.

'How often have you been to the gun range since the
shooting?'

'Look at my hands. Are they shaking? No.'

'They were earlier.'

'Yeah, yeah. And I know what you're going to say. You
need to trust me, you need to know if I have your back.'

'Do you? We all make mistakes, Aiboy, but I can't have you
freezing on me.'

Tonelessly. 'For a while afterwards I couldn't even look at a gun. When I went to the firing range for my assessment it was like . . . like drowning. I thought I was drowning. It felt like all the oxygen had been sucked out of my lungs.'

'You should have come to me.'

'You were too busy, *Gajah*, dealing with internal affairs and talking to the press. You didn't have the time.'

'I would have made time.'

'I know. But I realize I have to deal with this myself.'

'And are you?'

Aiboy stared at his hands. 'I try hard, very hard, not to think about Farah. I have to force her out of my head. But I can't. She's everywhere I look.' He shook the hair out of his eyes. 'We went for a long weekend to Ujung Kelon. Beautiful beach. Beautiful sunsets. But there were mosquitoes, lots of them, and Farah was bitten alive. There was a hole in the curtain. Less than a week later she fell ill. I often think what might have happened if we hadn't gone. She'd still be here, right?'

'Dengue's a bitch. You can't blame yourself.'

'But I do. I carry the guilt around with me all the time; carry it around like a stone in my pocket. The thing is, *Gajah*, she got sick and I didn't. How come? What, the mosquito didn't like the smell of my skin? So I got lucky and she didn't? Who rolls the dice? God? Fate? Sometimes, late at night, I have these bad thoughts, dark thoughts.'

'When you next feel down you call me, all right? Mate, you're a fine policeman. You worked hard to get where you are. Don't throw it away.'

All his life Aiboy Ali had wanted to join the police force. When he was seven his father, a cattle farmer from Madura, bought him a policeman's costume together with a plastic truncheon and whistle. It had been the best gift he'd ever received. After that he never imagined growing up to be anything else. He enrolled at seventeen, got transferred to Jakarta at nineteen, spent six years with the narcotics division DRN, two of those undercover. He had the necessary tattoos emblazoned on his arms and torso and in the webbing of his fingers, learned the appropriate lingo, grew his hair long, wore the right clothes, altered his musical tastes, and went from being a clean fresh-faced kid to a narc dealer specializing in ketamine and ice.

For twenty-two months he slummed it in a grotty tenement flat in Glodok, living in perpetual fear that his cover would be blown and some junkie would stick a knife in his throat – ninety-three weeks and five days of unbroken paranoia. His entire drug intake during that period was six tabs of ketamine and half a spliff, all taken in the company of lowlifes in order to look the part. Only when he pulled in a *preman* gang boss and had him put away for twenty years did he transfer to homicide.

He'd sacrificed too much to let a bullet in the leg drag him under. To him, there was no two ways about it. He had to pull himself together.

Ruud gave his friend a sharp look. 'How about taking some extra time off? Maybe go home to Madura and spend a week with your parents. Is that what you need?'

'No,' he objected, his eyes blinking. He went quiet.

Ruud let the silence fall, hoping Aiboy Ali would fill it with a grievance, a curse. He didn't. Instead, deep in thought, he peered into empty space.

Nearby, an ambulance siren erupted and hurtled down the street.

Ruud glanced up and to his right for a moment. Then he returned to staring at Aiboy.

A bead of sweat snaked its way down Aiboy's temple.

All of a sudden Ruud felt his colleague's isolation and loneliness. He saw the gauntness of his face, the private despair in his eyes, the empty, scar-threaded exhaustion. Ruud dug the heel of his left shoe into the ground. 'What do you want me to say, Aiboy?' He rocked the heel back and forth. 'That everything's going to be hunky-dory? That if you chant a mantra, touch the tip of your forefinger to your thumb and imagine you're in your happy place everything will turn out great?'

Aiboy hunched his shoulders.

'Let me tell you something you already know. Homicide's a tough job, mate. Really tough,' said Ruud. 'You can't let it beat you down.'

'I won't.'

'I'm here if you want me, you know that, right?'

'Yes.'

'And it's never as bad as you think once you talk about it.' Ruud thumped him on the shoulder. 'Lighten up, OK? Besides, I know what Hamzah would say.' Ruud parted his hair down the middle and spoke from the depths of his throat, as if exhaling a jet of cigarette smoke from his mouth. '"Best you find yourself a hot chilli pepper woman and go live with her water-buffalo style, *nih*. No more picking coconuts from a slope when whole tree is waiting by your bed."'

The other detective laughed and wiped the drop of sweat away with his biker cuff.

'Do you have my back, Aiboy?'

'It just so happens I do.'

'Well, Mr XTC heavy, do you also happen to have,' asked Ruud, his voice echoing off the ceiling, 'an address for this Suparman fellow?'

Aiboy made a what-do-you-take-me-for face. 'Three, at most four blocks from here, right next to the railway tracks.'

'Get Sabhara uniform to bring him in. Let's get this evidence bag to Solossa. After that, you and I are going to grab some breakfast.'

Chapter Twenty

Sunday morning.

The most activity the second level of the Central Police Station had witnessed in the last year was when a pewter plaque was presented to Police Commissioner Joyo T. Witarsa commemorating his twenty-five years of service.

That is, until today.

'What's happening?' asked Mrs Hapsari, the tea lady, poking her head out of the communal pantry. 'Every interview room is occupied. What with people barging in and out, the place is like a zoo and it's not gone nine in the morning.'

Werry Hartono rushed by, clutching several box files to his chest. 'The game is on, Mrs Hapsari!' he yelled. 'Absolutely no reason to panic!'

Earlier, someone had pinned a sheet of A4 to the corkboard of the Incident Room. It read:

Ruang Interogasi 1 – Suparman, aka Dr Stonor, aka Mario. Drug dealer.

Ruang Interogasi 2 – Imam Aflan Gunawan. Worship leader, Masjid Jami Darul.

Ruang Interogasi 3 – Matius Oskar. Security Guard. Grand Atlas Towers Condominiums.

With his hands full of files, Werry shouldered his way into Interrogation Room 1 (*Ruang Interogasi 1*), a stark chamber furnished with a single table and two chairs. At the table, Aiboy Ali sat opposite a thin, nervous, bird-boned man whose cheeks were braided with grime.

Aiboy Ali spoke into the microphone. 'The time is eight eleven a.m. and Second Lieutenant Werry Hartono has entered the room.' He took one of the box files proffered by Hartono, opened it and removed a recent photograph of a smiling Anita Dalloway. He pushed the photograph across the table towards the man.

'Do you know who this is?' asked the detective.

Full of jangly nerves, Suparman writhed in his seat. 'What the hell, *bang*? No.'

Aiboy extracted a second photograph and held it up for the man to see. It was a shot of Anita's blackened body. 'Maybe you recognize her now?'

'You can't be fucking doing this. There I was sleeping in my bed, the next thing I know every cop in Jakarta is shining his fucking flashlight in my face.'

'She was burned to death.'

'I'm in my home and then, boom! It's like a messed-up-bad Hollywood movie, *bang*.'

'Burned black. When we found her the flesh on her bones was rippling, as if it were alive, crawling.'

'No, no, no.' He gave his head a vigorous shake of protest. 'You can't be doing this to me. Bringing me in on no charges. It's like, "Hey Suparman, hands in the air, motherfuck, and press your nose to the floor, you're coming in for questioning!" This is bullshit, *bang*, pure bullshit. I mean, listen, what the fuck is going on? Are you arresting me?'

'Given that we found both marijuana and cocaine in your home, we should be arresting you. But today's going to be your lucky day, Dr Stonor, today we are going to sit and talk.'

'Yeah, right.' There was a single ten-centimetre strand of facial hair sprouting from a mole on Suparman's chin. He pulled on it nervously.

'Sit back,' said Aiboy Ali. 'Sit back, relax, chill out.'

'I'm sitting, I'm sitting.'

'Do you recall seeing this girl?'

'I don't remember.'

'Memory is a tricky thing when you're stoned.'

'I'm not stoned.'

'Try to remember, Suparman,' said Aiboy, 'and I'll make you a deal. You help us with our inquiries and give us information about the dead woman and we'll see what we can do about making those drugs disappear.'

'*Bang*, you should hear yourself. Yeah, you should, you should. You're giving me rope to hang myself. I know your police tricks. It's not fine. Not fucking fine. No way, no way.'

'The woman's name is Anita Dalloway.'

'Look, I don't know what you're trying to pin on me and I don't know why, but I want out.' He fidgeted through his pockets in search of a cigarette.

'You sold her drugs, didn't you?'

'I sell drugs, yeah, so what? I handle rasta weed. Sell some Thai sticks for some scratch. OK, no surprise, I admit it. You know I do, I say I do. Fuck, man, but then all of a sudden you're accusing me of killing this woman? No way, you prick, no way. I'll tell you now, this is a lie. A fucking lie. Fuck you, man.' He kicked the table but it was secured to the floor.

Aiboy Ali rose from his chair. He looked menacing in drill

trousers and bovver boots. 'On the night of Wednesday the seventeenth of February we have reason to believe you met with Anita Dalloway at an abandoned shoplot that was once the JK Café.'

'Says who? Who saw me with her? Who, who?' He fiddled with his face.

'We also have reason to believe that you sold her marijuana at said premises.'

'Dragging me in here on some souped-up murder charge. It's fucking bullshit, *bang*.'

'And that you may have abducted her.'

'No, *bang*, no.' He narrowed his eyes against the bright overhead lights. 'Stop, stop.'

'Raped her.'

'Listen to yourself. No way, no way. Remove that idea from your brain.'

'And killed her.'

'You can't fit me up for this! I don't know this woman!'

Aiboy held up an evidence bag in his left hand. 'But look what you left behind at the crime scene.' Inside the clear polyethylene pouch was a tartan Alice band. He stared at Suparman. 'We found traces of blood on it. Could be Anita's, could be yours.'

'I've never seen that before!' He wriggled in his chair, as jumpy as a Javanese click beetle.

Aiboy made tweezers of his forefinger and thumb and waggled the bag in the air.

Suparman rubbed the back of his wrist, rubbed the skin that imprisoned it. 'Not fine, *bang*, not fine. I've never seen that shit before.'

'Are you willing to do a swab test?'

'A *what* test?'

'We take a sample of your DNA from your mouth.'

'Fuck that. Here's my middle finger Mister Policeman.'

Hartono leaned in and whispered, 'He has the right to counsel, you know,' into Aiboy's ear.

Aiboy gave the young second lieutenant a withering look. He scrawled the words 'Only if he invokes it!' on his notepad and thrust it under Hartono's nose.

'Official procedure,' Werry countered with a nasal whine, 'is of paramount importance.'

Aiboy leaned into the microphone. 'For the record Second Lieutenant Hartono is about to leave the room.'

With that, Hartono kissed his pinky ring and turned on his heels.

The moment Werry shut the door to Interrogation Room 1 he turned left into the hallway and observed First *Inspektur* Pujasumarta giving instructions to Alya Entitisari. 'Now remember,' Ruud enjoined, 'learn to refine your cross-examination technique. You ask him a question and then you stare, longer than you should, even after he gives you an answer. Keep your eyes locked on him whatever he says. Ten seconds. Twenty seconds. Say nothing. Just look at him as if he's punched your mother in the stomach.'

'Yes, *tuan*.' She handed Ruud a book. 'Thank you for lending me this.' Werry glanced at the title, *The Psychology of Lying*.

'Keep the book for now,' urged Ruud. 'Read chapter eight again.'

'I will.'

'Remember the clues are in the eyes and mouth, look for rapid blinking or intense staring.'

'And the counterfeit smile.'

'Yes, the non-verbal behaviour. Test for weak spots.'

'Yes, *tuan.*'

'People are more likely to tell the truth between eight a.m. and eleven a.m., which is why we normally do this early in the day. As noon approaches individuals grow hungry, impatient and tired. They start to fib to get things over and done with, and their ability to judge what's right and wrong goes out the window.'

'I understand.'

'Are you ready for this?'

'Yes, *tuan.*' Alya beamed.

As soon as Alya entered Ruang Interogasi 3 and saw the security guard she sized him up: quite tall, broad shoulders, big hands, balding, thick moustache, hard eyes.

'Please state your name.'

'Oskar with an O. Why am I here?' Matius Oskar's voice trembled with subdued anger. He was still wearing his uniform. 'I haven't been home to see my family. I clocked off duty two hours ago. My wife is expecting me home.'

Alya sat in the chair facing Oskar. She crossed her legs. With his forelock, chiselled mandible, horseshoe tash and knotted physique, he brought to mind a combination of circus strongman and Village People wannabe.

'Is this about the Australian woman? I read in the newspaper that she was found dead. It said she worked in my building.'

'How long have you been a security guard at Grand Atlas Towers?'

'Three years.'

'What's it like?'

'What's it like? What do you think it's like?' He rolled his neck on his shoulders like a boxer about to enter the ring. 'It's lonely and dull. I do my rounds. I check on the cars. I breathe in their exhaust fumes.'

'Do you find it monotonous?'

'I do a fourteen-hour shift from four in the afternoon to six in the morning every day except Wednesdays.' He lifted his broad flanks. 'It may be boring but I have mouths to feed.'

'And what about Jillian Parker, the Australian woman, did you know her? Ever chat with her?'

The heavyset man rocked back and forth in his seat, rubbing his hands on his knees. Stubby hands with bitten-back thumbnails. 'She was nice. She always said good afternoon to me, and in the New Year she gave a box of chocolates for my wife.'

'Cast your mind back to Monday, fifteenth of February. Do you remember seeing anyone you didn't know on the premises? Or someone acting suspiciously?'

'No.'

'We're taking the view that Miss Parker was abducted from the car park and was driven away in her own vehicle. We think her abductor came in from the main road, walked down the ramp, passed the boom gates and waited for her to appear out of the lifts.'

Oskar clenched his teeth and shook his head.

Alya, poised, continued. 'Did you see her leave that day? Did you see her car exit the building? And if so did you recognize who was driving it?'

'Am I supposed to recognize every car that comes in and out of Atlas Towers? The car park holds three hundred cars!'

'But you said you knew Miss Parker. You must have known which car she drove.'

'A green Mazda.'

His reply came too readily and Alya made a mental note of it. 'Where were you between four forty-five and five thirty p.m.?'

'You're talking about last Monday, is it?' Oskar thought for a moment. 'I arrived at work at four and got changed in the cubicle. By five o'clock I'd have completed my initial patrol of the basement levels.'

'Did you see Miss Parker? The elevator camera has her exiting the lift at five oh four p.m. and captured her stepping out onto Basement Level One.'

'No, I didn't see her.'

'Did you hear anything? A scream or anything suspicious?'

'No.'

Alya pursed her lips.

'Grand Atlas Towers' building management allowed us access to their monitoring equipment. Unfortunately, it appears the security cameras on the basement floors are just for decoration. None of them work.'

'The building has another security guard. He's stationed in the lobby at the alarm centre. He looks at the monitors. Talk to him.'

'We have. Did you know the closed-circuit cameras were broken?'

'No.'

'I'm surprised. Isn't it your job to oversee them? All six cameras were blacked-out with paint. Vandalized. And you knew nothing about this?'

He wiped his hands on his knees.

She held his gaze, counted down from twenty. The stillness made Oskar squirm in his seat. Eventually, the silence forced the words from his mouth.

'The management people are cheap. If something is broken they only fix it if a tenant complains.'

'So let me get this straight. A woman is kidnapped from your building, snatched from the very place you are meant to protect, and you don't see a thing?'

He breathed faster. 'I'm telling you, I didn't notice anything wrong.'

'I find that hard to believe.'

The man heaved himself up off his chair, but a look from Alya's sharp black eyes made him sit down again. 'I'm not lying.'

'So let me ask you again, what were you doing between four forty-five and five thirty p.m.?'

She saw him hesitate.

'If ever there's a time to tell the truth, Oskar, this is it.'

He made a sour face.

'Oskar?'

'I might have been in my cubicle.'

'Doing what?'

He kneaded a bulbous forearm, which was covered with dark wiry hair. 'I was tired. I might have been taking a little snooze.'

'But nobody can corroborate this.'

A mosquito buzzed about before landing on Oskar's arm. He smacked it dead then examined the spot on his skin. 'I was asleep. What can I say?'

'Just one more question, Oskar. Can you drive?'

'Yes, I have a licence.'

'Do the building's tenants ever lend you their car keys?'

'What do you mean?'

'Do they let you look after their cars?'

'There's a car-cleaning service.' Again Alya heard the

166

hesitancy in his voice. 'Sometimes the car owners give me the keys so the cleaners can vacuum the interior.'

'Did Jillian Parker ever give you her car keys?'

He did not reply.

'Oskar?'

'No.' He wiped his hands against his knees. 'She never did.'

Meanwhile, in Interrogation Room 2 Imam Aflan Gunawan squeezed his eyes shut and recited Surah Al-Fatiha under his breath, promising to seek refuge in the prophet Muhammad from Satan, the accursed.

Ruud waited patiently for the cleric to open his eyes once again.

'Thank you,' said Ruud, addressing the imam. 'Thank you for cooperating with us, prayer leader. For the benefit of the tape I am showing the subject images of Anita Dalloway and Jillian Parker.' He arranged the photographs on the table so they faced the cleric. 'What do you know about this?'

'Two untimely deaths.' He tut-tutted, pushing the images aside.

With exaggerated care, Pujasumarta placed another pair of photographs in front of the imam. 'When we discovered the bodies we also found something else – a length of canvas – with Islamic calligraphy on it. A message. Or more likely a warning.' The detective pointed at the enlargements with an open palm. 'Can you read what it says?'

'It is in Arabic.'

'What does Surah An-Nisa, verse four: fifty-six, mean to you?'

'Like all teachings from the miraculous book, it is wisdom.

167

The verse says all disbelievers shall remain in hellfire for eternity.'

'Sounds pretty medieval to me.'

'It is punishment grounded on religion, on the Hadith precepts.'

'Where were you last Wednesday night?'

The imam, dressed in a white thawb and sandals, wore an expression of scorn. 'Is this because I am a strict advocate of sharia law and its disciplines, is this why I am here?'

'Please answer my question.'

'Sharia is the path.' He played with the akik ring on his right hand, twisting the silver round and round.

'You've been spreading some pretty hateful talk about foreigners.'

'Rumours, nasty rumours, which I strongly deny. Islam is about love. Why would I spread hate?'

'Violent, militant, extremist talk.'

'A misunderstanding, I am sure. Often when I speak in parables, the words can be misinterpreted, misconstrued.'

'There is speculation you have had ties with Al-Qaeda in the past, with their affiliate Jemaah Islamiyah.'

'All lies.' His attention turned to the photographs. The breath rushed from his nostrils and teased the black hairs of his upper lip. 'You say these Western women are dead. Regrettable, I am sure, but what of it?'

'Are you behind the killings?'

'Me?' He stroked his beard. 'Absurd.'

'We have three witnesses who claim you have spoken of punishing Western women for their sexual indiscretions.'

'As I say, people can sometimes misinterpret my message.'

'Where were you between the hours of five p.m. and midnight on the night of February fifteenth?'

'Offering religious counselling, which proves I had nothing to do with the woman's demise.' He folded his hands and rested them on the table, fingers locked.

'Who's to say you didn't order it? Some men kill from afar to keep their fingers pure. Did you arrange it? One does not have to look at the fire to know where the smoke comes from.'

Imam Gunawan made a fist and trained his akik ring at Ruud. 'An outrageous comment, without any truth or merit.'

'Two days later, February seventeenth, where were you Wednesday night?'

'At my mosque.'

'With?'

'With individuals I trust.'

'Someone you know is behind this. I can tell. Give me a name.'

'God in Islam shuns the treacherous.'

'He shuns murderers, too! Who burned these women? Who lit the match?'

'Even were I to know this fiend, you expect me to betray a man? Betrayal is the worst form of hypocrisy, detective.'

'It's someone in your congregation, isn't it?'

'Even the purest flocks can have a black dog masquerading as sheep, but to the best of my knowledge there is no such beast amongst my faithful.'

The imam kicked off his sandals and wiggled his toes.

'A name!'

The cleric's smile curled at the corners of his lips. 'I will suffer the fires of Jahannam before giving up a fellow believer.' He examined a fat big toe. 'And if you are to continue badgering me I think it is necessary I call for an attorney to sit by my side.'

'The interview with Imam Aflan Gunawan is terminated. The time is nine thirteen a.m.' Ruud rose to join Aiboy Ali in Interrogation Room 1.

'Here's how it stands, Suparman,' said Ruud. 'You were found in possession of three hundred grams of marijuana, a violation of Articles one one three and one three two of Law number thirty-five 2009 on narcotics in Indonesia. That's five to fifteen years and a minimum fine of one billion rupiah.'

'This is bullshit, *bang*. You going to get me for selling rasta weed? Come on, it's not like I'm pushing twenty-twenty or white mosquito or sweet stuff. It's light material, man. Does no harm.' He blinked, narrowing his eyes at the ceiling. 'Hey, can you turn down the lights?'

'Let me tell you something, my friend. You're nothing but pond scum to us, just a smear of muck on the bottom of our shoe. Frankly, we don't give a fuck what happens to you. Prisons in Jakarta are operating at almost three hundred per cent capacity. Cipinang was designed for eight hundred and eighty inmates and currently holds three thousand seven hundred. Latest government figures state that five hundred and eighty-two prisoners died in captivity across the whole of Indonesia last year. It's hell in there. Now, I see you've never been incarcerated but—'

'What do you want from me, man?' He fiddled with the pimples on his neck.

'A trade. We'll turn a blind eye to your misdemeanour if

you tell us what you saw the night you sold weed to Anita Dalloway.'

'No way, *bang*. I can't tell you.'

'Why?'

'Why? Because the man might have seen me. If I rat, he'll come after me. No way, no way.'

'Which man?'

'The man who took her.'

'What did he look like?'

Suparman glared wide-eyed at Aiboy Ali. His voice was tight, as though all the tension in his body had formed around his throat. 'If I squeal I'm dead. What if the guy saw me?'

'There are no mattresses in Cipinang. You all sleep piled up against one another. Thirty to a cell. Want to know what the prison-block leaders do to scrawny little blokes like you?'

'All right! All right, man. Yeah, yeah, OK, OK, I'll tell you. He was big.'

'Big strong or big overweight?'

'Strong. Thick-necked. I saw him from across the road after the woman bought the shit from me.'

'Where were you exactly?'

'Across the road from the old café, there's a small dark space I like to fold into.' He gnawed on his thumbnail.

'And where was the woman?'

'I think she went to inspect what I sold her cos she walked to the back of the café.'

'And then?'

'He just grabbed her, man, grabbed her and knocked her unconscious. One punch. *Whap!*' Suparman snapped his fingers. 'Then he bundled her into the back of his car. Took him no time at all.' He snapped his fingers again. 'One-two-three and she was in the boot. No time for her to scream or fight back. I'm telling you he was strong.'

'Did you see his face?' asked Aiboy.

'No, it was dark. You have to believe me, *bang*.' Suparman looked about the room as if searching for an escape route. He cracked his knuckles.

'What car was he driving?'

'Black. Expensive. You know the type, like one of those big European cars. The ones with the round badges on the hood, yeah. Mercedes Benzo, man, Mercedes Benzo. But just as he drove away, he turned, and I swear he saw me, man, saw me through his window.'

'Go on.'

'And he was wearing this, I don't know, like a mask thing. The crazy way he watched and stared, wearing this fucking mask. It was like seeing the devil stood before me.'

Ruud felt the back of his neck tingle. 'What kind of mask? What exactly did you see?'

Suparman's mouth contorted. 'It was straight out of a horror film . . . a pig, a goddam pig, man. *Bang*, it freaked me out.'

Ruud switched off the recording equipment and left the room together with Aiboy Ali.

Seconds later the detectives stood in front of the two-way mirror and watched Suparman through the glass. The overhead lights beat down on him relentlessly. For five whole minutes he sat staring at his hands, rapt, smiling to himself.

And then he got to his feet, turned, unzipped his fly and pissed on his own shadow.

Chapter Twenty-One

It was pouring. The tropical rain pelted down, hammering at the tin rafters and corrugated metal roofs in the shanty towns. As the brown water rose, the danger of *banjir*, a major tidal flooding, increased by the hour. Already there were perilous surges in lower Jakarta, where the yellow marker sticks showed water levels at 20 cms and rising fast. In places like Kalibata and Rawajati the flood channels were near full to the brim as the streams and rivers struggled to empty their loads into the Java Sea.

That evening Ruud slumped at his dining table and watched the rain make patterns on the window glass. He liked it when it rained – it meant he couldn't hear the traffic and the querulous bleat of motorcycle horns during the night.

He sighed audibly.

'Oh dear, dear, dear. Are you in a dismal mood?' asked Aunt Erica. 'A Van Gogh despair?' It was Sunday night and she'd offered to cook dinner at Ruud and Imke's apartment. Draped in Ruud's Victoria Bitter barbecue apron, she stood at the kitchen stove, sleeves rolled up, stirring a pot of soup with a spoon.

'He is always in mood at this stage of an investigation,' said Mrs Panggabean, Ruud's ex-mother-in-law.

Ruud bubbled up with laughter. 'Do I really look that miserable?' He sipped a cold Bintang.

Erica gave him a quizzical tilt of her head, then went back to stirring. 'Yes, First *Inspektur*, you do.'

'Look-see,' cried Mrs Panggabean, presenting him with a Manila envelope. 'I brought some old photographs to cheer you up.'

'What are these?'

'I found them in an old shoebox. Nothing valuable. Only memories. I'm giving them to you for safekeeping. My daughter doesn't want them.'

'These are my wedding photos.' He glanced at an image of himself smiling broadly, all teeth and stiff-collared. He handed them back. 'No offence, but I don't really want to see them lying around.'

'She has a new man again. The last one couldn't keep up with her.' Mrs Panggabean sighed. 'She is just like her father was – big head, small mind.'

Imke appeared from the bathroom with a thick white paste smeared over her top lip. She wore her fuchsia-coloured dressing gown and a pair of soft Turkish slippers.

'I like your bathrobe,' declared Mrs Panggabean.

'What, this old thing? I bought it for an apple and an egg.' A theatrical pause. 'That's a Dutch expression, if you're wondering.'

'Jeez! What's that on your face?' exclaimed Ruud, tucking the shoebox under his chair, desperate to change the subject.

'Plain yoghurt and lemon juice. I'm getting a tash,' she said, drying her hair with a towel.

'No, you're not.'

'Maybe, a little one,' said Mrs Panggabean. 'Plucking better than dying, Imke. I use thread. I show you later how it's done.'

Imke went to the sofa and curled her body around Kiki. 'Our boy is in a terrible mood,' said Erica.

Ruud turned back to face the kitchen. 'It's more a sense of frustration, to be honest,' said Ruud. 'The case I'm working on, the one I told you about, the pieces of the puzzle won't fall into place. It's baffling.'

Erica examined the wooden spoon in her hand. She was making split-pea soup for supper. 'Imke, *liefste*, can you take the rye bread in for me.'

Imke put her nose close and kissed the top of Kiki's head, leaving a little white smudge. She rose from the sofa and tightened the cord of her dressing gown.

At the fridge door she said, 'Ruud, have you been giving Kiki snacks laced with mustard again? Please stop, you know it makes her sneeze.'

Man and dog eyed each other guiltily.

Retrieving the dark loaf from the oven, Imke deposited it on a wooden board and brought it to the table.

'Do you want to talk about the case?' asked Imke, flopping down in the chair next to Ruud.

Pujasumarta didn't need a second invitation. Perched by the first-floor window, with car headlights winking through the blinds, he told her everything that had happened that day, describing what was said in the interviews with Imam Gunawan, with Suparman and with Oskar the security guard. He also briefed her about Gerhard Vosseler, Jade Watson and Timothy Greenleaf at the hostel. He even recounted his meeting with Shane Waters and Ambassador Beale at the Australian Embassy.

'And the only piece of solid evidence you have is the Alice band found behind the JK Café,' Imke recapped. 'Well, at least you have traces of DNA on it. How confident is Solossa that it belongs to the killer?'

'The blood on the Alice band could be the suspect's and we're working on the theory that the perp grabbed Anita Dalloway from behind. She was quite short. It's likely she reached back and scratched his face or neck. There's also a chance the skin from his throat and chin would have rubbed against the top of her head.

'But the DNA doesn't match any of the people we've questioned thus far – Suparman, Gunawan, Oskar and the people at The Paradies. We got the results back just moments ago.' Having fast-tracked it, Solossa's team had worked miracles to get the extraction, quantitation, PCR and DNA typing done in less than sixty hours. 'It's a clear sample, all we require now is a match.'

Kiki trotted over and sat on Imke's foot. 'Tell me about the pig mask?' Imke stroked Kiki's ears and massaged the dog's rump with her big toe.

'Not much to tell. Aiboy Ali is checking out the costume and fancy-dress outlets, going shop to shop to see which retailers stock the same mask.

'We have some footage taken from a traffic camera outside Grand Atlas Towers. It's a long-shot view but Tech enhanced it, fixed the blurriness and removed the digital noise, and sure enough it shows our man in a pig mask at the wheel of Jillian Parker's green Mazda.'

'A person drives through the centre of town wearing a pink Peter Porker disguise and nobody blinks an eye, hè?'

'This is Jakarta. People see crazy things every day,' offered Mrs Panggabean.

'You'd think a traffic cop might have stopped him.'

'Luckily for him, nobody did,' said Ruud. 'But d'you

know what? As he drives out of the car park we see him lean forward and swipe something off the windscreen with his left hand.'

'Like a bug or a fly?'

'Yes.'

'Why is that relevant?'

'Because he leans forward and to his right, like this.' Ruud stretched his arm across.

Imke registered. 'He's left-handed.'

'Most probably.'

'Have you questioned Shane Waters?'

'No.'

'Why in heavens not?' bellowed Erica from the kitchen. Ruud looked over and saw her adding a bay leaf and some sliced smoked sausage to the soup.

With what seemed like an awful taste in his mouth, Ruud said, 'We can't. Waters has diplomatic immunity. The authorities can't proceed with any legal action against him.'

'Do you honestly think it could be him?' said Imke.

'It's really too early to say. Suparman claims he saw the killer. He said he was big and strong, so Waters certainly fits the physical profile. And he also saw a car that was black and expensive-looking. Waters drives a black German-made car. The embassy has a *sopir* he can use, but he prefers to drive himself.'

'But what's his connection with Anita Dalloway? And what's the deal with the Quranic writing?'

Ruud rubbed his eyes. 'None of it makes any sense. I'm trying to wrap my head around it. Worse still, I was on the phone to both Anita and Jillian's parents earlier. All they want right now is for me to release the bodies. They want to take their children home, but I can't do that yet.'

'What do you know about him? This Shane Waters.'

'Next to nothing. Hamzah and Alya did some digging into Jillian's phone records, both landline and mobile.'

'Who's Alya?'

'Our new *ajun inspektur*. I told you about her.'

'No you didn't.'

'I'm sure I did.'

Imke's expression turned cool.

'Alya joined us from Commercial Crimes. Anyway, what they found is pretty odd. In the last fortnight Waters called Jillian on average ten times a day. According to the call logs, three days before she died he phoned her thirty-one times in the space of ten hours. More often than not he went straight to voicemail. She rarely called him back.'

'Harassment?'

'Could be. Seems like he had a fixation.'

'On his own cousin? That's pretty depraved.'

'True, but it doesn't mean he killed her.'

Mrs Panggabean, who'd been silent for some time, quietly playing Candy Crush on her phone, suddenly said, 'My grandparents were cousins. Both crazy souls.' She rose from her chair and went to give Erica a hand.

A thought struck Imke. 'What about emails?'

'The tech team got hold of Jillian's office computer. All electronic communication from Shane Waters was PGP encrypted. The security software belongs to the Australian Embassy; the tech guys can't crack it. We can't get in.'

'Surely you can do something,' Imke said on her way to the kitchen. Ruud heard the cutlery drawer slide open. She returned with forks and spoons and set them down, then she went back for the placemats, soup bowls and water glasses.

'We have him under surveillance, but as I say, if he is our man he has complete immunity from criminal jurisdiction. We can't arrest him or detain him. Hell, we can't even search his car or enter his premises.'

Imke laid the table. 'But if he's guilty . . .' She picked up a knife and slapped butter on a slice of rye bread.

'All we can do is report our findings to the foreign affairs minister, Imke. The only thing the ministry can do is expel him, rescind his diplomatic credentials.'

'That's it?'

He nodded. 'Yup.'

Imke searched Ruud's face. 'No, that's not it. What is it you're not telling me, *hè*? I know that look, Pujasumarta.'

Ruud smiled. 'I'm not sure', he whispered, 'that I should be telling you this.'

'Bollocks.' She bit into the slice of buttered bread. 'Come on, spill the beans.'

'Promise not to tell.'

Imke rolled her eyes.

He kept his voice low. 'I got Aiboy to attach a tracking device to Waters' car.'

Imke sat up straight. 'You did what?'

'Don't you dare tell a soul,' he said, making sure Erica and Nyonya Panggabean couldn't hear. 'Witarsa will go ballistic if he finds out.'

She nudged Ruud as Mrs Panggabean returned to reclaim her seat.

A few seconds later, Erica bustled in and planted the pot in the centre of the table.

'Smells good,' said Ruud.

'Are you both still talking about that fellow at the

179

Australian Embassy?' said Erica. 'It just so happens I'm going there on Thursday after lunch.'

'You are?' said Ruud.

'By invitation of Ambassador Glenn Beale. They're hosting an exhibition of contemporary Australian artists. My friends at the Dutch Embassy wrangled an invite for me. Doors open at one o'clock, which is a very odd time, if you ask me.'

Imke held out her dish.

Erica ladled a generous helping of soup into her bowl. 'When I get there I'll make a beeline for Shane Waters. I'll work my magic and see what I can learn from him?'

Ruud was mortified. 'Learn from him?'

'Yes, about his personal life.'

'Why would he tell you anything?' Ruud exclaimed.

'People always like to talk about themselves,' said Mrs Panggabean. 'I used to be a journalist. I know.'

'Erica,' said Ruud, 'with all due respect, you really can't get involved. This is a police matter.'

'I can help.'

'Don't be daft.'

'I can.'

'I doubt that very much.'

'You just wait and see.' She winked at Imke. 'You'd be surprised what an old hen like me can dredge up from pecking in the dirt.'

'No. Forget about it, OK? Just forget Waters. Look, why don't you and Imke go away for the weekend. Go on a day trip,' he continued. 'Take a drive to Cisarua to look at the Curug Cilember waterfalls.'

Erica puckered her lips. 'Waterfalls make me want to pee.'

'If Waters suspects anything, you could be putting yourself in serious danger,' said Ruud.

'Nonsense. Why should he suspect?'

'True,' said Imke. 'Are you going to tell him you're an artist?'

'Well, I'm hardly going to say I'm a pin-up girl or burlesque queen, am I?'

'Erica,' Ruud ran a hand over his face. 'I can't rope you into this.'

'Rope? You're not roping anyone into anything. I'm volunteering and that's that!'

Ruud threw up his hands. He knew better than to argue with the Sneijder women. 'All right, if you have to go, then go. But I'm going to make sure Sabhara have eyes on you. But promise me one thing: no drama.'

'Oh, but we can't resist a spot of drama.'

'Erica!'

'Yes, yes. I promise.'

Chapter Twenty-Two

Jalan Jaksa.

It was late evening and the backpacker's haven was getting busy.

Like a spectral presence hovering on the periphery, Aiboy Ali watched the blonde woman from the shadows. He reached into the glove compartment and retracted a pair of mini binoculars. The action made a thin rustling noise in the silence. He lifted the binoculars to his eyes and brought them into focus.

The tendons at the axes of his jaw, beneath his ears, twitched. He held back, waiting for the ache in his leg to pass. Almost twenty months and the bloody thing still acted up. The doctors put it down to extensive nerve damage. Nevertheless, he counted his blessings – the bullet had only just missed the femoral artery. If it had severed that, he wouldn't be sitting here now.

A bus roared past.

The woman was heading from west to east.

He trailed her every movement. She walked with a confident step, all loose swinging strides and nose aloft. Aiboy Ali turned, lifting himself slightly off his seat.

She disappeared into shadow, reappearing a second later.

The streetlamps were either broken or cast little light. They threw orange pools every twenty metres, illuminating her straight posture and the cotton skirt she wore: a rich quilt of colours.

She turned into a narrow pedestrian route leading to a set of squat buildings. He knew the area intimately from the time he worked undercover narcotics. It was full of cheap hostels, backpacker bars and low-cost eateries. The seedy hovels were murky, lit with fairy lights and neon tubes, washed with a dim yellow glow. He watched as she chose a stool at a watering hole offering 2-for-1 beers and Live FA Cup Football. It was Sunday night: Chelsea was hosting Manchester City at Stamford Bridge. The game flashed up on a giant screen, showing a close-up of Eden Hazard's face.

Aiboy Ali blinked, adjusting the focus on the binoculars. He lost her, but then with a quick correction found her again. Her golden hair was reflected in a dirty mirror behind the bar. The mirror was flimsy, held together with fraying threads of twine.

At this point in the evening, at this time of year, the 400-metre-long street was crowded with young Caucasians. Later on, after midnight, Nigerian drug dealers will mingle with the cockroaches, drunks and transgenders on the pick-up.

But for now, the focus was on cheap beer and football.

Aiboy Ali squinted through the binoculars, crinkling his nose.

He did a wide, fast sweep, checking out the other patrons one by one.

The men were mostly lanky. They wore grubby singlets and tie-dyed tank tops and swigged Anker straight from the bottle. Some looked unwashed; one of them wore his hair

long, matted and braided to resemble a lion's mane. Aiboy
Ali wondered if he was a rocker.

A podgy, pale redheaded girl came up to the lion's mane.
She had tattoos covering her upper arms and ankles. It wasn't
a good look on her. She reminded Aiboy Ali of a *banteng*
cow, with their buff hides and white rumps burned red by
a toasting fork left too long on the fire.

He threw the binoculars onto the passenger seat. He was
getting nowhere with this. He wanted to get close to the
blonde woman. Real close. He was sick of watching from a
distance.

He banged his head hard against the steering wheel.

A small red mark formed below his hairline.

And he felt his heart pound and race.

The brand-new Burgerkill album caught his eye – bought
only that morning from Pondok Indah Mall. He wanted to
hear the clash and chaos of sound. He wanted to drown
himself in noise. He was about to shove the CD into the
stereo slot and turn it up full blast, but then he realized it
would draw attention.

Instead, he glanced at the car clock. It was prayer time.
He hadn't prayed all day so he removed the Qibla compass
from under his chair and arranged it on the dashboard. He
consulted it quickly before shifting his weight clockwise in
the direction of Mecca.

Aiboy Ali took a few seconds to compose himself, then
brought his hands to his face, palms forward, thumbs behind
earlobes. He spoke a handful of words under his breath, his
voice lost in a gurgle of devotional mutterings. He looked
over his right shoulder at the angel, acknowledging his good
deeds, and over his left shoulder at the angel, acknowledging

his wrongful deeds, then wiped his cheeks with his palms and bowed his head low.

Rigid, he remained seated in the front of the car, in the dark, feeling the cool air conditioning rouge his skin. His heart rate tempered. Calmly, unhurriedly, he lifted his gaze.

And there she was.

The blonde woman had a cigarette between her teeth now but she was talking to someone new: a dusky-skinned girl with curly black hair.

Aiboy Ali retrieved his binoculars.

He increased the magnification using the zoom lever and watched her with both eyes.

Blood thrummed in his ears. His breathing became audible.

Yes, he decided, this was what he'd been waiting for. The dark girl did a little twirl for her friend and burst out laughing.

He wondered what her voice sounded like.

Swiping his lips, he continued to study her – the elongated limbs, the bounteous ebony hair, the shameless pose.

From a nearby mosque, loudspeakers crackled.

It was time.

In the space next to him, the piggy mask waited patiently, smelling of rubber and chemical wipes, all pink-snouted and floppy-eared with hollow inverted commas for eyes, a sly grin stretching its mouth.

Aiboy Ali flexed his thigh. An ache pinged through his lower back.

He gripped the mask and got out of the car.

Chapter Twenty-Three

On Monday morning Imam Aflan Gunawan was once more seated in Interrogation Room 2. His beard looked tatty and his white thawb was wrinkled all along the back. This time he had his solicitor by his side, a criminal lawyer called Triady.

Ruud switched on the recording device. 'Imam Gunawan interview. Reference number three eight five nine three. Present are *Inspektur Polisi Satu* Ruud Pujasumarta and *Inspektur Polisi Dua* Werry Hartono. Also present is D. Triady from the law firm Pidana & Associates. The time is currently,' said Ruud, 'a quarter past nine in the morning.'

'Why have I been brought here again?' demanded the Imam.

'We wish to question you further.'

'On what grounds?'

'Inciting hate crimes.'

'May I see the search warrant again, please?' requested the solicitor.

Ruud handed him the paperwork.

Sabhara had raided the imam's premises at 6 a.m., where they'd found bundles and bundles of leaflets promoting the establishment of a Khilafah that promised 'The Dawn of a

New Era'; several booklets calling on Muslims to condemn Israel and America, and a library of modern hate-texts, including *Mein Kampf, Protocols of the Elders of Zion* and *Did Six Million Really Die?*

They also confiscated a personal computer.

Triady slid the A4-sized sheet across the table to Ruud. 'Everything is in order.'

'This is completely uncalled for,' protested the imam.

Triady, a ratty-haired, bespectacled man in his sixties, rapped three fingers on the side of his chair. 'My client feels your accusations are baseless and you are using him as a scapegoat because he is different.'

'How so?'

'He does not vote like you, pray like you or share the same background.'

Ruud cut him short.

'In your client's personal computer we found downloaded files,' said Hartono. 'Several dozen pornographic images. Mainly bondage and S&M.'

'That computer is not mine,' said the imam. 'It was loaned to me.'

'The Anti-Pornography Bill of 2008 empowers the authorities to jail offenders for up to four years.'

'As I say, the infernal machine does not belong to me.'

'To whom does it belong?' asked Ruud.

The imam, quick to save his own skin, did not hesitate to give a name. 'Tantar. He is called Tantar.'

'Full name?'

The worship leader swiped the air lackadaisically with a hand. 'Al Sadawi something . . .'

'And what does Tantar Al Sadawi something do?'

'I don't know.'

'Yes, you do.' Ruud smiled. 'He works for your mosque, doesn't he?'

'No, he does not work for the mosque.'

'Tell me or I will charge you.'

'I believe he is a foreman at a construction firm.'

'Yet, he also answers to you.'

'He assists me.'

'How so?'

Gunawan did not respond. He stroked his beard. After a while he said, 'You have a white girlfriend, isn't it so? I've done some checking up on you, detective.'

Ruud was startled enough by the question to recoil. 'What's it to you?'

'It would be a shame if anything should happen to her. What with all these foreign women being attacked.'

'Is that a threat, Imam Gunawan?'

'Of course not, detective. I am simply saying she ought to be careful. Bad things can happen.'

Ruud steadied himself. 'Imam Gunawan,' he said, his tone biting, raw, dangerous. 'I will ask you politely once more. And please state coherently for the record. How does Tantar assist you?'

'Sharia is the path, First *Inspektur*.' He played with the akik ring on his right hand. 'Every so often people stray off course. Tantar is my, how-do-you-say, my morality police-man. On occasion I require him to administer Sharia regulations. There are times when members of my flock need a little ethical adjustment; a little reminder of what is right and wrong. For example, if I see a woman from my *masjid* sitting astride a motorcycle rather than sitting side-saddle, he tells her off. If I learn of an unmarried couple going to a hotel room, committing *khilwa*, he pays them a visit and does my bidding.'

'He roughs them up, shames them.'

'In Saudi Arabia they would receive forty lashes each. The Commission for the Promotion of Virtue and Prevention of Vice would see to that.'

'This is not Saudi Arabia.'

No reply.

Ruud went on. 'What else does Tantar do for you?'

Stony silence.

'Are you refusing to answer the question?'

More of the same.

Ruud spoke into the microphone. 'We are going to take a five-minute break. The interview will recommence at nine thirty-five a.m.'

He left the room and approached Aiboy Ali's desk. 'Where's Aiboy?'

Soentoro, the Office Manager, looked up. 'He hasn't turned up for work.'

'What are you talking about? Aiboy always turns up for work, even when he's sick. Is he ill? What the hell's happened to him?'

'I don't know,' said Soentoro. 'There's been no word. Maybe he *masuk angin*. Catch a cold.'

Ruud blinked his eyes. Something inside him, something cold, tightened around his chest. It wasn't a good feeling.

The first *inspektur* walked across the room and pulled open the middle drawer of a filing cabinet. He rummaged about for half a minute, then removed a yellow file with pink inserts. Moving briskly to his office, he logged into his computer, entered a password and a security code into the POLRI database and waited for the system to cough up a document. When the document flashed across his screen he cross-referenced a file number. A new page appeared. He pressed PRINT and waited for the Canon to do its job.

Retrieving the data, he returned to Interrogation Room 2.

'Now that we've had our little rest,' he said, flicking the switch to green on the microphone, 'let's go back to Mr Tantar, shall we?'

He opened the yellow cardboard file and whipped out the freshly printed report. 'Tantar bin Abdulaziz Al Sadawi, male, height 185 cms, weight a hundred kilos. Qatari national, born in Mesaieed in 1988. Arrived in Indonesia in 2011. Profession: gardening specialist. Arrested for aggravated assault, February twenty thirteen; charges dropped. Arrested again in May twenty fourteen on allegations of battery; case dismissed due to lack of evidence. Finally, in June twenty fifteen, charged with causing an affray and fined two hundred thousand rupiah; fine waived by magistrate. No plea record.'

Imam Gunawan stroked his beard and turned his gaze to the wall.

'Our man is certainly no puppy dog, eh?' said Ruud.

'What? For causing an affray?' said Gunawan. 'It was a misunderstanding. The magistrate thought the same, which is why the fine was waived. And those earlier allegations were all false, he was never prosecuted.'

'Perhaps he has a guardian angel looking out for him.'

'Where are you going with this, detective?' implored the solicitor.

'Two questions. Is Tantar responsible for the deaths of Jillian Parker and Anita Dalloway? Are you, Imam Gunawan?'

'Absurd,' said the prayer-leader.

Triady stepped in. 'Detective, your questions are completely groundless.'

'The videos on the computer show women being tied up, restrained, tortured even. Is that what you like to do, Imam Gunawan? Do you like to torture women?'

'I'm warning you, detective,' said Triady.

Ruud leaned back in his chair. 'All right, let me ask you this. If in time we prove that the terminal does indeed belong to this Mr Tantar, were you, Imam Gunawan, ever aware of its contents?'

'No, of course not.'

'Why would Tantar bin Abdulaziz Al Sadawi, one of your devotees, a devout practitioner of Sharia, have pornographic images on his computer?'

The Imam hesitated. Triady leaned in and whispered something in his ear. Imam Gunawan nodded. The solicitor replied on his behalf.

'If my client were to answer such a question it could be argued in court that he has knowledge of Mr Tantar's intentions.'

'What if he were to hazard a guess? Humour me, Imam Gunawan. Surely we're allowed to speculate.'

It was the imam's turn to whisper into the attorney's ear.

The lawyer adjusted his spectacles with his fingers, nudging them along the bridge of his nose until they balanced on the very tip. 'If my client were to speculate, his best guess is that Mr Tantar uses the files for research purposes.'

Ruud shook his head. 'Research, that's a good one.'

'The images of depravity are tools. He believes Mr Tantar uses them as teaching tools, as a template to educate our congregation, as a warning to the honest Muslims of this world of the West's growing and plague-like immorality.'

'You expect me to believe that?'

'You may believe what you wish,' said Triady.

'Please ask your client to formally provide us with Tantar bin Abdulaziz Al Sadawi's address.'

'You are planning to bring him in for questioning?'

'Too bloody right I am.'

'In which case I advise you to be careful,' said Triady in a whisper. The words felt like a warning.

'The time is nine fifty-nine a.m. This concludes the interview.'

Hartono rose with Ruud and followed him out of the room. 'Where are you going?'

'To make a phone call to my mother.'

'Your mother in Australia?'

'No, the one that lives in Timbuktu. Yes, bloody Australia!'

Ruud returned to his office and plonked himself down, flopping over his desk with his head buried in the folds of his arms. He was pissed off. Both Imam Gunawan and his solicitor claimed they had no idea where Tantar bin Abdulaziz Al Sadawi lived. This meant he'd have to waste several valuable hours looking for the bastard. And that wasn't the only thing pissing Ruud off. The GPS tracker placed under Shane Waters' car was no longer working. The system had gone dead.

He grabbed the handset of his desk phone, dialled the long-distance code for Melbourne, Australia, and punched in several more digits before pressing the receiver to his ear.

He chatted to his mum about nothing, asked after his father and after Arjun.

'Arjun has a new job down at the library,' she said.

'How's he enjoying it?'

'He complains about his workstation by the window. It gets too hot for him in the afternoon, so he's taken to wearing zinc cream at work.'

'Any problems with the neighbour's cats?'

'Not recently. Arjun's left them alone.'

'That's comforting.'

'Drop him an email. He misses you, Ruud. Drop him a line, will you promise?'

'Yes, Mum.'

Five minutes later, following the usual niceties and discussions about the weather, he had what he wanted. His mother had given him the number of Professor John Sharpe, Head of Fire Science at Victoria University.

'What can I do for you, Ruud? Goodness, I haven't seen your parents for ages. How are they?'

'They're very well, Professor.'

'I'm glad. Look, I'm sure if you're telephoning from Jakarta this isn't a social call. What's on your mind?'

Ruud explained the predicament he was in. He told him about the two dead women.

'Both were burned, eh?' said Sharpe.

'What's the significance of it, do you think? The fire?'

Sharpe thought for a moment. 'Fire is the great destroyer, Ruud. The great leveller. It is savage and violent. It doesn't pick sides. It can reduce a lush tropical forest into a barren moonscape faster and more completely than anything else. Yet . . .'

'Yet . . . ?'

'Yet the link between fire and life on earth is complex, deceptive even.'

'How do you mean?'

'It destroys but it also creates. Don't ever forget that. The way humans view fire has changed appreciably in the last hundred years. Many ancient civilizations believed fire to be vital and regenerative; even today a few societies remain in awe of it. Take the Mescalero Apaches, for example; they still believe it to be a sacred, magical force, a universal purifier. And in many ways they're right. Burning breaks down dead matter into nutrients. Grasslands burst into life just days after wildfires. That's why grazing herds like African wildebeests track the path of veld fires.

'Many ecosystems around the world are dependent on fire and have been for thousands of years. Some plants, like manzanita, chamise and scrub oak, look to fire to encourage regeneration – a pine cone, for example, requires temperatures of over one hundred and twenty degrees Fahrenheit to melt the resin that binds it. Without fire, the seeds would never disperse.'

'So my killer is aiming to rejuvenate the world through fire.'

'A moderate fire burns the forest's understorey, killing disease and nourishing the soil, so the established trees can thrive.'

Ruud thanked the professor for his time. He replaced the handset and buried his head in the folds of his arms again.

The phone rang.

'Guess what?' It was Alya.

'Given your tone I'd say you have riveting news.'

'Oskar the security guard, remember him? Well, he doesn't stay home on his weekly day off as claimed. He does a part-time job delivering bottled water. Every Wednesday he delivers five-gallon dispensers to restaurants and hostels in the Central Jakarta district. And one of the neighbourhoods he delivers to is?'

'Jalan Jaksa.'

'Correct.'

'Which is where Anita Dalloway's hostel, The Paradies, is located.' He put Alya on speakerphone and rubbed his temples with the heels of his hands. 'Well, that is a coincidence.'

'Yes.'

'I'll contact Herr Vosseler and find out who delivers his drinking water. And let's question Oskar again,' said Ruud. 'But not today. I'm shattered.'

'Fancy a coffee?'

'I've still got masses to do.'

'Me too,' there was laughter in her voice, 'but how about a quick coffee with a side order of *pisang goreng sambal roa*?'

Ruud felt a tingling sensation in his mouth. He was starving, and he loved deep-fried banana fritters with chilli. 'See you at the corner eatery in ten minutes.'

Chapter Twenty-Four

They sat on a faux-leather banquette with dappled sunlight streaming through the window. The coffee was hot, sweet and a little gritty.

Ruud had taken only a single mouthful of banana fritter when Alya's phone rang.

'You found him? Hold on,' she told the mobile. She seized a pen from her tunic pocket. 'Give me the location.' She scribbled an address on the back of her hand.

Ruud leaned across the plastic table. 'What is it?' he said, slurping his coffee.

Alya was on her feet now, aggressively eager. 'That was Hamzah. There's been a development. They've located Tantar. He's working on a building site at the corner of Damai and Lubang Buaya, near the Crocodile Pit Monument. Do you want Hamzah to send backup?'

'No, we're stretched too thin as it is. You and I can handle this. Are you carrying?'

She patted the side of her belt.

They left the remaining fritters untouched.

The *cendol* seller pushed his cart into the shade and watched the Toyota Yaris approach, but as soon as he saw the distinct-ive yellow-on-black police licence plates he turned his back on them. He wrapped ice in a towel and smashed it with a hammer. '*Es Cendol Durian!*' he cried. 'Sweet and delicious! *Dingin dan Menyegarkan!*'

Ruud parked the Toyota in a narrow alley and, together with Alya, stepped into the windless, close afternoon. The smog was bad today. The sky was watery grey and the air heavy with construction dust and smoke.

They walked up to a low-slung tumour of a building surrounded by H-frame metal scaffolding, past an old man getting a haircut on his doorstep.

A billboard announced that Stabilitas Contractors man-aged the project. Ruud pointed his thumb at the sign. 'It's the same firm behind the JK Café rebuild.'

A crew of workmen clambered up and down the steel-tube scaffolding, leaning on the guard rails, hopping on and off the toe boards. Their bodies were silhouetted black by the sun. Many were shirtless, covered in gangster ink. Only those on the roof, six storeys up, wore standard-issue yellow hard hats and galoshes.

As soon as they saw Alya, they stopped their work and balanced on the edge of the platforms, hooking their legs over the metal cross braces, hanging off the sides.

Bobbing their necks, arms dangling, they watched her approach like Sulawesi macaques tracking the movements of an advancing predator.

Alya felt their eyes on her. She looked up and counted ten, maybe a dozen, short, stringy men; all from the country-side; all manual labourers with arms made muscular from hours in the fields – swinging parangs and wielding axes, lifting logs, cultivating the land.

They came from the backwoods and backwaters, from the oil-palm plantations of Sumatra and the timber yards of Kalimantan. Hungry, hard, blunt-nosed men with hungry, hard expressions.

'Hey cop! *Ke mana . . . ?*' came a shout from above. 'Where are you going? What do you want?'

Ruud lifted his gaze. 'We've come to speak to Tantar bin Abdulaziz Al Sadawi.'

One of the men, his hair dyed purple and worn spiked up like a Warhol fright wig, tilted forward, hands flapping. 'There is nobody here by that name. Go!' He shooed. 'We are busy working! Go!'

'I'd like every one of you to come down, stand in front of me and show me your KTP card.'

The purple man pressed a thumb to his nostril and blew snot onto the floor.

'If you refuse to comply, a platoon of BRIMOB officers from Jalan Matraman Raya will turn up. And you know how clumsy they can be with their billy clubs. But don't worry, I'll be here to help pick your teeth up off the floor.'

One by one the men descended.

They lined up under the sweltering sun and emptied their pockets. Cigarettes, sweet wrappers, iron nails, keys, coins, cheap phones, matchboxes and tiny baggies of *Shabu* fell to the ground. Two of the men claimed not to have any form of identification.

'No ID means we take you down to the station.'

The remaining KTP cards appeared miraculously, taped to the inner soles of their shoes.

Ruud grabbed the purple man by his purple hair. 'I'm in a bad mood,' he said. 'My coffee break was interrupted, so let me ask you again, a little more directly. Tantar bin Abdulaziz Al Sadawi. Big Fucker from Qatar. Where is he?'

The purple man grimaced. His head was at an odd angle. Ruud gave his hair another tug, exposing the black roots. 'Do you mean the Bull? Why didn't you say? He's the foreman. He's not working today, he hasn't been here for a couple of days already.'

'Where's he gone?'

'*Saya tidak tahu*. I do not know, but I can show you his trailer. There!' he pointed.

Ruud let go of the fright wig. 'Show me.' He nudged the man in the back. 'The rest of you don't move. *Ajun Inspektur* Entitisari, while I take a look, I want you to check all their IDs with Central.'

'Yes, sir.'

Ruud followed the purple man to the back.

There were two trailers. One was a green UASC shipping container balanced on breeze blocks, the other was white with OOCL markings.

The purple man led him to the green one.

'This is it? This is Tantar's tin-can trailer?'

The purple man nodded. Ruud motioned for him to step away. Ruud mouthed, 'Is the door locked?'

The man said he didn't know.

Ruud mimed zipping his lip and then cutting his throat. The man took another cautionary step back. Ruud held his Heckler & Koch 9 mm at chest height with both hands.

The police detective examined the twin doors. There was a lock box welded to the right door, which when closed overlapped a staple welded to the left door.

'Open it!' he hissed.

The purple man hesitated.

Ruud levelled the gun at the man's groin.

The purple man rushed forward, deftly rotating the catches and yanking the leverage bars up. The massive right door leaf opened outwards.

Darkness.

Thin shafts of sunshine streamed through cracks in the roof panels. Particles of dust danced in the light.

Crouching, Heckler raised and aimed towards the end wall and corner fittings, Ruud searched for movement. Tiny claws – a mouse or a rat – clattered across the floor planks.

He advanced half a step and suddenly felt a pair of hands shove him hard in the back. He tumbled to the ground. Before he could swing his gun round, the door banged shut. In the blackness he heard a bar thud down.

He was locked in.

The heat and dust got to Alya. She was sweating under her cotton hijab and her head was beginning to itch. Her mouth was dry. She could feel the onset of a headache.

KTP cards in hand, she walked back to Ruud's Toyota in order to call Central dispatch on the radio. There were ten names and corresponding NIK numbers to validate. This was going to take a bit of time.

Her fingers pulled uselessly on the door handle. The car was locked.

She saw a standpipe ten metres away, nestled in a shaded nook. She went over, unhooked her utility belt and draped it on a nail in the wall. Her service revolver, walkie-talkie, cuffs and ammunition pouch weighed over three kilo-grammes. It was good to be free of them for a while.

Alya tucked the KTP cards into her tunic pocket and bent forward, turning the faucet anticlockwise.

The water felt so cool.

She patted her face with damp hands and ran a wet handkerchief over the back of her neck.

Better. Much better.

She half-straightened.

That was when she sensed them.

Slowly, Alya's gaze lifted to their faces.

Three men.

They'd approached noiselessly. One of them carried a brick trowel.

Instinctively, she went to unclip the .38 Special from her belt, but it was still on the wall.

She clenched her teeth.

The men looked right past the revolver straight into her eyes.

'I'm a police officer,' she warned. 'Step back. Now!'

The men did not say a word. Instead, Alya saw a dialogue of glances pass between them. A stirring.

They watched her, considering, as if pondering what they'd do if she lunged for her weapon.

'I said, step back!'

They came closer. So close she could smell them.

Three men.

Two to hold her down and one to . . .

'Maybe, *nih*, we will play a game of trust,' said the one with the trowel. He had the face of an eel. Round-snouted with an ugly, wide mouth. 'We will let you go if you hand back our KTP cards.'

'I can't do that.'

'*Nasib kamu malang.* You see, some of us do not like the authorities knowing where we are and what we get up to.'

'Get back,' she said. 'If you don't take three steps back, I'll—'

He shushed her with a finger to his lips. 'You will do what?' He smiled. A sea creature baring its fangs.

Suddenly, another man appeared behind her, knotting and unknotting a rope.

That made four in total.

A loop of rope fell like a lasso by her feet, hoping to catch an ankle. She waved her fist at him.

He swayed as she punched at the air.

'Fuck you!' she roared.

The man with the trowel jabbed her in the side, drawing blood. As she turned, he kicked her in the backside and she dropped to one knee. Naughty, naughty, said his puckered mouth.

The pack circled.

She heard the man behind unbuckle his trousers.

'Now, will you do as you are told?'

She hung her head.

'What a good girl.'

Stupidly, he'd left his mobile in the car.

Ruud thumped and clawed at the door, barging it with his shoulder.

The whole trailer shook and rocked, but the door would not give.

The tin can was sweltering. He shone his penlight in all directions. A moth flew through the beam of his torch.

Within a minute he found the small metal box containing all the outlets and switches. He flipped several on, and electrical fittings mounted on steel strips blinked into life.

There wasn't much to look at: a stack of old newspapers on the floor, a cot bed with dirty sheets, a hard hat, a chair, a desk. Ruud scanned the desk's countertop: nothing but blunt pencils, architectural drawings, a stapler, a clipboard, an ancient transistor radio and an overturned bowl of *cendol*. Ants were crawling all over the upset rice flour jelly.

He tested the *cendol* with his finger – still cool to the touch. Someone had left here in a hurry.

Sunshine spilled through the gaps in the door hinges. Ruud pressed his face to them, looked up, squinting, and saw a flash of blue sky.

Then suddenly the door to the trailer opposite tore open. A monster of a man, big and square like a giant filing cabinet, bounded out, looking left and right. His bulk filled the doorframe. Hopping on one foot, he pulled on a shoe before rumbling down the road, pumping his beefy legs, shirt tail flailing.

Tantar.

Fuck!

He fired a shot into the ceiling. The sound was deafening.

When the ringing in his ears cleared, he heard the shrieking of crows. No, not crows. Men. He heard men cheering and hollering, whoops of delight. 'Alya!' he shouted. The hollering continued. They were the sounds drunkards make at a floorshow or a stag do. He kicked at the door, kicked and kicked until his ankle buckled. 'Alya!'

He pressed his ear to the door again and felt his throat constrict.

The yelps of delight came to an abrupt stop.

Now, all he heard was screaming.

Alya was coiled on the ground, still on one knee. Her hijab had slipped, concealing the left part of her face. She stared at the dirt floor.

'Why are you doing this to me?'

'Why?' said the eel-faced man. 'Because some of us have a police record, and some of us, like my two friends here, are still wanted by the police. So when you and pretty boy come poking about, taking down numbers and addresses, it inconveniences us too much. *Kau mengerti?* It means we have to move on again, go underground for a while. This is cash-cash business. We give the boss a false name, he asks no questions. Simple. Now, shut your mouth or I will slice you.'

She waited, gritting her teeth, for the man behind her to make his move. He shuffled forward with his jeans around his ankles. The head of his engorged penis glistened in the late afternoon glare.

'Let this be a lesson to you interfering cops, *nih*?'

The men were hooting, making whoops of delight.

'Time for a feast, boys. Sapto, you hold her still. After me, it's Biscuit's turn at the table.'

Closer, she wanted him to get closer.

'If you struggle, girl, we will tie you with the rope and cut your pretty face to ribbons.'

Closer still.

'Understand? *Kau mengerti?*'

Real close.

'And afterwards you are going to wash yourself clean of

us. Understand? Use that tap and scrub yourself thoroughly. Pussy, mouth, fingernails, everything.'

Just a bit more.

She felt hands on her shoulders.

She lifted her chin.

Now!

Her hand grabbed for the holster strapped to her left thigh.

Fingers clasped the rubberized grip.

Springing up, she flicked her wrist hard and the impact weapon telescoped to its full length. The friction lock snapped into place.

She gave them no time to react.

With astonishing speed, she pirouetted on her heels and struck like a hooded cobra.

Fluidly and brutally, she smashed the expandable baton against the first man's collarbone.

A howl of pain escaped his throat as he dropped and crumpled.

The second man threw a couple of hooks. She swung at his right elbow, shattering the bone. The ulna cracked like a dry tree branch.

Enraged, Eel-face charged with his trowel, baring his fangs. She ducked. A punch deflected off her forearm. The recoil sent her backwards a step, but she kept swinging with horizontal, downward-slashing strikes.

He charged a second time.

She pivoted.

The flat, pointed blade tore into her clothing, missing flesh.

Feet together, she whirled like a capeless matador and brought down her stick.

'Show's over, you bastards.'

Sixty-six centimetres of solid steel thudded against Eel-face's forehead and his nose exploded in a shower of blood.

It had taken no longer than fifteen seconds.

Only the man with his trousers round his ankles was left standing.

Dumbstruck.

'I am a fucking police officer,' she panted, coolly reaching across and buckling her utility belt to her waist.

His penis was limp now.

'Understand? *Kau mengerti?*'

The baton swished through the air.

She aimed for his kneecaps.

Alya and Ruud stood, arms crossed, shaking their heads.

Three emergency vehicles were at the scene. The man with the busted kneecaps was lifted onto an ambulance gurney.

Two other men were cuffed together. The one with the broken arm in a sling was sobbing. 'We were only trying to scare her. Not planning on doing her any harm.'

A fourth man squatted by a police car drenched in blood, pressing an ice pack to his face. 'She broke my nose!' he squealed, glowering ferociously.

'Are you all right, Alya?' asked Ruud.

Alya's mouth was downcast. 'I've had better afternoons.'

'They didn't hurt you, did they?'

'Does it look like they did?'

Ruud had to smile. 'No, I guess not.' He indicated her side. 'But you're bleeding.'

'It's nothing more than a flesh wound. The female medic patched it up for me.'

'Right.' He could tell she was putting on a brave face. 'Bet you wish you'd never left Commercial Crimes.'

'Well, as an American politician once said, "One day you're a peacock, the next day you're a feather duster."'

Ruud laughed.

She watched the ambulance drive off. 'What do we do now?' she wondered.

'I'll ask Sabhara to dust the trailers for prints.'

'It's a shame Tantar got away.'

'Don't worry, he won't get far. Listen, Alya, take the rest of the day off. Go home.'

'No, I have to get back and follow up on the Oskar business.'

'You can do that tomorrow.'

'But . . .'

'No buts. Treat yourself to a decent night's sleep. Get your head down.'

'What about you?'

'I'll wrap things up here and sort out the paperwork later.'

He hailed one of the Sabhara cops at the scene. 'Bharada, do me a favour please. Take the detective to her place of residence, will you?'

Alya walked off with a little wave. She called over her shoulder, 'You take care, First *Inspektur* Pujasumarta.'

'You too, *Ajun Inspektur* Entitisari.'

She strolled off, leaving a faint scent of freesias behind.

Five hours later Ruud put a full stop to the day's activities.

He got into his car and took the Inner Ring Road and Tol Cililitan 2 all the way to Pulo Gadung.

When Ruud stumbled through his front door he found Imke sprawled across the couch watching *When Harry Met Sally* on DVD.

He lay down next to her, resting his head on her hip. He stroked her hand, she stroked his hair. Both of them were asleep by the time Meg Ryan faked her orgasm.

Chapter Twenty-Five

'Fuck you.

'Fuck every one of you piss-stinking scum.'

A musty, curdled smell of neglect, of things turned rotten, filled the room.

The ceiling blurred and the floorboards bobbed like a roiling sea.

'You hear me? Fuck you all.'

The apartment walls were quaking with noise. Motorhead's 'Ace Of Spades' blasted from the speakers. The song played on a continuous loop.

'And you! Death! *Malak al-Maut*, you son of a fat, hustling slut. Fuck you, too.

'Fuck you for taking Farah away.

'She was only twenty-six, twenty-fucking-six!'

There was a box of pills on the floor. Hissing, Aiboy Ali slumped down next to his single bed and popped three pills from the blister pack, jammed them between his lips. His head sagged. He couldn't hold it together any longer. He sobbed huge wrenching sobs.

There was a handful of blond hair still clutched in his hand. He let it fall into the plastic bucket.

Lemmy Kilmister's electric bass banged out the riff. His

rasping voice swamped Aiboy Ali. He needed the music to drown him, otherwise his thoughts would veer off to the darkest places imaginable.

'You fucking bastard. You fucking bas—'

He heaved and threw up into the bucket between his ankles. A thick acid burned his throat. He clutched the bucket with his knees.

Strings of saliva stretched and dangled from his mouth. The stench of rotten fish filled the room.

He wiped a hand across his lips and leaned back, exhausted, head against the wall. His clothes – the leather biker vest, the Burgerkill T-shirt, the camouflage drill pants – were soaked from the rain, and a pool of rainwater formed around him.

There was a gun on the floor, by his side, next to his muddy boots.

The pool of rainwater trembled to the thud of the music. A tear rolled down his cheek.

'*Malak al-Maut!* You bastard. Angel of Death . . . ? Fuck off. I'm the authority on death. Not you! Me!'

Quietly. 'Me.'

The tear plopped into the bucket and mingled with his vomit and the strands of blond hair.

'I'm not scared of you. I've stared a legion of demons down, stood eye to eye to them, smelled their breath.'

The wall behind Aiboy thudded three times.

Thump! Thump! Thump!

'Keep the noise down. My children are sleeping!'

Ibrahim the electrician. Nice man. Hands out *kue* and sweet dumplings during *Hari Raya Idul Fitri*.

Aiboy liked him.

'Piss off, Ibrahim!'

210

Aiboy Ali's face was in the bucket.

The reek of vomit was intoxicating. His face was bathed in sweat.

A demon was circling him. A devil-thing in his peripheral vision, always there, waiting, watching, ready to snatch him away.

'I should have drawn my weapon. When the demons pulled their pistols on me. A Ruger SR22 and two Smith & Wessons.

'But they weren't demons, they were boys. Three seventeen-year-old *Shabu* pushers.

'I should have drawn my weapon.

'But I froze.

'They could have shot me. They would have shot me.

'If it hadn't been for Hamzah firing into the air . . .

'Hamzah you fucking rock star! You fucking bastard! You fucking—'

Thump! Thump! Thump!

'Shut up, for heaven's sake, will you! It's four in the morning! Turn that music off! I don't care if you're a blasted policeman! I'm calling one one zero. My children have school tomorrow.'

Unblinking, Aiboy stared at the contents of the bucket. The clump of blond hair floated in the sick.

'Why the dreams? Why the white coffin? The open casket, my body lying there, arms folded, with my face made up like a pig, why?

'Why a pig?

'Why?'

Eyelids heavy. So heavy.

A black blanket dropped. Thick and comforting. Black as . . . black as . . .

The ace of spades!

Lemmy again.

The ace of spades!

Thump! Thump! Thump!

His body jolted awake.

Jolted as if it had touched a live wire.

Sleep?

No. Whatever that just was, it wasn't sleep. Only the edges of it. He hadn't slept for days.

He ached for sleep, but when he closed his eyes, dead souls penetrated his thoughts. They came at him like henchmen.

Murderous.

Henchmen.

Ready to flense his carcass raw, ready to strip the flesh from his bones.

Ready to gut him like a butchered hog.

And yet, when he looked carefully, he saw them for what they were. They were not gangsters, or *preman* hoodlums, or rapists or murderers. They were the souls of dead women, innocent women . . . all with wild hair.

Coloured wild hair.

He snatched at the blond hair in the bucket.

The strands were slick and slippery.

Misery filled him.

It sucked at his core, dragging him under, dragging him so far down he recoiled from himself, as if there were something deep in his soul that was too frightful to touch.

Earlier he'd thought about putting his head in the oven, but no.

He reached for his Glock 17 and held it with both hands.

He stroked the proof marks on the slide and on the frame with the ends of his fingers, then rubbed the cartouches at the top and bottom of the grip.

The rubber grip was sticky with sweat and vomit. He cleaned the gun with the front of his shirt and turned the backstrap round so that his right thumb was on the trigger.

The muzzle pointed directly into his face.

With the slide pulled back, the hammer was halfway cocked.

His breath came quicker and quicker.

And all of a sudden he was capsized in a wild sea.

With an anchor tied to his ankles.

Hundreds of tiny air bubbles exploded from his nostrils as his lungs filled with water.

The Glock 17 was in his face.

Wide eyed, he stared into the barrel, into the bore, into the narrow inkpot-black tube.

He wanted to see it.

The bullet.

But all he saw was grooves and darkness.

He thrust the gun hard against his forehead, so hard that the front sight ground into the skin between his eyebrows.

There was a single round in the chamber. A Winchester 9 mm NATO FMJ, 124 grain.

The Glock 17 had a trigger weight of only about two and a half kilos. There was no manual safety catch.

He knew the bullet would blow the back of his skull out.

His hand tightened around the grip and he thumb-feathered the trigger.

He knew a 9 mm NATO FMJ would leave an irregular exit hole the size of an orange.

The muscles strained on his neck. His arms shook.

He knew the resulting explosion would spray hair, skin and tissue all over the room like pink milkshake.

His mind was screaming, screaming, screaming.

He knew that Solossa's technicians would have to dig several centimetres into the drywall to excavate his cranial fragments and brain matter.

Three, two.

He puffed out his cheeks and whispered a name.

Farah.

Thump! Thump! Thump!

One.

BANG!

Chapter Twenty-Six

Tuesday morning.

The call came in at 7.35 a.m.

Another body. Ruud grunted as he took down the address: Sion Church in Taman Sari, bordering the Glodok district, Jakarta's Chinatown.

There were three areas of the city Ruud was wary of: Blok M in South Jakarta, Ancol Port in the north, and Glodok, which was a haven for pirate DVD salesmen, pickpockets and vendors of cheap electronic knock-offs.

The rain pounded down as Imke ushered Kiki into the back of Ruud's Toyota. Imke's turquoise windcheater was dripping wet as she climbed into the passenger side, with Ruud at the wheel. The windscreen wipers swished at high speed, shovelling rainwater, yet the metal blades did little to improve visibility. She shook off her sandals and stuck her feet into a pair of galoshes.

Hazard lights flashing, the car carved through deep puddles, throwing up jets of spray. On a good day, the drive from their apartment in Pulo Gadung to Glodok was a thirty-minute journey via the Jakarta Inner Ring Road, but due to the rising floodwaters, they were forced to abandon the Toyota at Kampung Bandan railway station. Here, the army had been called in to battle the elements. Dozens of soldiers unloaded sandbags, inflatable boats and other flood-related equipment from the back of lorries.

Runoff from the downpour had engulfed several main roads. Many of the streets were waterlogged, some impass-able. Earlier the *Jakarta Post* reported that the state utility firm Perusahaan Listrik Negara had shut down power grids in strategic parts of northern and central Jakarta to avoid electrocutions.

By the rail tracks a barefoot Werry Hartono, looking pale and shambolic with his trousers rolled up to his knees, met them in a rubber dinghy. He handed them an oar each. 'You should have worn your sarongs,' he shouted in a boyish treble, and threw Ruud a plastic disposable raincoat. Ruud slipped the raincoat on, and together they paddled up the boulevard leading to the Sion Church, blade tips plashing. Already the water was at 45 cms.

Silently they paddled the dinghy along, ingesting the stink of the glutted conduits, the faecal reek of sewage overspill and the oily trash-clogged waters of the Ciliwung River.

Imke heard a screech and looked up. Through the blur of rain she saw a pair of shrews squabbling on a stretch of tele-phone wire. They fought for a bit and then took refuge on a jumbled old rooftop.

All manner of debris floated on the rising tide. A rubber tyre bobbed past, quickly followed by twigs and tree roots, plastic bags and bottles, a pink bicycle, a traffic cone, poly-styrene boxes, a dead kitten, a live rat and every colour of flip-flop imaginable. A child's toy – a doll's head – surfaced fleetingly before it was slurped under.

At the mouth of Jalan Mangga Dua, they passed a series of low-rise apartment buildings in various stages of disrepair.

People calf-deep in water waded out of their ground-floor homes carrying cloth parcels on their heads, bearing little dogs in buckets and crying infants in their arms, lugging timber staves heaped high with possessions.

Ruud sucked in several lungfuls of sour air, steeling himself for what lay ahead. A chill came over him, and he halted mid-paddle to drape a protective arm across Imke's back. Something stirred deep in his chest, a foreboding. At first he wasn't sure why he felt so uneasy but then, all of a sudden, he saw where they were making for.

Jayakarta.

It was here as a young detective, in the cul-de-sac behind the Sion Church, that he'd come across his first dead body. It had been raining hard that night, too, almost as hard as it was now, and Ruud kept wiping his hands and licking his lips. The technicians set up a white tent. There were trees on either side. Solossa, thinner in those days and with more hair, signalled Ruud over. With a wicked smile, the forensic doctor seized him by the arm and made him crouch down by the side of the corpse. The stiff was a man called Tjoe. He was in his late thirties, a big shot in one of South Jakarta's illegal gambling rings. A rival gang had garroted him. Tjoe's eyes bulged from their sockets and his tongue had turned the colour of canned pears; it protruded from his lips like a small fish. But it was the sight of Tjoe's yawning throat that made Ruud's body shake and his larynx contract: a deep, broad gash stretched across his Adam's apple from earlobe to earlobe, exposing ruffled contours and a mash-up of yellowy fat, red muscle and gummy globules of inky-purple blood.

It was a moment stitched into Ruud's consciousness.

He was inexperienced, a rookie, and he remembered the fear and disgust he'd felt. Eight years and countless homicide investigations later, disgust had turned to professional curiosity, but the fear remained; it was an emotion that rarely went away.

'How much further?' cried Imke, head bent. Her face was flushed. The storm lashed her Day-Glo turquoise windbreaker, drowning her words. She slanted her eyes away from the weather.

'Another half a kilometre,' Ruud yelled back. They bumslid across the slick rubber seat.

When they reached Sion Church, Hartono and Ruud jumped out of the dinghy. Ruud stuck his arm out and helped Imke off the craft. The wet edges of her jeans clung to her thighs.

She gazed at the church. Built in 1695 and the oldest in Jakarta, it sat on elevated ground in the shadow of an ancient palm tree.

Hartono slipped on his shoes, rolled down his trousers and, with a bit of clumsy splashing, secured the dock line to a telephone pole.

Already they could smell it. The carbon scent of smoke turning the air.

Ruud cast the paddles aside. 'I'm guessing we're not the first to arrive.'

Imke noticed three other police dinghies hitched to a stretch of metal railings nearby. Twenty metres away, several Sabhara cops stood in a huddle under an awning, keeping dry, smoking Djarum Blacks, waiting for instructions. The static from their police radios crackled.

Hartono showed them his warrant card and they nodded their assent.

The rain slanted in. Ruud flipped his shirt collar up at the nape of his neck and pulled his raincoat hood tight. Together they hurried through the little garden and up the paved pathway leading to a set of solid wooden doors, squelching through slimy mud, picking through puddles.

Pushing through the wooden doors, they entered the church, dripping rain all over the floor, leaving a wet trail behind them. They crossed the white-walled antechamber, which was bathed in grey light streaming through the domed windows. The interior was void of worshippers. A soil-like, musty smell pervaded.

Imke clumped down the nave in her galoshes, the rubber soles squeaking against the stone. Kiki followed on a leash, a step or two behind, shaking herself energetically.

'About bloody time!' Witarsa bellowed from across the aisle. The commissioner, a long loose wrinkle of frustration, was standing next to Solossa, the forensic pathologist. 'What in hell's name is going on, Pujasumarta?' he raged. 'Three murders. Three! And we're no closer to finding the killer.'

Ruud, seeing the state Witarsa was in, kept his voice steady. 'We're doing all we can, sir.'

The commissioner's face muscles jerked in spasm. There was morning coffee at the corners of his mouth. He approached the nave and braced himself by gripping the backrest of a bench. 'What did you say?'

'I said we're doing all we can.'

'All you can?' he roared, panting as he spoke. His eyelids twitched. The Herbert Lom tic had returned.

Witarsa's foot slapped against the bench. He kicked it so hard it toppled over. Ruud bent down and righted it. 'Steady on, chief. Remember your blood pressure.'

'I've got the President of the country threatening to sack me, the Ministry of Home Affairs breathing down my neck, the British Ambassador raising a stink, Anita Dalloway's parents demanding we release her body for burial, Jillian Parker's family demanding the same, a hate-crime serial killer on the loose, the international press going nuts, and you want me to keep calm!'

He dug something out of his raincoat. 'And then, to cap it all off, we receive this from the head of Indonesian–Australian relations!' He tossed Ruud a small black box, no bigger than a deck of cards. It was a GPS tracker. 'The Australian Embassy did a sweep of the legation cars and discovered this little gem lodged under the First Secretary's vehicle.' Witarsa's eyes spun in their sockets. 'Are you responsible for this?' Ruud kept quiet. 'Well, are you? Have you any idea how many rules you're breaking?'

'Shane Waters should be treated as a *tersangka*, he's a viable suspect.'

'He's a bloody diplomat! You're lucky they can't pin the tracker on us, otherwise we'd have an international scandal on our hands. What the hell were you thinking?'

'I'm trying to solve this case.'

'By breaking the law? Eight days, three victims, no leads. Those are lousy numbers, Pujasumarta. Pull your bloody finger out.'

'We're working round the clock, double overtime as it is.'

'Do you know who's just been on the phone to me? Police Public Relations chief Anton Charliyan. And do you know what he said? He called it a shambles. He said heads are going to roll and wanted the name of the person leading this inquiry. You're on borrowed time, Pujasumarta.'

Ruud felt the heat rise in his cheeks. His face was as hot as a struck match. He lifted his hand and swept the hair out of his eyes with a knuckle. Instinctively, the other hand reached into his hip pocket for a HeadStart tablet.

Empty pocket.

Damn.

Force of habit, he told himself. He didn't need those pills any more.

Pained, he said, 'May I see the body?'

Witarsa stared at the floor.

Ruud waited for him to answer.

'Show him the body, Solossa! Not that it will do any good.'

Imke bristled. She knew Witarsa could be a bully sometimes, but he was completely out of order. Feeling protective towards Ruud, she jumped to his defence and went quickly to his side. 'Stop acting like an arse, Witarsa.'

'What is this? A wrestling tag team?'

'He's your most decorated homicide detective,' she said. 'His arrest statistics are second to none, and all you do when the pressure's on is shout at him like some jackass tyrant. You should be ashamed of yourself. I thought you were smarter than this.'

The commissioner flushed a dusky red. He stood under the copper chandeliers, facing the baroque pulpit. Outside, the hiss of rain abated. Chirping bulbuls, nesting in the eaves, filled the awkward lull with birdsong.

Gripping the leash tightly, Imke's jaw clenched and unclenched in time with her breathing. She wanted to hold Ruud's hand.

'I'm giving you seventy-two hours, Pujasumarta,' said the commissioner, his voice barely above a whisper.

The forensic pathologist closed in on Ruud and nudged his back. 'Come this way, First *Inspektur* Pujasumarta,' he insisted, embarrassed for him.

'After that you're done,' continued Witarsa. 'I'm handing the case to Natsir from Section Twelve. You're to be reassigned at a later date.'

'Natsir again?' said Ruud. 'That self-aggrandizing prick? You can't be serious?'

'We need a fresh perspective,' said Witarsa. 'Someone with a sure hand. You're on the ragged edge.'

'This is bullshit,' said Ruud.

'As your commanding officer I recommend you take extra leave.'

'What have I done wrong? I don't understand.'

'I got word you've been harassing a senior imam, questioning his integrity. There are allegations of intimidation.'

'That's crap. My interview with Imam Gunawan was completely above board.'

'The Ulema Council received a formal complaint from him.'

'Oh, come on.'

'Seventy-two hours. I'll make a formal announcement at the Friday morning press conference.'

Ruud allowed the implications of Witarsa's ultimatum to sink in. He stared fiercely into the commissioner's rumpled bloodhound face before wheeling round to follow Solossa through the transept door and into the extension at the back.

Ruud's eyes misted with rancour.

'Are you all right?' Imke asked as they entered the sacristy.

She could tell he was struggling to contain his emotions. 'Never better,' came the reply. He gave her hand a quick, reassuring squeeze before letting go. 'Thanks for sticking up for me.'

Solossa steered them to the far side of the sacristy and out through a low door that led outside.

Imke was immediately struck by the scorched smell of burned hair and fried muscle tissue. She pulled the throat of her windbreaker up over her nose and mouth.

The charred, naked body lay face up and spread-eagled on the sodden earth, arms spread wide as if nailed to a cross.

There were half a dozen red Versa-Cones placed around the victim, each one numbered from one to six. The blackened area was cordoned off with yellow *garis polisi* barrier tape.

Stationed next to the corpse, under an umbrella, Officer Hamka Hamzah, looking ragged and frayed in his battered brown police uniform, jabbed his teeth with a matchstick.

'Rain stopped for now,' said Hamzah, glancing at the sky. Above him the dark clouds were thinning. All around, the branches and leaves dripped. He pretended not to have heard the confrontation between Ruud and Witarsa. 'But coming again soon.'

A police photographer was snapping pictures of the crime scene. The battery of his camera whirred noisily every time the flash went off. Ruud waved him away.

'Exactly the same MO as before,' said Solossa. 'Like the others, I'd say she was burned alive. Reproductive organs taken out. And he left his usual calling card: a canvas banner marked with white Islamic writing.' Thin poles of sunlight pierced the clouds, illuminating a long scribble of Arabic script. The rain had made some of the paint run on the canvas. 'Only on this occasion,' continued the *dokter forensik*, 'our man didn't complete the job.'

'How do you mean?'

'He must have been spooked. Only half the body burned before the rain extinguished it. My guess is she's been dead five, six hours.'

Ruud sank down and examined the remains.

Solossa was bang on. From the thighs up, the burns were severe: her torso was crisped and crumpled, her arms kinked and knotted, and her head roasted black.

Ruud drew a pen from his hip pocket and prodded the pasty ash that had been the victim's hair. He then stared at her melted face. The woman's mouth was still locked in a grotesque scream. He gave the jaw a tap but it didn't close. It was evident that the city's crows had got to her first – the flesh was ripped away from her philtrum down to the angle of her jaw, exposing both rows of teeth.

Repositioning, Ruud ran his eyes down her body and saw for himself that the lower parts of her legs were only mildly cooked. There were dark patterns on her ankles and calves, full-thickness burns like purple ink blots, where the fire had licked the flesh and blistered the skin.

Ruud gazed at the once-pale feet and painted toes, at the tattoo encircling her ankle depicting a lotus flower. The tattoo was quite recent, its colours rich and sharp. 'Who is she?'

Solossa directed his attention to the lanyard on the ground, untouched by the flames. 'Her name is Emily Grealish. There's a lanyard and keycard that says she works at Plaza Atrium. It's a security pass allowing her to get in and out of the building. So far it's all we know.'

'You're right, this looks hurried, as if he couldn't wait to get out of here. Do you think our man is getting sloppy?'

'Possible,' Solossa surmised. 'Or someone, or something, scared him away from his kill. There's no sign of a violent melee so I think it's safe to say Emily Grealish was either unconscious or deceased when she was brought here and set alight. But, as I say, he might have been spooked by something as he didn't finish the job.'

Hunkered down beside Hamzah, some two metres to his left, on the outer periphery of the barricade tape, a priest in a black cassock knelt in prayer.

'Who's this?' demanded Ruud, taking a step to the side.

'Pastor Ignatius Kwong,' said Solossa.

'He's been down there for almost an hour now,' said Hamzah, yawning. 'Keeping vigil, murmuring words to the dead and whatnot, *meh*?' The little policeman waved his umbrella at a passing bug. A cloud of flying ants swarmed about, their excitement aroused by the heavy rains.

Taking no notice of the police officers, the priest scraped along the floor with his hands folded to his face. He inched forward every few seconds, thrusting his substantial hindquarters in the air.

Ruud went and stood in front of the man. The priest lifted his gaze. He was a fat diminutive Chinese man whose wide face was so puffy his eyes disappeared in the pillows of flesh. 'How could this have happened here?' cried Pastor Ignatius. 'Here of all places, on God's holy turf.'

'Was it you who discovered the body?' asked Ruud.

Pastor Ignatius gesticulated deliriously. 'This is a most terrible, terrible travesty. Who would do this? Who?' He raised his arms and opened his palms to the heavens.

'Please get to your feet, sir, and answer my question.'

Ignatius did as he was told. His shoes and trousers were caked in mud and mulch. 'Yes,' he said. 'I was the one who found the poor soul. Because of the high water I didn't return to my home. I slept in the church last night.'

'Alone?' Hartono asked, his pen and notebook poised.

'With the cat. I take Jaha with me everywhere. I woke this morning at five o'clock sharp to let Jaha out. As soon as I reached the annexe I could smell it. When I came out here a few minutes later I found the poor woman like this, the top part of her was still smouldering, bits of her were hissing. I called the police immediately.'

'Hissing?' said Ruud.

'Yes,' he blubbered. 'It was simply awful!' The priest tilted forward and theatrically rammed his forehead against Ruud's chest. The man's hair smelled vaguely sulphurous, as though he'd rubbed the root follicles with boiled eggs. 'Most terribly, terribly awful.' His mouth pecked at Ruud's shirtfront.

'Did you see anyone in the grounds? Anyone suspicious?'

Ignatius elevated his chin and eyeballed the sacristy door as though he feared Witarsa would come barging out, blathering and cursing. 'I've already told your colleagues that I saw nobody.'

'You didn't see or hear anything at all?'

'The bedchamber is windowless and the walls of these old buildings are thick. I usually fall into a deep sleep.'

'Deep sleep, you say,' said Hartono. He licked the nib of his biro and wrote in his notebook.

Ruud held the lanyard up to the priest's face, insisting he look at the photograph. 'Do you recognize this woman? Is she a member of your church?'

The fleshy lids of his eyes widened a fraction. 'Not to my knowledge.'

Ajun Inspektur Polisi Dua Alya Entitisari materialized from the graveyard gates at the back, walking confidently through a cluster of sprouting weeds, head held high. Two men in white overalls accompanied her, their uniforms clinging soggily to their bodies. One of the men carried a bag of Arrowstone casting material.

She flashed Ruud a smile. 'Good morning First *Inspektur* Pujasumarta.'

'Morning,' he replied.

'We have found drag marks as well as boot prints in the mud,' she said, looking Imke up and down. 'US size twelve. The forensic team is about to take outsole impressions and make a plaster cast. Also, we think there may be fibre traces left in the soil.' She glanced at Kiki. 'Hello. Nice doggy.'

'He's leaving footprints, and fibre samples now? Yep, he's getting sloppy all right,' said Ruud.

Alya went on. 'Our perpetrator tried to cover his tracks but botched it.' She jutted her chin at the desolate grass and ragged terrain beyond the chain-link fence.

'Where does that lead to?' asked Ruud.

'Over the fence to the east is a tangle of lanes, to the south a cul-de-sac. The Sabhara boys are going door-to-door checking for witnesses.'

'Right, expand the crime scene to the chain-link fence.' The first *inspektur* looked about. 'Where's Aiboy?'

'We don't know,' Alya said. 'I've been calling him all morning. Repeatedly. He's not picking up.'

The words hung in the humid air.

Ruud thought about his friend's fragile state of mind and a chill ran through him.

A police helicopter hovered high overhead.

'Would you like me to tell the office manager to dock him half a day's pay?' she asked.

'No, leave it for now.' Ruud ran a hand across his face. 'I'll chase him up and try to get hold of him myself. Werry,

227

please take Pastor Ignatius inside and run through the standard questions with him again.'

The priest thumbed the cross dangling from his neck and followed Hartono indoors.

While Hamzah smoked a *kretek* and the technicians prepared a cast of the footprint, Alya approached Imke and introduced herself. She wore her brown police tunic and hijab with pride, with a nickel-plated .38 Special clipped to her belt and a leather sling bag secured to her back.

Imke noticed the bag's strap was unbuckled and a book was peeking out from the top. She arched her brows. 'Is that Ruud's?'

'*The Psychology of Lying*. Yes, First *Inspektur* Pujasumarta leant it to me. He's been coaching me on interrogation techniques.'

'He has, has he?'

Ruud heard something in Imke's tone. Stepping between them, he broke in quickly. 'Tomorrow, as soon as the water subsides, I want you and Alya to return to the JK Café crime scene. From now on I want you working together.'

'Great,' Alya said. 'Should be fun.'

'As fun as rolling about in a bed of nettles,' muttered Imke under her breath.

'Why do you want us back at the JK site?' Alya asked Ruud pointedly.

'Because in just over thirty hours from now, at three p.m. Wednesday, we're issuing a press release saying we believe an item of Anita Dalloway's clothing is missing and was never recovered from the fire. That this piece of clothing is vital to our investigation, and if found may provide crucial DNA evidence leading to the killer's arrest.'

Imke nodded. 'You're talking about her Alice band.'

'Yes, her tartan Alice band. We'll provide a photograph of a replica headband and urge the public to come forth with any information. There'll be a fifty million rupiah reward attached.'

Alya's eyes widened. 'But we already have the Alice band.'

'Ah, but our man doesn't know that, does he?' said Ruud. 'The press release will also state that the police DNA database retains DNA samples taken from every person over eighteen with a conviction or caution over the last ten years.'

'What are you talking about?' said Alya, nose upraised. 'We don't have anything like that in place.'

'Again, he doesn't know that.'

Imke said, 'So you're going to attempt to draw him out.'

'I'm hoping this will unnerve him enough to retrace his steps. We'll have plain-clothes officers at Jakarta Kota Station and spotters on the nearby roofs. Isn't that right, Hamzah?'

The little policeman released a thin jet of smoke through his nose. 'Yes, boss.' He dropped his cigarette and ground it out with his shoe, then, remembering he was at a crime scene, hastily retrieved it.

'The same goes for the area around Jalan Jaksa and the streets leading to JK Café.'

'So what is it you want me to do, *hè*?' said Imke, crossing her arms.

'I'd like you and Kiki to do a sweep of the JK construction site. If our man's watching and he notices a K9 unit at work he may panic and show himself.'

'If he comes again, most likely it will be in the same black car,' said Hamzah.

'I know it's a long shot,' said Ruud, 'but it's worth a try.'

'Sounds like we're to be the cheese in the mouse trap,' Alya said to Imke.

'Great,' said Imke, drawing her windbreaker tightly around herself. 'Just great.'

Chapter Twenty-Seven

Ruud, stiff from the rain, stumbled out of the elevator at Central HQ and went straight to his office, slamming the door behind him.

He'd come from Sion Church via the morgue and his clothes now carried the smell of powdered bleach.

In the last thirty minutes he'd learned that Emily Grealish was thirty years old with blonde hair, 172 cms, fifty-four kilograms, with a tattoo of a lotus flower on her right ankle. She was born in Vancouver, Canada, and ran a business called Elite Protocol Management out of offices at Plaza Atrium, an upscale mall near the National Monument. She was single, lived alone and had resided in Jakarta for six years. According to Emily's Facebook page, she was a lapsed Catholic and now practised Buddhism. Her medical dossier, accessed from her GP at Metropolitan Medical Centre, indicated she'd been in very good health – the only blemish on her record was a detached retina suffered in 2013, which caused mild myopia in her right eye.

He looked at his watch and reckoned he had another sixty-odd hours left before Natsir took over. Captain Natsir (AKP), that spluttering, self-serving, obsequious twat from Section 12, was going to take his job again – what in God's name was Witarsa thinking? Ruud wanted to punch his lights out.

There was a gust of laughter in the corridor.

Ruud threw open his door and yelled for quiet, before banging it shut again. He then shoved his desk clear across the floor of his office until it collided noisily with the far wall. The large map of South Jakarta wobbled but remained hung on its pin.

Ruud heard a voice from outside the door. 'Is everything all right in there?'

'Yes, Mrs Hapsari.'

'Would you like a cup of tea?'

'No thank you, Mrs Hapsari.'

Ruud listened to her shuffle off.

Sixty hours.

Two and a half days.

He had until Friday mid-morning. Then it would be Natsir o'clock and he'd turn into a pumpkin.

He couldn't bear the thought of it.

But what the fuck could he do? With the initial interviews concluded and the investigative assessment ongoing, he still hadn't a clue what was going on.

He picked up his chair and positioned it on top of his desk.

Come on Pujasumarta, implored Ruud, get those little grey cells of yours firing.

The detective placed the police reports, case files, interview notes, photographs, tip-offs and other material on the ground in no particular order. He fanned them out and arranged them into a sequence, sorting them until they formed a ranking, creating a timescale of events.

He removed his shoes and cooled his feet on the concrete

floor. He waited for the cool from the floor to creep through his toes before climbing on to the table. He sat on his chair, hands on his chin, elbows on knees, staring down, looking like a Bondi lifeguard peering down from his tower.

Deep in thought, he pored over the landscape of information that lay scattered beneath him.

Mentally he made his way through the sequence of incidents. Tried to draw the strands together to create a link. He couldn't. He sketched scenario after scenario in his head, making up one storyline after another, but got nowhere. Covering his face with both hands, he smothered a groan before crying out in frustration.

What flummoxed him was the random order of the killings. There seemed to be no logic to it. The victims did not know each other. They came from different parts of the world (Australia, UK and Canada respectively). They did not share common friends or acquaintances. Apart from being Western, they appeared to be totally unconnected. Two of them were Christians, one was Buddhist. One was a divorcee (Jillian), one had a boyfriend (Anita) and one was single (Emily). Jillian had short mousy hair, Anita was a dark brunette and Emily had curly blonde locks. There were differences in age, height, weight and body type. The same could be said of their professions, the schools they attended and the types of people they hung around with. They had contrasting tastes in clothing and eyewear (Anita used contact lenses, Jillian had perfect vision, Emily possessed a pair of reading spectacles), and wore different brands of perfume.

Perhaps his first instinct was right: that these were religious hate crimes and the victims were killed for being unbelievers. Set alight and sent to hell. Hellfire and damnation. Fire the purifier.

No, something in his gut told him no.

He looked at the evidence again.

Three dead. Were there others the police didn't know about? Possibly, but for now he had to concentrate on the facts and figures before him.

Jillian was killed on a Monday. Anita was killed on a Wednesday and Emily died on a Tuesday, with no apparent astronomical pattern to the murders. Monday, Wednesday, Tuesday . . . would the next victim be killed on a Thursday? Perhaps. And were they killed according to some kind of lunar cycle? No, apparently not. Again, no pattern.

Yet all three victims had had their uteruses cut out. Why? He wondered. Were they pregnant? And if they were, why remove the foetuses? Because the mothers were non-believers, non-Muslim heathens being punished for bringing new infidels into the world? Solossa was running hGC tests on the victims' bone marrow to see if they were with child, but it would take weeks to get a definitive result. They must have been pregnant. But what if they weren't? Why would the perp take out their wombs if they weren't pregnant? Was it because he was a sadist with a talent for mutilation? Did he get an erotic thrill from it? Were they keepsakes? Ruud scratched his chin. None of this made any sense. All three victims appeared completely random – the only things tying them together were their gender, manner of death and the fact that they weren't Muslim.

So why did the killer pick such contrasting targets?

Was it a deliberate ploy?

Were they chosen indiscriminately or methodically? Casualties of chance or casualties of choice?

And what about Shane Waters and Suparman, Oskar and

Tantar? Were they connected to the murders? Were any of them suspects? Or was Ruud grasping at shadows.

True, Tantar had done a runner. But in Jakarta everyone ran from the police.

All this rattled through Ruud's mind in less than three minutes.

For a long while he stared into space.

He watched an opaque *cicak* crawl upside down on the ceiling. His ex-mother-in-law, Nyonya Panggabean, once told him that if a tiny gecko dropped on your right shoulder it was considered good luck, but bad luck if it fell on your left. Instinctively, Ruud stuck out his right shoulder. The *cicak* remained glued to the ceiling.

The minute Ruud took his leave from his office Alya and Hamka Hamzah intercepted him in the hallway. The little man waved a computer printout in Ruud's face. 'Emily Grealish had only the one mobile phone account, with Indosat. We got hold of her billing records and there's something damn-strange weird about the calls she made. Look, *nih?*'

Ruud grabbed the printout.

'Look at this one here, made to one of her clients.'

Alya cut in. 'Because we don't physically have her mobile phone we can't access any call content, the actual recording of her conversations, but we can look at the metadata.'

'Metadata,' repeated Hamzah.

'Which is information about the calls, who called who and when,' said Alya.

'I know what metadata means,' said Ruud. 'What did you find?'

'With the help of Emily's office staff, we separated the phone numbers into two lists – clients in one, family and friends in the other.'

'Please tell me Shane Waters was pestering her too.'

'This has nothing to do with Shane Waters, boss,' said Hamzah, a finger hooked to his belt.

Alya almost shouldered Hamzah aside in her excitement. 'It seems she was talking to one of her clients at really odd hours. See here, look at the date, Sunday seventh February.' She indicated a line highlighted in yellow. 'A ten-minute call was made at twelve thirty-seven a.m., then again at one a.m. – this time the conversation lasted for three minutes. Then a few hours later at six twenty-two a.m. Who the hell calls a client at that time of night?'

'The same pattern occurred the following day. It seems it had been going on for weeks, since mid-January.'

'Who's the client?'

'You're not going to like this,' warned Hamzah.

'Enough with the suspense, guys, tell me.'

Alya's voice gave a little tremor. 'Lieutenant General Fauzi, Director for International Cooperation, Ministry of Defence.'

Ruud's shoulders stiffened and the hairs on the back of his neck stood up. 'Oh, Jesus.'

He exchanged glances with Hamzah and Alya and saw the fear in their eyes.

He grabbed Hamzah's arm. 'Who else have you spoken to about this?'

'Only you, boss.'

Ruud felt something hard form in his stomach.

'What do we do?' said Alya.

'Nothing, and keep your voice down,' hushed Ruud. He

began to march towards his office, weaving through the row of desks screened by melamine partitions.

Alya followed him. 'There's only one reason why a woman calls a man at one in the morning,' she said.

'Keep it down,' hissed Ruud.

'Where are you going?'

He walked quickly, without breaking stride. 'To my room. I need time to think.'

'What is there to think about?' said Alya. 'She was sleeping with him. Emily Grealish was having an affair with Lieutenant General Fauzi.'

Hamzah caught up with them.

Ruud steered them into his office and closed the door. 'Listen to me very carefully. Right now we know jack shit. Everything you just said is conjecture and speculation. Even if Fauzi was sleeping with Emily it doesn't prove anything. It certainly doesn't mean he killed her.' He looked her in the eye. 'Right?'

'Recent homicide studies show that out of every hundred women killed, thirty-four of them died at the hands of a husband or boyfriend.'

'Do you know what you're saying?' Ruud glared at her. 'You're suggesting one of the country's top brass, a former member of the MPR, committed murder.'

'So what if he's top brass. It doesn't make him immune to prosecution; it doesn't make him untouchable.'

'We're on dangerous ground here.'

'I know,' she huffed.

'We can't rush blindly into this.'

'So what do we do?' implored Alya.

'We tell nobody, do you understand? Nobody.' He grabbed Hamzah's wrist. 'Hamzah, look at me.'

'Yes, boss.'

'Keep your mouth shut. Is that clear?'

'Yes, boss. I tell nobody.'

'Not until I speak to Witarsa.'

'You think this could land us in a lot of trouble, boss, *meh*?'

'Hamzah, my friend, this sort of information could get us killed.'

Chapter Twenty-Eight

Wednesday morning.

The photographs from the data-recording boys arrived on Ruud's desk.

With a cup of hot coffee in hand, Ruud locked himself in his office and kicked off his shoes.

Closing the window blinds, he shut himself off from the world and fished about inside the thick cardboard file that contained the images. He laid out five large glassine envelopes.

For the next two hours he studied the black-and-white enlargements of Emily Grealish's apartment. When noon came around, he dialled Werry Hartono's extension from his desk phone and waited for him to pick up.

'Second Lieutenant Werry Hartono speaking,' he announced in English.

'It's me. I want you to run something by me again.'

Werry's voice climbed an octave. 'I am at your disposal.'

'Did we find a computer, a MacBook, a laptop or iPad in Emily's flat?'

'No, sir, no portable devices. Nothing.'

Ruud switched hands and ears. 'What about at work?'

'Only her desktop computer, but Tech went through it

and found only business-related items. There was no personal correspondence or anything related to her social life. You know what? I have a theory.' It wasn't unusual for Werry Hartono to have a theory. These days he had a theory for most things homicide related, typically gleaned from an online blog like *The Science of Sherlock Holmes* or *The Mystery of Deduction*. 'I think someone broke into Emily's flat and took her tablets, phone and whatever other portable devices she had.'

'What makes you say that?'

'There were no hard disks, USB flash drives or memory sticks anywhere. It's as if the apartment had been swept of storage devices.'

'Were there any signs of a break-in?'

'The front door lock had bumping on it, nicks around the edges of the keyhole.'

'What about inside?'

'The place was messy, but not ransacked. It's hard to tell, to be honest, if anyone had been through her things. However, we did find one item of interest, an envelope in Emily's bedside drawer. It was a letter addressed to Pastor Ignatius Kwong. The note inside reads, 'If anything should happen to me, put everything on ice. EG.'

'What the hell does that mean?'

'No idea.'

'I thought the priest said he didn't know Emily Grealish.'

'That's what I thought, too.'

Ruud listened to Hartono breathing into the handset. 'What's your personal opinion?'

'I think she confided in Ignatius Kwong. She was probably part of his congregation. My guess is she confided in the priest because she was scared of someone. And I think that someone broke into her flat, searched the place, took her electronic devices, but failed to find what they were really looking for.'

'Like what?'

'I don't know, sir. Confidential files? Secret documents?'

'I've been thinking. You know what's odd, Werry? The first death, Jillian Parker, was almost made to look like an accident. But the next two victims were positioned deliberately out in the open. Why do you think that is?'

'I don't know, sir.'

'Also, why the hell did she chew off her own finger?'

'We spoke with her parents and learned that she was severely claustrophobic. Apparently as a child she was abducted by a crazy aunty and locked in a dark cupboard for two days.'

'I guess that might explain the finger. Anyway, have a think about it, will you? Also, go question Ignatius Kwong and find out what he's hiding from us.'

'I will.'

'All right. Listen, I want you to do something else for me. There are a number of inappropriate postings of Emily on Facebook, photographs of her in a bikini, drinking beer, that sort of thing. Speak to her father. As next of kin he can formally request to shut down the account.'

'Why is this important?'

'The press have a habit of categorizing women as either saints or sluts, pure or wanton. They like to speculate, insinuate. I don't want to give them an excuse to. Do the same for Anita and Jillian.'

Ruud hung up and called Alya.

'Do you have that list of Emily's phone records for me?'

'Give me one minute.' Ruud heard Alya tap her keyboard and click her mouse. 'I have it right here. I'm sending to you right now at twelve oh five. Check your inbox.'

'Good. Now grab Hamzah and Hartono and see me in my office.'

A minute later all four sat around Ruud's desk. 'Alya, run Emily Grealish's job data by me again.'

'Emily Tiffany Grealish: arrived in Jakarta in 2010. Initially worked for a PR firm before starting her own company in 2012. The company's called Elite Protocol Management. She had eight employees. All of them were women and Indonesian nationals. Says here she paid herself 62 million rupiah a month running etiquette training courses.'

Hamka Hamzah pulled on his *kretek* and stroked his chin. 'What does that mean, this ati-quake training, *nih*?' Smoke leaked from his nose.

'Teaching people manners,' said Ruud. 'Which knife and fork to use. How to speak in public, when it is polite to fart and burp, that sort of thing.'

'According to Google,' Alya noted, 'she did quite a bit of work with the Indo government.'

'Which explains her association with Lieutenant General Fauzi. OK, got it.' Ruud stood up and went to the door. 'Listen, has Aiboy Ali turned up for work yet?'

'Actually, sir, I should have said earlier. There's been some worrying news. Polda Metro's incident centre received reports of a disturbance on Tuesday morning coming from Aiboy Ali's apartment block. One neighbour said he heard loud music and screaming. Another neighbour claims he heard a gunshot.'

'Oh, shit.'

'A patrol car went to check it out. They knocked on his

door. When nobody answered they got a locksmith to open it. The flat was empty. Aiboy wasn't there, but the officer said he didn't like what he saw. The lights were still on and the place was in disarray. A total wreck. And he reported a rotten stench, like a locked-in smell.'

'Any sign of blood?'

'No, but someone had blasted a massive hole in the stereo, which probably accounts for the gunshot.'

'Right.'

'There's more. They found a lot of weird clothing. Leather stuff with zips and rivets.'

'Big deal.'

'And a pig mask.'

Ruud fought to keep the black panic at bay. He tried to make sense of it. 'I asked Aiboy to check out the costume and fancy-dress outlets. He might have bought one to . . .' He looked hard at Hamzah. 'Get Central Control to issue a KLO4. I want to make sure Aiboy is safe.'

'Yes, sir.'

'Don't mention the mask to anyone for the moment, OK? When did you last try calling him?'

'An hour ago,' Hamzah said. 'His phone is still switched off.'

Unnerved by the news, Ruud held his gaze. 'Keep on trying.'

'Yes, boss. *Nih*, there's something else.'

'What is it?'

Hamzah read from his tatty notebook. 'The night Anita Dalloway disappeared. One of the shopkeepers close to the JK Café was stocktaking and dealing with invoices when she heard a scream. Quick-hurry she goes to look out of the window and sees a black car race by. She remembers this because after dark cars and minibuses don't go down that road because of the potholes.'

'Good work. Now, leave me alone, will you? I have work to do.'

They closed the door behind them as they left.

Ruud returned to the black-and-white enlargements of Emily Grealish's flat. He examined every photo, appraising the images of cupboards, wardrobes and storage boxes, taking in the swathes of fingerprint powder dusting every surface, the clothing piled on the armchairs, the clean sheets in the tumble dryer. He viewed image after image showing countertops, dressers, lamps, books, embroidered cushions, silver picture frames and the interiors of desk drawers. Then he went back to the photograph showing her bed and nightstand. He tilted his head to the side. And that's when he spotted it, scanning the spines of the thick paperbacks on the bedside table: *Choosing Single Motherhood: The Thinking Woman's Guide.*

He snatched up his phone and dialled another extension. A woman answered.

'Damia, where's Witarsa?' said Ruud, up on his feet.

The commissioner's secretary said he was taking his lunch. 'He said he wasn't going far. What day is it today? Wednesday, isn't it? Wednesday is either fruit *rujak* or satays from Sapta's, depending on the weather.'

Commissioner Witarsa took his lunch on the streets, as he liked to on cooler afternoons when the clouds up above darkened and the air carried the threat of rain.

Ruud found him across the road from the station, standing on the pavement, eating satays from a *gerobak*. When he saw Ruud striding his way the commissioner raised a finger, telling him to wait a moment. Patiently, Ruud watched as Sapta the satay vendor turned the sticks on his grill and fanned the charcoal flames with a wicker fan.

Seconds later, Sapta handed a plate of hot satays to Witarsa. Smacking his lips heartily, the commissioner grasped a skewer and clamped a sliver of beef between his upper and lower teeth. He had to pull and snatch at it a bit but eventually the beef came free.

The satay man nodded his approval. Next to him his wife sliced cucumbers and threw them into a large enamel basin, which she covered with newspaper to keep out the bugs. On the floor was a bowl of sugar water to distract the flies.

As Witarsa chewed, peanut sauce dribbled off his thumb. He'd yet to touch the cucumber relish or the rice cakes.

'What do you want?' said the commissioner, taking another bite and washing it down with a swig of Milo. His brusque tone did not take Ruud by surprise.

'We have a problem. Aiboy Ali's gone AWOL.'

'And?'

'I'm concerned for his mental well-being. There was a gunshot heard at his home early Tuesday morning. Sabhara made a house call. He's not there.'

'Have you checked all the hospitals?'

'Yes. I'm worried about his state of mind, he's on the ragged edge.'

'I'll put in a call to one of the in-house support staff. Anything else?'

Ruud paused. He had to put his concerns regarding Aiboy Ali to one side for now. 'Yes, there's another matter.'

'What?'

'I need to ask a favour, well, not a favour as such, more a formal request. It's a bit tricky.'

'A favour? Listen, you're not exactly in my good books right now.' Witarsa's chewing grew agitated. He put the plate down. 'What are you playing at, Pujasumarta? When your eyes do that I know you're up to something.'

'When my eyes do what?'

'Slink off to the side like this.' Witarsa slid his gaze downwards and to the left. 'Bloody shifty look, I'm telling you.'

'Something's come up.' He dug out his shades and slipped them on.

'Tell me.'

Ruud kept his narrative simple and to the point. He told Witarsa about Emily Grealish's client list and the calls she'd made to Lieutenant General Fauzi. He decided, however, to leave out Alya's theory that the two of them were having an affair – for now.

Witarsa stopped chewing. The skewer slipped from his hands. 'Let me get this straight. You want to go sniffing around the Ministry of Defence.'

'Hardly sniffing around, more a little chat about the general's relationship with Emily Grealish.'

'*Sialan!* Have you lost your mind?'

'What's the problem?'

Witarsa wondered if Pujasumarta was pulling his leg. 'Did Hamzah put you up to this? How much did he bet you this time? Two minutes? Three minutes before I blew my top?'

Silence.

'My God, you're being serious.'

'I just want to talk to Fauzi. Why are you looking at me like that?'

'*Anda sudah gila!* I should check you into the psych ward in Magelang.'

'Maybe Fauzi has nothing to do with any of this, but I have to be sure. Will you set up the meeting?' said Ruud.

'Me?' he snorted. The question wrong-footed him. 'You've got two days before Natsir takes over and you want me to commit professional suicide?'

'It would be better coming from you.'

A splutter of disbelief. 'You want me to set up the meeting.' He laughed, a little unhinged. 'Bloody hell, you've got some nerve. You know there's a team from Scotland Yard flying in to assist with our investigation, don't you? Not to mention the two officers from the Australian Federal Police already poking about. I don't have time for this shit.'

'Just speak to one of his ministry sycophants.'

'Ruud, listen to me and listen very, very carefully. There are certain individuals – a handful of politicians, businessmen and legislators in the high echelons of this country – who POLRI do not "talk to". These are important people, influential people.' He folded his arms. 'Dangerous people. Men of power. Do you understand?'

'I'm not accusing anybody of anything. At least, not yet. But if we could get hold of Fauzi's mobile phone we'd be able to recover the texts sent to Emily.'

'You're not listening, Ruud.'

'All we have to do is get hold of the texts. Even if he's deleted them from his phone, we'd be able to read them in fragmented form.'

'Pack it in, Pujasumarta.'

Ruud whipped off his Oakley sunglasses. He took a breath. 'OK, I'm going to come straight out with it. I think Fauzi was fucking Emily Grealish. I did some digging. They were in Paris last October when he attended an armaments conference. In December Fauzi spent a week in London talking with munitions suppliers and helicopter manufacturers. Again, Emily was with him. In total they've travelled overseas three times together. The official line is that Emily Grealish went as Fauzi's etiquette and language coach. Yet, curiously, whenever Emily accompanied him on a trip, his wife and children stayed home in Jakarta.'

Witarsa shook his head. 'Enough, Ruud.'

'Her job was to advise him on decorum – from how to wear a pocket handkerchief to the colour of his shoes to the proper way to hold a teacup.'

The commissioner started to walk away.

Ruud grabbed his arm. 'Do you know what Fauzi does for the Ministry of Defence? He's the Director for International Cooperation. You know what that means? It means he negotiates weapon sales. He acts as a middleman. He deals with the Russians, the Chinese, the Pakistanis, the Iranians. Billions of rupiah exchange hands. Hundreds of billions.'

'I said pack it in,' snarled Witarsa.

'I can't,' said Ruud. He was starting to regret approaching Witarsa.

'Look, there's no way I am going to sanction this. He has a three-star military rank.'

'Where does it say I can't question a *Letnan Jenderal*?'

'Seriously, Ruud.'

'Hold on a second, Joyo. I'm talking about a *Letnan Jenderal* who's an adulterer, a cheater. I'm talking about a treacherous man who climbed into bed with a young woman and got her pregnant. A woman who knew all his private black-market dealings, a woman privy to every payoff, every kickback, every backhander and bung paid into his offshore bank accounts. I'm talking about a high-ranking army officer mixed up in corruption and murder.'

'Where are you getting this from? It's pure speculation. You've got no proof, Ruud.'

'I'll get proof.'

Joyo T. Witarsa exhaled loudly. 'And what about Anita Dalloway and Jillian Parker? Did Fauzi sleep with them, too? Was Anita blackmailing Fauzi as well? Was Jillian? Rein in that overheated imagination of yours.'

'Overheated imagination?'

'Seriously, Ruud. Listen to yourself!'

'I'm asking for twenty minutes with him, that's all.'

Witarsa reared up like a shying horse smelling danger. 'Lieutenant General Fauzi has nothing to do with this investigation,' he snorted.

'How can you be so sure?'

'Stop, Ruud. For God's sake, stop. It's too dangerous. What you're saying is too dangerous . . .' His voice died away.

'Jesus, look at you, you're shaking.' Ruud stared at Witarsa. The commissioner avoided his gaze. 'Shit, I don't believe this. Who's put the frighteners on you? What is it you're not telling me?'

Witarsa sucked in a huge gulp of air and lifted his eyes from the floor. 'These people are protected, Ruud. They have dark secrets and they will do anything to hide those secrets.'

'When did you ever duck out of a fight?'

'I'm trying to protect you.'

'You're trying to protect your own skin.'

'Everything I do, I do to safeguard this unit.'

'Oh come on, don't give me the selfless-boss crap.'

'You go after Fauzi with this cavalier attitude of yours and there'll be hell to pay. The top brass will rain down so much shit on you you'll wish you were never born.'

'I want to do my job. I want to know why Emily and Anita and Jillian died.'

'I'm sorry, I can't and won't sanction this.'

Ruud looked at Witarsa for a long while before speaking. 'Well, if you won't authorize it then I'll have to go to Fahruddin. The *Brigadir Jenderal* owes me a favour.'

Witarsa's jowly face paled to the colour of turned milk. 'You're putting yourself at risk. You're putting all of us at risk. You, me and everyone else on the team.'

'I'm attempting to get some answers.'

'Tell that to the angel Azrael when they put a bullet through your head in the dead of night.'

When he said this Ruud felt it: a rib-tightening contraction, a dread. 'Don't be ridiculous.'

'I'm warning you, Ruud.' He paused, allowing his words to sink in. 'Leave Fauzi alone.'

Ruud tipped his chin at Witarsa. 'Thanks for the advice. I'll let you know what Fahruddin says.' He clamped his jaw tight. Something hot burned a hole in his stomach. The thing was, in spite of Witarsa's irascibility, Ruud respected the man. They'd worked together for eight years and Ruud considered him as much a friend as a boss. He trusted him with his life. Defying the old bugger gave him little pleasure.

'So,' said the commissioner, rubbing his face. 'What now?'

'What now? After I talk with Fahruddin I'm bringing Tantar in.'

'Tantar?'

'Imam Gunawan's stooge.'

'You're still going after Gunawan? Despite the reprimand from the Ulema Council?'

'Tantar ran from the scene when I went to question him. His men assaulted Alya.'

'Yes, I read the damage report. She put four men in hospital.'

'Vehicle Crimes is delighted. Two of them are wanted for a car-dealership heist dating back six months.'

'I also gather a round was discharged from your firearm. A warning shot, was it?'

'Something like that. I reported the incident to the on-duty supervisor. The shot was fired because I believed my partner was in serious physical danger at the time.'

'Did you find any evidence linking Tantar to the victims?'

'Nope, not a thing.' He stuck his hands in his pockets and looked away.

Moments later he walked off.

The commissioner, loose-jointed and sprocket-hipped, swayed on his feet. He wanted to grab hold of Ruud and shake sense into him. Instead, head bowed and arms folded, he watched Ruud Pujasumarta go.

He wrinkled his forehead as small droplets of rain pattered down on his face.

The last fingers of sunlight disappeared as the growl and roll of thunder grew nearer.

It hadn't rained since early morning and as it began to come down hard, the streets emptied of pedestrians and the hawkers and peddlers packed up their things.

Witarsa, however, did not move. He stood motionless like a 500-year-old oak, watching Ruud disappear into the distance.

251

The commissioner's heart thumped hard against his chest, like a hammer on a hollow urn. He shuddered as a damp wind blew through him.

Rain rat-a-tatted against his bloodhound cheeks.

The black storm was closing in.

Chapter Twenty-Nine

Thursday.

When Ruud called Fahruddin, it took him only a minute to persuade the police brigadier general to arrange a meeting with Lieutenant General Fauzi.

But now that everything was arranged, Ruud was getting nervous.

He paced back and forth across his office in bare feet. There were files and sheets of A4 all over the floor.

How was he going to play this? Should he be chatty?

Or stern?

Stern. Yes, stern but polite. Polite, stern and professional. No silly jokes.

Ruud retrieved a file from the floor. It was a copy of Emily Grealish's phone records. Getting information out of Fauzi was going to be difficult, nigh on impossible; nevertheless he was determined to get the man talking. He was going to get some answers – by hook or by crook – even at the risk of losing his job.

But people like Fauzi never talked. They were too clever and too canny. They were experts at the art of deflection and diversion. Duplicity and guile were second nature to them. Ruud knew this from experience.

He stared at the call sheet. Two hundred and thirty phone conversations over a six-week period. That worked out at 1.3 calls per day.

What was their relationship? OK, let's say they were sleeping together. A hot and passionate affair. And then he decided to get rid of her. Not get rid of her as in ditch her as a lover, but get rid of her like in *The Sopranos*: shoot her in the back of the head and stick her in the ground New Jersey mob style. But what would be his motive? Was she blackmailing him? Did she discover something about him that could bring him down? Make him a laughing stock? Put him in prison? Had he killed her to keep her from talking? Had he burned her alive to keep her tongue still? What did she know that was so damaging?

Secrets, Ruud; dirty, dark secrets. Don't ever trivialize the potency of a grotty rotten secret. Corruption, sex and greed – the essential triangle, the triple attributes of all hardboiled scandals. Lift the lid and it will explode in your face, whether you like it or not. And the fallout is often incalculable: public uproar, a ruined career, families torn apart, a corporation brought to its knees, politicians exposed, a government destabilized.

Deep waters.

His conjecturing was interrupted when Hartono knocked on the door.

'Yes?'

The door opened and Hartono's head appeared through the gap.

'Time for your appointment with Lieutenant General Fauzi. I received a dispatch from Police Brigadier General Fahruddin. He'll be downstairs in ten minutes and he says you are to follow him in your car.'

'Has Aiboy Ali showed up yet?'

'No. We still haven't heard from him.'

'In that case you're coming with me.'

'I am?' Hartono's face lit up. He could hardly contain his excitement 'The brigadier general travels in a black armoured Land Cruiser with bulletproof windows. Also, guess what? Because the traffic's so bad, we're getting a motorcycle escort.'

Ruud tossed Hartono his car keys. 'Bring the Toyota round the front.'

'Do I need to bring anything?'

'Prepare for the worst.'

'Yes, boss!'

Ruud rubbed his eyes and climbed into his socks. He put on his shoes and tucked in his shirt. 'Right, let's smash this.'

While Ruud got ready to meet Lieutenant General Fauzi, Erica Sneijder was halfway across Central Jakarta nibbling on canapés and sipping sparkling wine from Australia's Piccadilly Valley.

Within a minute of arriving at the embassy, Erica had navigated the small crowd of invitees and latched on to Shane Waters. Ruud had mentioned he was stocky and gruff, with a thick mane of dark hair, and there was nobody more burly in the room than the fellow leaning against the plastic-topped table. He wasn't hard to spot.

'I think the KitKat in my bag's melted.'

'I'm sorry?' Waters looked puzzled.

'Thank heavens for air conditioning and chilled bubbly is all I can say,' she exclaimed, sidling up to the meaty-faced Australian. 'Forty-five minutes in the back of a taxi with no AC, a broken meter and sticky vinyl seats. Good thing I wore long trousers otherwise I'd still be peeling the skin on the back of my legs off the upholstery.' She sipped her champagne.

'That's Jakarta taxis for you,' said the First Secretary.

'*Goede God* above, it's a miracle I made it here. Why is it taxi drivers claim to know all ten thousand street names in Jakarta apart from the one I'm going to?' Imke's aunt extended her hand. 'Erica Sneijder.'

'Yes, yes, of course. I was told you might be attending our little bash. What an honour.' He bowed and gave her palm a hearty shake. 'Shane Waters at your service.'

Oh heavens, thought Erica, as she let go of his hand, he's got callouses as hard as the rinds of last year's Parmesan cheese. Proper strangler's mitts.

Erica waved an arm at the whitewashed space. 'What a triumph. I love the contemporary feel of the room. And is that who I think it is? Dame Edna Everage?' she cooed, referring to the stainless-steel bust of Barry Humphries on the solid teak table. Stooping, Erica gave an ambiguous *hmph!* as she stared Barry straight in the eyes. 'Well, he's got the nose just right, don't you think? Oh, now look at the vibrancy of this painting.' She clutched Waters by the arm, towing him along. 'The colours are like the tulip fields of Voorhout.'

'That's by a young Melbourne artist called Yvette Coppersmith.'

'Is that so? What a charming name. Have you any more bubbly by the way? You'll join me for a top-up, won't you?'

'I don't drink.'

'Mormon?'

'Muslim.'

256

Erica's eyebrows shot up. 'How *interesting*!'

'Funny how everyone reacts that way when I tell them.'

'Did you marry into Islam?'

'No, I converted. I lived in Kuwait for four years, Qatar for three and Istanbul for eighteen months. In the end I guess it just caught up with me.'

'And your wife followed suit?'

'My wife died in Twenty Twelve.'

'Oh, I am sorry. Stupid me putting my foot in it again.'

'That's all right. You weren't to know. Yes, Elsa died of ovarian cancer. We were college sweethearts. Her passing made me re-examine my faith, and I turned to Islam a couple of years after.'

'You say your name is Walters.'

'Waters. Shane Waters.'

'Didn't you have to change your name? To an Islamic one, I mean.'

'Well, yes, but I've managed to . . .' Before he had a chance to complete his sentence, the First Secretary's attention was diverted by the arrival of a VIP from the Jakarta Art Council.

He bustled away.

Erica reattached herself to him but Waters managed to shake her off; the first time to the Ambassador of Japan, the second time to a ceramicist from Borobudur, but she didn't give up.

The room grew fuller.

People mingled in tight little groups.

'Have you tried these delicious cheese straws?' she said, proffering her plate to him.

He grabbed one of the twists with his chunky fingers and chomped into it. 'Nice one, thanks,' he grunted, then walked away.

Unabashed, she stalked him from a distance, watching Waters from the corner of her eye. She listened with feigned interest to H.E. Glenn Beale's welcome speech and engaged in conversation with a British journalist. She clinked glasses with the Dutch Defence Attaché and the US Consular Agent for Bali.

Before she knew it, a whole hour had flown by and it was two o'clock.

Ten minutes later, munching on a mini chocolate and ginger brownie, Erica moved smoothly into Shane Waters' eyeline.

'Help me, Shane,' she mouthed.

Nonchalantly, Shane Waters eased his big body around a quartet of South American diplomats and stood alongside her.

'You look hot and bothered,' he said in a low, raspy voice.

'There's an awful little fellow here,' she breathed, indicating a man with pomaded red hair, 'who wants to paint me nude. Says he can envisage me naked and swinging my bits on a pommel horse. Something about creating the illusion of frozen movement.'

The pint-sized man stood a metre away and was busily examining a Stewart MacFarlane canvas.

'His name's Rodrigo Diaz,' Waters whispered, stifling a grin.

'Is he even an artist?'

'Not really, no. He's attached to the Embassy of Spain. His official position is Advisor to the Head of the Cultural, Tourism and Press Section.'

'Catchy title.'

'Isn't it just? He usually tries to chat up my assistant.'

'Well, you know what they say,' said Erica, eyelashes

fluttering like a Chinese concubine's fan. 'The longer the title the less important the job.'

'Oh, he's actually quite influential. He knows how to climb the diplomatic ladder.'

'The higher a monkey climbs, the more you can see his arse.'

Shane Waters burst out laughing.

'If I didn't know better, I'd say you were flirting with me, Erica Sneijder.'

'Don't be absurd, First Secretary Waters.' She slapped him lightly on the arm. 'I'm well past my sell-by date.' She giggled. 'To tell you the truth, I'm so pleased there's you to talk to. I don't know a soul here – makes me feel like a lemon.'

'I happen to adore lemons,' he said. 'I like to suck the juice from their flesh.'

Ugh! thought Erica.

He made a *shlock, shlock* noise with his tongue, which made Erica think of Hannibal Lecter.

As a waiter went past with a tray of crunchy crab parcels, Erica nabbed one. 'I suppose I ought to mingle a bit.'

'Listen,' said Shane Waters. 'I've got an idea. Do you want to see my mosque?'

'Now, there's a chat-up line to get a girl's heart all aflutter.'

'No, I mean it.' His eyes became narrow slits. 'The Luar Batang Mosque is beautiful, simple but beautiful. We could go now. I'd like to show it to you.'

'What?' Erica hesitated, glaring at him, the crab parcel halfway to her mouth. 'Right now?'

'Yes, right now.'

Warning bells went off in her head.

'Why not? Strike while the iron's hot, I say,' he added.

'Unless you and Rodrigo Diaz have more important things on your mind.'

'How far away is it?'

'Not far. I'll drive.' His teeth twinkled, a saliva-glint of white. 'I can drop you back at your hotel when we're done. Better than taking another dodgy Jakarta taxi, what do you reckon?'

She considered excusing herself and escaping through a bathroom window.

He placed a sports-hardened hand on her arm and squeezed.

Suddenly it was Erica's turn to shake free of Shane Waters. She took a step backwards.

His body drooped. 'Aw, look, if you don't fancy it, never mind,' he said. 'No worries. I shouldn't have been so impulsive. Maybe some other time . . .' He broke off.

'No no no,' she exclaimed, full of renewed pluck. 'It's not like I've got something on the hob or anything. There's no reason for me to rush back.' Her heart began to pound. She braced herself. 'Of course I'll see your mosque. In fact, I'd love to see it.'

'Good onya.' Straightaway, a smile brightened his face. 'Listen, I'll nip out back and get the car. You wait for me at the front entrance. I won't be long.'

He manoeuvred his way through the crowd and vanished with wide-rumped zeal.

'*Goede God* above! What in heaven's name do I do now?' Erica's fluting voice rang out. 'I'm going for a drive with a murder suspect.'

The Japanese Ambassador turned his head round and gave her a funny look.

'Oh, you wouldn't understand.'

Hastily, she brushed the worst of the cheese twirl crumbs off her cotton blouse before fishing her mobile from her bag to call Ruud.

His phone rang and rang and rang.

But nobody picked up.

She left a message: 'Me and my big mouth. I've only gone and talked myself into spending the afternoon with Shane Waters. If you don't hear from me by sundown call out the cavalry.'

The next thing Erica knew, she was outside by the embassy checkpoint, standing alone, waiting for the large black car to swing round, the sleeves of her blouse gently fluttering in the breeze, an exhibition catalogue clutched to her side.

She retrieved from her pocket a tube of lip gloss she'd bought from The Body Shop at Schiphol Airport. Deftly, she applied some colour to her lips.

The black car drew close.

A door swung open. The front passenger door.

She clambered in.

Chapter Thirty

Jakarta was caught in a snarled gridlock.

The traffic lights turned green but the cars in front didn't move.

Lieutenant General Fauzi's home was in Kebayoran Baru, one of Jakarta's most prestigious neighbourhoods.

Even with the motorcycle escort, it took two hours to travel the 15 kms from Central HQ to the tree-lined streets of South Jakarta.

Squinting through the windscreen as the logjam of cars nudged forward, lane-hopping, jostling for position, centimetre by centimetre, Ruud feared he might suffer a frustration-induced aneurism.

By the time he arrived at the imposing fortress on Kebayoran Baru with its scissor-perfect lawns, he'd run out of swearwords.

Boxed in at the guardhouse by a trio of Fauzi's security team, the convoy waited as they checked under the cars for bombs, before clearing the passengers.

The boom gate lifted and the convoy glided past a boastful line of trees.

A peacock strutted around the terraced garden. Four

massive stone cobras spat jets of water into the 25-metre swimming pool.

The cars and motorcycles pulled into the large compound. At the top of the drive Police Brigadier General Fahruddin climbed out of the armoured Land Cruiser and stuck his chin in the air. The gold stars on his uniform epaulettes glinted in the sun. With his peaked cap on, he looked remarkably sangfroid despite the two-hour journey. Ramrod straight, he marched up three flagged steps with his swagger stick thrust under an armpit.

'Now listen up both of you,' he jabbed his swagger stick at Hartono and Ruud. 'Switch off your mobile phones. I can't bear the thought of those blasted things trilling like songbirds every other minute.'

The detectives did as they were told.

'Now you, what's your name again?'

'Werry Hartono, sir.' He snapped erect.

'Wipe that gormless smile off your face; you look like a pug dog on uppers.'

'Yes, sir.'

'And Pujasumarta, tuck your bloody shirt in at the back. Look sharp. That's better. Right, are we ready? Splendid.'

'How do you want to do this?' asked Ruud.

'I'll take the lead and do the introductions, yes? After that I'll hand over to you, Pujasumarta. But keep your questions respectful. Remember we're dealing with a former member of the MPR. No mention of coming down to the station and taking DNA swabs and whatnot. Three words: civil, courteous, gracious. And you, Hartono, for goodness sake keep your mouth shut. A little stupidity can stretch a long way.'

Nettled, Werry Hartono pursed his lips and nodded sullenly. He scratched the ground with a shoe.

A clattering of boots made them look to the front door.

Two muscular bodyguards in black safari suits appeared. They stepped quickly to one side, allowing Lieutenant General Fauzi to emerge from the house with a raised palm. 'Hello!' he cried.

'Salam, my old friend. Peace be upon you,' said Fahruddin with a slight bow of the head.

'Salam, *Brigadir Jenderal Polisi* Fahruddin. *Selamat datang.* Welcome.'

Fauzi greeted each man with a warm handshake. He was soft-palmed, his nails manicured and sheeny. He wore a silk batik shirt and beige cotton trousers. 'Gentlemen, I take it you are not here to talk politics.'

'Perhaps another time, my friend,' said Fahruddin.

'Please, this way.'

They entered the house and stepped into the cool. Ruud took off his sunglasses. Despite it being mid-afternoon, the ceiling lights in the cavernous hall shone so bright they stung his eyes.

'No need to remove your shoes. We take a Western approach to footwear hygiene.'

Hartono had already shod one of his loafers, so he hastily slipped it back on.

'My wife,' said the lieutenant general.

Lestari Fauzi, lightly perfumed, received them with a soft smile. '*Selamat datang ke rumah saya,*' she said with a gently rolled R. A wisp of a voice. 'Come in, come in. This is my Noah and this is my daughter Harum.' Lestari Fauzi was a short lady with a round, friendly face. There were several moles and beauty spots on her chin – Indonesians like to call them *tahi lalat*, literally translated as fly poo.

She stood with her children – both in their twenties – at her elbow. 'Harum is completing her final year at the Bandung Institute of Technology. Noah, my eldest, is a captain with the Second Marine Cavalry Regiment.'

'We've met before,' Ruud reminded Noah.

'Come to poke around, have you *inspektur*?' He clamped his teeth around the word '*inspektur*'.

'I'm just doing my job, Captain.'

Noah Fauzi sniffed the air and quickly excused himself, saying he had to return to the naval base. Harum followed him out.

'Fine young people,' said Fahruddin.

'Do your children live with you, madam?' asked Ruud.

'Harum lives on campus but tries to be here whenever she can.' She fluttered her paraffin-manicured nails. 'Noah has a one-bedroom apartment to himself in Kemang for the weekends.'

'Please, come,' Lieutenant General Fauzi reiterated with a sweep of his arm. 'Let's move out of the hallway. Our voices echo in here.' He led them through a set of wide double doors and into a freezing-cold drawing room with lustre-tile copper wallpaper. The salon was a temple to nineties Versace baroque and high-end kitsch. It was large, too, the size of a petrol station forecourt, and with about as much charm.

'Do not hesitate to make yourselves comfortable,' said Lestari Fauzi, settling on an L-shaped settee with stiff cushions.

'My wife will join us, if you don't mind. I trust that is acceptable.'

Fahruddin sat in a high-backed leather armchair, crossing

his long legs at the knee, while Hartono parked himself on a lilac-upholstered Ottoman by the window with his notebook on his lap. Ruud remained standing, purposely deciding not to sit, and hoping height would give his questions added authority, making him appear more in control.

The military man passed around a humidor filled with Indonesian cigars.

'No, thank you,' said Ruud.

Hartono declined as well.

The police brigadier general chose a Tambo short corona, which he pierced with a punch cutter and lit with a Dupont Xtend.

Lieutenant General Fauzi selected a Grand Robusto.

Standing in the fog of Fahruddin and Fauzi's smoke, Ruud waited, listening to the gentle click of a carriage clock, as both men drew enthusiastically on their cigars. The fumes irritated his lungs.

'Emily Grealish,' Ruud said eventually.

'What a mess,' growled Fauzi. 'What an appalling tragedy.'

'Tell me how you got to know her.'

'May I first say that I only agreed to see you out of my great respect for Ms Grealish. Ordinarily, I would not involve myself in such things.' He sighed. 'Al-Fatihah. Heaven is her place now.'

A housemaid entered. She carried a pot of tea with gold-trimmed cups and saucers on a pewter tray. She set the tray down, poured out the tea and handed each guest a cup.

Ruud rested his Oakley sunglasses on a silver salver on top of a marble console table.

The lieutenant general waited for the housemaid to leave. When the door eased shut he said, 'I first met Ms Grealish two years ago.'

'How well did you know her?' said Ruud.

'Not terribly well.'

Lestari Fauzi got up from the L-shaped settee and crossed to the far window. She fumbled with her shirtsleeve, pulling on it.

'You kept her company, Elite Protocol Management, on a retainer. Is that correct?'

'Yes,' said the lieutenant general.

'How much did you pay her annually?'

'You will have to ask Prem, he's the member of staff who settles the bills.'

'Rumour has it she accompanied you on several trips to London and Paris.'

'In a professional capacity,' Lestari Fauzi said from the far window. She was standing there, looking out into the lawns, at the soft grey sky. 'Ms Grealish went as an advisor.' The window glass was misty with condensation.

'An advisor?'

'In this business,' said Fauzi, smiling, squinting through cigar smoke, 'first impressions matter. When one meets senior ministers from the British Ministry of Defence I cannot dress like a farmer and eat like a *kampung* boy. What's the saying in London? No brown in town. This makes me laugh.'

'Professional capacity aside, we have it on good authority that she contacted you at odd hours, non-business hours, often after midnight. What did you and Ms Grealish speak about?'

'I am sorry, I have no recollection of such conversations.'

'Were they personal matters?'

Uncertainty crept into the general's smile. He placed his

cigar on the lip of a glass ashtray. 'As I say, I have no recollection.'

'Perhaps if I could have your mobile phone we could clear this up. I promise to return it within two days.'

'We would like to take it for assessment,' said Hartono, sitting with his knees together.

'I am sorry, that's simply not going to happen.'

'But if you have nothing to hide . . .'

'There are matters of national importance on my phone. Much of which is classified.'

Fahruddin, alive to what was about to unfold, cleared his throat in warning. His jaw hardened.

Ruud backed off. Nearby, Hartono wrote in his notebook.

The room was so fiercely air-conditioned that when Ruud got round to sipping his tea it was lukewarm. He placed the cup and saucer down next to his shades on the marble console table.

'When was the last time you saw Emily Grealish, sir?' asked Hartono, wiping his clammy hands on his knees.

'It would have been three weeks ago. I don't have any business trips planned so we had little need to discuss anything face to face.'

'But you spoke on the phone,' said Ruud. 'Tell us how she sounded.'

'She sounded her usual self. Polite, polished, confident.'

'What did you talk about?'

'I cannot recall.'

'Did she mention anything about someone following her? Threatening her?'

'No. Nothing like that was ever discussed. She was normal. Businesslike and normal.'

'But you can't recall anything you talked about?'

'I've already said as much. Look, we seem to be going round in circles here.'

On Fauzi's right wrist, Ruud saw a Breitling with a large face, an onyx bangle and several silver bracelets. The fingers of the same hand were similarly weighed down with jade and emerald-studded rings. The left hand, however, was completely bare of jewellery.

It dawned on Ruud that Fauzi, from force of habit and military training, would have kept his shooting hand free of bling – it made drawing a gun or holding a dagger less burdensome.

'Are you right- or left-handed?' asked Ruud.

Fahruddin's iron-jawed expression hardened further.

Fauzi cocked an eyebrow. 'Why should you ask that?'

Measured. 'I have reason to suspect the killer is left-handed.'

Fauzi's laugh was savage, high and artificial. His eyes narrowed, he turned back to his cigar. 'You are, it would seem, a many-sided coin, *Inspektur* Pujasumarta.'

'Well, are you? Left-handed, I mean.'

'I am, how–do–you–say, ambidextrous.'

'How many cars do you have in the compound?'

'Three. A Range Rover, an Audi TT and a Mercedes.'

'Do you ever drive them yourself, without a chauffeur?'

'Yes, he does occasionally,' replied Mrs Fauzi on her husband's behalf.

He clamped eyes on his wife.

'Which car do you take and where do you go?' said Ruud.

'Usually the TT,' replied the lieutenant general. 'I cut her loose on the Jakarta–Tangeran.'

'What about the Mercedes?'

'I drive it once in a while.'

Ruud waited. 'Anything else you'd like to tell me?'

'There is little to tell.'

'Where were you between 8 p.m. on Monday and 5 a.m. Tuesday?'

Muscle tension along his jaw. 'I was here at home with my wife.'

'Can anyone else corroborate this?'

'The housemaid, Suli, the young lady who served us tea, can vouch for me. She served me a late supper of chicken with lime leaves on Monday.'

'Anita Dalloway and Jillian Parker – are these names familiar to you?'

'They are familiar to me.'

'How so?'

'My dear detective, I read the national newspapers every morning, just like any regular person.'

'I'd like to add,' said Fahruddin, 'that when the other murders were committed, Lieutenant General Fauzi was at his country house in Cirebon, some two hundred kilometres away.'

'That's all very well, sir, but if I may ask just one or two more questions. I'd like to eliminate the lieutenant general from our enquiries.'

'Please proceed, first *inspektur*, I am more than happy to cooperate.'

'Have you ever met Anita Dalloway or Jillian Parker?'

'No, never.' He puffed on his cigar.

'Did you have connections with either?'

'No.'

'Did Emily Grealish ever mention their names in passing?'

'No.'

'And are you aware that Emily, Jillian and Anita were all killed in a particular way?'

'Yes, the papers said they were all set alight. That this is a series of gruesome hate crimes.'

'They could be hate crimes, lieutenant general, but it's possible they're nothing of the sort.'

'But the message placed in front of the bodies ... the Surah An-Nisa.'

'Put there to distract us.'

'Distract us? Distract us from what?'

'You see, what the newspapers failed to report was that each woman had a part of her insides taken out.'

'What on earth are you talking about?'

'They were mutilated.'

Lestari Fauzi suppressed a gasp. 'Emily was mutilated?'

'Yes, madam, she had her womb removed,' said Ruud.

Fauzi looked across to his wife.

'Why? Why take her womb?' A hidden terror froze her features.

Ruud also turned to look at Lestari Fauzi with an enquiring glance. 'Perhaps he wanted her reproductive organs as a keepsake.' He paused. 'Or possibly each and every one of these murdered women was—'

'Pregnant,' said Lestari Fauzi, unaware that everyone was watching her. The word came out flat and low and hard. The corners of her mouth drew in. 'They were killed because they were with child.'

'It's a theory we are working on.'

'Gentlemen,' the general's wife breathed. 'If you will pardon me. I am feeling rather faint.' A blue vein throbbed on her neck.

Brigadier General Fahruddin slapped his thighs sharply. 'Time to go, Pujasumarta. We've outstayed our welcome.'

271

Lieutenant General Fauzi escorted the men from the living room. Outside, as they emerged into the afternoon glare and waited for the cars to be brought around, Fahruddin apologized to him. 'I hope we did not upset your wife.'

'No, please do not burden yourself. She has a sensitive temperament. I am glad she has gone to rest her head.'

The lieutenant general was about to shake Ruud by the hand when Ruud exclaimed, 'Oh hell, I've forgotten my sunglasses.'

'Allow me to send one of my men.'

'No,' said Ruud rushing back indoors. 'I won't be a minute.'

Chapter Thirty-One

The sun broke through the clouds. To the west, towards Bekasi, the pale grey sky was stirred through with charcoal. More rain was on the way.

Imke fastened the leash to Kiki's collar and looked up to see a smoke rope in the sky made by a passing jumbo jet.

As they crossed the road, an *ojak* taxi raced past. Imke noticed that the elderly woman passenger riding pillion was wearing a shower cap to keep the dust and rain out of her hair.

Imke smiled to herself. The quirkiness of Jakarta's commuters usually had that effect on her. The chug of a distant engine made her glance to her left.

It was the LPG man. 'Gas, gas, *elpiji*, gas!' cried the driver of the microvan. The orange cylinders rattled and clanked together noisily in the back of the open-bedded Daihatsu.

Alya, Imke and Kiki snuck under the yellow *garis polisi* tape surrounding the outer edges of the JK Café.

In the background, three Sabhara policemen patrolled the perimeter, their eyes peeled for a black German-manufactured sedan. Imke also took in the spotters on the Morrisey Hotel's roof two streets away.

The women made a quick assessment of the level ground and decided to do a preliminary inspection of the site.

'Where should we start?' said Alya in English.

Imke pointed with her thumb. 'Over there.'

At the rear of the building the ground was littered with broken bits of tile and slate and jute fibre.

Imke clicked her fingers twice. Kiki, with an alert expression on her face, waited for instructions.

Bending low, Imke whispered something and offered an unlaundered shirt belonging to Anita Dalloway. Tail rigid with purpose, Kiki stuck her snout into the clothing and quickly worked out what was required of her.

'What is she looking for specifically?' asked Alya.

'We call it scarf. Dried skin particles and blood. Ready, Kiki? Find!' cried Imke. Kiki sprang away at once, dashing right and left. First she pressed her nose to a coiled length of Fish tape, then into a mound of gravel and sand before venturing forward. She waded amongst scraggy strips of knotted weed and made her body small to squirm through a tight hole in the foundation wall. She shoved her head and front legs in the hole, snorted, sniffled a bit and hastily back-pedalled.

Imke spoke into her mobile, leaving a message for Aunty Erica, who wasn't picking up.

'Is that German?' asked Alya.

Imke looked up briefly before returning to her phone. 'Dutch.'

'You are from Holland?'

They followed Kiki as she inspected some wooden pallets stacked against one another.

'Yes,' Imke replied in Bahasa. 'My parents are from there. They live in Amsterdam.'

'You speak very good Bahasa Indonesia.'

'I was born in Jakarta. I picked it up as a kid.'

'Your mother and father are still here?'

'No, in Holland.'

'You must miss them.'

Imke could not pretend that she didn't miss Amsterdam, her mother especially.

Alya said, 'What did your father do here?'

'He ran coffee estates in South Sulawesi.'

'My ayah is a cloth merchant. He and my mother live in Yogyakarta.'

They made a slow, careful circuit of the property, following Kiki as she worked methodically, moving in semicircles, inspecting the ground, testing every centimetre with her nose.

'I regret not learning more languages when I was younger,' said Alya. 'That and African drumming. I would have loved to play the *djembe*. I watched a performance once at the Bandung Cultural Festival. I was riveted.

'I wish I'd studied French or Mandarin,' Alya continued, 'but I concentrated on science and sports instead. Swimming was my main activity. I learned to swim because I realized it's the one sport in which you can save someone's life.'

'Saving lives. I'm guessing that's why you joined the police force? Why did you leave Commercial Crimes?'

'Nobody took me seriously there. All the senior male officers treated me like a little sister with nothing to say,' she huffed. 'I could have worn a sandwich board and rung a bell and still nobody would have listened to my opinions.'

'You must have complained.'

'I did eventually. But then they just threw my words back at me.'

'So what's it like working for Ruud?'

The two women were now conversing in Bahasa.

'First *Inspektur* Pujasumarta is very capable and organized.'

'Organized? That's a new one.'

'But he is a little behind the times when it comes to technology.'

'More than a little. He's as tech-savvy as a cave dweller. The man has a Facebook page with no content and mistakes a selfie stick for a golf club.'

Alya smiled. 'And I find Commissioner Witarsa fair-minded. He is nurturing, and the type of leader who doesn't care about your background, sex or race. What matters to him is how you do your job.'

'He has a rotten temper, though.'

'Oh, he can be testy but that's nothing. My father is like that. A little man who likes to slam doors.'

'What about the others, Hartono for instance?'

'*Meh*, he simply wants to please.'

'And Hamzah? What's he like as a colleague?'

Alya faltered. 'Officer Hamka Hamzah has some strong points, but he can be a bit . . . how do you say . . .'

'Uncultured,' Imke said in English.

'Yes. In Indonesia we call it *kamseupay*.'

Imke laughed. 'Yes, I know *kamseupay*. Like a country bumpkin.'

'His clothes are always rumpled, in complete disarray.'

'Does he even own a mirror?'

'Probably not. And he belches a lot in my presence. I wonder sometimes if he does it to annoy me.'

'I think he's allergic to peppercorns.'

'He does it very close to my ear.'

Imke looked at her watch. She wondered if she had time after this to pop into Giant to pick up some milk.

'Men, eh?' said Alya.

'Yep, it's not easy working in a male-dominated profession.'

'Strong, competent women like us will always be under-estimated in the workplace.'

'I think we're much more than competent.'

Alya smiled again. 'I suppose we are.'

'Men, *hè*? Can you imagine what they'd say if we started burping and scratching our bums in front of them?'

One of the Sabhara cops who'd been eavesdropping on their conversation shouted to his colleagues, 'We'd say *isep kontol gue*.' He burst out laughing.

'You shut your bloody mouth, *asu*!'

'What did he say?' asked Imke.

'It's street slang,' said Alya, reverting to English. 'It means please suck my dick.'

Imke yelled back. 'A thousand cocks in your arse!'

'Bloody bonehead. *Tolol.*' Alya was laughing. 'You see? No respect.'

'You obviously like your job.'

'I do, but it's not easy being a woman in the force. I have to mind the way I dress and the way I speak. It is essential I do not appear slovenly. For a man it is different. Officer Hamka Hamzah, for example, can turn up for duty looking like he slept in a birdcage. Me? I cannot. My uniform must be perfect. I have to appear neat, clean and professional, yet at the same time reassuringly feminine. And we are rarely asked for an opinion. The top brass do not like it when we call too much attention to ourselves. It takes a long while for us to move up in rank.'

'The brass ceiling. Is that why there are so few women in the police force?' Imke crossed her arms.

'We have certain obstacles.'

'Oh?'

'Let me tell you the real reason why recruitment is so low. Women are still marginalized and belittled. Debased at the first hurdle. You want to know what they did before I was accepted into the police force? They gave me a virginity test.'

'What?'

'Every female applicant has to present herself before a police recruitment officer and a police doctor. It is *wajib*, compulsory. They ask a few questions and then perform the test.'

'I don't understand.'

Alya gave a slow, bitter laugh. 'This is sure to shock you, I think. When women are recruited by the police force we first have to be examined by a doctor. It's called the 'two-finger' test.'

'I don't follow.'

'During the physical examination the doctor sticks two fingers up your vagina to see if you're a virgin. It's painful, I can tell you.' She widened her eyes. 'A couple of girls I was with fainted.'

'But that's . . . that's appalling.'

Alya's cheeks turned a deep plum colour. 'Non-discrimination? Equality? Ha! It's all a sham.'

Disgusted, Imke told her to go on.

'At first, we strip down to our undergarments and the doctors look at our teeth, our eyes, our arms, legs and chest. Then we're told to enter a separate room and lie on a bed. A female doctor carries out the procedure to see whether our hymens are intact.'

'I can't believe they do that. It's humiliating. A violation of your dignity. Why? Why do they do it?'

Alya met Imke's avid stare. 'To uphold the moral integrity of the police force.'

'That's crazy.'

'They must think we're all prostitutes. It's all really very odd. They require us to be virtuous and strong women, but up until two years ago we weren't allowed to wear the hijab in the force.'

'I'm so sorry, Alya. I had no idea.'

'I was angry for a time, but I let it go. I wanted to become a policewoman and I became a policewoman.' She laughed again. 'They erected a statue to Kartini as a symbol of women's emancipation in Indonesia, and yet little ever changes.'

They took a break from circling the property to inspect the portable cement mixer that lay stranded on its side. Vines twisted up the towing tongue and the drum was mashed white with dollops of bird shit.

Kiki was struggling. Every few minutes she'd stop and sneeze. 'We may have to call it a day,' said Imke. 'The chemicals and solvents from the construction are confusing her. She can't get a scent.'

'I agree. It's getting too hot anyway. Look, across the road, it's the *es potong* man pushing his trolley. Let's get one to cool us down. D'you want chocolate or strawberry?'

Just then Imke's phone rang.

The traffic had eased and for once cars and buses flowed freely through the streets surrounding Medan Merdeka. Ruud whistled as he drove, steering with his wrists. 'Well, Hartono, I think we smashed that meeting, don't you?'

'We learned nothing.'

'Oh, I'm not so sure.'

'Fahruddin hates me.'

Ruud shoved a CD into the car stereo. 'He doesn't hate you. I thought you did well back there.'

'*Ai*, you piss on my head and tell me it's raining. He called me gormless.'

'No, he said you were sporting a gormless smile. There's a subtle difference.'

'I don't think I'm in line for a promotion, am I?'

Ruud lip-synched a Prince song from the 1980s.

Hartono waited for '1999' to come to an end. 'Perhaps I should have worn darker trousers. People always take me more seriously when I wear dark trousers.'

'What did you think of Mrs Fauzi?' Ruud turned right at Monas. He bounced in his seat and bobbed his head to 'Little Red Corvette'.

'She uses too much whitening cream.'

'Apart from that.'

'Hard to tell, sir.'

'I thought she was nice enough, in a fragile, haunted sort of way.'

'Don't let her nice manners fool you. I hear she has a tongue that can shred the skin off a durian.'

'Do you think the wife suspects the husband?'

'Possibly.'

'Is she protecting him?'

'Probably.'

'She seemed pretty upset when I mentioned that the victims had had their insides removed.'

They drove slowly in companionable silence for several minutes.

A fluorescent *ojek* cut into their lane. A peddler selling magazines tapped his fingers on their windscreen.

'Maybe one of his bodyguards did it,' said Ruud eventually.

'Did you see the size of the muscle man with the crew cut?' marvelled Hartono.

'I wonder where the goons live. Do you think they sleep in the house?'

'What a house! Marble and gold everywhere. Every corner garish and brash. How did he get to be like that, so *tajir*, so filthy rich? Even her eyeshadow was gold.'

Ruud laughed. For the first time in ages his natural bubbly self-confidence came fizzing to the surface. 'How indeed. From stealing and snatching.'

'Swindling and skimming.'

'That's what happens when you give the foxes the keys to the henhouse.'

'There's something wrong with that family.'

'You think?'

'It's like badness and corruption have permeated their bones and sunk into them like toxic dye. These are deep waters, Watson, deep waters.'

'No shit, Sherlock.'

Hartono stiffened and glared at Ruud with disdain. 'I fail to see how Benedict Cumberbatch's toilet habits fit into this.'

'Relax, Hartono. It's a joke.'

'What are you so happy about anyway?' asked Hartono. 'Our case is a mess. You have no witnesses, hardly any leads. Every avenue of inquiry turns out to be a dead end. Normally you'd be fuming.'

Ruud removed his Oakleys and flung them on Hartono's lap.

'Remember when I went back inside the house to get these? Well, when I was in the living room I also helped myself to something else.'

'*Ya ampun!* Not the silver teaspoons.'

'No, not the silver spoons, Werry. This.'

He showed Hartono a plain plastic evidence bag.

'A cigar?'

'Not just a cigar. It's Lieutenant General Fauzi's cigar, chock-full of his DNA.'

'You stole it!'

'Steal is such a derogatory word. No, I didn't steal it. I *liberated* it.'

'You're as bad as Fauzi.' Hartono went white. 'He'll know it was you.'

'And what if he does?'

'He'll tell Fahruddin.'

'No, he won't.'

'Even so, you can't use the cigar as evidence.'

'I don't intend to. I simply want to see if his DNA matches the DNA we found on Anita Dalloway's Alice band.' He shoved the bag in the glove compartment.

As they passed the National Monument, the tall marble obelisk cast its long shadow across the road. Ruud turned the car into a side street, and they spent the next five minutes in complete silence.

Determined to reply to Hartono's unspoken questions Ruud said, 'Look, we've hit a wall with Shane Waters, Tantar's done a runner and we're not allowed to bring in Fauzi for questioning. I need answers.'

'This sort of shady stuff is not in the Semarang Police Academy handbook.'

'Nope. It's not.'

The young detective kissed his pinky ring. 'I will turn a blind eye to it.'

'You do that.'

'I will.'

'You're a regular Stevie Wonder.'

'I don't know who that is,' muttered Hartono.

'That figures.' Ruud sighed. 'Anyway, now we've got that out of the way, tell me what's happening with Erica Sneijder?'

Hartono tapped something into his mobile phone. Moments later it pinged. 'The squad car stationed outside the Australian Embassy hasn't seen her leave yet.'

Ruud glanced at his watch. 'Four o'clock. Long party. What about Alya? Have you checked in with her?'

'Ten minutes ago.'

'What's the status?'

'So far everything is as it ought to be at the JK Café.'

Ruud fiddled with the police radio gear so that the display appeared on the dashboard.

'Werry, see if you can get this linked to Central Control and give Imke a call on your mobile, will you?'

'What's the matter with your own phone?'

'Battery's dead.'

Hartono dialled and passed him the phone. 'Hi, it's me. How are things? Yep. That's good. OK. Keep your wits about you. Promise? OK. You too.'

Ruud handed back the phone.

'Listen, Hartono, I'm going to make a quick pit stop. Are you peckish? Fancy a snack?'

'No, but I take my coffee extra sweet.'

Ruud drove along a narrow road marked by several temporary food stalls and vendors in rush hats. He swung the car onto the pavement and yanked the handbrake. 'You want to wait in the car?'

'No problem.'

Ruud lowered the front windows and killed the engine. Warm air displaced air-conditioned cool. The smell of bus exhaust rolled in.

They were at the corner of Jalan Kebon Sirih and Jalan Jaksa. The sun was struggling to break through the clouds.

Hartono's phone rang as Ruud climbed out.

Giant billboards of local pop stars smiled down on Ruud as he crossed the road to buy a paper cone of peanuts from a street vendor.

Five minutes later Ruud returned with coffee, peanuts and three portions of *nasi goreng* folded in greaseproof paper.

Hartono was sending a text, typing frantically with his thumbs. 'I got a call from the IT boys,' he said, helping himself to coffee and fried rice. 'They found something on YouTube concerning Shane Waters.'

'Dig in while it's hot.'

'They came across a four-minute clip of Shane Waters speaking at a gathering of reformists in a *kampung* town hall last November.' Hartono tucked a paper plate between his thighs and unravelled the parcel. 'My guess is the meeting was meant to be a closed forum but it appears Waters was filmed without his consent. There's secretly filmed footage of him speaking out against the Catholic Church and denouncing atheists. The images are a bit hazy but it's definitely him. He also talks about social segregation and his journey to discovering Islam.'

Ruud opened out the greaseproof paper, which was dark with oil. It left a stain on Ruud's trousers. 'He's Muslim?'

Chewing. 'That's what he says in the video. Here, take a look. I downloaded it onto my phone.'

Hartono propped the phone against the windscreen and pressed the white arrow on the thumbnail. They watched the clip and ate the *nasi goreng* off their laps with their fingers. The shaky recording showed a stout dark-haired man with a peculiar brightness in his eyes standing at a lectern, his face florid and sweaty from the overhead lights. Ruud recognized the First Secretary's gruff voice immediately. He spoke calmly but assertively against the Pope, the Holy See, the international Jewish conspiracy, and America's right-wing extreme Christians. He also voiced his support for Palestinian nationalism. Occasionally the image misted and grew fuzzy; however, there was no doubt that the man doing the talking was Shane Waters. After a while the camera panned round, revealing an audience of about twenty men sitting abreast, all dressed in white cloaks and skullcaps.

'So Waters is antipapal and an anti-Semite,' said Ruud, steam rising from his coffee. 'Not ideal diplomatic credentials, are they?'

'Still, that doesn't make him our killer.'

The video lasted another sixty seconds. As soon as they finished watching, Ruud said, 'Do you think it's genuine?'

'It looks and sounds genuine. The picture's too blurry most of the time to see his lips moving, but I don't think it's been doctored.'

'We'd better get an update on Erica Sneijder. If she's still at the Australian Embassy we should get her out of there.' Ruud took a sip of coffee from a styrofoam cup. 'Any news from Sabhara? They're meant to have eyes on her.'

By now, Hartono was into his second helping of fried rice. 'I'll get onto it in a minute.'

'I thought you said you weren't hungry,' said Ruud.

'My mother said never to turn down a free meal.'

Ruud glanced at his watch again. Four fifteen.

Stuffed full of *nasi goreng*, Hartono sucked the *sambal* off his thumb and licked his lips. His chin was shiny with grease.

Ruud wiped his hands with a tissue.

'D'you want chocolate or strawberry?' Alya repeated.

Imke held up a finger. 'Yes, I promise. Speak soon. Love you.' Imke rang off and replaced the phone in her pocket. 'Strawberry, please. That was Ruud.'

Alya strode off to get an ice lolly, Imke following in her wake. About ten metres from the *es potong* man, a funny feeling made Alya stop short. Her radar had picked up on something. It was the sensation of being watched. She thrust out a warning arm, barring Imke's progress. '*Berhenti.*'

'What's the matter?'

'Quiet.' Alya's eyes scanned up and down the street. Something was very wrong. Every fibre in her body was jangling. She felt herself grow cold. 'Go back and stand behind the police tape.'

'What's going on?'

'He's here.'

'Where?'

'*Sshh.* Don't move.'

Her eyes darted about. And then she spotted it. A car. Silver body, dark against the sun. 'Over there, do you see it? Across the road, sixty metres away, under the awning of the mechanic shop.'

Imke shielded her eyes against the glare. Alya, too,

screened her face from the late afternoon sun, her raised arm casting long shadows.

The silver car was motionless. Its blackened windows impenetrable.

'What are you talking about?' said Imke. 'We're looking for a black Mercedes.'

A little to Imke's left a group of small children were play-ing with a shuttlecock, alternating between laughing and shrieking, reeling in and out of her field of vision.

Slowly and deliberately Alya unclipped the firearm from her holster. 'Wait!' said Imke, looking about for the Sabhara cops who were nowhere in sight. 'We have to call for backup. There are bystanders.'

'Let go of my wrist.' Imke did as she was told. 'Stand over there and secure the dog to the fence,' Alya ordered, with-out taking her eyes off the car. She took a step forward.

Suddenly, in the noisy, traffic-laden city, all Imke could hear were her soft retreating footfalls and the sound of her own shallow breathing.

Nerves on high alert, Imke sunk to her haunches and held Kiki to her chest.

Alya levelled the double-action revolver. She took another step forward. Concentration locked. She cocked her head to one side as if gauging the driver's intentions. Was the engine idling? She couldn't tell for sure, but it seemed as though the engine wasn't running, and for a moment she imagined making out the car's metal exhaust system ticking and click-ing as it cooled.

Fifty-five metres away now.

Alya's progress was like a hunter's. Steady. Stealth-like. But unlike a hunter she did not seek cover. She tracked her target out in the open. Confronting it head-on. The Maasai warrior challenging the rogue elephant. She could almost hear the African drumming, the sounds of the *djembe* in her head.

Her breathing tightened.

Carefully, with her left hand. she freed her portable walkie-talkie from her side and brought it to her mouth.

But then suddenly, as if picking up her scent, the vehicle's 2-litre engine rocked awake, purring very lightly.

Imke felt the skin on the back of her neck prickle.

A crackle of static. 'Ten-seventeen, I have a visual,' said Alya, pressing the push-to-talk button. 'Silver Subaru WRX. Stand by. Approaching on foot.'

Fifty metres away. Firearm raised, the *ajun inspektur* called out to the driver. 'You are to exit the vehicle. Right now!'

Another step. Arms fully extended. Shoulders forward. Feet planted a hip's width apart. 'Exit the vehicle now!' she commanded. But her words were drowned by the squeal of front and rear tyres kicking and spinning.

The car accelerated fast.

All 268 horsepower and 258 pounds per foot of torque.

Bucking, throwing up dust, it charged like a bull from its enclosure.

Imke sprang up. 'Move, Alya!'

But Alya did not move. She stood rooted in the middle of the road with her .38 Special held steady. A female Dirty Harry sans the .44 Magnum. She fired once. Her upper body recoiled. She fired again. The car windscreen spiderwebbed just as the front bumper and grille slammed into her legs and knee joints, throwing her thighs on to the bonnet. Her hips and torso rotated. Limbs catapulted. Her head smashed into the cracked windscreen.

THE BURNINGS

A mist of red sprayed up as her beige hijab ripped away. Over a thousand kilograms of aluminium and steel tore the skin from her face, separating her jaw from her skull. The base of her spine hit the roof.

Snapping her like glass.

Chapter Thirty-Two

The dashboard radio squawked, 'OFFICER DOWN! OFFICER DOWN! Shots fired!'

A different voice on the radio, calmer, more authoritative, said, 'Control to all units. Eleven ninety-nine. Officer needs help. Four eighty in progress. Location – corner of Gg. eight and Sirih Timur Dalam. Requesting Korlantas and Tactical Firearms.

Ruud: 'That's where Imke and Alya are!'

'Suspect is driving a silver Subaru WRX, heading north towards Kebon Sirih.'

'Battle stations!' cried Hartono, buckling up and chucking his coffee cup out the window.

'Which way?'

'Down here. Two blocks.'

Ruud stepped on the gas, yanking the steering wheel to full left lock. The tyres squealed and threw up a pillar of dust as the car screamed out onto the main road.

Out of the corner of his eye Ruud saw a bus coming. There was a loud, deep blast of horn as the bus thundered past, ripping off the Toyota's side mirror, then braking violently, forcing its standing passengers off their feet.

'There he is!' Hartono shouted.

Up ahead, the silver Subaru wove in and out of the traffic 100 metres in front. There were several vehicles between them.

Hartono reached his hand out the window and fastened the magnetic blue light. Lights flashing, he turned on the siren.

Ruud pushed the Toyota hard, picked up speed, skidded sharply left and then right, before straightening up on the outside lane.

A taxi slowed down in front. Red tail-lights flashed. The Toyota's nose rammed the taxi out of the way with a screech of metal on metal.

Hartono keyed the hand mike. 'Unit *Kuda Zebra* Sixty-three giving chase along Wahid Hasyim, heading north toward Menteng Raya.'

A voice crackled a reply on the police scanner.

The Subaru mounted the pavement, scattering pedestrians, upending carts and trolleys. Men, women and children dived out of the way. A teenager on a Suzuki 50 cc moped was knocked sprawling.

Ruud followed in pursuit, tearing along the footway and narrowly avoiding colliding with the moped's bumblebee engine.

'Slow down!' howled Hartono. 'You're going to kill someone!'

Ruud ignored him. His fingers clasped the steering wheel tightly, his eyes locked on the chaotic activity ahead, his left palm pressed down on the horn. He sliced past people who didn't know which way to run. Voices cried out. Those that didn't crash into one another either stood motionless or crouched low in fear.

'Get out of the fucking way!' Ruud yelled. A cluster of school kids outside the Gedung Sindo Building jumped back in unison.

Paper bags, cans and tangles of trash flew up into their path. A plastic stool went soaring. An old man's walking stick cartwheeled away.

Hartono twisted round to retrieve something from under his seat, and emerged with a Remington 870 pump-action shotgun. He saw the look of surprise on Ruud's face.

'What the fuck is that?'

'Express Synthetic Tactical. I came prepared. I borrowed it from a friend who's with the Mobile Brigade Corps. He wants it back by Saturday.'

'What's it doing in my car?'

'You said prepare for the worst.'

'Is it loaded?'

'Six in the magazine and one in the chamber.'

He pressed the 12-gauge shotgun into his shoulder, at the same time shoving a box of 3-inch shells into his hip pocket.

Hartono unbuckled his seat belt and stuck his head and half his body out the passenger window, his shoulders and arms dangling.

The wind whipped up his hair, buffeting the young detective. He swivelled the barrel of the shotgun to his left.

'I'll aim for the wheels!'

'Aim for the guy's fucking head!'

'We're not meant to use excessive force when arresting a suspect.'

'Fuck excessive force! Take him out!'

Fifteen metres ahead, the Subaru smacked into a parked bicycle. Hartono ducked back inside.

The bicycle flew up and the handlebars smashed into Ruud's windscreen, splintering the glass.

'I can't see!' Ruud shouted.

Hartono battered the rifle butt against the glass, kicking out part of the windscreen so that a portion of the laminate folded in on itself.

'Can you get a clean shot?'

Ruud veered off sharply, then straightened, narrowly missing a couple of street urchins.

Hartono rammed the shotgun barrel through the windscreen debris.

BANG!

Ruud felt the heat from the gunshot blast sear the right side of his face. His ears rang.

The back of the Subaru was riddled with jagged holes.

'Bring the bastard down, Hartono!'

BANG!

The back window of the car in front shattered.

Suddenly, the silver car turned sharply down a small side street, taking out a phone booth on its way.

Ruud braked hard and his head whiplashed and spanked against the seat's headrest. He spun the steering wheel, skidding through a red light.

'He's doing a one eighty, heading for Srikaya!'

Ruud screamed into a hairpin turn and gave chase, but they'd lost ground.

A voice crackled on the police scanner.

Sunshine poured through the clouds at an angle, temporarily blinding Ruud.

The Subaru exploded out of the side street and hit a ramp, spraying yellow bollards this way and that.

'Can you see him?'

'He took a left down here.'

'We need eyes in the sky!' screamed Hartono into the hand mike.

The siren and roar of the wind drowned out his voice.

Hartono turned to Ruud. 'He's taking Ridwan Rais?'

'It's a smart move. The road's under repair for several kilometres, so it's closed off to traffic. If he can get a clear run, he'll turn off at one of the exits and we'll lose him.' Ruud raced past construction vehicles, zigzagging to avoid tarmac trucks.

A metal drum rolled across the road, chiming and clanging.

'Where is he?'

Horn blaring, Ruud swerved and slid beyond a HMI trailer, wheels spinning.

'There he is!'

Pumped with adrenaline, Ruud floored it. Both cars shot past an asphalt paver.

'You're closing on him!'

Thirty metres away. Twenty.

Rushing headlong, Ruud ploughed into the tail of the Subaru. He slammed into the rear bumper, hitting it just above the right back wheel.

The car in front wobbled.

For a tantalizing moment the Toyota drew abreast of the Subaru.

'Watch out!' shrieked Hartono.

Ruud counter-steered to stop the Toyota from hurtling into a parked dump trailer.

The Subaru scudded left then right.

Hartono raised the Remington and took aim at the tyres.

He fired. A shower of rubber tread and wire sprayed the air.

The Subaru veered hard to the left. Ruud followed it and rammed it again. This time both vehicles pivoted.

The Subaru flipped.

Ruud desperately tried to regain control of the Toyota by slamming on the brakes. The wheels locked. The world blurred. There was a terrific bang somewhere to the side.

For a split second Ruud winced, bracing for the airbag pillow to hit him full in the face. But the fabric bag didn't inflate; there was no cushioned collision.

On the contrary, the impact force was brutal. His head jounced on his neck. He felt his brain crash against the inside of his skull and his heart thud violently into the back of his ribcage.

Glass showered his eyes.

Ruud was conscious of Hartono pitching through the windscreen, aware of his colleague bouncing off the hood.

Ruud gasped. And a moment later the air was crushed from his lungs.

Under his lids he saw the colour red and the colour green, whirling shadows.

Followed by a black void.

Chapter Thirty-Three

Imke dropped to her knees and bent over Alya's ripped face and broken body. She listened for breathing. Her fingers tried to find a pulse on the policewoman's throat next to her Adam's apple. Recalling her first-aid training, she was about to begin CPR when she felt a faint throb coming from the carotid artery.

'Talk to me, Alya. Tell me where you are and what day it is.'

Imke shifted her position to support Alya's head. 'You've been in a hit-and-run accident, Alya. It's important you don't move. Paramedics are on the way.'

As she said this, Imke noticed she was kneeling in blood and her hands were wet and sticky. And the moment she tilted her gaze she saw that Alya had a ten-centimetre length of thin black plastic protruding from behind her ear. It took Imke a few seconds to realise that the car's front windscreen-wiper arm had broken off and embedded itself in Alya's neck.

Intuitively, Imke pulled two Kotex napkins from her back pocket and tore open the packets with her teeth. Because she could not apply direct pressure on the injury as something was embedded in the wound, she pressed the pads against either side of the protrusion.

'Can you breathe, Alya?'

Three words roared in Imke's head: ESTABLISH AN AIRWAY. But she didn't know what to do. Alya wasn't choking. Was her upper respiratory tract open? There was no way of telling. Somewhere in her training she recalled having to 'remove all foreign objects'.

She took Alya's hand. Skinned raw from the fall. The *ajun inspektur's* eyes flickered open.

Conscious, shivering, Alya attempted to speak, but her lower face was too mangled to form words. The blood glutted her tongue and mouth, pink bubbles popped on her lips. Alya stared at Imke. She was mahogany eyed. But her eyes now were wide and terrified. Prey eyes. Antelope eyes with a lion's jaws clamped to her throat.

'Don't be scared, Alya. I'm here.'

Imke gazed into the brown irises, into the rich, watery gleam. She smoothed down the young woman's hair. 'Help is coming, Alya.'

Imke looked up and around. There were shocked faces all about her. Children were crying. A mother yelled from a window above. Imke heard the shriek of a girl who'd bent to look at the body.

'Get back! Back!' The Sabhara cops shouted.

The force of the impact had been so strong that Alya's gun lay fifteen metres down the road. Her beige hijab more than twenty metres away. Somewhere in the distance her walkie-talkie crackled.

Tenderly, Imke lifted a strand of hair from across Alya's cheek.

Alya turned a tiny fraction and a gout of blood trickled from her ear. Her breathing grew ragged, stuttering.

Leaning close, Imke whispered gently. 'Stay with me, Alya.'

Alya blinked rapidly, petrified. Her throat rattled.

People were yelling all around them. Shrill cries of panic.

Imke's head swam. She couldn't believe this was happening. Her legs shook.

A faraway siren.

'Help is on its way, Alya.' Imke's legs shook even harder. 'Do you hear that sound? It's the ambulance. Help is on its way. Please don't die.'

Imke squeezed the policewoman's hand.

Alya's eyes howled and shrieked.

And then her stare grew fixed.

The little pink bubbles stopped popping on her lips.

Unflinching, Imke held Alya tight to keep her warm.

The shivering stilled.

'Alya! I'm still with you, Alya! I'm not going anywhere. Do you hear me?' Imke pressed her forehead against Alya's. 'I'm not leaving you.'

A few minutes later, voices spoke to her. Told her to let go. Stubbornly, Imke squeezed Alya's hand tighter.

The ambulance crew had to prise her fingers away.

Chapter Thirty-Four

Dazed.

Head floating.

The sun bright and low, dazzling his eyes.

Ruud shook himself to life.

Pain somewhere near the top of his head. A wound on his scalp was weeping thickly, trickling down his cheek.

Ruud touched the scarlet slash and winced.

The police radio crackled. A jumble of staticky words.

Ruud patted and prodded himself with a tentative hand. He felt a twinge when he inhaled. The back of his neck ached. It hurt to swallow. But nothing was broken. All bones still intact.

The Toyota, too, was in one piece, having skidded hard to a halt.

'Bloody airbags. Fucking locally made piece of rubbish,' he hissed, climbing out of his vehicle. 'Should've gone for a Honda.' As he hauled himself out of the front seat, his legs shook; the ground felt spongy under his feet. Splinters of glass fell from his clothes and hair.

Hartono was on the ground some twenty metres back, groaning and sighing deeply. He was coiled into a sphere, his

299

face a bloody mess. A long slender string of blood leaked from his mouth.

'Werry! Don't move, OK? Werry!'

Ruud did not go to him. Instead, he bore down on the silver car to his right.

The Subaru lay on its back, turned turtle, four wheels and a black underbelly facing the sky. Its radiator hissed. There were bits of debris all around it.

Ruud tugged his Heckler & Koch 9 mm free from its holster. He searched his pocket for his mobile. It wasn't there. It must have fallen out in the crash.

The ground was sprinkled with shards of glass. Engine oil spilled into the breakage. Ruud moved neatly to the side of the spill; firearm raised, tracking up and down, left to right, searching for the target. 'Police officer! Come out with your hands on your head!' he ordered.

No response.

Shading his eyes from the bright setting sun, he stepped forward and immediately smelled the warm reek of scorched rubber, followed by a sudden waft of petrol and brake fluid.

One half of the car was in sharp shadow.

Ruud crouched low, tilting his head, Heckler held at eye level. He edged closer to the wreck and bent his knees.

No signs of movement. Nothing. He inched closer still.

The front seats of the Subaru were empty. Anterior and side airbags had crumpled and deflated; everything was coated with dusty particles like talcum powder.

He shifted focus to the back seats. Scrunching down, he saw a jumble of Kleenex boxes, candy wrappers, a neck cushion, dangling seat belts.

There was nobody there.

No driver.

Ruud gaped.

The voice in his head told him to take cover. To get the fuck out of there.

That was when he heard the sound. Three muffled words from behind: 'Oink! Oink! Oink!'

Ruud sprang up.

He twisted round.

Waiting for him. A man in a pig mask. Ugly plastic mouth grinning at him. Pistol barrel aimed at his face.

Staring down the muzzle, Ruud had no time to react. No time to flinch.

A cannon crack splintered the air.

But Ruud never heard it.

The force of the impact seemed to break him in half.

Lifted off his feet, Ruud sailed backwards, landing with a thump on a bed of newly laid asphalt dappled with engine oil and splintered glass.

For a while Ruud couldn't work out why he was lying on his back, why the curve of his skull rested on the ground.

He moved one of his hands ever so slightly, felt his fingers curl. His fingers were syrupy wet, the asphalt warm to the touch.

He wanted to get to his feet. If only he could get his legs working. If only he could figure out what to do. But his body refused to budge.

Blinking rapidly, trying to focus, he stared up at the evening sky, at the blue horizon banded with pink and fuchsia streaks. Behind his left shoulder, the sun sank behind a skyscraper.

Fuchsia.

The colour of Imke's dressing gown. Suddenly, he saw her face. He wondered where she was. Whether she was taking

Erica out for a meal later that night. They ought to go somewhere high up, a penthouse bar, somewhere with a view.
Imke always liked sunsets.

First *Inspektur* Ruud Pujasumarta breathed in. He felt his
ribcage expand and his lungs gently bloat. The air felt good.
He held the air in his chest for as long as he could, before
breathing out, turning his head to catch the twilight.

The pink pennants and fuchsia bands were turning
vermillion.

A beautiful luxurious vermillion.

Like a butterfly opening its wings.

Seconds later, vermillion became auburn, and later still
auburn became rosewood.

A noise somewhere behind him. The sound of someone
coughing.

Was it Werry?

Or was it the man with the gun?

He didn't care. He was beyond caring.

Still, he wanted to see how Werry was doing. Offer him
his hand, tell him help was on its way. But he couldn't. He
felt cold. His legs wouldn't move and his mouth wouldn't
work.

He listened for more, yet all he heard was a distant hum,
the white-noise from the underpass traffic below.

Werry, good old Werry.

Battle stations. Ruud allowed himself a little inward smile.
Who but Werry Hartono would say something as absurd as
battle stations.

He hoped Werry was going to be all right.

Trembling, he bit his lip to stop his teeth from chatter-
ing. A frigid ice cube swelled in his chest, spreading,
lengthening up and down his spine.

He thought about his family; he thought about his brother. The life they'd spent together. It all seemed so far away now.

Overtaken by shivers, he blinked into the evening sky. The rosewood horizon grew darker and darker, disintegrating, fading to ash. A murky slate.

A minuscule breeze tossed flakes of sparkling talcum powder in the air. Infinity expanded and crackled before his eyes.

When the rosewood dwindled altogether, his ribcage inflated one last time.

And he stopped breathing.

Chapter Thirty-Five

Yuliana was distraught.

Earlier, her husband vanished halfway through his plate of grilled *ikan bakar*. They were eating at a streetside seafood outlet on Jalan Hidup Baru famous for its butterfly-cut pomfret and blackened cuttlefish. They hadn't been seated for more than five minutes when he suddenly got up, spilling tamarind sauce and *ketjap manis*, grabbed a bag of Tanjung prawn crackers and scarpered without saying a word to her, leaving her to settle the bill.

All day Bayu had been preoccupied with his telephone, looking as miserable as one of the crabs in the restaurant's fish tank.

Yuliana didn't know what to make of it. He'd been cantankerous and on edge. She wondered whether he'd started gambling again. No, please, no, she said to herself. The thought of Bayu falling into debt again made her blood pressure soar. Last autumn he'd thrown away over two million rupiah on the opening games of the German Bundesliga season, placing illegal bets with a *preman* syndicate – it was money they simply couldn't afford to lose.

At first she'd been oblivious to it all. Until two men

showed up at her door. They had toothpicks in their mouths and razorblades for eyes.

'Tell him he has until Thursday,' they'd said.

'What is this about?' she'd demanded.

'It's about paying his debt.' They'd smiled slyly.

That night, Bayu had told her there was nothing to be concerned about.

He was on top of it.

On top of what, she'd asked.

Nothing, he said, nothing to worry your pretty head over.

Thursday came and went.

On Friday she'd discovered their savings had been wiped out. Bayu arrived home at dusk and she took him to task. To his credit, he'd apologized profusely, and assured her, hand on heart, that it would never happen again. He'd sworn on her life that he'd acted out of character and would make it up to her.

That was then.

Now, sitting alone amongst the clouds of barbecue smoke and the smell of burning charcoal and charred cuttlefish, she was more concerned and confused than ever. What on earth had just happened? She stared at the half-eaten dishes on the plastic laminate table. The streetside stalls grew busier and busier. The sizzle of oil and the clanging of woks got louder.

Was Bayu coming back to finish his meal? Was he feeling unwell? Was he ill? Why had he abandoned her like this? Maybe he has a woman on the side. Some cheap *pantat besar* girl.

Yuliana waited and waited. Flies and motorcycles buzzed about.

She went over what she'd witnessed: soon after settling in his seat he'd received a call, which he took with an anxious look on his face. He'd spoken seven words into the receiver – 'Yes.' 'Tell me where?' 'How much?' 'Agreed.' – then he'd risen to his feet, walked outside and jumped into his car, that beat-up Perodua Kenari of his.

She wanted to call him, ask him what the hell was going on. Instead, she did something drastic, something she'd never done before. She plucked up the courage and telephoned Azni, Bayu's supervisor at the Gatot Soebroto Army Hospital, somebody she rarely spoke to but whose number she retained for emergencies.

What Azni told her shocked her to the bone. He said Bayu hadn't worked there for three months.

'Three months? But that's impossible.'

'He's been suspended without pay.'

'He never mentioned anything about being suspended. He's been going to work, Azni. He tells me he's been working nights. How can he have been suspended? Only yesterday he paid the air-conditioner man in cash. How has he been paying the household bills without a salary?'

'Yuliana, your husband is under investigation for stealing medical equipment and pharmaceutical drugs.'

'Stealing?'

'Oxycodone, fentanyl and hydromorphone, to name but a few.'

So where had he been going these last evenings? What in heaven's name had he been doing?

Azni said he couldn't help her, but assured her that Bayu would be disciplined. 'I'm so sorry to break this news to you,' he said.

Yuliana dropped the phone into her lap and burst into tears.

Chapter Thirty-Six

Imke sat hunched on a bench in the hospital corridor and rocked back and forth, yanking at her eyebrows, pulling the hairs out one at a time. Her lifeless hair was scrunched into a messy ponytail and the orange sweatshirt she'd been wearing hung loosely over her shoulders, crusted with Alya's blood, the fibres glinting rust-brown under the corridor lights.

Perched on the edge of the bench, tilting it onto its front legs, she stabbed at her mobile phone. For what must have been the hundredth time, Imke pressed redial. Time and again, she got Ruud's voicemail.

Needing to speak to someone, anyone, she called Djoko, the head of the K9 special unit. 'Is Kiki still with you? Good, yes, thank you for looking after her. I'll come and fetch her later.'

She got to her feet and paced about. She was too wired to sit – her entire body felt stiff with dread. An hour went by. She checked her mobile over and over again.

Finally, exhausted, she sat back down with her head on her knees.

When the door leading from A&E crashed open and Witarsa appeared with a female family liaison officer, Imke sprang up like a jack-in-the-box.

'What happened? There's talk of a shooting. Nobody will tell me anything. Where's Ruud?'

'Please sit,' the liaison officer advised.

'No. I want to know what's going on.'

The woman wore spectacles with translucent frames. Gravely, she removed them from her face. 'Earlier today, *Ajun Inspektur Polisi Dua* Alya Entitisari was involved in a hit-and-run. She didn't make it. She was pronounced dead thirty minutes ago. You were at the scene. Can you tell us what you saw when *Ajun Inspektur* Entitisari was run over.'

'It was a silver car. A Subaru, I think. A sedan. The windows were blacked out. No, I didn't get the licence plate.'

'That's all you saw.'

'Yes. The officers in the car park outside said someone was shot.'

'Second Lieutenant Werry Hartono and First *Inspektur* Ruud Pujasumarta were the first responders to the hit-and-run. They gave chase, attempting to apprehend the culprit. Their car was involved in an accident. Second Lieutenant Hartono has suffered head injuries and concussion, but he is in a satisfactory condition. His vital signs are stable and he is conscious and speaking.'

'And Ruud? What happened to Ruud?'

'Imke.' Witarsa's voice was soft. 'It's not good news.'

'Oh God.'

The commissioner pinched his brow with thumb and forefinger. 'Hartono described to us what happened. He said Ruud survived the collision but was subsequently shot at point-blank range by the assailant. He says he saw the perp sneak up on Ruud and fire a round into his chest.'

'How badly injured is he? Is he here? I can donate blood. We're the same blood group. If he's still undergoing surgery, let me help. He's blood type A negative, it's rare, so I can help if they need—'

Witarsa placed both his hands on her shoulders to steady her. 'Imke, Ruud's . . .' he wavered. 'Hartono says Ruud was shot and killed. He saw it with his own eyes.'

'Killed?'

'I'm so sorry.'

'Joyo, what are you saying?' The blood drained from her face. 'My Ruud? Killed? No, no, that's not possible.' She shook her head. All of a sudden she felt incredibly cold. Her voice cracked and her teeth chattered. 'I only spoke to him, what was it, four hours ago.'

A sudden flurry of images flashed before her eyes: Ruud sipping iced Milo, gurning through a brain freeze. Ruud wearing a paper hat on his head, singing 'Happy Birthday'. Ruud rolling about with Kiki on the carpet, laughing. Ruud in bed, holding her tight, keeping her safe.

Witarsa: 'It's three in the morning, Imke. You've been here all night. Call your aunt. Tell her to come and collect you.'

'My aunt. Oh, God. I forgot all about her. Where is she? The last I heard she was with Shane Waters.'

'The diplomat?'

'I haven't spoken to her since lunch.'

'In that case I will arrange a squad car to take you home. You have to rest now.'

'You don't understand, I have to find Aunty Ecks.'

'She is probably at home waiting for you. Go to her. There's nothing more you can do here.'

For several moments Imke stood her ground. Then she looked into the commissioner's face and saw the unbearable sadness in his eyes. 'Ruud's dead,' she whispered. 'He's really gone?'

'I'm so sorry.'

She balled her hands into fists and wrapped them across her shaking chest. Heart thudding, she said, 'Let me see him. Before I go, I want to see Ruud's body.'

The commissioner shook his head. 'I'm afraid that's not possible.'

'Why not?'

Witarsa wavered and looked at the liaison officer for assistance.

'Because,' the woman interjected, translucent-framed spectacles firmly reattached to her face, 'the killer took First *Inspektur* Pujasumarta's body away with him. He carried off the corpse.'

Chapter Thirty-Seven

Smelling salts.

Ruud jarred awake violently, coming up for air. Inhalation reflex working overtime. He choked. Retched. Tasted grit.

Ammonia burned his nostrils.

A sharp trilling alarm went off in his head. Heart thudding, he struggled, body angry and aching, to make sense of things. Where the fuck am I? What the hell happened? Am I still alive? Then, all of a sudden, he remembered.

Suddenly, the terror of it, the surprise, kicked in hard.

Eyes gluey and distended, he glared about. There were shapes and shadows in the foreground, dark contours behind. Everything was charcoal-grey, almost black.

Gasping for breath, his brain told him to get up, to grab for his gun, to reach for his phone. But his limbs were torpefied, rooted to the spot. His arms and legs wouldn't do as they were told. He looked down and saw wrist straps. He was tied to a chair. His legs were secured too. And he was naked.

Mind racing, he took in his surroundings: a dim room with cavernous ceilings, a large neglected industrial space, rust-stained panels, corroded duct shafts, dripping waste pipes. To his right, at two o'clock, was a sturdy metal door with a heavy iron latch. Even from this distance he could see the latch was unclasped.

The tall airless chamber was thick with subterranean damp – a soupy, fungal, squalid vapour.

Suddenly.

A scuffling noise.

Motion to his left. A dimly outlined figure. A man. His silhouette appeared misshapen, distorted. There was the sound of muted jangling, of metal instruments rattling in a metal dish. A far-off lamp was switched on. The rattling got nearer. A small table on casters was pushed close. Ruud flinched. He spied the dish. It was sitting on the small chrome table. The dish was kidney-shaped, bone white with a navy blue trim. He also glimpsed several different-sized knives and skewers, some double-pronged, some with mouths like nail scissors. Torture tools.

Ruud pulled his knees together to protect his exposed genitals. Feet turned inwards, he tried not to shake, thinking about what was going to happen to him.

The man made a tut-tutting sound. He wore a cream lab coat and latex gloves.

Ruud strained to snatch a look at his captor's face, and caught a glimpse of chin, cramped white teeth, pink gums, receding black hair and safety goggles.

Scarcely a couple of metres away, in the gloom, the man regarded Ruud silently. Ruud began to piece the man's facial features together, reconstructing a possible likeness – desperate to fashion a PhotoFit match.

Suddenly a bright light blinded him. A 100-watt bulb shone what felt like jagged glass into the backs of his eyes, searing his retinas.

The man's voice told him to say hello to number nine.

What the fuck is number nine?

Corneas stinging, Ruud heard a tinkle of metal.

A ping of titanium on tin.

And then.

Pain.

It shot through him.

Every muscle in his body tightened and went rigid.

The man was sticking something into his flesh.

Ruud cried out. He bucked and wrestled and kicked against his leg braces. Fighting to climb out of the torture chair. But the straps held. After what seemed like an eternity, the pain subsided.

He looked down again. There was blood everywhere. He'd been stabbed and the weapon was still in him. There was a twenty-centimetre finger ring retractor stuck inside him, below the shoulder. It was made of stainless steel with a cam ratchet lock that drew back the tissue, laying bare the surgical site.

The curved metal arms protruded from his flesh, twitching. He wanted to grab it with his teeth and pull it out but the neck fasteners kept his head in place.

Squinting, Ruud studied it. Half-terrified, half-fascinated.

A voice, a man's voice, informed him that he'd been shot in the deltopectoral triangle, just below the right shoulder. The bullet had passed right through him. 'Your circumflex humeral artery's been partially torn, but currently there's a clamp put in place to stem the bleeding.'

'What am I doing here? What do you want from me?'

He told Ruud that he was going to ask him some questions, and if he was a good boy he was going to receive a treat. He shook a syrette in front of Ruud's face. Liquid morphine, he explained. One jab under the skin if he behaved himself. No jabs at all if he was a naughty boy.

'Who are you?'

'Me? Just a man.'

'Your name.'

'Now, why should I give you my name?'

He selected something spiky and evil-looking from the tray. 'I suppose if you must, you may call me The Physician.'

'I take it that's not your real name?'

'Oh, what makes you think that?' The man dug the long, thin implement into Ruud's flesh, skewering him like a moth pinned to a mounting board.

Every muscle in his body squeezed tight, constricting.

Pain ripped through him.

The Physician twisted the implement, like pasta on a fork. He told Ruud he was about to release the bulldog clamp.

Ruud convulsed, shaking uncontrollably.

He heard himself roiling and blowing.

The wound was deep. Each time his heart contracted the Weitlaner retractor shivered and a spurt of blood sprayed up. It splattered Ruud's face and chest, dousing the barber's chair and dribbling down his stomach until it reached his pubes and balls.

Ruud wrestled against the wrist and neck straps, thrashing and heaving.

But the buckles held.

The Weitlaner retractor shivered.

Haemorraging. The blood spattered. It spilled down his bare shanks onto his ankles and feet. Untended, the blood glutted the spaces between his toes, pooling on the footrest. It was as though someone clever had done a magic trick and concealed a water pistol somewhere below his collarbone. *Stffff-stffff. Stffff-stffff.* Squeeze the plastic trigger, cowboy! Quick Draw. *Stffff-stffff.*

The Physician restored the bulldog clamp.

The blood stopped spraying.

A slow hissing sound escaped Ruud's mouth.

Sixty-seven types, the man said almost jauntily, the words dancing off his tongue.

He raised a scalpel, held softly between the thumb and forefinger of his left hand. Silver in the spotlights.

Pausing to watch Ruud's reaction, he told Ruud there were sixty-seven types of scalpel blade. Blade No. 12, for example, had a sharp crescent-shaped tip – he showed him – and was used to disarticulate small joints during digit amputation, or for cleft-palate procedures. He picked up another. No. 15 had a small curved tip used to make short, precise incisions – good for excising skin lesions or opening coronary arteries.

'Where, where, where to make the incision . . .' The Physician attempted a few practice stabs with his wrist. Then he sliced Ruud open along his left forearm.

'Now that I have your full attention, I have a few questions for you. First up, what is your name and rank?'

Ruud informed him he was a first inspector.

'Age?'

Ruud stared at the raised scalpel, but didn't say anything.

'I'd say you were in your late twenties, perhaps thirty, thirty-one. You look pretty fit. We're about the same age, you and me, but I don't keep myself in shape. I should, I know, but you know what it's like. Running shoes never used. Gym kit abandoned in the cupboard.'

He slipped the tip of the scalpel under the fingernail of Ruud's index finger. 'So, are we ready for the next question? Yes? *Boleh.* Something important went missing not long ago, an item that's become central to your investigation. Do you know what I'm talking about? Of course, you do. The all-important hair garment. So. Tell me. Where is Anita Dalloway's Alice band?'

'Honestly, I have no idea.'

'Please don't make this any harder for me.'

'I'm telling you the truth.'

The scalpel slid underneath the fingernail and levered it out.

Ruud flailed and writhed, spat in the man's face. He would have hit him square in the eyes but for the man's goggles.

A glob of phlegm rolled down the man's cheek.

'Naughty, naughty. You shouldn't have done that,' said the man, his voice full of sharks' teeth. 'No more magic morphine for you.' He picked up a crimpled packet of metallized plastic film and tore it open. 'Have a guess what this is?' He ran the packet under Ruud's nose.

Ruud smelled shrimp paste.

'*Krupuk udang*. My favourite brand of prawn crackers. This was meant to be part of my supper. Don't you just love them with *gado-gado*?' He took one in his mouth with a crunch. 'Available at most roadside food stalls and hurts like hell when rubbed into an open wound. Want to see?'

He crushed then sprinkled a few on top of the gash on Ruud's forearm.

Ruud gnashed and ground.

'Must be the salt that does it. The chilli powder helps, too. Now, the Alice band. Did you find it?'

'No.'

'Where is it, *inspektur*?'

The Physician worked the broken pieces into the cut with a forefinger.

316

Ruud screamed.

A minute later, Ruud, panting, conceded. 'It's with LABFOR,' he wheezed. 'We had it all along. The Alice band's with the forensic lab at police headquarters.'

'Very good. See how easy it can be, coming clean?' He wiped his hands with a towel, but his cuffs and cuticles remained smudged with blood. 'Now that you seem willing to talk, let's see what else you can tell us. We have so many more questions.'

The man's eyes trained on a spot somewhere behind Ruud. He wanted to follow his gaze but couldn't. He couldn't move his head.

'We?' said Ruud.

The man's voice dropped a notch. 'Me and my friend.'

'What friend?'

The man tossed the empty salt sachet aside.

'Aren't you acting alone?'

'Alone? Goodness, no. I'm merely an employee. I do as I'm told.'

With all his remaining strength Ruud tried to pull free. 'Look, I don't know anything. Whatever you're thinking of doing to me you've got to stop.'

'Got to stop, got to stop.' He mimicked. 'You sound like a ten-year-old in the school yard.'

'Tell your boss I don't know anything!'

'You want to relay a message? No problem! *Tidak apa-apa!* You can tell him yourself.' A sideways glance. 'He's standing right behind you.'

'Who's standing right behind me?'

'*He* is. Watching the entertainment.'

Ruud imagined slippery hot breath on the back of his neck. He struggled, heaving his quadriceps against the leg bonds.

'*Shhhh. Shhhh. Shhhh.* Come now, you know you can't escape.'

Ruud heard something or someone shift about behind him. A stirring. Furtive footsteps. His muscles strained at the clasps, but he couldn't move his head to see. He could sense it, though, this demon slouched in the dark like a witch in black robes.

'Who are you?' Ruud shouted. 'Stop hiding in the shadows, you fucking coward. Show yourself. Say something!'

Silence.

'As you can no doubt tell, my friend is not the talkative type, detective. He leaves all that to me. At any rate I want to hear you do the talking, not him, isn't that right?'

A scalpel with a head as thin as a razor blade caught the light, so shiny Ruud spotted his reflection in it. 'Now then, where were we? Oh, yes. We were playing twenty questions.'

The scalpel pierced skin, sliced away a comma of flesh, a freckle on Ruud's wrist, leaving a wet mushy mark the size of a penny. 'Question number three. Where is Emily Grealish's USB flash drive?'

Ruud told him they'd never found any flash drives in Emily's apartment, nor in her office.

'Is that so?'

'Yes.'

He hovered over Ruud like a giant predatory bird. 'I will ask you one last time, Detective Pujasumarta. And if you do not give us the right answer my friend over there will get angry.'

'I'm telling you the truth, we didn't find anything!'

'Hmmmm.'

'There weren't any thumb drives anywhere!'

'Tell us about the USB drive and we will put you to sleep quietly. No pain.'

'I don't know shit.'

'Lie to us or tell us you know nothing and you'll die painfully and slowly.'

'There weren't any USB drives in her apartment!'

'Your girlfriend from Holland, your family in Australia. We can get to all of them. Do you understand? We'll go after the people you love.'

'Leave my family out of this!'

'Do you understand?'

'It's the fucking truth. There was nothing in her apartment.'

'Why don't I believe you?'

The Physician's free hand dug the long pin back into Ruud's shoulder, into the gristle of his rotator cuff muscles. It felt like he was shoving bent nails under his skin.

A searing pain shot through Ruud's body.

And something inside him popped.

Ruud had compressed recollections of pain breaking over him like a wave. Of yowling, pleading, shrieking. Of harpoons and lances twisting inside him. Of metal splinters and leaf-shaped blades. Of time expanding and contracting.

Somebody nearby was screaming. Dreadful cries that made Ruud want to rush over and help. But something held Ruud down, prevented him from moving his arms and legs. And then Ruud realized he was the one doing the screaming.

★ ★ ★

A fly landed on Ruud's eyebrow. He shook it off and took a breath. Disorientated, exhausted, his muscles were slack and spent. Perspiration cooled his skin. He blinked. Eyelids gummy, glued together as if they'd been closed too long. Had he lost consciousness? It seemed like he had. How long for? A few minutes? An hour? More?

He remained strapped to his torture throne.

The light now shone at an angle, no longer directly into his face. The 100-watt bulb still stung his eyes.

The pain in his upper chest and shoulder remained but it was manageable, not the sharp agony from earlier. More a throbbing, tense ache. He looked down. The Weitlaner retractor was gone, and in its place he saw what looked like a giant hair clip. The spongy wound appeared as smooth and shiny as a cherry Popsicle. He was no longer bleeding.

Ruud wiggled his bare toes – a sticky sensation. They were pasted with dried blood.

In the background, somewhere behind Ruud, where he couldn't see, he heard a low ominous rumbling, two men in conversation. Both were talking at once. Ruud listened but could not hear what they said.

A current of fear burned through him. He had told them what he knew and didn't know, and now they would execute him.

He heard a barked order, followed by a door in the rear opening and closing.

Footsteps approached.

The Physician again. The front of his lab coat was so blood-spattered it was more red than white.

He pulled Ruud's head up by the hair. 'We have concluded you know nothing of the USB drive. You are a stubborn one. I suppose my friend will simply have to search the apartment again more thoroughly. I am sorry, First *Inspektur* Pujasumarta,' he said, letting Ruud's head drop. He took hold of Ruud's arm and searched for a vein in the crook of his elbow. 'I am sorry it has to end this way.'

'Don't do this. You can let me go. You realize that, don't you? He's gone hasn't he, your friend? I heard the door shut just now. He's left. You can let me go. Please, just . . . just loosen these ties and I'll walk out of here.'

'I cannot do that. This is the way he wants things done.' Regarding him, the man offered Ruud an apologetic smile.

Ruud saw a hypodermic needle in his hand with an orange syringe hub. 'What is that? What are you sticking in me?'

'Something to put you to sleep. It will be painless. The first injection is a pre-mixed cocktail, Tiletamine and Zolazepam. A sedative. The second injection, containing barbiturates, will induce cardiac arrest.'

'No, you can't do this.'

The Physician removed the needle cap with his teeth. 'Be thankful. Boss man wanted you to bleed out but I insisted this would be more humane.'

'Fuck him. Fuck what he wants. Who is he? Is he paying you to do this? Listen to me, look at me, I can pay you more.'

The Physician did not speak for several moments. He stood motionless, like a still from a black-and-white horror movie. Eventually, lips drawn back, he said, 'How much are you willing to cough up?'

'Wh-whatever you want.'

With keen curiosity he contemplated Ruud and smiled. 'Let's talk US dollars, shall we? Shall we say half a million?'

'I'll get you whatever you want. Just let me go.'

'A whole half million? Really?'

Ruud said nothing.

'You must think I'm an idiot, first *inspektur*. You've seen my face.'

'I can say I never saw you.'

'Sorry.' He turned a small vial of clear liquid upside-down and filled the syringe. 'The boss man will find out and that's not a good thing.'

Ruud shrank into the chair. 'Listen, let me go and we'll forget all about this. I won't mention you. I'll tell the police I never saw your face. For God's sake, don't do this!'

The man pinched the vein on Ruud's inner elbow. The short orange needle punctured Ruud's flesh. 'Best not to struggle.' His thumb pressed the rubber plunger.

Ruud watched the number calibration slide from 3 cc to 2.5 cc.

'Please, no.'

When the syringe ring reached halfway down the barrel, he began to feel drowsy.

Then all of a sudden, Ruud heard another sound. A clanging noise. Both he and the white-coated man turned their heads to see the sturdy metal door with the heavy iron latch shudder.

A boot slammed into the door with the force of a cannon shot, and it flew open.

There was a cry of '*Polisi!*', followed by the ear-sting of gunfire.

One minute The Physician was standing over him, the next he was knocked off his feet and sprawled across the floor with a hole blasted into his face, just a couple of centimetres from his gaping mouth.

Chapter Thirty-Eight

Behind the sharp light, Ruud spied Aiboy Ali, his long hair dripping over his eyes.

'*Gajah*, it's me. You're not dead! Fucking hell, what did they do to you?' Aiboy stared at the trauma written all over Ruud's flesh. 'My God.'

'They did a number on me, mate.'

'You're telling me.' His eyes were as round as golf balls. 'And you're butt naked, too. The nurses are going to have a field day.' Aiboy Ali loosened the restraining buckles and set Ruud's limbs free. 'We'll worry about your modesty later, yeah?' He tore off his own T-shirt and covered Ruud's shoulders with it. 'But this will have to do for now. I can't see any sign of your clothes. For the record, this is my favourite Burgerkill T-shirt, so don't go bleeding all over it now, will you?'

'Get me to hospital, Aiboy.'

'Doing the best I can, *Gajah*.' With measured care, Aiboy draped Ruud's left arm over his shoulder and pulled him to his feet. He forced Ruud upright. 'Can you walk without shoes? One step at a time. We'll do this at your pace. Ready?'

Ruud nodded, grimacing. His skin and hair were stiff with blood, and it hurt each time he took a half-stride.

Together they lurched through the metal door into the courtyard, Aiboy's right hand gripping Ruud's waist and the other cupped under his chin.

Suddenly, Ruud found himself out in the open, inhaling vehicle smoke and burning trash. The hot morning sun tore at his eyes. 'It's morning? How can it be morning?'

'It's eight a.m., *Gajah*. POLRI have been looking for you for hours.'

'Where am I?'

'You're near the docks in Kali Baru. He had you in a *gudang*, an abandoned chemical depot.'

Aiboy's face leant into Ruud's, so close Ruud could count the pores on his nose.

'I don't remember what happened. I can't remember.'

'Enough talking, *Gajah*. Let's get you some help.' Slowly, they executed a clumsy three-legged-race stagger along the loose ground towards Aiboy's car.

Not far away, the streets beyond were bustling with activity.

Ruud squinted. A mass of blue, yellow and green *ojeks* raced by. Their colours swam in his head.

Lifting his gaze, Ruud spotted his Toyota Yaris on the opposite side of the forecourt. 'What's my car doing over there?'

'I'm guessing that's how you got here,' said Aiboy, opening the passenger door of his car for Ruud. 'Hartono said the man in the mask bundled you into the back and drove off.'

Ruud had no recollection of this. Out of breath, he grimaced as he lowered himself into the sitting position. 'Hartono's alive?'

'Yes.'

'The bloke in the white coat, is he dead?' Ruud stammered, close to blacking out again.

'I shot him in the head.'

'What about the other guy?' he said between gasps.

'What other guy?'

Ruud felt his scalp tingle. 'There are two of them, Aiboy.'

Aiboy Ali stopped in his tracks. 'What are you talking about?'

'There was someone else in the room.'

'Not when I got there.' He looked sharply over his shoulder. 'Fuck it, there's nothing I can do about it now. I have to get you to a doctor.'

Once in the car, Aiboy, bare-chested, reached over to the back seat and grabbed a police-issue rain jacket. Ruud took the jacket and arranged it across his stomach and thighs.

Aiboy fastened the blue strobe to the roof and switched on the siren.

He drove cautiously but quickly, careful to avoid the jarring potholes. He called Central to report the shooting, to request units to search the scene and to alert Persahabatan General that he had an injured officer who needed immediate treatment.

'Water,' Ruud urged.

Aiboy Ali unscrewed the top from a bottle of 2 Tang and handed the bottle to Ruud. He drank greedily.

'Better? Good. Now drink this too. You have to remain conscious.'

'What is it?'

'Cold coffee.'

Ruud grimaced as he took two long gulps. He glanced at Aiboy, shaking his head. 'Where the fuck were you this entire time?'

Aiboy shut his eyes briefly and took a breath to compose himself. 'Thinking. Hiding.'

'What are you talking about? Hiding from whom?'

'From myself, *Gajah*, from myself. I needed time alone.' Aiboy tightened his lips. 'Witarsa's livid with me.'

'I'm not surprised. What did he say?'

'TO GO MISSING during an investigation of this magnitude is unacceptable.' Aiboy said, parroting the commissioner's way of speaking. 'UNACCEPTABLE AND IRRESPONSIBLE.'

Blinking hard, Ruud saw signs telling drivers that Tangarang was 40 kms away. Beyond the signage he recognized the cityscape of Jakarta Utara.

'This isn't the way to Persahabatan General.'

'I changed my mind. I'm taking you to Royal Progress. It's closer.'

Ruud turned his head to the left to look at Aiboy Ali. His mind was racing. Thoughts entered his head that a week ago he would never have considered, could never have imagined. 'Where's your Glock? Procedure dictates I take possession of your firearm. I'm going to have to pass it to the crime lab.'

Aiboy dug it out of his hip holster and placed it on the centre console. Not for the first time, Ruud registered his colleague as left-handed. His insides lit a warning flare.

'A clean shot to the head. A week ago you couldn't hold a gun without shaking like a leaf.'

'Put it down to instinct.'

Ruud eyed him suspiciously. 'Well, I guess I should thank you for saving my life.'

He waited for Aiboy Ali to take a wide turn into Jalan Kalibaru Bar. As the detective leaned his body fractionally away from him, Ruud reached for the Glock 17.

He disengaged the safety and pointed the gun at Aiboy's

temple, doing everything in his power to stop the barrel from shaking.

'*Gajah, bego lu!* what are you doing?'

Ruud struggled to remain conscious. 'How did you know where I was?'

Aiboy Ali whistled through his teeth. 'So it's come to this, has it? You think I'm behind it all. Seriously?'

'You go AWOL in the middle of a murder probe. You turn up miraculously out of nowhere to save the day. You take out the suspect before he has a chance to surrender himself. I get this cock-and-bull story that you're scared of guns, but then you shoot the bastard between the eyes. It doesn't add up.'

'I can't believe I'm hearing this.'

'You shot him before he could say anything, before he could identify you.' He breathed rapid, shallow breaths. 'You're the second man, Aiboy, aren't you?'

'You've known me for six years,' Aiboy replied, his voice measured.

'And there's the pig mask. Sabhara found one in your apartment.'

'You're crazy, *Gajah*. That was one of the masks I picked up in Glodock, at the fancy dress outlet. You told me to go there.' He reached towards the glove compartment. 'Look, I'll show you.'

'Keep both hands on the wheel, Aiboy. I will shoot you if I have to.'

'I might hit a pothole. What if the gun goes off by accident?'

Ruud fiercely sucked air through his mouth. 'You'd better hope it doesn't.'

'Should I stop the car? You don't want to shoot me when I'm going fifty on the highway, not in the condition you're in.'

'Keep driving.' Ruud opened the glove compartment with his free hand and pulled out a cartoon mask. The effort of using his injured side sent shooting pains along his arm.

'Did the man you were chasing have that one on? With all that blond hair? Thought not.'

'It's a bloody Miss Piggy mask.'

'How did you know where I was?'

'POLRA wanted to trace your phone but it was discovered at the crime scene smashed to bits.'

Ruud tightened his grip on the Glock. 'So? How?'

'Remember when you asked me to put a GPS tracker on Shane Waters' car? Well, I stuck one under the bonnet of your Toyota Yaris too.'

'What the fuck? Why?'

'I don't know . . . instinct, intuition, gut feeling. Anyway, when I heard you were missing I legged it to Central and reported directly to Witarsa. This was about three hours ago. And here I am. Now, don't do anything rash, but I'm going to slowly retrieve my phone from my pocket.' Aiboy pulled out his Nokia and showed Ruud the display. A detailed city map of Jakarta appeared on the screen with a red dot blinking to indicate the location of Ruud's vehicle.

'You slapped a tracking unit on my bloody car.'

'That tracker saved your life, *Gajah*.'

'You bastard.'

'Hey, fire me.'

'Jesus.' Ruud lowered the Glock. 'You stupid mad bastard.'

'You've got some fucking nerve sticking a nine millimetre in my face.'

He allowed his head to fall back on the headrest. 'Sorry, mate. What the hell did you expect me to do? No hard feelings?'

Aiboy glanced at his friend. 'How are you doing?'

'Not good. Pretty ropey.'

'Hang in there. We'll be at Royal Progress in under five minutes.' Aiboy called Central and informed them of his change of plan.

Ruud felt his head spin. 'Keep talking to me. Tell me what's happening with the case.'

'Bad news. Alya was killed. Hit-and-run. Same guy you were chasing.'

Ruud looked down and away. His face contorted. 'And Imke?'

'She's shaken but unharmed. Traffic police reported a silver Subaru WRX was stolen from Jalan Benda in Kebayoran Baru at around three p.m. yesterday. The same one our pig friend was driving.'

'That's less than a kilometre from Fauzi's house.'

'Coincidence?'

'Hartono and I left Fauzi's place at two forty-five. The one-one-nine-nine call came soon after four p.m. More than enough time for Lieutenant General Fauzi to get his shit together.' Ruud blew out his cheeks. 'Are LABFOR checking the Subaru for DNA?'

'The bastard torched the car. Even so, they're picking through it for clues.'

Ruud shut his eyes as the pain closed in on him.

'Hang in there, *Gajah*. Hang in there.'

Chapter Thirty-Nine

Three nights in Royal Progress Hospital.

The surgeon told Ruud he'd sustained a gunshot wound to the right shoulder, that the bullet nicked some bone on the way through, tearing an artery. That overall he'd been pretty fortunate. Radiographic images suggested a tiny fracture to the surgical neck of the humerus. Most likely he would experience some right-arm abduction problems and temporary loss of sensation on the lateral side of his right shoulder, but it was nothing that pyshiotherapy couldn't fix.

Ruud shut his eyes and turned his head away.

He hated hospitals. He loathed the smells, the sounds, the feeling of helplessness and confinement, the clickety-clackety trays and heavy-handed nurses.

He didn't care for doctors either. Ever since the age of ten, when Dr Purnama shoved a rectal thermometer up his backside, cupped his balls and asked him to turn his head away and cough. It had scarred him for life, that had.

And why was the matron always so keen to wake him whenever he drifted off to sleep? Did she really have to take his blood pressure and change his intravenous drips every few hours? Did she enjoy shoving pills down his throat each time he took a catnap? Perhaps she was some kind of sadistic fiend, a tyrant of the wards.

Still, it was far better than being strapped to the barber's chair.

And he had Imke's pretty face to stare at, too.

Imke spent every moment with Ruud post surgery. Watching him sleep. Praying for him, head bowed, sometimes with her fist in her mouth.

When he woke, she was the first person he saw.

Her hands smoothed the hair on his head. Her kisses warmed his cheeks. She looked deep into his eyes, as if searching for something lost, and in hushed teary tones told him how much she loved him.

It made him feel good to hear it.

But she was exhausted. The trauma of the last seventy-two hours had taken its toll. But Ruud was alive and Erica was safe. Her aunt, thankfully, hadn't been kidnapped. Erica had simply returned to her hotel room and switched off her phone.

'Go home,' he said, his voice croaky from disuse. 'Kiki needs you.'

'Kiki's with Djoko. She's fine.'

Ruud squeezed Imke's arm. She refused to leave his side.

She held out until the third morning when, finally, after some persuading, she'd taken the matron's advice. Genuine rest was required, together with home-cooked food, a shower and her bed.

So Imke returned to their apartment to get a proper lie-down. She'd also agreed to leave Jakarta for a few weeks. 'The killer saw your face, Imke,' Ruud argued. 'It's too risky for you and Erica to stay here.' They were already under twenty-four-hour guard.

331

Reluctantly, she consented to head back to Amsterdam. She and Erica were scheduled to fly the following day.

With the machines beeping softly, Ruud lay on the bed, his wrist, index finger and forearm bandaged, his right arm strapped tight and in a sling. There were two uniformed policemen stationed at the entrance to his ward. Like Imke, he too had round-the-clock protection.

He fiddled with the hand control pad, played with the electric motor, first lowering and then raising the bed so that he was sitting upright. He was parched. He thought about letting down the side rails, climbing out of bed and grabbing a soft drink from the machine down the hall, glugging down the orangey carbonated contents in three giant gulps. There were something like 42 grams of sugar per serving. Death in a bottle, he called it. In the bedside locker drawer next to him he found an envelope of loose change left by Imke. He shook free some coins and notes.

Five minutes later, alone at last with his ice-cold Fanta, Ruud perched on the edge of his hospital bed, leaning his good forearm against the bedside locker. He placed his fingers and thumb on either side of the bottle and lowered his lips to the straw.

After two sips his phone rang.

'I'm downstairs.'

'Oh, hello Erica,' said Ruud.

'May I come up to see you?'

'Sure.'

'Please tell the goons at reception to let me through.'

A few minutes later he heard her feet clomping down the corridor. 'Shane Waters!' she cried, her voice echoing across the ward.

When she reached Ruud's bed, he said, 'What about him?'

She gave Ruud three kisses on the cheek. 'I wanted to see you before I fly. The nurses wouldn't let me visit before today. Here, for you.' She handed him a box of *kue* – bite-sized snacks made from steamed rice flour, palm sugar and grated coconut. These particular sweets were electric green, as if they'd been slathered in mint jelly.

'How are you?'

'Desperate to get out of here. I've started dreaming about bedpans. Tell me about Waters.'

'Ah well, my meeting with him went a bit . . . what do the British like to say . . . tits up.'

'How do you mean?'

'Well, I was sent to entrap him. In the end I got nothing. He's odd, for sure, and he's a bit of a religious kook. He loves his faith. I think he's a . . .' she made inverted commas with her fingers, 'a born-again Muslim. But I don't think he's your killer.'

'No?'

'He fancied the pants off Jillian Parker, that's for certain. Probably drove her potty with emails and phone calls. They may even have had a fling, after which she suffered dreadful postcoital regret for all I know. But burning, mutilating, hate killing? No, I don't think he'd do that.'

'You've been wrong before.'

'Have I?'

'I recall you quite liked Nakula. And he murdered five women.'

She swiped the air. 'That's different.'

'So we're back to square one.'

'Still can't connect the dots? No new developments?'

'Afraid not,' said Ruud. 'At any rate, I'm off the case now.

Natsir has taken over. Coffee? Soft drink? I can ask a nurse to run down to the cafeteria.'

Erica said no.

Ruud rubbed a hand over his face. 'Anyhow, run me through what happened. You got into Waters' car and then what?'

'I was getting to that. He decided to take me to see the Luar Batang Mosque. He recently converted to Islam.'

'So you said. But we knew that already. Who drove? His driver?'

'He drove himself.'

'Did he behave suspiciously? Was he nervous, looking in the car mirror, acting as if he had a tail, worried he was being followed?'

'No, he drove as if he didn't have a care in the world.'

'What about the scratches on his arms and neck?'

'I came right out and asked him. Very bold of me, I thought. He does martial arts. Grapples with other sweaty men – judo or jujitsu or something. I think I wrote down the name of the club in case you need witnesses. Did I ever tell you about the time I watched two fat men oil wrestling in Istanbul?'

'What else did you talk about?'

'Bosch.'

'The kitchen people?'

'No, you twit, the artist. Hieronymus Bosch. One of history's most fascinating artistic minds.'

Ruud was unimpressed. 'Was Glenn Beale at the exhibition?'

'*Goede God!* What a frightful gasbag! The man's a *schaamhaarvlechter*!'

Ruud was about to ask when . . .

'It's Dutch for someone who twines his pubic hair,' Erica explained.

'Charming.'

'And then there's that Murray Pocock, their press relations officer, as bland as skimmed milk. Poor chap never quite got round to developing a personality.' She dug into her bag. 'Fancy a Bath Oliver?'

Ruud declined.

She went on. 'What about a cookie? Surely you won't turn down a cookie. What with hospital food and all that.' She held out a manky chocolate digestive wrapped in tissue. 'Did you know cookie is a Dutch word? In Dutch it's *koekje*. Anyway, as I was saying, we talked about Bosch and his most ambitious work *The Garden of Earthly Delights*. Waters said he was twelve when he first laid eyes on it, the glorious triptych. His family had gone on a two-week break in Spain and his parents insisted they visit the Prado. He thought it was modern art and hated the bloody thing.'

Ruud checked his phone for messages.

'Funny isn't it,' she continued. Erica now had a box of Beech's chocolate assortment balanced on her lap. 'He thought a five-hundred-year-old painting was contemporary. But he wasn't far off, you know. Many still believe Bosch to be the first surrealist artist. Anyway, Waters blabbered on about the terrifying demons and bat-winged monsters and how the artist used the images as tools to elicit dread and dismay. Bosch gave him nightmares. Made him question his faith.'

'He said that?'

'Yes.'

'Interesting.'

'What are you thinking?' asked Erica.

Ruud held his forehead in the palm of his hand. 'I'm wondering if . . . no, it's probably nothing.'

'Come on, out with it.'

'Waters. If, and it's a big if, but if Waters is our man, let's try to break this down. He lives alone. Lost his wife. He's lonely. Feels dislocated. Converted to Islam to find meaning and truth but came away disappointed. Maybe he needs to talk, maybe he feels misunderstood, maybe he wants to tell someone what's driven him over the edge. An outlet.'

'He did seem very eager to chat,' admitted Erica.

'And he fits the physical profile. There's an athleticism about our murderer. Moving those women around; they weighed over sixty kilos each. That's no mean feat. He has to be strong and fit.'

Erica took a bite out of a chocolate triangle. Ruud watched her make a face and toss the teeth-marked tablet into the wastepaper bin. 'I don't care for the ones with the vanilla centres.'

'Perhaps without you realizing it, Waters was confiding in you. Do you think he's given us a motive, drawing a parallel between Bosch's depictions of good and evil and radical Islam? The opposition of light and dark. If he's our killer, maybe he's telling you why he kills.'

'Why tell me?'

'You're harmless and totally unconnected to the case.'

'Seems unlikely.'

'It's just a thought.'

'What do you know about Hieronymus Bosch?'

'Next to nothing,' admitted Ruud.

'Well, let me enlighten you, my dear. He grew up during the Renaissance, when Europe was experiencing a complete cultural reawakening. Many believe this blossoming of culture was a result of the Black Death, which spread throughout Europe and wiped out a third of the population. Those that survived reckoned that God had grown deaf. Many turned against the Church.'

'Why?'

'If you lost your entire family, wouldn't you grow distrustful of the Church and the divine order of the universe?'

'Maybe. So you're saying people rejected Christian teachings in favour of science, art and literature,' said Ruud.

'Precisely.'

'Sounds like the Western world today.'

'People don't go to Lourdes to see miracles any longer, they simply stare into their iPhones to witness the magic.'

'So it's possible Waters is comparing modern-day society with that of Bosch's sixteenth-century Holland?'

Involuntarily, Erica straightened her spine. 'Bosch's visual imagery is a warning to those who are morally corrupt. He's saying, 'Look, sinners, look and beware what will become of you if you fail to live a pious and faithful existence.'

Ruud scratched his chin, then worked his fingers under the hospital smock to scratch his stomach.

'What's more,' said Erica. 'Hieronymus Bosch was a pseudonym. His real name was Jeroen van Aken. Not many people know that.'

She broke off.

'Is that relevant?' asked Ruud.

'Well, if you consider Shane Waters converted to Islam and took a Muslim name, which nobody seems to know, then yes, I think it's relevant. Both he and Bosch are hiding behind aliases.'

'Go on.'

'Bosch's portrayals of turmoil and lust, where a pregnant Virgin Mary becomes a lizard, spoonbills sprout human feet and the world is a living nightmare, reflected the horrors of his time.'

'A society gone mad,' said Ruud.

'Where temptation, depravity and perversion are the cause of all evil.'

'Perhaps that's what the killer is telling us. That we're living in a sick society only radical Islam can cure. Otherwise all humankind will be condemned to hellfire.'

'Yes.'

'"Indeed, those who disbelieve in our teachings, we will burn them with fire. Every time their skins are roasted through we will replace them with other skins so they may taste the punishment once more. For God is majestic and all-wise."' He stared hard at Erica. 'Surah An-Nisa. Verse four fifty-six. You can see the connection, can't you?'

Erica, proffering some Mint Imperials, made a face. 'It gets better. There are three panels in Bosch's *Garden of Earthly Delights*. The left panel depicts scenes of the Garden of Eden. Adam, Eve and God in paradise with a few animals thrown in. The central panel depicts mankind gone insane with sin, eating, drinking and shagging wantonly. Finally, the right panel shows a hellscape. The scene is set at night. Cities are on fire, animals feast on human flesh. The damned are tossed into a pit of flames. There's also a pig in a nun's habit.'

Ruud's head tilted sideways.

'Your killer wears a pig mask and he burns his victims at night,' said Erica.

'He does indeed. Interesting theory.'

'It's a bit thin, to be honest.'

Ruud rubbed his chin. 'Emaciated. Bulimic even, but we've little else to go on. So back to your date with Shane Waters. You got to Luar Batang and then what?'

'Well, that's just it. We never got as far as the mosque. He drove to the corner of it and, next thing I know, he receives a text message and informs me he has something urgent to go to.'

'Did he mention what?'

'No, but he seemed rather agitated.'

'What time was this?'

'About three o'clock.'

'That's exactly the time POLRI issued a press release about Anita Dalloway's Alice band.'

'The swine dropped me on the side of the road and raced off. Took me an age to hail a taxi.'

'Maybe he got a tip-off and panicked. He ditched his car and got into the Subaru.'

'It's possible.'

Ruud looked at Erica and smiled. 'Thanks for helping out.'

'I'm sorry I couldn't get more out of him.'

'How's Imke?'

'Still in shock, I think. She was told you were dead, Ruud. That hit her very hard. Not to mention the poor female officer dying in her arms.' Erica shook her head. 'She's also pissed off that I didn't call her when I got back from the Australian Embassy, but I was so tired. Champagne does that to me, especially in the afternoon. I crawled into bed and took the hotel phone off the hook. Silly girl thought Waters had abducted me.'

'A few weeks in Amsterdam will do her a world of good. It's about time she made up with her father.'

The phone on the bedside locker rang. It was Hamzah. 'We've found something. Tech boys at LABFOR did an image search on Google and spotted Shane Waters in the society pages of Indonesia *Tatler*. Guess who he was photographed with? Emily Grealish.'

'You're joking,' said Ruud.

'They were both at the Maple Leaf Ball last March, sponsored by the Indonesia Canada Chamber of Commerce.'

'Keep digging. Even if Witarsa says to stop, keep digging.'

Later that morning, the commissioner was one of four visitors to Ruud's bedside, together with Hamka Hamzah, Solossa and Aiboy Ali.

'We recovered your firearm, your wallet and your warrant card,' said Solossa. 'Sabhara also took your clothing left at the scene as evidence. You'll get it all back when forensics finish with them.'

Ruud got stuck into the questions straight away. 'The man who tortured me, what have we got on him?'

Witarsa paced splay-footed around Ruud's bed. 'His name is Bayu. Aged twenty-seven. Married. No children. Until recently, he worked at Gatot Soebroto Army Hospital. He was suspended February first on grounds of stealing medical equipment and pharmaceutical supplies. In the meantime, it seems he was moonlighting. Our BNN undercover boys say he did jobs for the *preman* underworld, stitching up stab wounds, treating gunshot injuries, that sort of thing. Injuries the organized gangs didn't want the authorities to know about.'

'Seems like he also ran a sideline in torture.'

'Word is the *preman* boys paid Bayu handsomely for his discretion.'

'What about the second man? The one giving him instructions.'

Witarsa adjusted his shirt cuffs. A tic on his face started up. 'Ruud, are you absolutely sure there was another person in the room with you?'

Ruud held his gaze. 'Yes.'

'There is no evidence to suggest anyone else was at the Kali Baru site. Forensics are working on what they found but so far nothing's come to light.'

'I'm telling you there was. He was standing right behind me.'

'Did you see him? Can you recognize his voice?'

'He was there. What about my car? Did they search my car?'

'It's been impounded. They're going through it now.' Witarsa folded his arms. 'Ruud, I should tell you that Fahruddin wants to close the case.'

'I can't let him do that. Bayu was just a pawn. The killer's still out there.'

Ruud put the Bosch theory to his colleagues.

Everyone nodded uncertainly.

Hamzah had a blurred expression on his face.

They all admitted to never having heard of Hieronymus Bosch.

'You may well be right about Waters,' said Witarsa. 'But there's little we can do about it until we have some hard evidence to put in front of the foreign affairs minister. We need conclusive information. So unless we make further progress, Waters remains untouchable.'

Ruud sat up in bed. 'We have to catch this bastard, Joyo.'

'You're taking this personally, aren't you?'

'What the fuck do you expect? He had me tortured and he killed Alya. A week into the job and she's dead. I should have sent a more experienced team to the JK Café.'

'She knew the risks, *Gajah*,' said Aiboy.

All five men were silent for a while.

Hamka Hamzah extended both arms. 'I brought you some *makanan*.' He presented Ruud with a clear plastic bag of fish head curry. 'I got it from the Singapore-style restaurant, *nih*.'

'Thank you, Hamzah.'

The officer smiled broadly and reslicked his centre parting, segregating his hair down the middle with his fingertips.

Witarsa rubbed his tired eyes, which were rimmed with red. 'Ruud, I want you to know that I'm not replacing you with Natsir.'

Ruud eyeballed the commissioner. 'You're not.'

'No. The case has stalled badly enough already. We need you at the helm. If you're right about a second man then you're the only one who can find this *jancok*.'

'And I will find him, as soon as they let me out of this godforsaken place.'

'It's true, the morgue facilities are pretty poor here,' Solossa said. 'They're much better at Persahabatan General.' He cleared his throat. 'Anyway,' he sniffed, 'as instructed, Sabhara searched your Toyota's glove compartment and found the item you wanted put forward for DNA testing. We'll have the results in a few days. Also, we have some developments on the fibres discovered at the Sion Church crime scene. The fibres we found came from a cotton-polyester blend. Dark blue colour. Most likely it is trouser material. We carried out extensive brand comparisons and guess what? This specific cotton-polyester blend is only available at military stores.'

'You're saying the guy is a soldier?'

'It would appear so. What's more, the fibres do not match any clothing in Bayu's household. At any rate, General Medical Officers at Gatot Soebroto Army Hospital are issued with white trousers and coats made from an entirely different cotton and polyester variety.'

'So he either has or has had a military background,' said Ruud.

'Fauzi!' Hamzah said in a stage whisper.

'Possibly. Although the clothing could be stolen.'

'Yes, but,' said Witarsa, his voice dropped an octave, 'fibres from a pair of blue trousers won't stand up in court. Defence counsel will argue that there are four hundred thousand armed forces personnel who wear the same brand.'

'But it's a start,' said Aiboy Ali.

'OK,' said Ruud. 'Let's put all our efforts into our two main suspects: Shane Waters and Lieutenant General Fauzi.'

'What about the others?'

'We're dumping Oskar, the security guard. No motive.'

'What about Imam Aflan Gunawan?'

'The imam's a hate preacher so I want eyes on him.'

'Understood. Meanwhile, we have Tantar in a holding cell at Kebon Nanas,' said Aiboy Ali. 'He's been locked up since Thursday morning.'

'Good. Keep him there for now. Hamzah, I want Fauzi under surveillance too. Get your Sabhara friends to put a twenty-four-hour watch on his movements.'

'And Waters?'

'Aiboy, you're on Waters' tail. He's a slippery fucker so stay close. The moment he leaves the confines of the embassy I want you on him like a dog tick.'

'Yes, *Gajah.*'

'The top brass won't like the sound of this,' said Witarsa.

'In that case don't tell them,' said Ruud. 'Hamzah, get me all you can on Bayu. The bastard said he was being paid. Find out by whom. Check his bank account, check his wife's bank account, check under his mattress. Also, go through his phone records. I want to know who his friends were, who he went to school with, where he ate, who he ate with, who he slept with, everything.'

'That will take time, boss.'

'Get started on it right away.'

'Yes, boss.'

'Any other developments?'

Aiboy said, 'Yes. Soentoro, our office manager, says he went to school with Fauzi's ADC. Soentoro thinks he can coerce the ADC into revealing some of Fauzi's activities.'

'Excellent.'

'There's one more thing,' said Witarsa. 'Pastor Ignatius Kwong. He met with an accident. His body was found in the Ciliwung River yesterday morning. Drowned. Looks like suicide.'

'This case is a bag of surprises, isn't it?'

'There's more,' continued Witarsa. 'Emily Grealish's apartment was broken into two nights ago.'

'Damn it.' Ruud kicked off his bed sheet.

'The locks were broken. There was nothing subtle about it, the door was smashed in. But it doesn't appear to be your common curry-sauce-variety burglary. The TV wasn't taken nor the CD player.'

'Who reported it?'

'Neighbour. A Mrs Mashud. She called the police when she saw the damage to the front door.'

'He was after the USB drive. Right, we have to move fast. How's Hartono?'

'Discharged last night.' Aiboy twirled his hand around the top of his head. 'He's wearing a white protective turban. He's at home recuperating.'

'Get him back to work as soon as possible.' Ruud climbed out of bed. 'Imke brought me a fresh set of clothes. They're in the bag over there. Pass me a shirt.'

Aiboy handed him some clothes.

'I'll need a new phone, too.' Ruud tore at the strings of his hospital gown and pushed his legs into a pair of trousers. 'Give me a hand with this sling, will you? And someone's going to have to do my shoelaces.' He thrust aside the IV pole. 'I'm busting out of here.'

Chapter Forty

Shane Waters' voice boomed over the phone. 'First *Inspektur* Pujasumarta, how may I be of assistance?'

Ruud was in the Incident Room. He disengaged the speakerphone button and held the handset to his ear. 'Sorry to intrude on your day, First Secretary Waters, but I wanted to follow up on Jillian Parker's murder. No, we still haven't made an arrest, but we have several suspects. Yes, that's right. Sorry? No, I can't go into any details, as I'm sure you're aware, but I do need to ask you a question. Did you know either Emily Grealish or Anita Dalloway personally? Yes, the women in the papers, the other two victims. Very tragic, indeed. Did you ever meet either of them? No? You're absolutely certain? OK. That's strange because we have a picture of you and Emily Grealish taken at the Maple Leaf Ball last March, sponsored by the Indonesia Canada Chamber of Commerce. Yes, that's right, last March. Yes, of course you meet loads of people. The thing is, was that the only time your paths ever crossed? I see. As far as you know.

'What about Lieutenant General Fauzi? Do you know him? Oh, you do. Interesting. And how many times have you met? Twice to your knowledge. And both times at diplomatic events? Please tell me when was the most recent meeting. Let me just write that down. The Australia Indonesia Business Council lunch last November. Thank you, that's all I wanted to know. You've been very helpful. We'll be in touch if necessary.'

The wound in Ruud's shoulder throbbed like a fever pulse. There were painkillers in his pocket if he needed them. Buprenorphine – 400 micrograms every six to eight hours.

Ruud limped across the corridor and into his office. Inside he found Werry Hartono bent over an ironing board, arranging a pair of trousers under a sheet of newspaper. The iron hissed in his hand. His left thumb was in a splint.

'What are you doing?' said Ruud.

'What does it look like I'm doing?'

The right side of Hartono's face was so swollen he couldn't open his eye. His chin was all scratched and he had a bandage wrapped round the top of his head like a turban.

'This is my office, not a bloody Chinese laundry.'

Hartono disconnected the iron from the outlet and placed it on the metal tray. 'I'll let it cool before putting it away.' He regarded Ruud. 'When were you released from hospital?'

'I discharged myself a few hours ago,' said Ruud.

Both of them moved stiffly, still feeling their injuries.

'You look like shit,' said Ruud.

'I've been working. What's your excuse?'

Ruud smiled. 'Put your trousers back on and come with me.'

'Where are we going?'

'To the seaside.'

* * *

Kali Baru.

A neighbourhood of warehouses, boatyards and garbage-strewn waterways.

Five hundred metres from the waterfront in an abandoned chemical storage plant.

Ruud's torch penetrated the darkness of the *gudang*, throwing light on to the ceiling of the chemical depot and into every nook, cranny and cubbyhole. He didn't stop to look at the barber's chair or the dried blood on the vinyl upholstery and floor.

Sweat formed on his brow. It was warm inside and the interior walls were streaked with scummy damp. He shivered at the memory of the place.

By torchlight he navigated the maze of empty corridors and found an exit in the back, where the dormant cooling units were housed.

A doorway, an escape route.

So, this was how the second man had made his way out.

The fucker got away just in time.

Perhaps he'd sensed Aiboy coming.

Ruud's torch shone brightly. He retraced his steps, prowling back and forth, back and forth, along the passageways. There was a strong smell of urine and his shoes were smeared with rat pellets.

He couldn't find any clues.

He straddled the yellow *garis polisi* barrier tape and emerged into the open.

He blinked hard. The sun stung his darkness-accustomed pupils.

'Boss!' someone called.

Ruud shielded his face with a hand.

Unlike him, Werry Hartono was fit to drive. The young

second lieutenant was waving at Ruud, leaning against a purple Mitsubishi Lancer signed out from the Polres Metro car pool.

'What is it?'

'Turn on your phone. The Commissioner wants to speak with you.'

'I'll call him back.'

Ruud turned away from Hartono and made a mental note of his surroundings. Everywhere he looked he saw trash. The gutters were choked with rubbish and debris from the recent floods. Rocking on his toes, right arm in a sling, Ruud gazed at the crap tossed across the forecourt. Indonesians were terrific at ignoring shit on the streets. There may be bottle tops, soiled newspapers, crushed milk cartons, coconut husks, styrofoam cups and household batteries scattered in their path, plastic bags hanging from trees, but they walk on by.

The sun on his face, he wheeled away from the abandoned storage facility and imagined the second man making his way down here on foot, on to the narrow road and disappearing into the press of people. Had he gone east towards the river or west towards the theme park?

Ruud thought of the Saturday afternoons he'd come here as a kid. His dad would drive, park close by, just down the road really, near the docks, and they'd both stroll through the fish *pasar*, selecting tiger prawns from buckets and barracuda and tilapia for the Sunday barbie. His dad would stick all the fish in the esky and afterwards they'd head to the theme park for twenty minutes.

It seemed a lifetime ago.

A black crow picked through a jumble of scrap. Ruud kicked a styrofoam cup at it. He was sore, his shoulder and chest still stung and his head felt full of rocks.

Behind him the thrusting city bustled with activity. Clots of three-wheeled *bajaj* gathered at a set of lights. Vendors sold fried rice and grilled chicken. Hustlers pushed fake Ray Bans and counterfeit watches. Street kids played *mencolek* – tapping one another on the back, then running away.

Ruud watched them for a bit, wondering if anyone had seen anything sinister. No, of course they hadn't.

Across the roofs came the sound of prayers. He tuned out the engine rumbles, motorcycle horns and incantations.

A bus idled by a stop. Great swirls of monoxide fumes belched from its backside.

Ojeks zipped past.

Dark crescents of perspiration formed under his arms. He thought he still smelled of hospital, of cetrimide and Savlon. It was in his hair and in his lungs.

Ruud turned once again and stared at the busted metal door, the one Aiboy had kicked in, looking but not seeing, his mind miles away.

Something nagged at him; it had bugged him all morning: the note that had been found in Emily Grealish's bedside drawer. 'If anything should happen to me, put everything on ice.' What the hell did it mean? And why was it addressed to the priest? 'On ice. Everything on ice.' The words billowed inside his head, hounding him, badgering him.

And then, just like that, he heard a bell: the sound ribboned out into the afternoon and a little ice-cream cart rolled into view.

You fuckin' beauty, Ruud said to himself.

He snatched his brand-new ASUS phone from his left trouser pocket and dialled a number. 'Aiboy, it's me.' He talked over the traffic, a finger in one ear. 'When Sabhara got into Emily Grealish's apartment, how badly turned over was it? Yeah. OK. Total ransack. What about the kitchen? Was the fridge disturbed? Yes, the fridge. Right. Meet me at her place in half an hour.'

Emily Grealish's lifeless apartment was a mess: piles of clothes on the floor, books and papers thrown everywhere, crockery and cutlery scattered here and there. Picture frames lay broken underfoot. The backs of mirrors smashed. Chairs overturned. Pillows shredded, feathers settled on the tops of tables and under settees.

In the kitchen, Ruud pulled at the bottom handle of the Maytag refrigerator and felt the suction release.

'Electricity supply in the flat still works,' said Aiboy Ali, slouched against the far wall. 'According to the landlord, Emily Grealish paid her rent well in advance and settled her utility bills on the first weekend of every month.'

Ruud stuck his head in the fridge. 'Everything in the flat's been demolished except the ice box. Lucky old us.'

All that was left was a bottle of Perrier, an empty egg carton, a tub of peanut butter, several cans of tonic water, some pickles in a jar and two tubes of mustard. 'Landlord's been in, has he?'

'He's putting the place back on the market next week. He says he dropped by to bin the milk, cheese and other perishables.'

'When was that?'

Aiboy Ali blew a strand of hair off his nose. 'He entered the premises on Thursday morning, as soon as forensics finished up and Sabhara released it from police custody. He came because he didn't know when Emily's parents were planning on packing up her possessions.'

'And when was the place broken into?'

'Some time on Saturday evening.' Aiboy's bovver boots crackled, crushing broken glass underfoot. The floor was slippery with olive oil. 'The neighbour noticed the state of the front door and called the police. She didn't see anyone entering or leaving.'

'Did the intruder leave anything behind?'

'No, *Gajah*.'

'When I was a kid my mother told me a story by Roald Dahl about a doctor who treated an Arabian prince, saving his life. In payment the doctor received a massive diamond. Soon after, the doctor and his wife went on a trip abroad and decided to stash the diamond in their freezer. To cut a long story short, their house got burgled while they were away and the kitchen got trashed, including the things in the fridge, and the diamond was gone. But as fate would have it, the next day the doctor was alerted to a patient in surgery who had a piece of bone lodged in his intestine. It wasn't a piece of bone at all, though, it was a diamond, and the patient was the very same cat burglar who'd broken into his house and fixed himself a drink in the doctor's kitchen, swallowing the diamond thinking it was an ice cube.'

Ruud went to the freezer compartment. The door made very little noise when he tugged it open.

Two trays of ice. That was what he found.

He pulled them out and inspected each tray, tapping the ice cubes with the ends of his fingers.

'Now, what have we here?' Ruud held one of the trays up to the light. 'You clever girl, Emily.'

'What is it, *Gajah*?'

'Pass me a knife from one of the drawers, will you, mate?' Aiboy Ali found a steak knife. 'Actually, you'd better do this. I've only got one arm. You see how those two middle squares sit higher than the rest? There's something hidden underneath. Take the tray apart, but mind your fingers. We don't want another visit to A&E.'

Chapter Forty-One

Back in the Incident Room, Werry Hartono fumbled clumsily with the tripod projection screen. His left thumb splint kept catching on things.

Police Brigadier General Fahruddin, Commissioner Witarsa and Aiboy Ali watched the proceedings with bemused expressions on their faces.

'There,' he said finally. 'Ready now, sir.'

Ruud thanked him and asked everyone to take a seat. He held a sheaf of papers, which he farmed out to each man.

They all looked at the screen, faces turned upwards.

'Gentlemen, there's been a turn of events, and, owing to the nature of this investigation, I've invited the Brigadier General to join us. *Terima kasih, Pak*, we appreciate you coming at such short notice. Earlier today we recovered a USB stick from Emily Grealish's apartment. She'd wrapped it in cling-film and hidden it in her freezer. Luckily for us, the cold didn't damage any of the data. Stored within the USB stick are bank account numbers, photographs, secret documents, audio files and emails. A great deal of material. Material that points to fraud and corruption on a massive scale.'

'Fraud and corruption perpetrated by whom?' asked Fahruddin.

'A high-standing figure. It's rather sensitive.'

'For God's sake, Pujasumarta, give us a name.'

'Lieutenant General Fauzi, Director for International Cooperation, Ministry of Defence. It's my belief that Fauzi not only committed acts of fraud against the Government of Indonesia but also killed Jillian Parker, Anita Dalloway, Emily Grealish and Alya Entitisari.'

'Do you have proof? Do you have motive?'

'Yes, I believe I do. We're trying to piece it all together, but let's just say there's compelling evidence to take to the Chief Justice.'

The screen lit up with images. 'Shell companies. Offshore bank accounts in the BVI and Cayman Islands. Names, dates, account numbers.' Ruud double-clicked on a window and several images popped up. 'It's all here.'

It took Ruud's superiors several moments to process this information. Ruud watched their throats stiffen and their bodies tense. The shock on their faces was undeniable.

'How many people know about this?' said Fahruddin icily.

'Apart from our OM, Soentoro, only the people in this room.'

Witarsa pored over the handouts and graphics. 'How the hell did Emily Grealish get her hands on all this?'

'She spent days with Fauzi when abroad. The two were having an affair. She kept an online journal. When she suspected he was doing deals on the sly she started looking into his activities. She made copies of his bank statements. She took audio recordings of his conversations. There's video, too, of Fauzi discussing money transfers with representatives from a Liechtenstein bank. I imagine she filmed it surreptitiously on her phone. It would seem that she also got into his computer.'

'How could he be so careless?' said Witarsa.

'Because he trusted her. He might even have been in love with her. Unfortunately, for Fauzi, she didn't feel the same way about him. I think it's fair to say that Emily Grealish was an opportunist.'

'She was blackmailing him.'

'That's what it boils down to. There's certainly enough information here to suggest that he paid her off. However, things took a turn for the worse when she got pregnant. If you turn to page six of the handout, you'll see texts sent from Grealish to Fauzi, dated January twenty-ninth and thirtieth, informing him of her condition and demanding a million US dollars. "We can keep this a secret but I will require a nest egg to do so. It would be awful if everything I know somehow got leaked to the press," she writes.'

'What did she have on him?' asked Witarsa, rumple-faced.

'A great deal.'

'Explain.'

'Page nine. Indonesia agreed to buy a squadron of utility helicopters in twenty fifteen. The contracts were signed in London in December. It appears the price was decided on but the purchase fee adjusted to ensure Fauzi took a percentage. A sweetener. Why choose Bell over Eurocopter? Sikorsky over Atlas? Well, now we know. The middleman made sure Fauzi was generously compensated for choosing particular aircrafts. How do we know this? Well, Emily Grealish took a voice recording of the meetings.' Ruud played the audio accompaniment.

Lieutenant General Fauzi's voice came across clearly and succinctly as he talked about inducements. The men listened in silence.

When the recording ended, Ruud carried on. 'Fauzi made

a killing on that deal. The same can be said of the fleet of military vehicles acquired earlier this year. Six armoured personnel carriers, a dozen light tanks, three self-propelled howitzers. On this occasion we do not have audio; instead we have evidence of funds being transferred to a Cayman Islands account.'

'How much money are we talking about here?' said Witarsa.

'Paid into Fauzi's accounts? Last year alone? I'm guessing over a hundred million euros. Transfers were made in euros rather than American dollars to avoid going through the US dollar clearing system and alerting the US Treasury Department.'

'But what does this have to do with the other victims?' said Witarsa. 'Jillian Parker and Anita Dalloway? They weren't associated with Fauzi.'

Werry Hartono stepped forward. 'That's precisely the point. We believe they were murdered to mislead us, to make the investigative team look left when we should have been looking right.'

Ruud clawed a hand through his hair. 'The Quranic text, the burnings, the pig mask – they're all an elaborate deception. Kill three white women, rip out their insides and make it appear like a homicidal Islamic fanatic, a religious maniac, is on the loose, pull the police this way and that . . .'

'The thing is,' said Hartono, 'we were always trying to find a cause and motive that involved all three victims. We wasted time looking for patterns, hoping to link the women in some way. But there was never any link.'

'Wait, hold up a minute. You're suggesting he killed Jillian Parker and Anita Dalloway for no reason whatsoever?' said Witarsa.

'He left a false trail of bodies. He wanted us to think there was a serial killer out there, but the only person he wanted dead was Emily Grealish.'

'Physical evidence,' said Fahruddin. 'What have you got on him?'

'Solossa has LABFOR working on DNA evidence that should put Fauzi at the scene of crime.'

'How long until he has confirmation?'

'Two or three days.'

Fahruddin looked unsettled. Ruud's words seemed to freeze the blood in his veins. For the first time in Ruud's experience the brigadier general appeared vulnerable, breakable. Blinking rapidly, chewing his lip, he placed both hands flat on the rim of his peaked cap. 'What,' he said, his vowels clipped and dry, 'do you propose to do with this information, Pujasumarta?'

'I was going to ask you to get the Chief Justice to issue an arrest warrant.'

'First *inspektur*, I admire your tenacity, but I will do nothing of the sort.' Fahruddin rose from his chair. 'Not until I discuss the matter with the Minister of Home Affairs. I want the case files transferred immediately to Medan Merdeka Utara. For the minister's eyes only. Understood?'

'What are we meant to do in the meantime?'

They stood facing each other.

'You sit tight.'

'With all due respect, sir, I don't feel like sitting tight.'

Fahruddin turned and jabbed Ruud in the chest with his swagger stick. 'I couldn't give a blind fuck how you feel, detective. Do as you're damn well told. And keep your mouths shut, understood? All of you. You're not to discuss this Fauzi mess with anybody. This is now a State Intelligence

Agency affair. Witarsa, gather up the handouts and take possession of the flash drive. Get hold of the head of NCB Interpol and meet me in my office in an hour.'

A nerve above Witarsa's eye began to jiggle independently to the rest of his face.

Witarsa watched Fahruddin barge out of the room. He held his head in his hands. His hands were shaking.

Chapter Forty-Two

Sit tight, he was told.

Wait it out.

But Ruud refused to wait it out.

Bollocks to that.

For two days running he and Aiboy Ali had staked out Fauzi's home on Kebayoran Baru, taking it in turn with Hartono and Hamzah. Eight hours on, eight hours off.

On the third morning, at six o'clock, minutes after the throaty rumble of Sunrise Prayers, they parked thirty metres across from the gatehouse and shut off the engine. It was an hour before dawn, before daylight replaced the spectral grey with splashes of colour.

The neighbourhood was quiet. Sparrows and pigeons were yet to awaken. The only sound was the radio jingle of JAK! FM spilling from the guard station opposite.

'I can't stand that local pop music,' said Aiboy, who shoved a Burgerkill CD into the car stereo and turned the volume up high. The music screeched.

A coarse-faced guard appeared at the mouth of the gatehouse. Ruud watched him from the shotgun seat of his Toyota Yaris, windows down, death metal blaring. For once, the appalling clatter made Ruud grin.

Aiboy Ali sat on the car bonnet, his feet not touching the ground. He ate *Tahu isi* out of a paper bag. The fritters tasted good and he grunted approvingly with each mouthful.

The coarse-faced guard used sign language, gesturing that they turn the music down.

Both detectives ignored him.

He lurched across the road. Angry. It was a ruse, of course – a similar hard-edged pantomime to the previous morning.

He'd berate them. Aiboy would flash his warrant card. They would pretend to argue a bit, and in exchange for some information the guard would receive a fold of cash in the parting handshake.

They stood away from the streetlight and had a muted conversation, the guard looking past Aiboy, eyeing the distance to see whether the other guards were watching.

With their business concluded, Ruud killed the music as Aiboy climbed into the driver's seat.

After a while it started to drizzle and Ruud felt his elbow grow damp from the spray.

'Fauzi senior knows we're out here and he's not happy. Do you think he's complained to Fahruddin?' Aiboy produced a thermos and poured out two cups of hot coffee.

Ruud eyed the overcast sky, studying the bank of low clouds. 'What's on the menu today?'

'According to the chauffeurs and maids, we have a full house. Both children are in residence. The daughter, Harum, is home for a few days. Where is she at college again?'

'Bandung Institute of Technology.'

'Right, anyway, she's home. The son, Noah, is also here. He arrived late last night. They had a nice family dinner together.'

'Did Noah drive himself?'

'Came on his motorbike. Daddy bought him a Harley.'

'Lucky bastard.'

'According to our office manager snitch, Soentoro, Noah is scheduled to fly to Bangkok around noon. He's helping to coordinate a joint military exercise held in Thailand. This news came direct from Fauzi's ADC.'

'Tell me what the *sopir* had to say?'

'As of last night's instructions, at nine a.m. Mrs Fauzi will be driven in the Mercedes. She has a nail appointment at Grand Indonesia Mall at ten. A little later, Harum will be collected to join her mother for lunch.'

'Go on.'

'At eleven o'clock the second *sopir* will be on standby to take Noah back to his naval base in the Range Rover, and from there he will make his own way to the airport. The Harley's got a fuel filter problem so it's going into the workshop for repairs.'

'Which leaves us with Fauzi senior.'

'Lieutenant General Fauzi apparently has no engagements today. However, he has requested that the Audi be ready with a full tank of petrol. Destination uncertain.'

For the next two hours Aiboy watched YouTube clips on his mobile device, while Ruud, huddled in his seat, worked on several Sudoku puzzles.

At a quarter past eight, Ruud, tapping the side of his head with a pencil, looked up to see a gardener in green overalls materialize at the mouth of the driveway, raking leaves and stuffing them in a sack.

'More coffee?' asked Aiboy. Ruud proffered his cup.

The gardener looked at them, then looked away.

Forty-five minutes later, the Mercedes, windows blackened, departed on schedule at nine. Ruud saw a shadow in the back seat and assumed it was Lestari Fauzi on her way to the nail salon.

After that the boom gate lifted again at nine ten and the Audi TT tore past the gatehouse.

'Did you see who was at the wheel?'

Aiboy Ali swept the hair from his eyes. 'Noah Fauzi.'

Ruud's insides pinched. 'I thought the father was taking the Audi.'

Aiboy Ali shrugged and returned to his YouTube viewing, his mouth moving as he lip-synced song lyrics.

At nine forty Ruud received a call from Solossa. 'Did I wake you?' said the *dokter forensic*. 'Listen, I've got the genetic fingerprinting results back from LABFOR.'

'And? Does the cigar DNA match the Alice Band DNA?'

'Yes and no.'

'What the hell are you saying?'

'We compared the two samples and the STR strands and minisatellites are similar but not identical. But it's close. The string of numbers is a fifty per cent match.'

'Meaning?

'The two individuals are related.'

Ruud straightened. The pinching in his chest turned into a fluttering sensation.

'The Alice band sample,' Solossa went on. 'The amelogenin shows both an X and Y chromosome, so it's not the daughter.'

'Oh Jesus.' Ruud looked at Aiboy as Solossa expounded. 'That means we've been chasing the wrong person all along.'

Chapter Forty-Three

'Go!' Ruud slapped the glove compartment. 'He's making a run for it!'

'Who?' said Aiboy, gunning the engine.

'He's heading for the airport! We've got to catch him!'

'Who?'

'Noah Fauzi.'

'Is Solossa sure?'

Scrambling, Ruud stuck the blue light to the roof and turned on the siren. 'Stop yapping and step on it, will you?' The car accelerated down the road. 'Turn into Jalan Jend Sudirman and head for the underpass.'

Ruud dialled a number on his phone. 'Damia, it's Pujasumarta. I need to speak to Witarsa!' he yelled. 'Tell him it's an emergency!'

Aiboy shot Ruud a look. 'D'you want me to call Soentoro and ask him which flight Noah Fauzi's on?'

'Yes! Do that now.'

The car hit a pothole and juddered violently. Ruud strapped on his seat belt. 'Damia? Yes. Put him through. Witarsa, it's me!' he cried. 'I need you to issue an arrest warrant for Noah Fauzi. Yes, the very same. We have a DNA match. How long? Fuck. All right, I'll hold.'

The car swerved viciously, performing a wild overtaking manoeuvre, passing three buses and a lorry.

'Take the Inner Ring Road.'

'Let me do the driving, *Gajah*.'

Witarsa's voice came back on. 'Yes, I'm still here,' said Ruud. 'What? You're shitting me.'

Ruud put the commissioner on speakerphone. 'You're to stand down,' said Witarsa. 'Orders from the top. Fahruddin says we need to obtain MOJ approval.'

'Fuck you.'

'WHAT was that?' demanded the commissioner.

'We can't hear you,' shouted Ruud.

'Your orders are to stand dow—'

Ruud hung up and phoned the airport police. It took an age for his call to be transferred to the supervisor. He described Noah Fauzi in detail. 'Detain him for as long as you can,' he pleaded. 'We're working on getting a warrant. I don't care. I said we're working on it. Look, just do me a favour, OK? If you see him, hold onto him as long as you can.' Ruud cut the line and turned to Aiboy. 'What did Soentoro say?'

'He said there are three flights to Bangkok around noon. Thai, Garuda and AirAsia. He's finding out which one Fauzi's on.' Aiboy wove past oncoming traffic. He made quick jerking movements with his elbows. '*Gajah*, I've been thinking. If Noah Fauzi thinks we're onto him, why would he risk getting stopped at an airport.'

'What options does he have?'

'I don't know. What would you do?'

A vein pulsed on Ruud's temple. 'North. I'd head north.'

'North? You mean Sumatra?'

'Yes. Via Merak. I'd take the ferry from Merak to Bakauheni, then make for the east coast of Sumatra.'

'And cross the Straits of Malacca to Malaysia.'

'Exactly. It's not hard sneaking into Malaysia illegally. There'd be no record of him leaving Indonesia, so while we piss about searching high and low for him here, he could lie low for a while in some Malay *kampung*, purchase a fake passport, then fuck off to some shithole country we can't extradite him from.'

'What do you say, *Gajah*?'

'Witarsa's no help. We're going to have to do this alone.'

'It's a hundred and fifty kilometres to Merak Port.'

'I won't let this bastard get away, Aiboy, I won't.'

Chapter Forty-Four

The waters of the Sunda Strait were dark grey and murky, coloured here and there with oil rainbows and bits of bobbing plastic.

Like most days Merak Port's operations were teetering under the increased commercial traffic between Java and Sumatra. A long line of trucks waited along Jalan Pantura, ready to board the 1.30 p.m. ferry in an hour's time.

Ruud stood on the gangplank of the *Andhika*, glancing at the words 'We Bridge the Nation' painted bright and bold on its starboard hull. He'd just spoken again with the airport police supervisor. The cameras at the terminal's car park and departure zone hadn't spotted Fauzi's silver Audi, and there was no evidence a vehicle with the corresponding number plate was in the vicinity of Soekarno-Hatta. Furthermore, there was no indication that Noah Fauzi had boarded TG 434 to Bangkok, the Thai Airways flight he was booked on.

Ruud ran a palm across the nape of his neck; it came away glistening. His shirt stuck to him like a second skin. He checked his phone: seven missed calls from Witarsa.

With his good arm, Ruud shielded his eyes from the sun and studied the cars parked by the water's edge.

Here, too, he saw no sign of the silver Audi. With the ferry's ramps raised, Ruud could only surmise that the vehicle was somewhere on the *Andhika*'s car deck.

Aiboy appeared on the gangplank. 'Witarsa got hold of me. He's ordering you to cease whatever you're doing and return immediately to Central.'

'Fuck him.'

'That's what I thought you'd say. I hung up before I could respond.'

'What have you got?'

'I spoke with the captain. The last crossing was eighty minutes ago. Fauzi had a forty-minute head start on us. All the same, he wouldn't have made the earlier sailing.'

'So, if he's here, he'll be on this boat. Take me to the bridge.'

Ruud followed Aiboy up some steps.

'We're going to have to evacuate the ferry,' Ruud informed the captain.

The captain, a portly man called Tirto, studied Ruud's warrant card. 'I can only allow that if there's a risk to the safety of those on my boat. What is this about, *nah*?' He tugged the ends of his thick moustache. 'Already, you've delayed departure by ten minutes.'

'I told you. We're after a fugitive,' said Aiboy.

'This is highly irregular. I speak to one of your superiors, *meh*?'

'How many people do you have making the crossing today?' said Ruud.

'On this journey?' He glanced at his log. 'One hundred and forty passengers and thirty-two vehicles.'

'One hundred and forty passengers, not including crew.

He could easily take one of them hostage. We have to act fast. Do you have closed–circuit cameras on board?'

'Cameras? No.' He laughed uncomfortably. 'No cameras. The company is looking to install a system soon. Is this man dangerous?'

'He's killed four people.'

Tirto's eyes widened. He took a backward step and stood amongst the monitors and radar screens. 'Listen, in that case I should contact the Merak Port Authority. KP Three also.'

'Yes, call the Sea Port Police. But first do as I say. It's crucial that you cooperate fully. Do this our way and you'll be a hero. The papers will say you saved your passengers and crew.'

'Really, *meh*?'

'For sure, man,' said Aiboy.

Ruud put his good arm around the captain's shoulder. 'Make an announcement that there's a problem with the engine. Ask everyone to disembark in an orderly fashion. Inform them it's a temporary situation and they are to leave their vehicles where they are. Keep the bow doors shut. OK?'

'Will my name really be in the newspapers?' Captain Tirto thrust his chest out; he already had the intercom microphone in his hand.

'For sure, man,' said Aiboy. 'What paper do you read?'

'*Tribun Jabar.*'

'Your family's going to be so proud of you. Get everyone safely off the boat and let us do our job, OK?' said Ruud.

The captain cleared his throat and held the microphone to his mouth. '*Bapak-bapak dan ibu-ibu . . .*' His voice resounded from the PA system.

★   ★   ★

A quarter of an hour later, the captain gave Aiboy Ali a thumbs-up signal, indicating that the vessel had been cleared of people. 'Secure the bridge door once we've gone,' Ruud instructed Tirto.

Ruud watched the passengers disgorge from the ferry and assemble on the pier, spilling onto the concourse, studying each man's face through the captain's binoculars. He saw people arguing, men gesturing to the sky, spotty adolescents jabbing their phones, a woman fanning herself with a magazine, a child clinging to his mother's leg.

'Any sign of him?' asked Tirto.

'No. He's still on board.'

Aiboy Ali pulled out his Glock 17 and checked the magazine.

'Are you up for this?' Ruud asked him.

'Trust me, *Gajah*, I want this guy as much as you do.'

'Let's try to take him alive.' Ruud lifted his bad arm a fraction. 'Get this sling off me, will you?'

Aiboy Ali helped Ruud untangle himself, undoing the reef knot and sliding the triangular bandage free. Ruud flexed his fingers.

Captain Tirto guided them out the door and engaged the locks.

With caution, the two policemen descended the stairs to the passenger lounge, Ruud's Nike sneakers trailing behind Aiboy's bovver boots. Their feet made light tinny sounds on the metal stairs. Featherlight footsteps.

His nerves on high alert, Ruud released the safety on his Heckler.

Keeping low, both hands gripping the Heckler & Koch 9 mm, Ruud did a sweep of the doorways and snack counters. He went up and down the aisles, row by row, checking the seats. There was a child's stuffed toy left on the floor. A little further on he found a guitar case propped up against the emergency doors.

The *Andhika* was eerily quiet.

A television screen mounted on the near wall ran a silent advertisement for ASDP Ferries on a continuous loop.

Thick shafts of sunshine streamed in through the lounge windows. The sunlight shone on metal armrests, tray tables, fittings and storage bins, dazzling Ruud momentarily.

Squinting, Ruud made his way along several seating areas and took cover behind a vending machine. He signalled to Aiboy across the room and hissed, 'Toilets!'

Aiboy Ali crept into the Gents' rest room, then the Ladies'. He emerged with a shake of the head. 'Clear. Now where?'

Ruud pointed to the floor.

To the car deck.

Chapter Forty-Five

Aiboy Ali descended the stairs first.

Ruud followed close behind. As soon as he came off the bottom step he could smell it: the stink of the farmyard. What the hell is down here? he wondered.

He took a half-step forward. With the bow door closed it was dark down below. Ruud had to wait several moments for his eyes to adjust to the lack of light.

Ruud kept his foot-shuffling to a minimum. He had to be quiet. But he could hear his heart thrumming in his ears. It was going crazy in his chest.

Wordlessly, Aiboy Ali indicated that he was going to creep up the port side. His hand accidentally brushed against the iron railing, and the railing called out. Every sound was amplified. Ruud felt his heart rate increase even more. It became hard to see, his peripheral field narrowed.

But then things came back into focus. There were eight rows of cars and lorries. Four to each row.

The pickup truck in front was stacked high with wooden crates. Ruud immediately saw that the crates were full of live chickens. The movements of the birds unsettled him. He wasn't sure where to train his eyes.

Thirty-two vehicles.

Noah Fauzi could be crouched behind any one of them, he thought. Is he armed? Yes, Ruud decided, he'll definitely be armed.

Control the distance to the threat, Ruud told himself. Stand two metres away from each car. Eyes on the target. Remember your training. One man searches. One man covers.

Motion to his left.

Ruud flinched.

Swivelling round, he held the Heckler at shoulder height, ready to fire. The chickens screeched and clucked in surprise. There was nothing there.

Ruud inched forward.

Five tiers from the bow doors he saw the silver Audi TT.

And then, somewhere ahead, the sound of glass shattering. A windscreen? A bottle breaking?

Shit.

Ruud bolted upright and advanced, accelerating sharply in response to the sound.

Breathless. Heart rate off the scales. He lunged at a silhouette. Everything was crisscrossed with shadows. His vision blurred.

Suddenly, Noah Fauzi was upon him, eyes bulging.

Slashing. Stabbing.

Bone and flesh collided. An eruption of pain exploded across Ruud's shoulders, knocking him off balance. The world tumbled.

Ruud was on the floor.

Fauzi's hands were clasped around the neck of a broken bottle and he thrust the jagged end at Ruud's head. Thrusting like a farmer driving a stake into the ground. The ground to one side sprayed a shower of glass. Ruud felt a sharp pain across his nose and cheeks, but his knees were drawn up and he kicked out.

He caught Fauzi in the chest. Within a second Ruud was up. He swung his left arm and the stock of his Heckler whacked against bone and jaw. He swung again and again until Fauzi's face hit the floor with a wet crack.

Fauzi struggled to his feet, but before he could rise, Aiboy Ali was kneeling on his back, pulling at his hands and snapping handcuffs to his wrists.

'You're under arrest, you sick bastard!' Aiboy yelled. 'We've got you.'

Ruud's head was swimming. There was blood in his mouth. He could taste it.

Aiboy hauled Fauzi upright.

Ruud wiped the blood from his face. He felt dizzy, yet he looked the man in the eyes.

Noah Fauzi had a sly smile on his face. He was speaking and Ruud had to concentrate hard to take in the words. 'Enjoy this while you can, gentlemen. If you think I'm going to jail then think again. I'm untouchable. My father's untouchable.'

'Then why make a run for it, Noah?' said Aiboy, discovering a canvas rucksack close by.

'I was taking a vacation.'

'A vacation. That's a good one. What's in the bag, Noah? Money? Enough to set up a new life somewhere?'

Aiboy pushed Fauzi into Ruud's arms and looked in the rucksack. Without thinking, Ruud held onto the man's elbow.

'Fuck me *Gajah*, it's full of US dollars. There must be over two hundred grand in here,' said Aiboy.

'When my father hears of this you'll be finished.' Ruud

listened to Fauzi talking. There was a smirk on the man's face. 'Mark my words. I'll be out on the street again by tomorrow morning. You idiots have just made the biggest mistake of your lives.'

'I suppose you're going to tell us you're innocent now, are you?' said Aiboy. 'That you didn't kill Emily or Jillian or Anita?'

Noah leaned in, putting his mouth close to Ruud's ear. 'Oh, I killed them all right. I watched their eyeballs burst in their heads.' He smiled. 'And there's fuck-all you're going to be able to do about it.'

Chapter Forty-Six

The Mighty Overlord himself occupied the penthouse offices of Polda Metro Jaya.

Usually, riding the elevator to the top tier made Ruud nervous. The last time he'd been up here was during the Nakula case. Back then, his nerves swam about in his stomach like a bloom of jellyfish.

No longer.

These people didn't intimidate him any more.

Not since Alya was killed. Not since he'd come so close to death himself.

A woman in a white blouse and navy skirt greeted him when the lift reached the top.

She led him down a plush corridor and tapped her nails on a door.

He entered the conference room and took in his surroundings: a square conference table, bare but for a wooden tray lined with bottled mineral water. Oil portraits lined the walls, eleven on either side of the window – all twenty-two of Indonesia's past and present Chiefs of Police, from General Said Soekanto Tjokrodiatmodjoto to General Badrodin Haiti.

'Please wait,' the woman commanded. 'They will be with you shortly.'

Five minutes later, seated at one end, Witarsa and Fahruddin faced the door. Opposite them slouched Ruud Pujasumarta, his right arm still in a sling, his nose and cheekbones pocked with butterfly bandages.

The sun streamed through the tall, skinny windows, warming the teak floorboards.

Fahruddin had a low stack of shiny pink files by his water glass. The gold stars on his uniform epaulettes glinted in the light. He offered Ruud a chilly smile.

Commissioner Joyo T. Witarsa was the first to speak. 'Thank you for joining us today, Ruud,' he said, wobbly-chopped.

'Did I have a choice?'

Forehead creasing, Witarsa ignored the petulance. His voice dropped in pitch. 'We wanted to update you on the Noah Fauzi case.'

'Top brass not joining us?'

'They will be briefed later. There are matters we must discuss first.'

'I'm all ears,' said Ruud.

'First of all, a job well done. You went above and beyond the call of duty to apprehend him.'

'Thank you.'

'You did, however, disobey direct orders to stand down. You were told on more than one occasion by a superior officer to refrain from making an arrest, which I believe you either ignored or misinterpreted.' His voice tailed away.

Ruud's face went still. He looked hard at his boss, kept his mouth shut.

'Having said that, I must commend you on your actions. However . . .'

'Here we go.'

'However, your arrest of Noah Fauzi seems to have opened up a casket of worms.'

'A great big fucking casket,' said Fahruddin.

'We've been placed in a particularly difficult situation, Ruud,' continued Witarsa. 'A situation that puts us in a bind.'

Fahruddin waved a hand in the air. 'Oh for heaven's sake, Witarsa, get to the point, will you?'

The commissioner cleared his throat. 'BNN have been in touch, Ruud. The National Narcotics Agency believes Fauzi has links with several of Jakarta's *preman* drug lords. There is strong talk he might have been laundering money for a Maluku smuggling ring led by Antonio Irawan, who is rumoured to go by the name SpongeBob.'

Ruud nodded. 'I've heard of SpongeBob.'

'Irawan is a ruthless bastard. One of BNN's informants was found stuffed in a barrel of acid earlier this month. A SpongeBob doll was placed beside the plastic barrel. It's his calling card. A warning to others, I suspect. All I can say is we were lucky to have the informant's DNA on record – there wasn't much left of him.'

Ruud grew agitated. 'So, you're saying Fauzi and Irawan are connected. Well, let's try them all together. Fauzi junior, Fauzi senior, SpongeBob, the lot.'

'It's not that simple.'

'Why not?'

'There are people at the top who owe other people favours.'

'Could you be a bit clearer?'

The commissioner tilted his head and squinted at the ceiling.

'Why did you ask me here today?' said Ruud.

Witarsa's hands appeared from under the table. He spread out his fingers. 'We're going to have to put everything on hold for the foreseeable future.'

'On hold? We have hard evidence that will put both Noah Fauzi and his father away for years. We have to act now.'

'The MOJ don't agree.'

'What are you talking about?'

Witarsa clawed a hand over his face. The pouches under his eyes grew heavier. His left eyelid fluttered like an angry bee. 'They are suggesting we don't go to the public pros-ecutor with this.'

Police Brigadier General Fahruddin cut in, his voice hard and sharp, 'It is to be handled internally.'

'What the hell does that mean?' said Ruud.

'What the bugger do you think it means? Use your bloody imagination, boy.' The *Brigadir Jenderal* stuck his chin out defiantly.

'He's getting off scot-free.'

'Both the Ministry of Justice and the Indonesian Prosecution Service are in full agreement regarding both of the Fauzi men: we are to avoid criminal proceedings.'

'Oh, right, they're in full agreement. Is that meant to make me feel better? Is that meant to make the victims' families feel better? Noah Fauzi is guilty. You know he did it. I know he did it. Everybody in the department knows he did it! He should be in a cage, locked up in Cipinang, not driving around in his father's Audi TT.'

'Calm down, Ruud,' Witarsa commanded.

'What about the KPK? Have you cleared this with the Corruption Eradication Commission?'

Fahruddin pursed his lips. The chin remained defiant. 'This sticks in my throat too, Pujasumarta, believe me.'

'He had me tortured! I'd be dead now if it hadn't been for Aiboy Ali.'

'We must protect the reputation and sovereignty of the country.'

Fired up, Ruud strangled the neck of a bottle of mineral water, ripping off the cap. 'Reputation? What reputation?'

'A scandal of this magnitude will do Indonesia incalculable damage on the international stage, Pujasumarta. Have you any idea what the repercussions would be? Better to have three dead foreigners on the front pages of the *Wall Street Journal* and the *Sydney Morning Herald* than one megacorrupt local general and his murderous son. Can you imagine the backflow of shit we'd get if the world learned the truth? Imagine the headlines: GENERAL'S SON KILLS THREE INNOCENT WOMEN TO HIDE HIS FATHER'S CRIMES. No, this must not come to light.'

'Four innocent women. You're forgetting *Ajun Inspektur Polisi Dua* Alya Entitisari. Not to mention the suspicious death of Pastor Ignatius Kwong.'

'Cities are dangerous places. There are going to be murders and hate crimes no matter what we do. If people start regarding Jakarta as an unsafe city, then so be it. Our mayor will come under pressure. The Police General, too. Tourist numbers may drop this quarter, maybe next. But high-end money laundering and fraud? Our top people don't like the sound of that. It's very bad for our new image-conscious government. It would not reflect well on them. The world believes we are cleaning up our act, which means we have to keep a lid on the truth. Absolute discretion is required. Once the door to the rice *lumbung* is opened there's no resealing it.'

'Reporters have a habit of digging up dirt; dirt we find hard to scrub away,' said Witarsa.

'We have confiscated the Fauzis' passports. Both men have been fitted with ankle monitors. They are not a flight risk,' said Fahruddin.

'Jesus!' Ruud threw the bottle of water across the room.

'I'll ask you to keep your composure, first *inspektur*,' Witarsa said in a voice Ruud hardly recognized.

'Doesn't the truth mean anything to you, Joyo?' His voice cracked.

'You're tired,' said Fahruddin.

'This is madness.'

The brigadier general glanced at his files. The line of his mouth cracked. 'So are we clear, then? There's to be no further mention of the Fauzis.' Fahruddin jabbed his finger against the tabletop. 'Not from us, not from the journalists, not from anyone. We control the local media, the media controls the story, the story goes away. Understood?'

Ruud curbed his anger and kept quiet. But he wanted them to see his anger, his hurt. He clenched his jaw. It brought out a vein on his neck.

'I *said* is that understood, Pujasumarta?'

The air prickled between them. Ruud glowered at Fahruddin, whose face leaned towards him, a face badly in need of a fist.

Ruud took a breath and exhaled slowly through his nose. 'Yes.'

A superior smile. 'How awfully wise of you to agree. Now, let's turn to some housekeeping matters. Do you have any further copies of Emily Grealish's thumb drive?'

Ruud bowed his head, defeated. His jaw tightened further. 'No.'

'And all your case notes and files are stored where?'

'On my office computer.'

Fahruddin tongued the top row of his teeth. Ruud wanted to knock those teeth out so they fell jangling from his mouth, like coins from a fruit machine.

'Please supply Commissioner Witarsa with your password and log-in details. Tech Support will have the files scrubbed by tomorrow morning. Yes?'

Ruud slouched forward. He glared at the brigadier general and gave a slight nod.

'Good, then we can put this matter to rest. Officially, the case will be classified as cold. The relevant foreign constabularies will be notified and that will be that. The rest of the world considers us an incompetent and amateurish bunch of cowboys, so not bringing anyone up on charges won't surprise too many people.'

'What about Alya Entitisari? Her death goes unanswered, does it?'

Fahruddin ignored him, his attention elsewhere, already turning the pages of one of his pink files. His movements calculated, precise. 'You are to be granted two weeks' injury leave so that you may recover fully from your wounds.'

'I asked you about Alya Entitisari.'

'Furthermore, Pujasumarta, you've been promoted to Police Commissioner Adjutant.'

'*Ajun Komisaris Polisi.*' Ruud shook his head slowly. 'I see what you're doing.'

'It's well deserved.'

'A promotion to keep me quiet, right? You want me to toe the line, so you're promoting me.'

Police Brigadier General Fahruddin's mouth thinned into a line. Without expression he said, 'That will be all, *ajun komisaris.* Meeting concluded. Close the door on your way out. And pick up that bottle while you're at it.'

An hour later.

Harried, Commissioner Joyo T. Witarsa thrust through the doors of Polda Metro Jaya, his flat feet slapping against the ground.

Outside, Aiboy Ali stood talking with Ruud, who sat in his Toyota with the engine running. They were out in the main road, beyond the parking lot, with pedestrians and motorcycles hurrying past. As soon as he saw Witarsa, Aiboy slapped the roof, indicating that he'd better be off.

Witarsa strode past the enormous flagpole and the *kaki lima* selling fried bananas into the din and racket of the streets. He managed to catch bits and pieces of their conversation, something about disabling an alarm and bypassing CCTV cameras.

'Remember, you have a meeting with internal affairs in thirty minutes,' said the commissioner, all twitchy and blinky. 'PROPAM want to hear your version of Bayu's shooting. I'd like to sit in on it.'

Aiboy Ali used both hands to pull his long hair from his eyes and watched Ruud drive away. A blue minibus roared by, assaulting them with exhaust fumes. 'Sure, whatever,' he said dismissively, both fists now deep in his cargo pants pockets.

'Don't keep them waiting,' warned Witarsa, his lips turned down.

'I won't.'

Witarsa blinked hard, tired red marbling streaked the

whites of his eyes. 'Also, I spoke with Alya's parents just now. Her funeral will take place tomorrow afternoon.'

The features of Aiboy's face stiffened. Back turned, he glared at the sprawl of motorcycles bunching by the traffic lights. 'I'll be there.'

'Aiboy, you have to understand, there was nothing I could do.' He placed both palms on his chest. 'Fauzi has powerful allies, he's connected. You can't reason with these people. To them, Fauzi is a problem they wish to solve internally, behind closed doors. Justice gets blurred. The Ministry of Law has been leaning on everyone to keep this quiet. If I could I would have issued an arrest warrant . . . but my hands were tied.' His voice trailed away.

'Your hands were tied,' repeated the detective, veiled hostility in his tone. 'Surely, you can talk them out of it.'

'It's too late. The rice is cooked. The situation can't be changed.'

'Thank you for restoring my faith in the Indonesian justice system.'

'I feel the same way you do.'

'Try telling that to Alya's mother and father.'

'I'm sorry,' he mumbled with a sad, tight smile, his hang-dog face engraved with wrinkles, his jowls dense and spongy. 'Thirty minutes.' He slouched away.

Aiboy Ali waited a few moments before heading back towards the entrance to the station. He cut a path through the stream of pedestrians and glared at the POLRI crest hanging above the doors. '*Rastra Sewakottama?*' he spat, glowering at the desk sergeant. 'The People's Main Servant my arse.'

★ ★ ★

Soaked by a recent rain shower, Ruud sat on the steps outside Jakarta Cathedral. The steps were not completely dry, but he didn't care.

He was at the entrance to a church, which was odd because he rarely went to church. He wasn't a practising Christian. He wasn't a practising anything. Yet today he needed solace, a place of calm to think things through.

He held his resignation letter, a single sheet of A4, with the envelope balanced on his knees, drying his damp hands in a sunbeam.

Ruud thought about the cases he'd solved, the families he'd helped, and all of a sudden it got to him. He squinted at the memories. The anger overwhelmed him and his face screwed up. He broke down and started to cry.

He felt useless, pathetic even. Like a drunkard yelling at the rain.

He told himself it was a natural reaction, symptomatic of the shitty injustice he was experiencing. With a shake of his head he got to his feet and entered the cathedral, making his way to the southern side, where the Pietà stood. Ruud glanced at the statue of the Virgin Mary clasping the dead Christ in her arms. Ruud bowed his head slightly and lit four candles.

Keeping his eyes on the dead Christ, he held the letter to the candle flame. The sheet of A4 caught fire and he watched it burn.

Hell in a handcart, he whispered under his breath. Hell in a handcart.

Epilogue

Kemang, South Jakarta.

The curtains in the second-floor apartment weren't yet drawn and the solitary light within cast faint shadows on the slate-toned walls.

A block away Ruud watched the trio of windows. For over an hour he'd waited in the dark, bleached of colour, hidden in a narrow passageway between two shophouses.

It was stifling and cramped. There was little air. His face felt clammy and sweat moistened his hair at the temples and trickled down the back of his shirt. The night was beginning to suffocate him. He felt as if he were wrapped from head to toe in gauze. His shoulder ached and the waterproof bandages itched. He wondered whether he was getting a rash on his neck.

A solitary motorcycle appeared in the distance and buzzed past. Ruud took a step back, retreating further into the shadows.

He could hear air conditioners humming in the small residences above him. Condensation dripped from PVC pipes to his left and right.

The minutes ticked by.

He stared at the entrance to the apartment building across

the road and tried not to imagine his mother watching him, judging him. Or Imke for that matter.

Ruud withdrew the cheap Telkomsel phone from his bag and dialled a number in Holland. He shielded the blue light from the mobile with his hand.

'Hi.' He spoke in a low voice.

'____'

'No, I'm using a different phone, a pre-paid one. The ASUS was giving me trouble. I can hardly hear you either. Must be the reception. How's Amsterdam?'

'____'

'Great. Say hi to Erica for me. No, I'm at work. Nothing much going on, just finishing off some paperwork.'

'____'

'The Toyota's still in the garage. Aiboy's downstairs standing by in his car. We're calling it a day soon. He'll drop me home.'

'____'

'Yeah, it's pretty late, about two a.m.'

'____'

Ruud laughed softly. 'Yeah, OK, I'll tell him to get a haircut.'

'____'

'I miss you, too. Remember to bring me back some cheese.'

'____'

'Yep, I've got your flight details. See you in three days.'

'____'

'Kiki's fine. I took her for a stroll around the block this morning.'

The *bee-bop* sound of a car horn rose from the street beyond. His expression soured.

'Listen, I have to go.'

Ruud killed the call.

Aiboy Ali's voice came through the earbud microphone fitted to Ruud's ear: 'Target approaching.'

'How long?' said Ruud.

'Two to three minutes.'

'Roger that. Where's the night watchman?'

'Night *jaga* is at the back entrance having a cigarette.'

'You sure this is a reliable tip-off?'

'As clean as they come.'

'Is the street clear?'

'Not a soul in sight. It's a quiet neighbourhood.'

Ruud pressed his back against the wall and waited, tight-jawed. A set of headlights lit up the street. He hesitated for a moment, fingering the 9 mm Heckler attached to his waist, before leaving it to sit in its holster. He was damp through with perspiration. His mouth felt dry. He hadn't had a sip of water for hours.

He spoke quietly into the mic. 'I've spotted the Range Rover.'

Ruud licked his lips and straightened his posture. His tongue clung to the roof of his mouth.

'Do you see him, *Gajah*?'

'Not yet. Hold on a second,' replied Ruud. 'OK, that's him getting out of the car. He's now on foot.'

'What are you going to do?'

'I don't know.'

'Standing by.'

The line went dead.

Counting down from sixty, Ruud remained very, very still. He watched the silhouette of a man approach the front entrance of the building across the road, his footfalls echoing off the pavement.

The pressure built in Ruud's chest. His stomach churned like a ball of snakes. When he got to twenty-five he made out the sharp rattling of keys.

Ruud counted down: Twenty-three, twenty-two, twenty-one . . .

A motorbike engine croaked nearby. Ruud saw a Suzuki RMZ 250 carrying two men ease into his eyeline.

Ruud heard the building's front door locks release.

The automatic lamp sensor on the porch blinked on, spilling watery light into the street.

The man riding pillion swung his leg free and jumped off the back of the Suzuki. His face was hidden behind a black helmet and tinted visor.

Ruud stiffened.

The front door was about to open when the man in the helmet spoke.

'Hello, Noah.'

There was a moment of startled silence as Noah Fauzi blinked into the darkness, unable to comprehend what was going on.

'I have a message from Antonio Irawan.' The voice sounded muffled behind the helmet and tinted visor.

'Who are you? What the fuck do you think you're doing?'

'Tying up loose ends.'

'W . . . what the hell is this?' Noah stammered.

'Goodbye, Noah.'

The helmeted man raised the SIG and fired two shots into Noah Fauzi's chest and one into his face. Three neat percussive pops.

The back of Noah Fauzi's skull exploded, spewing bone and brain tissue.

Noah's mouth opened and closed without a sound escaping. His body slumped backwards to the ground, boneless. It gave a little shiver before settling in a motionless mess.

Ruud wrinkled his nose.

The small blob in the middle of Fauzi's face began to widen, dark red spreading like butterfly wings.

Bending low, the gunman gathered up the spent cartridges. He unscrewed the twenty-centimetre Mystic X suppressor attachment and slid it into his waistband with the SIG Sauer P320C. Then he placed something on Noah Fauzi's chest, turned and walked unhurriedly towards the idling Suzuki.

Ruud watched the motorcycle gun its engine and squeal away.

He waited for someone to scream and shout, for a neighbour to run out and raise the alarm, but nobody seemed to have seen or heard anything. Still, he bided his time.

After about ninety seconds, Ruud spoke into the mic. 'All is calm.'

'All is bright.'

'I'll meet you at the corner of Kamboja and Jambu in ten minutes. Bring the car round.'

'OK, *Gajah*.'

Unblinking, Ruud crossed the road, keeping in the shadows. Five metres away the SpongeBob doll sat wetly on Noah Fauzi's chest. Ruud ran his eyes over the body, conscious of the growing pool of blood that was spreading like a red rag.

'When the one-eight-seven call comes in we should be first on the scene.'

'Understood, *Gajah*.'

Ruud shut his eyes, mouthed a quiet prayer for Alya Entitisari's soul, then headed east in the direction of Jalan Jambu.

He could see the headlines now:

Marine Cavalry Captain gunned down by *preman* hit squad.

He'd have to have a word with Witarsa in the morning. These gangland-related drug killings were getting out of hand. Nobody was safe.

With a backhanded swing, he smashed the Telkomsel phone against a wall, dropped the broken components into a storm drain and tossed the earbud microphone over a metal fence.

His shoulder ached and itched. He wanted to scratch it but he let it be.

Seconds later he half-vanished into a dark alleyway, stepped between a pair of parked cars and merged completely with the darkness.

Acknowledgements

I am hugely indebted to a number of people who have helped make this book possible:

To the families and friends in Jakarta who opened their homes and hearts to me.

To Krystyna Green at Constable, for your unwavering support and encouragement.

To Shauna Bartlett, my brilliant copy-editor, for your wonderful eye for detail.

To Viki Cheung, Rachael Hum and Paul Kenny at Hachette, for your enthusiasm and professionalism.

To Amanda Keats at Little, Brown, for your invaluable input and diligence.

I must also show my appreciation to the KL Bookish Babes – Orla Govaerts, Amy Schneider, Mary Kosco, Patricia Peterson, Marilyn Mak, Neha Dave-Manoharan, Isabelle Martinez Primavesi, Nancy Follett and Leisa Puri.

And as always, most notably, an enormous thank you must go to my phenomenal agent, Kate Hordern.